Rachael Stewart adores co[...]
from heartwarmingly roman[...]
She's been writing since she could put pen to
paper—as the stacks of scrawled-on pages in her
loft will attest to. A Welsh lass at heart, she now
lives in Yorkshire, with her very own hero and
three awesome kids—and if she's not tapping out
a story she's wrapped up in one or enjoying
the great outdoors. Reach her on Facebook,
on X @rach_b52, or at rachaelstewartauthor.com.

Justine Lewis writes uplifting, heartwarming
contemporary romances. She lives in Australia
with her hero husband, two teenagers, and an
outgoing puppy. When she isn't writing she
loves to walk her dog in the bush near her house,
attempt to keep her garden alive, and search for
the perfect frock. She loves hearing from readers;
you can visit her at justinelewis.com.

SUMMER WITH THE BILLIONAIRE

RACHAEL STEWART

JUSTINE LEWIS

MILLS & BOON

First published in Great Britain 2025 by Mills & Boon, an imprint of HarperCollins*Publishers* Ltd, 1 London Bridge Street, London, SE1 9GF

www.harpercollins.co.uk

HarperCollins*Publishers*, Macken House, 39/40 Mayor Street Upper, Dublin 1, D01 C9W8, Ireland

Summer with the Billionaire © 2025 Harlequin Enterprises ULC

Cinderella's Fling with the Billionaire © 2025 Rachael Stewart

Italian Tycoon to Remember © 2025 Justine Lewis

ISBN: 978-0-263-41757-9

09/25

MIX
Paper | Supporting responsible forestry
FSC
www.fsc.org
FSC™ C007454

This book contains FSC™ certified paper and other controlled sources to ensure responsible forest management.

For more information visit www.harpercollins.co.uk/green.

Printed and Bound in the UK using 100% Renewable Electricity at CPI Group (UK) Ltd, Croydon, CR0 4YY

CINDERELLA'S FLING WITH THE BILLIONAIRE

RACHAEL STEWART

MILLS & BOON

For Daphne.

Thank you for showing Dad the true wonder of Australia.

He's one lucky guy to have you in his life!

xxx

CHAPTER ONE

TIMOTHY CAMPBELL SCANNED the grand ballroom of the Ritz-Carlton, the incessant rumble of Melbourne's elite an irritating buzz in his ear. Didn't matter that they were all here for him, his company and their latest win, every vibration mocked him and his lack of cheer.

A waiter approached, offering out a tray of champagne, and he waved him away.

He didn't want more alcohol.

He didn't want more small talk.

What he wanted was an escape.

'Great evening, Campbell.' Connor, his biggest investor and closest friend sidled up, a whisky in hand, his blond hair looking like he'd just rolled out of bed. His overbright blue eyes and flushed cheeks suggesting he hadn't been alone in the tumble either.

'The champagne not good enough for you?' he murmured.

'Not when you have a fifty-year-old Macallan behind the bar.' Connor raised the crystal tumbler in salute. 'Thanks, by the way.'

'It comes out of your pocket too.'

'Damn, I forgot that bit.'

'Sure, you did.'

'Great party though, can always rely on you to throw the best.'

'Can always rely on you to lower the tone too.'

He gestured to his friend's slackened tie and unbuttoned collar. 'Who was it this time?'

Connor raised a lazy brow.

'Don't want to tell me?'

'Do you really want to know?'

He huffed. Connor had him there.

'What does it matter how we look anyway? No one cares when you make as much money as we do.'

'*You* should care.'

But then Connor wasn't a father. Hadn't been a husband. Hadn't felt the responsibility of wanting to be the best you could possibly be for those you loved.

And at forty-eight, Tim was in the best shape of his life. Physically. Financially. But mentally...

'You up for sailing next week? I'm taking the yacht out to Gabo...'

'Gabo?' Hell, Tim hadn't been there since... 'Maybe.'

'Maybe?' Connor raised the other brow. 'It appeals that much, hey?'

It did appeal—the open water, the fresh air, the freedom—but the memories...

'If we hadn't been friends for years, I'd be insulted at the face you're pulling.'

'And if I hadn't known you for years, I'd think there was a real risk of you being insulted.'

Connor laughed. 'My God, you need to get laid.'

'Getting laid,' he ground out, 'is the last thing I need.'

'Okay, laid is too crude.' Though he grinned as he said it. 'What I mean is, you need the love of a good woman to turn that frown upside down.'

'*Seriously*?'

'What?' Connor said, wide-eyed innocence all the way.

Did his friend really need reminding that the love of a good woman had been the instigator of said frown—the love and its loss?

'You're acting like I suggested you take a running leap off the nearest skyscraper.'

'You might as well have.'

'It's been seven years, buddy.' Concern softened Connor's tone, his eyes too, and Tim turned away—he couldn't bear that look.

'And it'll be another seven and I'll still stand here alone.'

'Why?'

'*Why?*' Tim snapped back around. 'Are you for real?'

'Yes! Is it guilt? Are you worried about Ellie turning over in her grave? Or are you worried about Sasha, because last I checked, Sasha was nagging *you* to date?'

'Coming from my daughter I'll take the nagging, but from you, the biggest player I know…?'

'Hey, before Ellie, *you* were the biggest player, or have you forgotten those days?'

No, he hadn't forgotten, but he'd been a different man then. He'd been younger for a start. Zero responsibility and all the drive to succeed.

'You worked hard, but you played harder. You had the best of both worlds.'

'How many times you been in love, Connor?'

'Alright, don't rub it in. We can't all be as lucky in love as you.'

He grunted. Lucky?

He'd *been* lucky, for sure. *So* lucky. He'd met Ellie at twenty-two, fallen in love and had Sasha within a year. His mates had thought he was crazy, tying himself down so young, but they were his motivation, his reason to succeed. And he had. His tech startup had made him one of the world's youngest self-made billionaires by the age of thirty.

For a long time, life had been perfect.

But luck came with its own expiry and his had run out. Seven years, one month and two days ago…or eight years if you counted the day that Ellie's oncologist had delivered his blow. A terminal diagnosis with a grim prognosis.

And no amount of money had been able to save her—*them*—from that.

'You might try dating women your own age for a start,' he muttered, tugging himself out of the gloom to focus on Connor. Far easier to beat on his mate than himself.

'Ha! Can I help it if women half our age take a shine to me?' He nudged his head in the direction of the bar, where two young women were brazenly checking them out.

'You're old enough to be their father.'

'*And?* It's the experience they're after. Boys their age don't have a clue what they're doing.'

'And you think you do?'

'Ouch.' He palmed his chest. 'You really are on one tonight.'

'Sorry.' Tim ran a hand through his hair, blew out a breath. 'I'm just…'

'You're just in a melancholic spin. I know, I get it, I'm used to it. We're *all* used to it. But don't you think it's time you found a way out of it, before it's all you know too?'

His words chimed so readily with what Sasha had been saying on repeat for the past few years that he couldn't take it any more—time to bail.

'Campbell?' Connor hurried after him as he made for the exit. 'Where are you going?'

'Anywhere but here,' he said, his smile fixed in place for the guests as he wove through the crowd, his speed making clear he wasn't for stopping.

'But it's still early and, if I'm not mistaken, those two look very much in need—'

'If you say getting laid again, I swear to God…'

Connor held up his hands. 'I was actually going to say *scintillating conversation*.'

'Of course you were.'

Connor's grin didn't waver. 'So, sailing next week, yeah?'

'You know your yacht has no sails, so technically it's not—'

'All right Mr Pedantic, just answer the question—you coming?'

'I'll think about it.'

'You need to stop thinking so hard because those wrinkles…' he drew a circle around his face '…they're only going to get worse.'

'Cheers for the tip,' Tim said with a slow, exaggerated nod. 'Now goodbye, Connor.'

And then he exited the room. It would be of no surprise to anyone that he'd scarpered without a formal farewell. He had form.

Initially, it had been a way to avoid the look in people's eyes, the pity. Then he'd lost patience with the platitudes and the meaningless conversation. Always eager to move on to the next thing that promised to occupy his mind and prevent it from turning to the past, to the pain, to Ellie.

Work and Sasha. They were his focus. But work no longer fulfilled him and Sasha—hell, Sasha was twenty-five and living her own life how she saw fit. She didn't need him any more.

And Tim… Tim had no idea what he needed, but it wasn't this.

Maria Thompson wiped down the bar and scanned the clientele.

To her mind, customers could be grouped into three camps:

Those who came for the company.

Those who came for solitude in said company.

And those who came looking for trouble, whatever form it took.

Tonight, Mickey's Bar rocked all three and her feet had barely touched the ground all evening.

'Hey, Mom.' Her eighteen-year-old daughter Fae set a tray of empties on the bar and stretched, arching her back with a groan that Maria felt all the way to her aching toes. 'Can I get another schooner for table four?'

'Already?' Maria frowned over at the guy. She'd served him not ten minutes ago and put him in the seeking solitude camp, but it was oh-so easy to slide into trouble with a few too many bevvies.

'Says he's had a day.'

He caught Maria's gaze and she gave a brief smile.

'Haven't we all...' she murmured, pouring him a fresh one as she looked back at Fae, concern deepening as she took in her daughter's pallor, the dark shadows under her eyes... Not that the hair dye helped, the jet-black tone washing her daughter out so completely. But they'd been pulling long shifts lately, covering for two sick bar staff and another on holiday, and though it was great for the savings, it was clearly taking its toll.

'Why don't you get off? We'll be closing soon enough and Trix and I can cope until then.'

Trix was Mickey's niece and Maria's closest friend. Usually serving onboard superyachts, Trix was between charters and had stepped in as a favour to her uncle, giving up on her downtime to help them out.

'Nah,' Fae said, stifling a yawn. 'I'm good.'

'You're not good, you look ready to drop.'

'Gee, thanks.'

'It's meant in the nicest possible way. You've been working late all week, and were up early this morning to chip in with the cleaning.'

'So were you.'

'And I'm your mother. Now go. And make sure you eat! There's a slice of leftover lasagne in the fridge with your name on it.'

'What are you going to have?'

'Bob will see me right.' Bob was Mickey's chef, a giant of a man who scowled more than he smiled but had the biggest heart. He was also their neighbour in the flat above the bar. 'There's sure to be something left over after tonight's shift.'

And failing that she'd grab a bag of chips on her way up. Easy-peasy.

'Okay, but call me down if you get a sudden rush on.' She sent a hesitant glance in the direction of table four. 'And—'

'Watch him, I know. Don't forget, I taught you all that you know.'

Fae smiled and heaved herself over the bar to plant a kiss on her cheek. 'I learnt from the best.'

Maria smiled tightly. If best meant learning from someone who'd been through the worst courtesy of the opposite sex, then yup, that was her. 'Sweet dreams, honey.'

''Night, Mum. 'Night, Trix!' she hollered.

Trix looked up from clearing table six, her brown skin radiant, her eyes bright—what Maria wouldn't give to have half her friend's glow right about now. She waved, and Fae skipped off, yanking off her apron and shaking out her hair— her petite frame and elfin features catching more than a few lingering stares.

Maria gritted her teeth. She knew this was no environment for her kid, yet it was the only environment they'd known for the last four years. And Mickey was a star. He'd given them a roof over their heads when they'd needed it, jobs too, a life safe from the past. Safe from Fae's father.

And though the men might leer, Fae, just like her mother, knew how to handle them.

Maria just wished her daughter didn't *have* to know.

But then she wished for a lot of things, and wishes were for the foolish, and the hopeful. Not for those who'd been burned enough times in life to think any would come true.

She'd like to think it might be different for Fae though… that one day her daughter might break away and reach for better things. Work to live rather than live to work. Get out of the suburbs and see the world.

'Fae okay?' Trix joined her behind the bar and set about prepping a fresh line of drinks.

'Yeah, she's just tired.'

'Poor darl.' Her phone pinged and she pulled it out of her pocket. 'That girl could do with—' She broke off with a curse.

'What's wrong?'

'I'm still a stew short for next week's charter and my last hope is already at sea.'

'Did you ask Fae?'

'I did but, as you suspected, she turned me down too. Said she'd rather work back-to-back bar shifts than spend a long weekend on water.'

Maria shook her head. It was one thing for her daughter to turn down the lucrative job offer, another to miss out on the added adventure. A change of scene. A new environment that wasn't the same old, day in day out.

'Did she say why?'

'Something about keeping her feet firmly on the ground.'

'I knew she had a fear of flying, but sailing…'

'Anyway, she's out, so are you in?'

'Ha!'

'I'm serious.'

'And so am I.'

'Like daughter, like mother.'

'It's not the sailing I object to.'

'It's just like working here only doing it on water, and you used to be a housekeeper, right? The work will be a breeze in comparison to this place.'

It wasn't the work she was objecting to either.

'It means leaving Fae alone…'

'You were going to trust her with me on a yacht for a few days.'

'That's different. I'd hoped she'd enjoy it. See it as an adventure.'

'She'd probably enjoy having her own space at home more. She's eighteen—an adult. You have to stop mollycoddling her.'

'I don't—'

Trix cocked a brow.

'Okay, I do. Maybe. Just a little. But she's my baby girl.'

'And she'll always be your baby girl, but these charter guests have deep pockets. You could earn enough to take you and Fae on holiday. Have some real mother and daughter time outside of this place.'

'A holiday?' She huffed out. 'What's one of those again?'

'My point exactly. And how do you expect Fae to go off and live her life if you won't do the same?'

Maria's mouth twisted up.

'And Bob is just across the hall, she can call him if she has any issues, and in the meantime, you can have some fun on board a superyacht with me.'

'Fun?'

'Yeah, Montgomery, the owner, he's pretty chill. I reckon we might even get some beach time in.'

Fun. Sun. A whole heap of money. She'd be a fool to say no. And she knew Trix was right about Fae. How could she expect her daughter to leave these four walls if she herself wouldn't?

'And before you say it, Uncle Mickey can already cover the shifts. I checked before asking Fae.'

'You have an answer for everything.'

Trix grinned. 'It's the only way to be, so you in?'

'Hey, hot stuff, is that drink going to walk itself over, or shall I come round there and get it?'

Maria blinked to find Table Four stood where Fae had

once been, his eyes now glassy up close. Not his first bar of the evening then…

She gave Trix a nod. 'Yeah, I'm in.'

Then sliding his drink across the bar, she gave a well-versed smile. 'Can I get you some chips, pretzels, nuts to go with that?'

'You upselling me?'

'You look like you could do with something more substantial than beer.'

He took up his drink. 'Are you offering your services?'

She cocked a brow. 'My services?'

His gaze dipped to her chest.

'I'd quit that thought right now if you know what's good for you.'

'Everything okay here, Maria?' Bob appeared from the back and the guy immediately backed away.

'All good, mate. All good.'

She set her exasperated smile on Bob. 'I had him handled, you know.'

'Yeah, you did,' Trix cheered as Bob grunted.

'Yeah, well, I didn't fancy breaking up a fight this evening.'

Maria laughed as she cleared the empties off the tray Fae had left. 'He would've been asking for it.'

'You say that every time.'

'Well, they shouldn't underestimate a woman.'

'Sometimes I fear you underestimate them too.'

The bar door swung open, and she glanced up—everything in her stilled, then kicked into overdrive at the sight of the man stepping inside. Now *he* was a whole different kind of trouble.

Bob nodded his way. 'Looks like someone took a wrong turn.'

'I'm sure he'll work it out soon enough.'

Because a guy dressed like that didn't belong in a joint like this…

Suave, sophisticated, swanky suit and tie.

Trix's superyacht, yeah. Mickey's bar, no.

'Or not,' she added, her bemused smile spreading as the guy's gaze landed squarely on her. A shallow breath, two… and then he was striding towards her.

'You know him?' Bob asked.

'No.'

And he had a face you couldn't forget.

'He sure acts like he knows you…'

'Or *wants* to get to know you,' Trix murmured.

'He can *want* all he likes…'

Trix laughed. 'Now I just feel sorry for him.'

Bob gave a low rumble—possibly a laugh, maybe a warning. 'I'm almost done out back, you come get me if you need me.'

'Will do,' Maria said, only half aware of him disappearing behind her as she stiffened her spine and refused to acknowledge the little skip to her pulse as her body appreciated all that was coming towards her.

Strong chiselled face. Salt-and-pepper hair. Carefully groomed stubble. And eyes…it was those that held her captive. Piercing as they remained fixed on her, their colour impossible to identify across the distance, but she could feel their interest—blatant and hot with it.

Tiny flutters kicked up in her abdomen and she promptly quashed the lot. He was *definitely* trouble. The kind of trouble that belonged firmly in her past.

She had no time for it in her present.

No desire for it in her future.

Zero. Zilch. Zippo!

If someone had asked him where he was, Tim would have struggled to answer. He hadn't been ready to head to his hotel room. And he hadn't wanted to stay where he'd run the risk of bumping into someone else he knew. So he'd taken a cab out of the city and then he'd walked.

Walked and walked, until eventually he'd come across a dated little side street with an equally dated little rock bar and found himself inside.

Thirsty for a drink with no questions on the side.

Thirsty for a time in his life before he'd made his money, before he'd fallen in love, before his responsibilities had multiplied exponentially and he'd forgotten how to sit still. Be happy. Just be.

Thirsty for…peace.

But the brunette with the caramel highlights and eyes of the same warm colour had him thirsty for something else entirely, the sensation so sudden and so shocking he'd rocked back on his heels. Then she'd smiled and it had streaked right through him, warming parts of his body he'd thought long since dead.

His lips had curved up, his legs had moved and he was at the bar before he knew what he was about.

'You lost?' she said.

'Do I look lost?'

'You really want me to answer that?'

She plucked a glass off the side, expertly polishing it with a cloth as her fiery gaze drifted over him. He couldn't remember the last time he'd been looked at with such…not hostility, but something. And it sure as hell had him *feeling* something in return.

He scanned the rest of the joint—the array of rock shirts on display, the gruff beards and piercings aplenty—and slackened off his tie.

'Oh, yeah, that helps,' she said with a wry twist of her luscious pink lips. 'What can I get you?'

He checked the array of spirits on the mirror-backed wall. 'Johnny Walker Black. Neat.'

'Sure thing, sugar.'

Sugar? He wanted to laugh. He'd never been called sugar in his life.

'You want to take a seat and I'll bring it over?'

'I'd rather sit here, if it's all the same to you.'

She shrugged. 'Suit yourself.'

He slid onto the bar stool, his mouth still tugging at the corners as he watched her grab the bottle off the shelf and slap a glass down in front of him.

'So,' she said as she poured a double without asking, 'what did you do? Bail on your bride-to-be?'

'W—what?' he laughed out.

'The penguin suit, the neat whisky—gotta be on the run.'

Was she serious? Or teasing?

'I think, technically, I need to be wearing a bow tie for this to be classed as a penguin suit.'

Her lips pursed off to the side—was she trapping a laugh? A laugh at *his* expense?

'Whatever.' She slid the glass his way. 'You're a long way from home.'

'Is that a problem?'

'No, everyone's welcome so long as they're not bringing trouble with them.'

'Define trouble.'

'A jilted bride. An angry father, brother, mother…'

'So a lone guy walks into your bar and you immediately leap to wedding?'

'No…' elbows planting onto the bar top, her eyes sparkled up at him '…a guy walks into my bar in a tux and orders a whisky neat, *then* I leap to wedding.'

'Not a fan?'

'I'm not the one in need of a whisky straight up.'

'Just the one jumping to conclusions.'

'Very true.'

'If you must know—'

'Which I don't…'

'Noted.' The impulsive smile made a return. 'I've come from an event in the city.'

'And chose to finish off your night here?'

'I wouldn't say I chose *per se*…more that I found myself here by chance.'

'So you *are* lost?'

'If one can be lost on purpose, yes.'

He took a sip of his drink, acknowledging that Connor probably had it right ordering the Macallan. Though the pleasing warmth of the drink had nothing on the heat of her gaze as it slid down his throat.

'Mind if I ask why?'

'Thought you said you didn't want to know.'

'I lied.'

'Do you make a habit of lying?'

'Only when it suits me.'

He chuckled. A real, genuine chuckle. The sound as surprising as it was rare. He could almost imagine the look on Sasha's face had she witnessed it. Connor's too.

'Duly noted. Again.'

'So…?'

He sensed the other barmaid leaning closer, the sidelong glances of the other patrons too, and shifted on the stool. Maybe he *should've* taken his drink to a discreet corner. Ducked out of sight, just like he had at his own party.

And here she was asking him why he'd done just that, and he was struggling to come up with an answer that wasn't the plain ugly truth…

But hell, he was tired of denying it.

And what harm was there in admitting it to a stranger anyway? A stranger who he wouldn't see again come tomorrow. A stranger with a smile that had the power to make him feel again. Feel and forget.

However temporary that relief might be…

CHAPTER TWO

GOD, HIS *EYES*...

Maria struggled to look away from the ghosts lurking in their stormy-grey depths.

'Would you think me a coward if I said I was running from my reality?'

'A coward?'

She frowned. No, she'd say he was being brave. Admitting as much to her. Risking his masculinity to show such weakness. Putting a voice to what half this room likely wouldn't, even though they were probably doing the exact same.

Four years ago, she'd done it herself. Run from her life. And she understood why, knew those demons of old. What were his? And could he outrun them like she had?

'Do you want to talk about it?'

The question slipped out before she could stop it, driven by the memory of what it had been like for her, having no one to confide in. How lonely she'd felt, how trapped...

'Does anyone ever want to talk about what pains them?'

'Sometimes.' She shrugged. 'It's what us bar tenders are good for, pouring drinks and lending ears.'

Though lending an ear to him...with the way he made her feel by look alone...she'd be better off letting Trix step in. Before the rebellious little flutters within danced her headlong into trouble.

'Though if you'd rather not...'

She started to move away but he reached out, the gesture turning every flutter into a full-on surge. The warmth consuming her as she blinked up at him.

'Actually…' He wet his lips, the action like pouring gasoline on the already simmering fire within—*Trouble, Maria! Total trouble!* 'At the risk of sounding in need of therapy, that might be kind of healthy.'

She gave an edgy laugh. 'You sure about that, because your face says otherwise?'

'Talking is a new one on me.'

She considered him quietly. 'Yeah, I imagine it is. Consider me honoured.'

'You should be.' He gave a tight chuckle. 'My daughter's been trying to get me to talk to someone for years.'

'Daughter?' Her knees weakened. Her heart too.

'Yeah.'

He took a swig of his whisky, and she checked his left hand. No ring. Though that didn't mean he wasn't married, or was once, or wasn't still with his daughter's mother. And hell, her head was spinning as much as her heart.

'What about her mum?'

A shadow fell across his face, taking up camp in his ghost-ridden eyes.

'She died.'

His pain reached across the bar, clawing at Maria's chest, stealing her voice.

'Seven years ago.'

Regret slammed into her. 'I'm so sorry.'

He let out a slow breath. 'Yeah, me too.'

'Is she—is she the reason you don't talk?'

'When everyone around you knows about your loss and either tiptoes around it or wants to make it the focus of every conversation, talking loses its appeal.'

'Even now? Seven years on…?'

'Even now, because the talk becomes that of moving on, and I have less interest in moving on than I had talking about it in the first place.'

'Of course…'

'And when it's coming from your own daughter too…'

She pulled a face. 'Ouch. How old is she?'

'Twenty-five. And she likes to think she knows better than her forty-eight-year-old father.'

'Ha. Tell me about it.'

'You too?'

'My daughter's eighteen going on eighty.'

'Dad around?'

'No, thank God.' And she meant that with every fibre of her being. 'We're better off without him in our lives, believe me.'

'Do *you* want to talk about it?'

She gave a tight laugh. 'Hell, no.'

He raised his drink. 'To stories we'd rather not share and daughters who think they know best.'

She gave a soft smile. 'Cheers to that.'

'Can I buy you a drink to toast with?'

'I don't drink on duty.'

'After then?'

She bit her lip. It was tempting. *So* tempting.

And she hadn't been tempted by a man in years.

She didn't *want* to be tempted by a man now.

So what in the hell was she doing indulging in this?

Wake up, Maria!

'I better not, thanks, though.' She pushed back from the bar. 'Enjoy your whisky.'

And then she walked, fighting a backward glance or several.

'Okay, spill!' Trix demanded as she approached.

'Spill what?' Maria said as she kept on walking, putting

as much distance between her and him as she sought refuge at the other end of the bar.

'I don't know, his entire life story. You chatted long enough. Looked to be an intense convo from over here.'

She laughed it off. 'Hardly!'

'And now he keeps checking you out.'

'No, he does not.'

Trix raised a brow. 'And you've been back all of ten seconds and looked back just as much.'

Maria flicked a tea towel at her. 'I have not!'

'Have so! And I gotta say if he was looking at me like that,' Trix said out of the corner of her mouth while pulling a beer, 'I wouldn't be in any hurry to leave his side.'

'Trix!'

'What? He's hot.'

'He's also a widower grieving for his wife seven years down the line.'

'Nooo…' She slammed the tap to off and pressed a hand to her chest. 'I think he just got even hotter.'

'I'd tell you that's insensitive, but I fear it would land on deaf ears.'

'And you expect me to believe you're not interested,' she drawled, shoving the schooner in front of the waiting customer and taking payment.

'I'm not!'

'Pull the other one, darl.'

Maria rolled her eyes. 'I'm beginning to regret asking Mickey for extra help tonight.'

'You love having me here really.'

'Debatable.' Though she smiled as she said it, nodding to a fresh customer and taking his order.

'Come on, darl,' Trix said in her ear while she served. 'Don't tell me you're not itching to unwrap him.'

'Hell, no.' She shivered, fearing it was more through the

thrill of it, than repulsion. 'Men with his kind of money, his kind of charm, they're a recipe for disaster and I want no part of it.'

She'd been there, lost her heart, and almost broke her daughter in the fallout. She'd be a fool to go there again.

'So you discussed his bank balance then?'

'What? No! You can just tell these things…'

'Sounds a little prejudiced to me.'

'I'm not prejudiced.'

'A man-hater, then.'

'I'm not a man-hater either.'

'You're something, darl, and I'm not entirely sure it's doing you any favours. When was the last time you had a bit of fun in that department?'

'It's not that simple. I have Fae to think about.'

'When it comes to sex, the only person who matters is you.'

Maria choked on her own laugh. 'When you're a mother you'll understand.'

'You saying mothers don't need sex too because—'

'Trix!'

'What? It's healthy to want it. Your problem is you keep insisting the two go hand in hand, sex and relationships. Flings are all about the sex, a temporary rush of meaningless fun. And you ought to keep that in mind because if I were you…' she checked him out across the bar '… I'd be locking him down before he scarpers and leaves you with nothing but regret.'

'I've no room for any more regret, believe me.'

'I wouldn't be so sure about that.'

Maria glanced in his direction, Trix's words echoing through her as his eyes lifted to hers and her breath caught, her cheeks warmed, those areas of her body that he'd reawakened after so many years begging to be listened to.

But who was to say he wanted her?

Who was to say it wasn't all in her head?

Her body alone?

Then his eyes dipped over her and the fire in their depths set her soul alight.

He wanted.

And heaven help her, so did she.

Tim didn't believe in love at first sight. Love was the kind of thing that took time and patience and understanding. But he believed in a certain kind of lust—the kind that felt like a lightning bolt from above. Sudden, fierce, powerful. And as rare as rain in the desert.

He'd only ever felt it with Ellie and figured it was a one-time-only deal. The closest thing to love at first sight he was ever going to get. Until now.

And he was pretty convinced she felt it too.

She might have run to the other end of the bar but her gaze kept drifting back. Her words might have said she wasn't interested but her eyes…

He wasn't the kind of man to assume desire. Far be it for him to put words in another person's mouth, but as he met her gaze again, he devoured every other outward sign. The way her mouth parted, her cheeks warmed, her chest lifting with a sudden breath—the bolt?

And she wasn't looking away. Not this time.

The beat of the music, the hum of the people, it all fell away. It was just them and this. The heated thread drawing them together.

Her colleague gave her a nudge—a customer was waiting at the bar. It took a second for her to blink, another for her to snap into action and break the connection.

He shook his head and raked his fingers through his hair. What was wrong with him?

He'd blame the drink for his chaotic thoughts, but he'd

hardly touched a drop. Not of his whisky or the champagne flowing at the party. Drunk on lust? Him?

He wanted to laugh at the very idea.

But he *was* something...

And as last orders were called and the customers started to leave, anticipation thrummed through his veins. Her looks became longer, more daring, as though she was contemplating, imagining...

The lights were dialled up and the music dialled down.

Her colleague bade her goodnight as a guy emerged from the back. Big enough to be the muscle of the place, but his white get-up and authoritative air singled him out as the chef. He was showing people the door and Tim would be next.

Time to go.

Whatever this was, it wasn't for him.

He downed the last of his drink and stood, lifting his jacket off the back of the stool, but before he could shrug it on, she was there, her hand on his empty glass, her eyes on him.

'Hi...'

Her voice was softer, less sure now the lights were up and her job was done.

'Hi yourself.'

He scanned her face, the way she bit down on her bottom lip, the way her cheeks filled with colour and her pulse flickered in her neck. Nerves?

'Did you change your mind...about the drink?'

'I guess I did.'

His mouth quirked up. 'You guess?'

'Unless you've changed your mind, because that's—'

'No,' he was quick to say. 'I haven't changed my mind.'

'Maria, you good?' the guy in chef whites called out.

'Yeah, I'm good.' She threw him a smile. 'You get yourself up to bed.'

He gave her a nod, his eyes narrowing on Tim.

'We're just…' Her eyes flitted back to Tim too. 'We're gonna get a drink together.'

'No worries.' Though the guy's gaze suggested he was none too sure about that. 'Holler if you need me.'

'Will do. G'night.'

She waited for him to head out through a door in the back before saying, 'Sorry about that. Bob can be a little overprotective.'

'Only a little?'

Her lips curved up, her eyes warming with affection for the guy. 'He likes to look out for us.'

'You and your daughter?'

'Yeah, he lives across the hall from us, upstairs.'

'That's handy. I mean the living upstairs from work, not the bodyguard across the hall…though on second thoughts, that's pretty handy too.'

She laughed. 'I suppose it is. Though not so handy when it means all your eggs are in one basket.'

'Eggs?'

'My livelihood and my living quarters, especially with the developers closing in, but it is what it is,' And dialling up her smile, she gestured to the bar. 'So, what can I get you to drink?'

'Your shift's over, it's my turn to ask you.'

She studied him for a beat.

'Okay. Give me two minutes to finish clearing up and I'll bring the bottle over.'

'Whisky?'

She cocked a brow, the self-assured barmaid making a return. 'Is that a problem?'

'Of course not.'

'Good,' she said with the same wry twist of her lips. 'For a second there I thought you were going to suggest it's too manly a drink for me.'

'I don't think I'd dare.'

She set his empty glass on the tray. 'Glad to hear it.'

'Can I help clear up?'

'You want to help?'

'Why not?' He took the tray from her grasp. 'I'm more than capable of collecting glasses.'

She grinned as she came out from behind the bar. 'Any breakages and you pay.'

'Wouldn't have it any other way.'

'Off you go then.'

He sensed her watching in bemused stillness as he swept around the room, collecting up the glasses.

'You just going to stand there and watch?'

'I was considering it,' she said, laughing as she moved to lock up the front and pull down the blinds.

She set the lights back to their muted glow and he joined her behind the bar, balancing the heavy tray while handing her the empties to load into the dishwasher. They moved in perfect synch—until his fingers brushed hers. She jolted. He jolted. Their eyes met and the glass fell, shattering against the floor and drowning out their shared curse.

'I'll pay for it,' he said, sliding the tray onto the side and crouching to gather the shards.

'Don't, you'll—'

Too late. He hissed as a sharp fragment pierced his finger.

'Oh, my God!' She dropped to her haunches and reached for his hand. Her sultry, spicy scent washing over him as her fingers wrapped around his wrist…talk about an assault on the senses.

He cleared his throat. 'It's fine.'

'It's not fine,' she blurted, 'you're bleeding.'

'I'll survive.'

'Come with me.' Her tone brooked no argument, and he was in no position to give one, not with her touch licking a fire right through him. They rose as one and she urged him to the sink, turned on the tap to let the water run over it. 'Didn't your mother ever teach you not to mess with broken glass?'

'I wasn't messing, I was helping.'

'Funny kind of helping, making a greater mess for me to tend to.'

She pulled out a first aid kit from under the counter, his hand still clutched in hers and taking him with her every step of the way.

'Are you calling me a mess?'

Her mouth twitched up as she tended to the cut, checking it for stray glass before pressing a strip of gauze to the fresh well of blood. 'If the shoe fits...'

Their eyes met, her words playful but everything else—her gaze, her care, her touch—this close, this sincere, this *intense*...

'What would you say if this mess told you he wanted to kiss you?'

She drew in a breath, her chest lightly grazing his.

'I'd say nothing.'

'In that case, what would you do?'

She rose on tiptoes, her lashes lowering as her lips inched closer...

'This.'

Boom!

Fireworks. That was what Maria felt as she threw caution to the wind and kissed him. The explosive rush of being this close to another person again, of letting the heat and the need take over. It was everything she'd been missing and everything she'd walk away from again come tomorrow, but right now... Trix was right.

He wrapped his arm around her, tugging her close, the groan caged within his throat rumbling through her chest.

'You taste like heaven.'

She wanted to laugh, wanted to tell him that was the expensive whisky they'd planned to consume, but they hadn't got to that yet. He had though, and he tasted divine. Lush and masculine. And she couldn't get enough.

'This is crazy,' she said, barely breaking away for fear it would stop.

'If crazy means good, I agree.'

'But your hand…'

'All better, thanks to you.'

His grey eyes seared her, the flush to his handsome cheeks too.

And then she kissed him, deeper, harder, revelling in the heat of his body pressed against hers as she released his hand to bury her own in his hair.

'You should know,' he rasped against her lips as he lifted her onto the counter. 'I don't do this.'

'This?'

'Lose all good sense in a heartbeat.'

She laughed against his mouth, wrapping her legs around him. 'Neither do I.'

'Then what are we doing?'

'I don't know that either.' She leaned back just enough to meet his gaze, the fire in his leaving her as breathless as his kiss. 'I just know I haven't felt like this in a long time, and I don't want you to walk out of here and regret what could have been.'

His eyes dipped to her mouth and back again. 'Ditto.'

'Then maybe we should quit talking,' she said, reaching closer.

'I won't argue.' He supped on her bottom lip, the briefest of caresses that had her thighs flexing around him, her fingers tightening in his hair. 'But if you want me to stop, you only have to—'

'If I want you to stop…' she stared into his eyes as their foreheads locked together, their breaths coming in shallow, synchronised puffs '…you'll know about it. But right now, I'm telling you I want this.'

She sealed her words with a kiss, her hands falling to the buttons of his shirt, fingers trembling as she hurried to undo each one. Safe in the knowledge that this was temporary, and it was mutual.

And for a night she could roll with it. Trust him with it.

She shoved the shirt from his shoulders, her palms recognising before her eyes could see that he was a mortal god. Every muscle honed to perfection. *Holy moly.* She bit into her lip and drank him in.

'Do you think we should…?'

Her eyes shot to his. He gestured to the door.

'It's okay, no one's coming back in here.'

'In that case…' He slid his hands beneath her T, his palms hot and sure as they moved over her skin to the curve of her breasts… Heat rushed to greet his touch, her nipples pressing against the lace of her bra as his thumbs teased each peak.

'You feel so good,' he murmured.

'That *feels* so good.' She arched back, her hands planting into the bar top as her head rolled back. How had she gone so long without this pleasure in her life?

'Do you have protection?'

His question snapped her back to earth. 'No.'

He swore under his breath and her panicked brain raced for a solution. 'The vending machine!'

'The what now?'

She shot off the counter. 'We have a vending machine.'

'You do?'

'In the ladies…'

She pulled him to the till, grabbed some coins.

'Add it to my bill.'

She laughed. 'Oh, I will, don't you worry.'

Then she tugged him into the loos, his chuckle deep and throaty right behind her. 'This is a first for me.'

'The ladies or the vending machine?' she said, slotting in the coins and pressing the button, her hips rolling against him as he closed in.

'Both.'

He wrapped his arms around her, his lips grazing her throat, the rough scrape of his stubble sending tiny ripples of excitement down her spine. The pack dropped and she snatched it up, turning in his hold as he guided her back against a stall.

'One night, yeah?' she blurted before his lips could claim hers, needing that reassurance, that reminder that this was all it was. A moment of madness, nothing that could hurt and everything they could enjoy as two consenting adults.

No promises. No commitment. Just fun.

He nodded. 'One night.'

CHAPTER THREE

TIM WASN'T SURE what roused him from his sleep—the soft snoring in his ear or the warm, silken body wrapped around him. All he knew was that he hadn't known a peace like it in too long. And he didn't want to leave.

Which was a sure sign that he should. Giving into lust was one thing, getting attached again...never.

She stirred, her head travelling down his chest until her cheek rested against his pec, her limbs tightening around him. He exhaled, abandoning all thought of leaving. A few hours wouldn't hurt. The amber glow slipping through her blinds said it was still early. Maybe they could grab coffee, some breakfast. It was Saturday after all—a day of rest for many. Maybe it was time he fell into that habit too.

His phone buzzed beside him and he reached out to silence it.

Okay, so maybe his world didn't agree.

He checked the caller ID. Sasha?

He frowned. She was supposed to be hosting a gala for her charity in London right now. A function that he should be attending too. But his corporate commitments had taken precedence—or at least that was what he'd said.

In reality, he still struggled to walk the same halls Ellie once had and the UK was full of them. Not to mention that the charity itself had been set up in her honour. If ever there was an event where people would want to talk about her, it was there.

A message buzzed through and Maria nuzzled in deeper, setting off a string of vibrations within him. How could he want her again already?

He felt like a hormonal teenager, not a man of his years. *Three* times they'd succumbed. Three times they'd completely lost their minds to it. The last session a very sleepy but very satisfying coming together that had seen her drifting off in his arms and he hadn't wanted to leave. Much like he didn't want to leave now. But he had to check on Sasha.

Easing out from under her, he scanned the room for his clothing. Where on earth…? They'd been otherwise engaged when they'd stumbled in during the night, but it had to be here somewhere. Not that he could see in every corner and he wasn't about to turn on a light.

Giving up, he grabbed the only obvious thing he could find—her kimono off the back of the door—and tugged it on. It would have to do.

Out he crept, straight into the living area where the early morning rays seeped through the thin curtains, bathing everything in gold. For the first time, he truly took in the space… The hodgepodge of old chairs, tables and cabinets that shared no cohesive quality but somehow worked together. Fresh flowers bloomed on the tiny coffee table. Books and plants lined the shelves. Photos too. Most depicting landscapes from around the world, while others were pictures of her and a young girl. Her daughter?

His phone buzzed again, reminding him of his own kid.

Call me back x

He dialled her number and crossed the room to the window, lifting back the curtain to eye the street below. A far cry from the fancy city block he'd left behind, the rundown strip was in dire need of a cash injection. Boarded-up businesses. Overflowing rubbish bins. Graffiti-laden walls. Connor would have a fit if he could see him now…and the thought only made him smile further.

'Dad!'

'Hello to you too, darling,' he murmured, careful to keep his voice down. 'Do you know what time it is?'

'Don't pretend you're not already awake and checking your email.'

'Actually, I—'

'And don't you darling me. Connor says you bailed on your party. The party you told me you couldn't possibly miss to come to the gala.'

He caught sight of his guilt-ridden grimace in the glass. 'Says the girl who's supposed to be at that very same gala now, entertaining her guests, but instead is berating her father for not being there.'

'I got sick of covering for you.'

'Covering for me?'

'Yes. *Everyone* is asking where you are. One day they'll realise that it's me running this charity and not you. Until then, it would be nice not to spend most of my time fielding questions about you.'

'I'm sorry, darling.'

'So am I. Not because of that, but because you're not here. And you should be.'

'Maybe next year.'

'You said that last year and the year before and…'

'I know, I know.'

She fell silent. In the background he could hear the gentle hum of chatter, laughter, music too.

'You should go back to your party.'

'It's really not the same without you here. It helped me, you know, coming back here, seeing the people who helped Mum, being around the family. You can't blame them all for asking where you are, Dad. Gran hasn't seen you since you flew her out to Paris.'

'That was a good trip, we should do it again.'

'It would be a lot easier on her if you came here.'

Sasha was right. Ellie's mum was getting on in years. But visiting her in the home where Ellie grew up, with her pictures in every room and, no, just no.

'Please, Dad.'

He cleared his throat. 'I'll see what I can sort.'

'And while you're doing that, will you sort your diary so that you can get out on the boat with Connor next week? He told me he asked and you flat-out refused.'

'I didn't refuse, I said I'd think about it.'

'Which is code for no.'

'It isn't code, it's an "I'll think about it".'

'You need to get a life, Dad. One that doesn't revolve around work and me.'

'I'm on it.'

Sasha's laugh of disbelief rippled down the phone. 'Being on it would be you saying yes to Connor for a start. He says you've not had a boys' trip in years.'

'Maybe because we're not boys any more—young, free and single.'

'Knock it off, Dad, you're hardly over the hill. And you're definitely free and single.'

'Doesn't make me ready to mingle like he wants to.'

'I know Connor can be a bit wild, but you could do with a little bit of that in your life…'

Hell, if Sasha only knew where he was now. What he *looked* like right now. He tugged at the floral fabric of Maria's kimono. His confession stuck on his tongue.

'Don't you think it's time?' she said softly.

He looked back to the view, though he wasn't seeing the street now. He was seeing the past. A premature goodbye and the guilt at feeling something for another, no matter how different it was.

'Pardon me if I don't want to take life advice from my twenty-five-year-old daughter who should be living her own life rather than interfering in mine.'

'I'm not interfering, I'm advising. There's a difference.'

'Well, whatever you're doing, you need to stop and get back to your party before you're missed. I hear you're set to smash last year's target, you should be proud.'

'I don't do it for me.'

'I'm proud of you, and I can be proud enough for the three of us.'

Because he knew Ellie would have been bursting with pride for all their daughter had achieved. Hitting the ground running with her charity venture at the young age of twenty and turning it into the multi-million-pound charity it was now, five years on.

'Thanks, Dad.'

He smiled. 'You're welcome, darling. So…how is the party?'

Maria shot up with a start, eyes wide, hands clutching the bedsheets…

Someone had screamed. She was sure of it. But her room was empty, the flat now quiet. Had she imagined it, or had—

'Who the hell are you?'

Her gaze shot to the door—*Fae!*

Oh, God, Tim!

She threw off the covers and darted for the door, pausing belatedly to snatch her kimono off the back and grasping thin air. She stared at the empty hook. What the—

'Mum!'

'I can explain,' came Tim's voice.

'I very much doubt that! Mum! What are you wearing? Is that—is that *Mum's*?'

Oh, God, oh, God, oh, God. She dashed around the bedroom, pulling on her knickers and grabbing the first thing that came to hand—his shirt, half-visible beneath the bed! Shoving her arms in, she buttoned it as she raced out.

Fae was in her bedroom doorway. Tim was before the living room window. Her floral kimono, a ridiculous sight on his too tall, too broad frame. What was he *thinking*, wearing *that*?

'Mum?'

'It's okay, Fae.'

She raised a placating hand while running the other through her hair that felt as wild as her daughter's looked.

'Is *it*?' Fae wrapped her arms around her pyjama-clad middle, eyes brimming with accusation as she pinned Tim with a glare. 'Who the hell is this?'

'This…' She glanced his way, wishing she'd woken sooner, wishing she'd thought to exercise more caution, wishing for anything but the current situation.

She wasn't about to wish the night away though…she wasn't an idiot and Fae wasn't a child. She was still her kid though and this was her home too. She had a right to be upset at his presence.

'This is Tim,' she said, like that explained everything, copying Fae's crossed arm stance and wishing his shirt was thicker, longer…that her kimono wasn't showing off far too much of him.

Hell, she needed to explain properly, but she couldn't think straight. Not when her body was overheating with remembered scenes from the night before, of the things he'd done, that *she'd* done—

'Since we're all up, shall I put the coffee on?' She averted her gaze and made a run for the machine. Coffee made everything better.

'Coffee?' Fae squeaked.

'Do you have tea?' Tim said.

'Do we have *tea*?' Fae repeated, mimicking his accent that had suddenly become very English. Maria was sure he'd sounded Aussie the night before. Maybe he was an ex-pat, or so well-travelled he'd picked up various accents along the way. It only served to highlight how little she knew about him and how reckless she had been, and now she was seeing it all through Fae's eyes maybe regret *should* be more forthcoming.

'I'm afraid not,' Maria said, loading the coffee machine and sensing her daughter's aghast frown continuing to flit between them.

'Did you— Did he— Did...'

Maria's head snapped in her direction—*for the love of God, don't say it!*

Fae shook her head, her cheeks colouring. 'I don't believe this.'

Then she turned and fled to her room, the slam of her door making them both flinch.

'Oh, God,' Maria grumbled. 'Shoot me now.'

'I'm so sorry,' he said.

'You have nothing to be sorry for...'

Maria, on the other hand. So much for no regrets.

'Oh, I do.' He came towards her and her pulse kicked up. How could she still find him hot in *that*? 'I think I'd be the same if I came across me dressed like this.'

He gave her a smile that had her toes curling into the wooden floor, warmth swirling through her lower belly despite her unease. Seriously! How was it possible? Anyone else and she'd be laughing at the ridiculous sight he made...

'It shouldn't look good on you, but...'

She reached out, her hand coming to rest upon his chest as her eyes lifted to his. Her intention had been to stop whatever he'd been about to do. Instead, the feel of his hot, hard body through the silk had her wishing for it all.

'I know what you mean,' he said, lifting his fingers to the

open collar of the shirt she wore, the lightest sweep of his fingers against her collarbone making her breath quiver. 'My shirt will never look plain again.'

She wet her lips—*take it down a notch, take—it—down!*

'Mind telling me *why* you chose my kimono?'

'It was the quickest thing to hand.'

'In a rush to escape me?'

'My daughter called.' He raised his phone. 'I didn't want to risk waking you.'

'Oh…' Thoughtful, sweet, the reminder that he was a parent too—a *caring* one—warming her in other ways.

'I have a feeling she'll be calling back very soon demanding an explanation for the girl she could hear screaming in the background.'

She grimaced. 'She heard?'

'Oh, yes, she heard.'

'What did you tell her?'

'That I was with a friend.'

'A *screaming* friend?'

'Hence why I'll have questions of my own to answer soon enough.'

'I'm sorry.' Maria glanced at Fae's door. 'She isn't used to me bringing men home.'

'You said as much last night, though it's nice to know I truly am a special case.'

A special case that you were supposed to be waving bye-bye to come morning...

She pulled away, freeing herself of his touch as much as his gaze.

'Dressed in that, definitely,' she said, deploying humour as a shield.

He gave a gruff laugh. 'Okay, there's only so much teasing a man's ego can take. Do you mind if I shower?'

'Help yourself.' The sooner she had space, the better. 'Towels are in the cupboard behind the door, use whatever you need.'

'Cheers.'

She set the coffee going and leaned back against the counter, taking a breath, then another, seeking calm and finding the opposite.

One night wasn't supposed to become a morning too. A morning where she craved it turning into another and another…

'Is he taking a *shower* now?'

Her head snapped up to find Fae gawping at her from across the room, hazel eyes firing sparks.

'Yes.'

Fae cursed.

'Language!'

'I need the loo!'

'He won't be long.'

'He's been here too long already.'

'I invited him.' Maria sighed. 'If you want to be mad at anyone, be mad at me.'

'I *am* mad at you!'

Maria's mouth fell open. She scrambled for something to say, something that wouldn't make the situation worse. Because truth was, she'd enjoyed having him with her for the night, and the whole point had been to indulge in a little fun and wake up with no regrets.

Not have them pile on by the plenty.

'I'm sorry, Mum,' Fae suddenly blurted, her shoulders slumping, eyes softening as she stepped forward. 'I don't mean to be…to be an arse. But I got up to get a glass of water, I walk in here and get the fright of my life. You could've at least warned me you had someone coming back.'

'I know, I'm sorry. It wasn't like I planned it. He came into the bar for a drink last night and we got talking and things… things just happened.' She bit her lips together as her daughter's eyes fired once more. 'What I mean is—'

'What you mean is, you just hooked up with some *random* guy? A guy you didn't even *know* before last night?'

Maria felt her cheeks burn. Who was the mother in this relationship?

'I know it looks bad but…'

'Too right it looks bad, you'd blow a fuse if I'd done that.'

'That's different.'

'How? *How* is that different?'

Her daughter had a point. 'I'm your mother for a start.'

'You are and you should know better.'

No argument there…

'Who even is he? He sounds like a right stuck-up—'

'*Fae,*' she warned.

'What, Mum? We know his type. He'll use you to get what he wants and leave you for dust when he's done.'

'Keep your voice down, love, he'll hear you.'

'I don't care if he hears me. He's gonna be just like all the rest. Just like…'

'He's *not* your father.'

'Yeah, well, don't say I didn't warn you.'

'You don't need to warn me, I know well enough.'

'Bullsh—'

'Fae! It was just a night, honey, nothing more.'

And now she was stressing she'd indulged in a one-night stand. To her own *daughter.* For crying out loud, could this get any worse?

Fae frowned. 'You're *not* planning on seeing him again?'

She shook her head, the 'no' sticking in her throat.

'Okay.' Fae raised her chin, gave a nod. 'Good.'

It was good. So why did it feel like anything but…?

'It's not that I don't want you to be happy, Mum. But this is our life. We spent so long living under Dad's thumb and now we're finally free of him and have things just how we want them… To have another man come in and…'

She broke off, her bottom lip quivering, and Maria was across the room in a heartbeat.

'Oh, honey, come here...' She pulled Fae into her arms. 'I am never letting a man take control of our lives again. I promise you that.' She kissed her hair. 'This is our home. Yours and mine. Okay?'

Fae sniffed against her chest, nodded. 'Yeah.'

She held her for a long moment, centring her thoughts on Fae and their life and why there was no room for a man. Especially one as distracting and all-consuming as Tim.

'You know he was talking to another "*dah-ling*" on the phone when I came in...' Fae murmured, glancing up at her. 'A bit dodge, don't you think?'

She gave a twisted smile. 'His daughter. Not another woman.'

'How can you know that for sure?'

She couldn't, not really. Just because he'd *told* her he didn't do this often didn't make it true. People made great liars when it suited them. Fae's father, Fraser, had been one of the best. He'd fooled her. And he'd fooled his wife. For years they'd danced to the tune of his lies and she wouldn't dance to the tune of another now, lies or otherwise.

The door to the bathroom swung open and he emerged in a cloud of steam, the look on his face telling her he'd overheard plenty. Bugger.

'I'll just throw my clothes on and get out of your hair.'

She nodded, unable to trust her voice. Especially when faced with him in nothing more than a towel, his hair and skin still wet, grey eyes shimmering with an emotion she didn't want to explore but felt to her core...

Damn it. He made her feel, made her want, made her put another first in the heat of the night—and that was why he had to go.

End of.

CHAPTER FOUR

TIM KNEW ENOUGH of teenage girls to know that Fae wasn't acting out because of him. He was pretty sure any man would have elicited the same response.

Even so, he dressed as quickly as he could. Stalling when he realised Maria still wore his shirt. As much as some men might consider a dinner jacket and trousers an outfit, he wasn't one.

But thinking of her in it…the way the white fabric fell to mid-thigh, shifting against her skin as she moved…he cursed as his body tightened.

So many years of zero interest in women and now he couldn't put a lid on it. What was that saying about Pandora's Box? And why the hell did that feel a euphemism? He groaned as he dragged a hand down his face, slapped his cheeks.

Get a grip!

He just needed to get his shirt and get the hell out of there. He glanced at the door, more than aware of the women still talking on the other side. He'd hoped Fae might disappear again, hide out until he was gone. More for the girl's benefit than his. But it wasn't to be…

Pocketing his phone, he grabbed his jacket off the floor and headed out. He found them in the kitchen, sipping coffee, the mood in the air suffocatingly thick as they both turned to him.

He cleared his throat, feeling every exposed millimetre of his chest. 'I'm going to need that back…'

He gestured to her—*his* shirt.

'Oh, God, of course! Sorry!' She slapped her mug down. 'I'll just change.'

She hurried from the room and the temperature dropped to freezing. Why the hell hadn't he thought to follow her?

Fae muttered something under her breath, her hostile glare enough to make him want to wilt— *Wilt*, him?

Be a man, for Pete's sake. Own it. Apologise. Move on.

He couldn't be afraid of an eighteen-year-old...could he?

'I really am sorry,' he tried.

'Yeah, you and me both.'

Okay, maybe he was, a little...

He rocked on his feet, paying great attention to the furnishings—the scuffed leg of the coffee table, the stitched-up sofa cushion, the damp seeping into the corner wall... Maria hurried back in, thank God!

Now dressed in shorts and an oversized T that had seen better days, she was a sight for sore eyes.

'There you go,' she said, passing him his shirt and snapping around as Fae tried to sneak out behind her. 'Where are you going?'

'I'm going to take my coffee to the park. That okay?'

'You don't have to go,' he said, tossing his jacket on the sofa and pulling on his shirt. 'I'll call a cab and be gone in—'

'It's fine,' she said to her mum. 'I want to get some air, and it'll give you chance to see *him*...off!'

She made it sound like he was about to *be* offed, particularly as she grunted the word while tugging on the door that was in dire need of a good planing.

He swallowed a crazed laugh and buttoned up his shirt. All the assurances he wanted to give about not being *that* guy—the guy to take the sex and run—dying on his lips because, a, that was precisely what they had agreed to do. And b, she looked in no mood to hear it.

The door slammed shut and Maria pressed a hand to her

mouth, the other fisted on her hip as she stared after her daughter. Was she upset? Nervous? Mortified? All of the above?

Whatever the case, she was no longer the confident barmaid willing to give in to the chemistry that had taken them both by surprise last night…

No, she was Maria the mum and the father in him could understand that and sure as hell sympathise.

'Funny how our kids can bring us back to earth with such gravitas.'

'Gravitas?' She gave a tight laugh as she turned to him. 'That's one word for it.'

'Anyone else dare judge us for last night,' he said, tucking in his shirt, 'and we'd tell them where to go, but our kids…'

Her smile twisted off to the side as she gave a slow nod. 'Yeah…'

'You're okay though?' he asked, the idea that she was now regretting what had been one of the best nights of his life giving him pause.

'I will be.' She glanced up at him, her smile not half as bright or as easy as he wanted it to be. 'Can I get you a coffee?'

'It's okay.' He was more than aware he'd overstayed his welcome. 'I can get one on the road.' He took up his phone, opened the app to request a taxi. 'It shouldn't take long to get a cab.'

'Honestly, it's no bother. At least have a coffee while you wait.'

He glanced up. 'Are you sure?'

She nodded. 'Fae won't come back until she knows you're gone if that's what you're worried about…'

He searched her gaze. 'I'm more concerned about what you want and whether you're only offering to be nice.'

She gave a laugh, her eyes sparkling with it. Now *that* was the woman he'd met last night. 'You should know, I don't do anything for nice's sake.'

'Well, in that case…' he returned her smile '… I'd love one.'

She headed to the kitchenette while he chose a cab twenty minutes away. Long enough not to drink and run, short enough not to become any more of a burden. He pocketed his phone and browsed the photos on her shelves while he waited.

Most were of cities around the world, interspersed with photos of Fae, or her and Fae together. He picked one off the shelf, smiling at the heartwarming moment captured between mother and daughter.

'That was the day we moved in here,' she said as she handed him a mug. 'Mickey took it.'

'Mickey?'

'The owner of the building, he owns the bar too.'

'Nice guy?'

'One of the best.'

His brows twitched as he kept his focus on the pic and his thoughts to himself. Because in his honest opinion, Mickey needed a lesson in How to be a Responsible Landlord if the damp and the dodgy door were anything to go by. The memory of them crashing through it the night before flashed through his mind and he promptly quashed it.

'If it wasn't for him—well, let's just say back then, we needed him more than he needed us.'

Why? He wanted to ask. But questions like that…they were hardly easy morning chat, easy goodbye chat. And that was what they were supposed to be doing.

He placed the photo back down. 'It's a great picture.'

'It was a great day.'

Her eyes warmed, her smile reminiscent.

'How so?' he couldn't stop himself from asking and immediately tried to backtrack, 'Or does this come under the same banner as the ex you'd prefer to forget?'

'It *is* the same banner as the ex.'

She sipped her coffee and he figured she was done, but then she surprised him with more. 'Up until then, he wasn't just in our life, he controlled it. Where we lived. Who we saw. Where Fae went to school. It took a lot to break away. But once we had…' She sighed. 'I'm afraid it's part of the reason she was so hard on you.'

Her explanation should have made him feel better. The confirmation that it wasn't about *who* he was, rather than *what* he was. A threat.

'I'm only sad that I didn't see sense sooner. I could have saved her a lot of heartache.'

'I don't know,' he said softly. 'It's hard when you live with someone for so long to imagine life without them. Whether the relationship is good or bad, it's what you know.'

'We never lived together, not in the way you're thinking…' She licked her lips, shifting tempo as she walked away. 'And this is way too deep a conversation to be having over our morning coffee.'

'I'd like to have it though,' he said, following her. 'If you're willing to talk about it.'

So much for keeping it light and easy…

But damn it, he *wanted* to know. Maybe it was because she'd got him talking about Ellie. Maybe it was because she got him feeling like Ellie once had. Maybe it was because he wasn't ready to walk away, no matter that his survival instincts said to do otherwise.

'You know we're not friends, right. You don't have to be all sweet and interested just because we…' she nudged her head towards the bedroom and he urged his mind not to travel in the same direction '…hooked up.'

'Hooked up?' He gave a chuckle as tight as his body now felt. 'It's been a long time since I hooked up with anyone.'

'Really? Because last night you seemed to know your way around like an expert.'

Her cheeks glowed, her eyes too, and hell, it took every bit of restraint not to tug her to him and work his way around her all over again.

'I could say the same about you.'

She laughed with him. 'Some skills you never unlearn, I guess.'

'I think it's more about the person than the skills. A rare connection that just…works.' He held her gaze as he accepted the truth. He didn't just want to talk today, he wanted to see her again tomorrow and quite possibly the next and the next. 'Maria, I know we said this was a—'

'Don't say it,' she blurted.

'You don't know what I'm going to say yet.'

'It's written in your face.'

'It is?'

'*Yes*. And I can't.'

'Why?'

'I just can't. We agreed. One night and then you go your way, I go mine. No complications. No muddying the waters and making this into more than it needs to be.'

'That still doesn't answer my question—why can't we see each other again?'

'I… I don't want to.'

Maria stared up into his grey eyes while her head screamed, *'Liar!'*

Yes, she wanted to see him again. Yes, she wanted to continue this conversation. Out here, back in the bedroom, wherever and whenever he wanted it to happen. And that was all the warning she needed.

'I don't want to see you again,' she repeated, as much for her own benefit as his, 'because there's no room in my life for a man.'

'You make it sound like I'm after forever.'

She choked on a laugh. *Imagine?*

'Not forever, no…' Though his words weren't too dissimilar to Trix's, berating her for seeing sex and relationships as one and the same thing. 'But I think it would be unfair of me to say yes, when I barely have a moment spare for me and Fae as it is. My life revolves around her and working to keep a roof over our heads.'

'Everyone needs some downtime.'

'Are you talking about work or parenthood now, because any decent parent knows you never get off that particular roll-ercoaster of responsibility?'

'No, our worlds revolve around them, for sure. And when they're young, when they need us, they come first absolutely. But she's eighteen now, she has her own life to lead, and so do you.'

Wasn't that another flavour of what Trix had been saying to her? Though Trix had been more about leading by example and showing her daughter there's more to life than this place and work.

'I know that, believe me, I do.'

But getting caught up in whatever this was between her and Tim, that wasn't the example she wanted to set. In fact, it was the exact opposite. She wanted to show Fae she could do it all on her own. Having spent over a decade with her happiness hinging on Fraser, she wanted Fae to know that she didn't need a man to be happy. That she didn't need a man to secure her future, to have fun either.

'But this is hardly setting her the best example.'

He gave an abrupt laugh. 'No, I don't think this morning was our finest parental hour either, but given time to adjust, time to…'

His voice trailed off as she shook her head. 'I can't.'

She knew from experience just how vulnerable you were at eighteen and she wanted to be there for her daughter, not distracted by him. She was already starting to hate herself enough for exposing Fae to Tim's kimono-clad self that morning…

And that wasn't his fault, it was hers. She'd been the one

to bring him back. To put her needs over her daughter in the heat of the moment.

'I'm sorry.'

'No.' He sighed. 'I'm sorry. We agreed this was a one-night deal and I shouldn't be trying to change that up at the eleventh hour.'

He returned to the wall of photos and she watched him go, her heart racing, body and mind adjusting to his acquiescence.

Damn, he was sweet, kind, thoughtful. So freaking understanding and everything Fraser hadn't been.

Which made him even more dangerous....

'You're well-travelled,' he said as she came up alongside him.

'In my dreams.'

He glanced her way. 'You didn't take these?'

'No. It's more a visual bucket list.'

'So, what, you take them off the wall after you've been?' She sipped her coffee. 'Maybe—I'd have to visit one first.'

'You haven't...'

'I've never been out of Australia. What about you?' she said, swiftly moving on. 'Which ones have you been to?'

He scanned every snap and she got the distinct impression the list was too long to share...or rub in her face.

'Okay.' She gave him a small smile. 'How about telling me your favourite instead?'

He looked back at the wall. 'Impossible to say, they all have different qualities. The gothic beauty of Edinburgh, the romance of Paris, the garden city of Singapore... Have you always wanted to travel?'

'Yeah. As a child, I'd cut pictures out of my mother's magazines, stick them in a scrapbook and tell myself one day I'd get there. I'd escape and see the world.'

'Escape? Is that how you saw it as a kid?'

His eyes narrowed on her and she knew he'd read so much in that one sentence.

She tried to give an easy shrug, but it was awkward, stilted by the memories that never really stayed silent.

'Who doesn't want to escape their home life at times, right?'

'I don't know. If anything, my parents sheltered me, made me feel safe and secure. I was adrift when I first went to boarding school and would fantasise about running back home.'

Her chest warmed with his honesty. 'That's kind of sweet.'

'Not the image you want when you're at boarding school, believe me. It forced me to grow up and find my feet though. What about you?'

'Well, I didn't go to boarding school,' she joked, then admitted softly, 'But I think I would've liked it.'

'Because it wasn't home?'

She gave a soft huff. 'Yeah.'

'Why?'

'That's a tale for another day…'

The day that wasn't ever going to happen. She knew it. He knew it. Time to move on. Because she wasn't dredging up that sorry tale to have him pity her more.

'Where are you from?' she asked. 'Originally, I mean. You sounded English just now, when you said "tea"…' She couldn't help mimicking him like Fae had done. 'But I would have pegged you as a fellow Aussie last night.'

'I'm from Sydney,' he said, taking her change of topic and running with it, though she sensed his question still hanging in the air between them. 'I lived in England for a while. My wife, Ellie, she was English. We met while I was there on business, fell in love, and the rest, as they say…'

'Is history,' she finished softly.

He nodded. 'Sasha, my daughter, she went to school there too.'

'Where's home for you both now?'

'Sasha splits her time between the UK and Sydney.'

'And you?'

'I travel a lot with work. I don't really consider myself as having a base any more.'

'Hence the yo-yo accent.'

'Yo-yo?'

'Yeah, from Aussie to English and whatever else you have going on there.'

'I guess *tea* is one of those words that's quintessentially British.'

She cocked a brow. 'Quintessentially?'

'You know, if I'd known my dialect was going to take this kind of beating come morning, I would have left in the night,' he teased, the weighted mood lifting with it and then shifting into something else as he sobered. 'Do you wish I had?'

The one question she couldn't answer. Not truthfully at any rate. Because it would be so easy to slip into the other truth, that she didn't want him to leave. That she wanted to let this chemistry run its course and pay no heed to what came next. A risk she refused to take.

His phone buzzed and she looked to where it sat in his pocket. 'Do you think that's your ride?'

He stared back at her. 'I guess I have my answer then.'

'It's not that I didn't enjoy last night, Tim.'

'I know, I believe you.'

'I hope so.'

She gave him a weak smile and he threw back the rest of his coffee, grabbed his jacket off the sofa and placed his mug next to the sink. She was waiting for him at the door, tugging the stubborn thing open.

'You really should get that seen to.'

'Tell me something I don't already know.'

'That you are quite wonderful, Maria. And whatever last night was for you, it meant something to me. So, thank you.'

He leant in to sweep a soft kiss against her cheek and she inhaled her own shampoo on his hair, felt his warmth caress her, and then he was gone. And *oh,* how she wanted to run after him. Tell him she'd changed her mind.

But the last time she'd succumbed to a connection like this, a connection that felt like it was meant to be, she'd stumbled away broken. Her daughter suffering all the more for being the unwanted product of an affair. Fraser choosing his *real* family over Fae, protecting them, putting them first.

And Maria had sworn Fae would never feel second-best again. Her daughter was everything. And that was how it would stay.

'Goodbye, Tim,' she whispered into the hallway that was as empty as her chest now felt.

'He's gone then?'

Her head snapped around to find Fae stepping out of Bob's across the way.

'I thought you said you were going to the park.'

'Yeah, I lied.'

Maria shook her head. 'Get back in here.'

Suitably sheepish, Fae crossed the hall and wrapped her arms around Maria's waist.

She hugged her daughter tight. 'Are we good?'

'We're always good, Mum. I love you.'

She kissed her hair. 'I love you too.'

And that was all that mattered. Her and Fae. Tim was just a distraction, a tiny blip. She'd forget about him soon enough... honestly, she would.

'Fancy pancakes with all the trimmings for breakfast?'

Fae's head shot up. 'Now you're talking!'

CHAPTER FIVE

'So sorry I'm late, Trix.' Maria barrelled on board the yacht, tugging her small suitcase with her. 'Some surveyor rocked up at the flat as I was trying to leave and I had to show him in.'

'A surveyor? Uncle Mickey finally putting some money back into the place?'

'It would seem that way.'

'Huh.' She nodded. 'Things must be looking up.'

'Let's hope so, yeah.' She paused on deck and looked around, a low whistle escaping. The sleek black vessel was by far the most exclusive-looking yacht currently docked. Bold and daring and radiating wealth... 'How rich did you say this guy was again?'

'I don't know, world's rich list rich. I'd give you a full tour but the boss is due on board any minute and you need to change. I'll point out the main areas on the way to our cabin and the rest we'll pick up later.'

'Sounds good, I'm sure I'll get my bearings soon enough.'

She followed Trix inside, working hard to stop her mouth from hanging open as she listened to her point out various things.

Get my bearings soon—yeah, right! This thing was huge! Huge *and* luxurious. Split over several floors, too.

From the apparent helipad and swimming pool up top, to the state-of-the-art gym, spa pool—yes, two pools!—cinema room, dancefloor, multiple bars and dining areas, before one even got to the master staterooms and VIP suites. This super-yacht had everything anyone could want. And with its teak floors, sumptuous furnishings, monochrome colour scheme and high-end tech, every bit of it oozed money.

A true billionaires' playground—and it had been a long time since Maria had been surrounded by such wealth. Though even Fraser's wealth as a world-renowned cosmetic surgeon paled in comparison to this.

'You're going to have to close that mouth of yours before we meet and greet,' Trix said with a laugh, shoving open the door to their cabin. 'Mind if I take the bottom bunk?'

She gestured to the beds and Maria swung her case up top. 'No worries.'

'So, you going to tell me what happened after I left the other night?'

Maria rolled her eyes. 'I've only just got on board. Do you wanna help me find my sea legs first before interrogating me?'

Trix chuckled and tossed her a neat stack of clothing. 'Your uniform… So something *did* happen?'

'I admit nothing.'

'Well, while you're admitting "nothing", can you get into the top set—white shirt, navy skirt? They're your whites for greeting the guests. You'll need the blues for daywear, and blacks for evening service.'

'*How* many outfits?'

'You'll be glad of them. It gets hot and dirty on deck.'

Maria cocked a brow. 'Why do you have to make every-thing sound so X-rated?'

'Hey, it's not the mouth it comes out of, darl…'

'So they say, but in your case they'd definitely make an exception.'

'Enough with the insults.' Trix tossed a pillow at her. 'Do you want this gig or not?'

'Yeah, I want the gig,' she said, stripping out of her travel clothes. 'You want to give me the lowdown on our boss and his guests while I change?'

'On it.' Trix plonked herself on the bottom bunk and ran through the preference sheet on her phone, giving Maria the highlights as she went.

There was the owner of the yacht, a Mr Montgomery. Forty-six. Old money and on the face of it easy to please. Trix loved working for him. Then there were his guests. Two women, of no relation. Twenty-six. Models, with *all* the dietary requirements and *all* the demands. They were going to be a hoot!

But three guests versus an entire bar—it had to be easier, right? And it certainly paid better. And if they were demanding enough to keep her extra busy, her mind would quit trekking back to the very same night Trix wanted to unpack.

And Maria had done enough unpacking this past week to last a lifetime. She did *not* need to go back over it. Verbally, especially.

It was supposed to have been one night of fun, of letting go and living in the moment. Not living in it every moment since. But Tim was proving hard to shift. His smile, his eyes, his warmth and his honesty...*no regrets, remember.*

She tucked the shirt into her navy skirt and turned to face the mirror on the back of their bathroom door, smoothing her hair back into the same functional bun Trix was sporting. 'How do I look?'

'Like you belong here, darl.'

'Attention all crew, attention all crew...' Trix's walkie-talkie crackled to life. 'This is your Captain speaking. Guests are on the dock. I need you all on the aft deck for meet and greet.'

'It's showtime,' Trix said, tossing Maria her own walkie-talkie to clip to her skirt and launching to her feet. 'You good?'

'I'm good.'

She followed her back upstairs to the grand saloon. 'Grab the face towels from the fridge, won't you? We'll take them out with the champagne.'

'Face towels, on it.'

Trix popped the cork on a bottle and filled three glasses, while Maria arranged the chilled towels into a neat triangle on the tray, topping it off with a fresh flower head from the display beside the bar.

'Nice touch,' Trix said. 'I knew you'd be a natural at this.'

Making things look pretty had been her speciality once upon a time. As a live-in maid in Fraser's household, she'd often been called upon to prettify a room or two. The odd flower on a pillow. A welcome arrangement in the hall. A full-on themed display for a house party.

A flower could lift the plainest of things—they'd made Fraser smile too. And the pleasure she'd got from receiving that simple gesture as a teenager made her recoil in horror now. How stupid she had been. How young and gullible and foolish. Selfish too.

'Hey, it was meant as a compliment.'

Her head snapped up, eyes blinking through the pain of her past to her present and Trix.

'You okay?'

'Sorry, yeah, head elsewhere.'

Which it had been a lot this past week. As if seeing Tim had somehow stirred it all up.

'Well, get it back, you need your game face on.' Trix slid the tray her way. 'Remember, it's just like serving on land with the occasional rock 'n' roll of the water.'

'Easy-peasy,' she said, taking up the tray with a well-prac-tised smile.

'That's the business!'

They joined the receiving line out on the aft deck and Trix quickly introduced her. There was Captain Kali, Chief Engi-neer Danis, First Officer Russell and Chef Rio. Running back and forth on the gangplank, hauling luggage on board, were Bosun Anya and her number two, Deckhand Bobby.

'Smiles at the ready, folks!' Kali murmured as a trio came

into view. A tall blond guy flanked by two women hanging off each arm. One of them raised her shades and gave a little squeal, clapping her hands with glee.

'Oh, God, we've got a squealer,' Trix said under her breath, rousing a giggle from all in earshot.

'Trix…' Kali warned.

'Don't worry, Captain, they can squeal all they like. Their wish is my command.'

'Glad to hear it…'

The sun was already beating down and Maria was grateful for the shade being gifted by the flybridge above. She was used to working indoors—her lightly freckled skin and the sun didn't mix. No matter how much she lathered herself in sunblock.

'Mr Montgomery,' Kali said, stepping forward as the man himself came up the gangplank. 'Welcome aboard, sir.'

'Hey, Captain!'

The man saluted before shaking Kali's hand. He was every-thing Maria had envisaged. Designer shades atop his foppish blond hair, blue eyes, all smiles and bronzed skin. His clothes too—chino shorts and a white polo with a sweater draped over his shoulders as if he was between tennis matches, not land and sea. And though he acted casual enough, men like him, like Fraser, like Tim, they radiated wealth like the yacht itself.

As for the models, they looked identical save for their hair colour. Cherry was blonde. Dana, a dark brunette. Golden tans, oversized shades, bright white smiles, triangles for bi-kini tops and the smallest strips for skirts.

What she couldn't work out was the connection between models and man? Friends? Associates? Lovers? She gave a discreet shudder. She hoped not. He was old enough to be their father.

Says the girl who fell in love with her boss twenty years her senior!

Maybe that was why it turned her stomach while her smile

ached upon her face, her mask staying in place as Captain ran through the introductions and she held out the tray.

'Towel?' she said smoothly. 'Champagne?'

'Thank you,' Montgomery said, his eyes narrowing on her as he took a swig. 'I've not seen you on board before, you're new?'

'Last-minute addition to the crew,' Trix said for her. 'Sadie's done herself a mischief skiing in Switzerland.'

'Ouch, hope she's okay?'

To his credit, Montgomery looked genuinely concerned.

'Nothing a bit of plaster and bedrest won't fix.'

'Get her some flowers, won't you, Trix?'

Generous too. Then again, with his kind of money, he could afford to be.

'Sure thing.'

'Something big with—' He froze midsentence, his gaze snapping back to the dock as a broad grin spread across his face. 'Well, bugger me, he actually made it.'

'Who made it?' Cherry asked, sipping her champagne and squinting towards the dock.

'Captain, make it a charter for four,' he said over her, slapping his glass back onto Maria's tray before striding towards the gangplank as every eye followed.

Four it is. Maria turned to head inside for extra supplies—then she saw him.

Her breath hitched. Her step faltered. The tray wobbled in her grip.

Tim?

No. It couldn't be.

But it was.

'Ohmigod,' Trix murmured close behind her, 'isn't that—'

'Yes,' Maria said through clenched teeth. 'Yes, it is.'

She watched, frozen in a strange mix of fascination and dread, as Montgomery embraced the man she'd sworn she would never see again.

'Trix,' the captain prompted, glancing their way as neither of them moved. 'We need refreshments for our new guest.'

'On it.' Trix gave her a gentle nudge and Maria tugged her gaze away, forcing her leaden limbs to move.

'Now you're *really* going to have to tell me what happened,' Trix said as soon as they were inside.

She slid the tray onto the counter behind the bar and shook off her trembling fingers. 'What's he doing here, Trix?'

'Damned if I know, he's never been on board before and I've been working *Celeste* for a couple of years now. But Connor has a lot of friends and, judging by that scene out there, I'd say they're pretty close. We'd best get the other stateroom made up.'

'Stateroom?'

'The other master suite.'

'Oh, God, right. Yeah.'

He'd be sleeping on board. For days. For nights.

She'd thought the yacht huge before, now it was nowhere near big enough!

To set sail with the man she had slept with not one week ago…to wait on the man she had slept with…

In the bar, it had been different. They'd been in her domain, it had been on her terms. Here, she was a fish out of water, on a boat with no escape. She'd laugh if it wasn't so messed up.

If Connor and his young guests hadn't put Fraser in her head to begin with, this weird twist of fate surely would have. She couldn't be that person again, sleeping with the man she was supposed to serve…the gossip, the looks, the subservience.

But how could she possibly press reset on their relationship when that ship had already sailed?

'You sly dog!' Connor leapt down the gangplank, his blue eyes as bright as the sky above. 'Making me think you weren't going to show and then rolling up in the nick of time.'

'Sorry, wasn't intentional. A last-minute change of plan.'

Because for the past few days, he'd been fighting the urge to return to a bar in the suburbs—and to a certain barmaid he couldn't get out of his head. But she'd made her feelings clear. And if he was on a boat at sea there'd be no risk of him going against them.

Hell, he'd probably done enough 'interfering' striking up a deal with her landlord, Mickey, and seeing to it that the building got the work it needed. It was time to move on. And sailing away from temptation made that much easier to do.

'Hey, Connor-baby, you going to introduce us?'

He looked over his friend's shoulder to see one of the young women from the party the other night teetering down the gangplank, closely followed by the other. 'I thought it was just going to be us?'

'What can I say, you bailed, they asked, and I thought what the hell?'

'Right,' he drawled, his frown building. 'In that case, I'll let you get on.' This wasn't the boys' trip he wanted or needed. Throwing his bag over his shoulder, he started to turn away. 'We'll catch up when you're back.'

'Oh, no, you don't.' Connor jumped in his path. 'There's plenty of room for us all and Cherry and Dana are great company. We'll make sure you enjoy yourself, won't we, girls?'

With tinkling laughs, the girls flanked Connor, curling into his side and blocking Tim's exit.

'This is Cherry.' The blonde gave a flutter of a wave. 'This is Dana.' The brunette blew a kiss. 'Girls, this is my friend, Campbell.'

'Hi, Campbell,' they cooed.

'Hi,' he said, his smile strained. 'But despite what Connor just said, I'm heading off. Look after him out there, won't you?'

Cherry jutted out her bottom lip. 'You're not going to stay?'

'Please say you'll stay,' Dana said with her, perfecting the same pout.

'As much as I'd love to...' He wouldn't. He'd rather stick pins in his eyes than play third wheel to this trio. But he didn't want to offend them any more than his quick exit already would. 'I'm afraid I'm going to have to take a raincheck.'

'Come on, Tim.' Connor's easy demeanour shifted into concern. 'You need this break.'

'You're not leaving because of us, are you?' Cherry purred, blue eyes blinking rapidly. 'Because that'll make us feel bad.'

'And you don't want to make us feel bad, do you?' Dana added in the same pleading tone.

My God, had Connor *paid* them to do this? Though it wasn't their eyes he saw now, it was Sasha's. His daughter pleading with him to get a life again. But this wasn't the kind of life he wanted any part of. It might work for Connor, but it didn't work for him.

'Nothing to do with you ladies, I can assure you.'

His friend cursed under his breath. 'Can you give us a moment, ladies?'

'Of course,' Dana said, peeling herself away.

'Just don't be too long,' Cherry murmured. 'That yacht's too big for the two of us. Not to mention the beds...'

They sashayed their way back on deck and Tim forked a hand through his hair. 'Don't you get tired of it?'

'Tired of what?'

'The meaningless hook-ups?'

Because yes, he'd hooked up with Maria, but it had felt far from meaningless.

'Those girls are fun, serious fun. And before you say anything else about me being old enough to be their father, at least they don't make me feel twice my age, which is what you do when you're being all...' He waved a hand at him.

'All what? Mature? Sensible? Need I go on?'

'Look, I just want my old mate back, the guy who laughed easily, smiled even. Is that so much to ask?'

'I'm all for a bit of fun. I just wasn't expecting…' He gestured towards the boat and the two girls giggling on board.

'I'm telling you, they're fun.'

'To you maybe. I prefer my women a little more…'

Words failed him as Maria launched to the forefront of his mind for the umpteenth time…the stewardess now serving the girls a fresh glass of champagne making him think of her too. He could only see her from behind, but her hair bore the same caramel streaks as Maria. And there was something about the way she held herself too.

Great! Now he was *seeing* her everywhere. He really did have it bad.

'See! You can't even remember what you like, it's been that long.'

'That isn't true,' he said, dragging his eyes back to Connor's. 'I just know they're not it. I honestly think you'll have a much better time without me.'

'You know what your problem is, you *think* too much these days. It's eat, sleep, work, repeat, and it's time to break free of the cycle. You used to love getting out on the open water. *We* used to love getting out together,' his friend reiterated.

'That was before.'

'*Everything* was before in your world, but it's all still here for the taking. And the sun is shining, the sea is calling, so no more thought, no more work, no more worries, yeah. And it'll make Sasha happy too.'

'You need to stop conspiring with my daughter.'

'Who says we're conspiring?'

'I do. It's why you invited me, is it not? Some kind of intervention to get me out of this perceived rut I'm in.'

'Intervention?' Connor chuckled. 'If you want to see it that way. I prefer to see it as a long overdue boys' trip.'

'And the women?'

'A healthy addition. But you can leave them to me and get out on the water, get some diving in, if you want, spend time with the fish if you prefer their company to ours. We won't be offended.'

'You're really selling it.'

He grinned. 'I know. When was the last time you scuba dived?'

'Too long to be doing it again now without a refresher.'

'And what the hell is that about? You *loved* diving! And you always squeezed in a trip to Gabo Island when you could.'

Ellie. It was all about Ellie and the fact that she had loved it too. And enjoying the same stuff without Ellie only made her absence all the more pronounced.

'Don't you think you owe it to her?'

It was as if his friend was in his head, reading his very thoughts...

'Sasha gets enough out of me,' he said, deliberately misunderstanding him.

'I meant Ellie.'

'I know who you meant.'

'You just didn't want to acknowledge her.'

'That's not...' He rubbed the back of his neck, giving up on the lie.

'You know, the more you talk about something the less power it has to hurt you.'

He'd fight back if not for the fact that Connor knew it from experience. He'd lost his entire family at the age of twenty-one—mother, father, sister, brother, all gone in a road traffic accident. Overnight, he'd become one of the wealthiest men alive, and the loneliest.

And no matter what Connor said about facing it and moving on, Tim was convinced his friend ran from his past daily. Hence the parties, the yachts, the girls...*everything* was fun in Connor's world.

But saying it was fun didn't automatically make it so.

'Tim, I'm serious. She was the one who died, not you. You owe it to her to live your life for the two of you.'

'And is that what you're still doing, living it for the five of you?'

Connor's lashes flickered, his blue eyes flashed. Shit.

'I'm sorry, mate, I shouldn't have.'

'No, I'll own it. And so what if I am?' he threw back. 'It beats the alternative half-life you seem to insist on living.' He looked to the boat and sighed. 'Look, if you truly hate it after one night, you can send for the chopper...or we can evict the chicks. Bros before—'

'Connor, so help me, if you finish that phrase.'

'But you know what I'm saying.'

'I do.'

He glanced at the yacht just as the stewardess with the champagne turned and his body jolted. *Maria?*

The crew uniform dulled her individuality, but he'd know her anywhere. The high cheekbones, the soft arch of her brows, the quiet intensity of those almond-shaped eyes. And that mouth...full, teasing, the faintest tilt at the corners.

My God, it really was her.

'See,' Connor said, 'she has a glass of champagne with your name on.'

His head wasn't playing tricks on him. She was here. On Connor's yacht. Questions raced as fast as his feet—*How? What? When? Why?*

'Best not keep her waiting any longer then...'

'You're *coming*?' Connor said, hurrying after him.

Another stewardess approached the rail and he did a double-take—the other barmaid! *She* was on board *too*. A hell of a coincidence. Or fate.

Either way, he was wholeheartedly on board with it.

'It's going to be great,' Connor said, full of cheer again. 'I promise.'

But the only person capable of making good on that promise was the woman staring back at him...her eyes getting wider by the second.

CHAPTER SIX

MARIA'S PULSE TRIPPED—one minute the two men were in deep debate on the dock, the next Tim was closing in at pace, Montgomery hot on his tail.

Just breathe.

Breathe and smile.

She backed up when he stepped onto the deck, his familiar grey eyes more dazzling than the sun. Especially when they shone with such joy at her presence. 'What are you—'

She stiffened, her eyes flaring, urging him to stop.

Don't out me. Don't out us!

Heat flushed her cheeks as every gaze on deck turned their way and he frowned, clearly trying to make sense of her reaction.

Wasn't it obvious? She didn't want the crew to know they knew each other. Worse still, that they'd slept together!

Not that one automatically led to the other, but…

'What are you—what?' Montgomery cut in, coming up alongside him and taking a fresh drink from her tray.

'What are you serving?' Tim said smoothly, following her cue. But her stunned brain lagged, too slow to answer.

'Bolly, of course!' Montgomery clasped Tim's shoulder. 'Now, grab yourself one and I'll introduce you to the crew.'

He reached for a glass, his intense gaze burning with a thousand questions, not that she was about to answer any. She kept her smile steady, but inside...inside *everything* raced. Her heart. Her pulse. Her mind.

'This is Maria,' Montgomery said.

He nodded. 'Maria.'

The memory of him saying the very same against her ear made her shiver. Her body reliving it and all the rest. Eager to remember...and reacquaint herself all over.

'Welcome aboard, Mr Campbell.' *Damn.* Was it the blood in her ears or did her voice really sound that thick? 'Towel?'

His mouth twitched. 'Do I look in need of one?'

She wet her lips as heat fractured right through her. He looked hot. So hot. And he knew it. His eyes sparked back at her, daring her to say it too.

'No.' She swallowed, feeding off his provocation to regain the fight. 'You look perfectly refreshed.'

Montgomery was watching their exchange with interest—hell, the entire crew were! She turned away before her mask could slip any more and Montgomery continued with the introductions. Though her eyes wouldn't be told, they kept drifting his way. Hungry for more.

He looked good in the sun. The deep grey polo shirt and pale grey shorts working with the grey of his eyes, his salt-and-pepper hair, his lightly bronzed skin...

And here she was, plain Jane. Her own style swapped out for the uniform of the yacht. The single stripe to each shoulder denoting her first stew, bottom-rung status. Whereas he was very much top rung and then some.

He caught her eye and she glanced away, ears ringing, cheeks burning, her heart beating too hard and too fast...

'Is that all of your luggage, sir?' Trix asked him as soon as the introductions were over.

Maria couldn't blame her friend for checking. Not when the others had brought a series of cases on board, most of them large enough to house the possessions of an entire family.

'It is.'

'Wonderful. If you just leave it here, Maria can unpack it while I take you for a tour of the yacht and the facilities.'

'A tour?' Cherry giggled. 'Is that really necessary?'

'You'll want to know how everything works,' Trix explained while Maria's heart did cartwheels at the idea of being in his room, unpacking his things, even without him there. 'Especially the spa pool and the dancefloor.'

'Oh, yes!' Dana hooked her arm through Cherry's. 'Show us the way.'

Trix sent Maria a look that said *Wish me luck* and started to guide them away.

'Actually,' Tim said, 'do you mind if I come with you, Maria?'

She gave a startled, 'Huh!', her jaw snapping back together so tight she swore she felt a tooth crack.

'Don't mind, do you, Connor?' he said, hoisting his bag onto his shoulder. 'I could do with making a few calls before signing off.'

Montgomery paused at the stairs to the flybridge as Trix led the girls up. 'No worries, just make sure you leave your phone down there, yeah? Boys' trip, remember!'

Maria's stomach clenched. Boys' trip? Wasn't that code for... Her eyes lifted to the flybridge above, to where the two girls were now cooing over Montgomery joining them. Was one for him and one for... Her eyes returned to Tim, her heart jerking as he gave the smallest shake of his head. Was she that obvious?

And hell, she wasn't jealous. She had no right to be jealous. She didn't care.

Only she did.

'Mr Campbell,' Captain Kali said, snagging his attention, 'I'll leave you in Maria's capable hands. I'm sure you'll find everything to your satisfaction but any problems, please don't hesitate to let us know.'

'I'm sure everything will be just fine.' His gaze flitted her way, like she had some say in it. 'Thanks, Captain.'

Everyone dispersed. They were alone. And she couldn't feel the tray in her hands any more, couldn't feel the warm wood beneath her feet either. Her senses were all about him. His scent, his heat, his proximity...

'Do you want to come this way?' she said, belatedly remembering her role and what she was *supposed* to be doing—showing him to his room—not *actually* doing—ogling him.

Trix had pointed out the second master stateroom, but she had no clue what awaited beyond the door.

She would get in and out as quickly as possible. Stock up the supplies, unpack his case, make the bed. *The bed.* She gulped as she pushed her way through the saloon, leaving the tray on the bar as she went.

'I don't think your room is made up yet. It shouldn't take me too long to have it ready for you though.'

She didn't look back as she said it. Didn't pause either as she hit the stairs. It was hard not to appear as if she was running from him but everything about this situation had her screaming to do just that.

'You don't need to panic.' He sounded amused—or was that bemused? 'I've seen an unmade bed before.'

It wasn't the *state* of the bed she was panicking about.

All around her, the shiny grandeur of the yacht had her feeling ever more out of place. As for his presence now in it... She'd known he was money. In the bar, she'd known. But here, now, with their roles on board accentuating their differences... It was hard to believe that less than a week ago he'd been in her bar, in *her* bed, making her forget her worries and her strife—and now she sounded like freaking Baloo in *The Jungle Book*!

What was wrong with her?

'Maria…?'

Him! He was what was wrong, her body pulsing over her name on his lips like it was everything she needed to hear when it wasn't.

'This is you,' she said, pushing open his door and losing herself in the showy display ahead because losing herself in him was *not* an option.

He walked ahead of her, his tall, broad frame a tiny blip in the room that seemed to extend forever. The colour palette was softer here, the muted greys and whites soothing on the eye, the accent lighting too. As for the panoramic view of the open sea, breathtaking.

She couldn't imagine wanting anything else. Not when every need was catered for. Space to eat, space to work, space to bathe, to relax, to…sleep. The giant bed, floating on an illuminated platform in the heart of the room, was already made up, its crisp white bedding like an inviting cloud calling out to be…

'Looks like your room is made up already,' she blurted, snapping her gaze away.

'So it is.'

He showed no sign of sharing her stress as he tossed his bag on the tempting cloud.

Just her then. Great.

'If you let me know when you're done with your calls, I'll come back and sort the rest.'

She was on the threshold when he came upon her. 'Wait!'

She blinked up at him, surprised by his sudden shift, surprised even more by his sudden proximity. She forced her face to relax, aiming for polite indifference, probably achieving lemon-sucking standard if his furrowed brow was anything to go by.

God, this was hard! She'd never needed to *feign* politeness in the bar, but here, on a superyacht, it was all change. In every way. 'Yes?'

'I don't have calls to make.'

'No?'

'I wanted to talk to you.'

Of course you did... 'About?'

'Isn't it obvious?'

She took a breath. Time to lay some ground rules. 'Look, Mr Campbell—'

He flinched. *'Just* Tim. Please.'

The smallest huff escaped. 'I'm afraid that's above my pay grade.'

'Seriously? After everything we shared the other night, you think I'm going to be okay with you addressing me in that way?'

She stiffened, glancing down the hallway. Thank God, it was empty.

'Things were different then,' she said under her breath. 'You weren't my boss for a start.'

'I'm not your boss now.'

'You might as well be.'

He raked a hand through his hair, took another step towards her. 'I don't need waiting on by you. By anyone. I'm more than capable of unpacking my own case, fetching my own drinks—'

'You going to cook your own dinner too, because Chef Rio won't like that.'

'Maria, please...'

'What?' She gave an awkward laugh, trying desperately to make light of a situation that was anything but. 'It sounds like you want to put us out of work.'

And she didn't care if she sounded extreme. Her job on board was to serve, and serving them well could see her earning a tip worth more than a month's wage at the bar. Not that he could even begin to understand that, so she had to be the one to make it clear to him.

'This job is important to me. Please don't make it any more awkward than it already is.'

'I'm not. Or at least I'm trying not to. But having you run around after me…it's not right.'

'It's perfectly fine,' she assured him as smoothly as she could. 'This is my job.' *Now draw the line and don't cross it.* 'What we shared the other night is in the past and I'd like for us to keep it that way.'

'You don't want anyone to know we slept together?'

'Of course I don't!'

Too loud, Maria.

'Why? Are you ashamed of me?'

'Ashamed? God, no.'

'Good. Because, the way I see it, we were two consenting adults, getting to know one another and having a good time. At least, I thought that was the case and now we're here—'

'That *was* the case.'

She wasn't about to lie about that.

'Then why on earth pretend we've never met?'

'Because I don't want it getting out.'

'Why?'

'Because on this yacht I'm the crew, you're a guest, we don't mix.'

'We more than mixed.'

'Tim!'

His mouth quirked to one side. 'At least you're calling me Tim now.'

Heat bloomed in her cheeks and her chest and her belly… but she refused to bow down. 'This isn't funny.'

'You think I think it is? You're out there wanting me to pretend nothing happened between us, that I don't even know you, when I know *every* inch of you.'

She cursed, her, 'Yes!' a panicked hiss.

'But that friend of yours, the other stewardess, she was working with you in the bar the other night, wasn't she? She knows we know each other.'

'She knows you were there having a drink. She doesn't know what came after.'

'Right. So what am I to be, your dirty little secret for the next few days because I—what? What did I say?'

She knew she was pale, her past draining the blood from her face, but she'd been the dirty little secret, her daughter Fae even more so... Tim could give himself the label all he liked, but his superior status would forever ensure he was on the right side of that equation.

'Maria? What is—'

'I need to go. Like I said, let me know when you're finished in your room, and I'll take care of your things. Or Trix will, if that makes you more comfortable.'

It would certainly be Maria's preference.

And then she legged it, before she went back on every word, every warning, and acted on the chemistry threatening to break her. But how long could she resist when they were on a boat in the middle of the ocean together and he wanted to...?

He wanted to what? She hadn't let him finish. She'd been too scared of what he would say. Too scared he'd see this weird twist of fate as a reason to extend their one night into several...and the idea of that...the temptation—gah!

Some flamin' pickle to be in when there was no way out of the freaking jar.

Tim stared at the door as it clicked shut. She didn't slam it. No, that would be too unprofessional, and she was being professional to a fault.

Hell, he could understand her need to set them both apart. To keep her place amongst the crew. But he'd never had to lie about knowing someone before and it didn't sit right. Especially when he got the impression that something else was amiss. Something that had nothing to do with him and everything to do with her.

His phone buzzed in his pocket and he pulled it out, glanced at the screen: Sasha.

Happy sailing, Dad! Enjoy it! Xxx

How did she— Connor! He shook his head and sent a reply:

Thank you. You can stop keeping tabs on me now x

Never. LOL x

He laughed softly. This was *not* how it should be. A daughter keeping a close eye on her father. Worrying about her father. It was time to show her he was good. That life was good. Even if he didn't truly feel it.

Though a week ago…a week ago it had shone with possibility again.

All because of a woman, and that in itself was a problem.

His happiness had once centred on Ellie and look how bereft that had left him.

He should be grateful to Maria for seeing sense when he couldn't. Keeping him at arm's length was as good for him as it was for her.

Even if it went against his every instinct…

'Everything okay?'

Trix was mixing drinks in the saloon when Maria came up a short while later.

'Yup.' Though she couldn't look at Trix as she said it. 'The room's already made up, but I said I'd sort his stuff once he was done.'

'I wasn't referring to the room.'

Maria's Spidey-senses tingled… 'Hmm?'

'He *is* the guy from the bar the other night, right?'

She nodded, taking up a sofa cushion and fluffing it with more focus than it needed.

'Of all the bars in all the world,' she murmured, 'and all the yachts in the sea…'

'Yeah, yeah, I know.'

'You think it's the universe trying to tell you something?'

'Like what, Trix?' She threw the cushion down and met her friend's sparkling brown gaze. 'Hey, Maria, here's that guy again, you know, the one you liked, now go serve him while he enjoys the company of two women a thousand times more beautiful and at home in his world. How's that for fun?'

Her friend laughed. 'Are you for real? Did you not *see* the way he was checking you out again?'

'I think he was in shock.'

Liar.

'Na-ah, those were full-on puppy-dog eyes out there. And if I had a rich widower taking a shine to me, I wouldn't be denying all knowledge of him. What was that about, anyway?'

'I don't want the crew thinking we…thinking there's something going on between us,' she said, swiftly adding, 'when there very much *isn't*.'

'And you think people knowing you've met before would give them the wrong idea?'

She shrugged. 'I don't know. Maybe.'

'Do you not think you're being an itty-bit paranoid?'

She didn't answer.

'There are plenty of *innocent* ways you could have met, the bar included, and no one would have thought it strange. Strikes me as your guilty conscience talking…'

Maria pressed her lips together.

'Something *did* happen, didn't it? That's why you're acting all kooky?'

Her teeth ground together.

'I *knew* it.'

'Trix, please, I don't want to make a huge deal of it. And I really don't want the crew finding out.'

'No one's gonna hear it from me, I promise you that. Good on you for finally getting some fun in!'

'And look where it's landed me.'

'It's hardly the end of the world.'

'You might not mind running around after a guy you had *sex* with,' she said under her breath. 'But it freaks me out.'

'Feels like a good excuse for some cheeky role play, if you ask me.'

'I didn't ask.'

And now her gut was rolling because *that* kind of role play had once been her life. For better or for worse. Memories she didn't want to face playing out in blazing Technicolor as the sickness welled.

She turned away before Trix could notice her pallor, busied herself rearranging the flower display on the bar.

'Sorry, darl, I was just teasing.'

'I know.'

Though Trix wouldn't have said it if she knew her story. If she knew who Fae's father was. But no one knew that sordid tale, except for Fae and the man himself. The staff had suspected enough and made her life hell. Never Fraser's though, because that had been more than their jobs' worth.

'It really isn't all that bad, you know. All sorts happen on these yachts.'

'You saying it wouldn't bother you at all?' she said quietly. 'A stew carrying on with a guest?'

'Of course it would, but this is different.'

'How?'

'You weren't my stew on land, for a start.'

'And now I am?'

'Before you turned ghost like, I was just happy to see you glowing.'

'Glowing?' she blustered. 'That's ridiculous.'

'You clearly haven't looked in the mirror lately.'

Actually, she had. And she knew Trix was right. He'd lit a spark within her, and now she couldn't put the damn thing out.

'All I'm saying is, don't be so quick to dismiss it. Especially when he appears to be one of the good ones.'

'The good ones…?'

'I've never seen a guest carry his own bags before.'

'He had one, Trix. One!'

'Yeah, not seen that before either. A wealthy man that travels light, a rare breed indeed. You really do need to lock him down.'

'Enough! Tell me what you want me to do next…and keep it clean!'

Trix pursed her lips to the side, her eyes dancing. 'Okay, spoilsport. The lads have taken all the bags down. You okay to tackle Cherry and Dana's room while I keep the drinks flowing?'

'Sure.'

It would also give her a good hour or so tucked away from Tim.

Out of sight, out of mind.

She could hope…

CHAPTER SEVEN

HOURS LATER, TIM was trying to relax in a lounger on the upper deck. He had a book in one hand, a soda and lime in the other and, on the face of it, looked to be having an idyllic afternoon beside the pool.

They were due to anchor in Refuge Cove for the night before continuing on to Gabo Island come morning. Weather conditions along the Bass Strait were good. Smooth sailing all the way. What more could one want?

Not the question to ask when it had been hours since he'd last set eyes on Maria. And the idea that she was avoiding him had him all at sea—*at sea?* Great. Even his conscience was having a laugh at his expense.

A squeal from Dana pierced his eardrums and he peered over the edge of his book.

She was reclining along the water's edge, supposedly sunbathing, with every curve angled just so. While Cherry was splashing about with Connor in the water.

It was the splashing that had Dana squealing.

'I'm going to have to wash my hair before dinner now, you pair of beasts,' she admonished, shaking out her ponytail and resuming her position.

'You were going to wash it anyway, darling,' Cherry said. 'Be honest.'

'I suppose I was.'

'But, speaking of dinner...' Cherry hooked her arms and legs around Connor. 'Shouldn't we be getting ready?'

'Ready? It's at least two hours away,' Connor said. 'And we're not going anywhere but the aft deck, so bikinis are perfectly acceptable.'

'You'd like that, wouldn't you?' Cherry rocked in his arms, her body moving in tune with the low, sultry beats coming through the sound system.

'What man wouldn't?' Connor said, nuzzling into her neck and making her moan unashamedly.

Tim rolled his eyes and leaned back. If this was how it was going to go, maybe he—

Movement to his right caught his eye. Caramel hair, lightly sunkissed skin, pale blue polo, navy shorts and a whole lot of leg—Maria!

Any thought of jumping ship swiftly quit.

'Three Sex on the Beach?' she called out, lifting the tray of colourful cocktails and carefully avoiding his eye.

'Perfect timing,' Connor said. 'Trix work her special magic with them?'

'An added twist of coconut?'

'That's the one.'

'Sounds divine,' Dana murmured, getting to her feet and stretching out her body in the barely-there bikini. Tim didn't know where to look. And from the way Maria glanced his way, she didn't either. He gave her the smallest of smiles, which she *almost* returned, then Dana swept between them, pulling on her sheer robe and taking up a glass.

'Thank you, sweetheart.'

Maria's smile tightened. 'You're welcome.'

'Time to get ready—you coming, Cherry?'

'Not yet she isn't,' Connor said, shamelessly nuzzling her neck still, 'but give us a minute.'

For the love of...

Tim closed his book. Not even the chill of a good thriller could distract from Connor in full-on playboy mode. 'There will be nothing left of her to get ready if you keep that up.'

'Promises, promises,' Cherry cooed, easing out of Connor's grasp and pushing up out of the pool. If Dana's bikini was barely-there, Cherry's might as well not exist, the white fabric having turned transparent with the water. Not that Connor or Cherry seemed to mind the design flaw.

She took her cocktail from the tray as her gaze found Tim's and she smiled around her straw. 'You want to swap that soda for one of these, baby, and come join us below deck?'

Tim exhaled slowly. 'I'm good, thanks.'

'Party-pooper,' Cherry pouted.

'Am I not enough for you?' Connor said, easing out of the water too, his rash vest clinging to his torso. His clothed state at total odds with the company he was keeping, but then, Tim knew what that vest hid. Scars that ran deeper than just the surface.

'You're always enough, darling.' Cherry trailed a hand down Connor's front as he wrapped a towel around her shoulders and drew her close. 'But your friend looks like he could do with cheering up and we're nothing if not cheer-inducing.'

Maria made a noise which she quickly masked with a cough, her averted gaze catching Tim's again. His mouth twitched with hers. The laughter in her hazel depths unmistakable.

'Can I get you something else?' she asked, finally sparing him more than a glance as she gestured to his glass.

'What's on offer?' And then he cringed as Maria blushed and Connor chortled. In any normal situation, that question would have been perfectly innocent. But hot off the back of the trio's antics… 'I meant drinks—what drinks do you have?'

'Sure you did, buddy,' Connor said, urging Cherry towards the stairs. 'And you know my yacht is as well stocked as any bar on land when it comes to drinks of your variety. Come on, ladies, let's leave Tim to dig himself out of that hole while we go get ready. Maybe he can find his funny bone while he's down there.'

'Remind me why we're friends again,' he muttered after him.

'You love me really.'

'Yeah, yeah…'

'If you change your mind…' Dana said, trailing her hand across Tim's bare shoulder before slinking off down the stairs behind them.

He rubbed away the goosebumps she'd fired up and dragged his gaze back to Maria's. The tightness around her eyes putting a fire under him as he launched to his feet. 'I'm so sorry about that.'

She gave a flustered laugh. 'You don't need to apologise.'

'Oh, I do, and I fear it won't be the last time either.'

He threw back the last of his soda water, but it did nothing to quench his thirst. Not when every inch of his body wanted to reacquaint itself with hers. Not helped by the fact that he was half-naked.

He raked a hand through his hair and her eyes dipped to his chest, colour surging to her cheeks before they snapped back to his. What he wouldn't give to act on that heat…

'Sometimes I think he shouldn't be let out in public.'

Now she laughed, a true easy tinkle that warmed and relaxed every tightened muscle. 'I've met worse.' Then she nipped her lip as her eyes flared. 'And I shouldn't have said that.'

'Don't worry, I won't tell if you won't.'

She met his smile curve for curve, her eyes warming as she blinked up at him. 'How did you two become friends? You don't seem anything alike.'

'We were at boarding school together. He was a couple of

years below me, but we played sport together. Hit it off. He's more of a brother than a mate.'

'Is that why you tolerate him?'

He chuckled. 'He's really not so bad once you get beneath all the bluster.'

'No?'

'We actually used to be quite similar.'

'Is that so?'

'Could barely tell us apart…'

She arched one brow, her eyes dancing. 'Like Tweedledee and Tweedledum?'

'Something like that.'

'So…' she lifted the empty tray to her chest '…what happened?'

Ah, so much for easy…

'Life.'

'That old chestnut, hey?' Then her smile faded with his. 'Sorry, that was really crass. Your wife…' She ran a hand over her smoothed back hair. 'Forgive me, I should go.'

She moved off and he intercepted her, gripping the handrail to stop himself from reaching for her. 'You have nothing to apologise for either.'

Her gaze lifted to his, guilt still shining in her eyes as her lips softly parted. And he couldn't look at them when he was trying to tell her this.

'Losing her did change me.' He turned to face the sea, watching as the sun slowly dipped behind the horizon. 'Most would say not for the better, too. Connor was no different…'

'Connor was married?'

'No. God, no. Connor can't imagine anything worse than giving himself to someone in that way. To love someone. Crazy thing is, he does still love. He loves me. He loves Sasha. He loved Ellie.' He gave Maria the smallest smile.

'Who did he lose?'

'His entire family.'

She gasped softly and he gave a slow nod. 'He was the only one to walk away from their car after a lorry sideswiped it on the motorway. Mother, father, sister, brother. All gone.'

'Oh, my God. That's awful.'

'He was twenty-one. Too young. He lost himself in his grief for a while and then, when he came out of it, he took the whole "life's too short" motto to a whole other level. There's no such thing as too much fun and there's no time to settle. He won't be tied down, to anyone or to anything. He's very careful about that.'

'So the women?'

'Are as committed to having fun and enjoying the single life as he is.'

Her brows knitted together. 'And what about you?' She turned to lean back against the rail. 'I assume from all the noise, he's hoping you and Dana might…hell, even Cherry… they all seem rather open to sharing.'

He angled his body to face her, his eyes reading every outward sign she dared to give. 'Would it bother you if I did?'

How had she gone from keeping him out of sight, out of mind to this…?

Maria opened her mouth to lie and his brows nudged north, his grey eyes searing her with their honesty, and she couldn't do it.

'Now you're just avoiding the question,' she hedged.

'*I'm* avoiding the question?'

'Yes.'

She took a breath, trying to regain her common sense, but instead she caught his scent. Oh-so familiar to her senses. Deep, spicy and inviting.

She turned to drag in the ocean air instead, willing it to soothe away the excited flurry within.

'I went through a phase,' he admitted, his voice low and gravel-like.

'A phase?' she murmured, resisting the urge to glance his way when it was all her eyes wanted to do. To drink him in up close. To study those eyes that gave away so much and those lips that succeeded in teasing her with words alone.

'I guess you could call it phases, plural.' He rested his forearms on the rail and looked to the sea with her. 'When I first lost Ellie, I couldn't bear being in company. I wanted to be there for my daughter but there were days when even she would tip me over the edge. She looks like her, acts like her... I'd catch sight of her at times and do a double-take before remembering all over again.'

She inhaled softly, her heart aching for him. 'That's hard. But it's something to cherish, having so much of her mother in her.'

'I know that now. I guess I knew that then too, but some days it was just too hard. I was bitter, angry, and I struggled to see past that. Life lost its reason. I'd worked so hard to get to where we were in life, to have all this money, and not be able to save her...to get her prognosis and know there was nothing I could do. Having to be strong when all I wanted to do was scream, *Why her? Why us?*'

'Why anyone?' she murmured, thinking of all those without the money, the connections, who suffered the same fate.

'Precisely. Those were Sasha's words too when she told me she wanted my support to set up a charity in memory of Ellie. She was only nineteen and full of all these incredible ideas. Bursting with them. She ploughed her grief into a venture designed to help others, save others, and I couldn't have been prouder.'

'She sounds amazing.'

'She is. She's an inspiration, not just to me but so many others. And there was a time when I saw that strength in her and realised she didn't need me to provide it any more. I found myself without any real purpose and Connor was there, coaxing me back into the land of the living.'

'Let me guess, then came the phase?'

'Yeah.' He rocked back, looking to the ground as he gave a brusque, bashful laugh. 'It didn't last long, much to Connor's dismay. I think he was happy having a wingman again. Different cities, different women, but I don't know…' he lifted his gaze to the setting sun once more, a crease forming between his brows '…it felt…soulless.'

'Soulless?'

'Yeah.' A small smile played about his lips. 'To be honest, I figured Ellie had ruined me for other women. And then I met you…'

He looked at her, his eyes awash with his words, an emotion she couldn't—*wouldn't* trust.

'Me?'

He gave the smallest nod. 'And for the first time since Ellie, I wanted…'

She swallowed as he turned to her. 'You wanted…?'

The entire world fell away as she lost herself in his eyes…the yacht, the sea, the reality of who they were and what they could never be. She'd blame the dreamlike quality of the sky, its soft pink hue as it turned the sea to liquid gold, but it was all him. Him and his words and his eyes that were all too captivating.

'I wanted you, Maria.' Slowly, he raised a hand to sweep an errant strand behind her ear, his gaze following the move and setting off a gazillion flutters in her chest. 'I still really want you.'

'You shouldn't.'

There were a thousand reasons why he shouldn't. Reasons she could throw at him now, reasons she *should* throw at him. But she was struggling to string a coherent thought together as the fire in the sky spread to his eyes and through her middle.

'It's true.' His hand came to rest beneath her chin, his eyes on her lips. 'I don't want the pain of losing someone I love again. But I can't deny what I feel for you.'

A rush of desire and something far more potent rose up within her, causing her lips to part and her pulse to race.

I want you too… The words were there, pushing at the line she'd sworn she wouldn't cross.

'And I'm not ready to walk away from this. Are you?'

Yes. She had to. She couldn't be that woman again. Hoodwinked by a man. Ridiculed by her peers. Feeling like a puppet controlled by her feelings. But she couldn't find her feet to walk.

Then he kissed her and she melted. It was the briefest sip against her lips, the lightest sweep of his tongue, and *oh, my God,* she wanted more. So much more.

His lashes lifted, his eyes connecting with hers. 'Maria…?'

The soft sound teased at the protective wall around her heart, hurting and healing and confusing as hell.

'I wish you wouldn't say it like that.'

'Like what?'

Like it was the most beautiful name in the world. A pleasure-filled sigh. A whispered caress along her skin. She gave the smallest shiver as he traced her lower lip with his thumb.

'Like I'm yours,' she whispered. Because to be his…to be loved like he had loved his wife. To be worthy of that kind of love from a man who cared so deeply, felt so deeply…

'I don't mean to. But I am trying to be honest with you.'

'You don't even know me.'

'I know enough. I know how you make me feel. I know I want to know more.'

'No, you don't.'

Because if he knew more, he'd know about Fraser. He'd know she'd betrayed another woman in the worst possible way. He'd know she'd almost torn apart a family and for what…to be a man's mistress, the dirty little secret, the money-grabbing whore to the select few who thought they knew.

Stay in your own flamin' lane, Maria!

'I can't do this.'

She pushed him away, running...

'Maria!'

He was hot on her tail and she spun to face him, hands raised to ward him off as her unshed tears blurred him and the sky into a kaleidoscope of colour.

'Please let it go. I don't deserve your attention. I don't *want* your attention. Just leave it alone.'

And then she fled.

CHAPTER EIGHT

TIM FELT LIKE a jerk. A complete and utter jerk.

She'd made her thoughts clear and then he'd pressed her to the point that she'd felt she'd had no choice but to run. Literally, run. From *him*.

Again.

He'd messed up. Big time. If only he could get her alone, explain, apologise properly...but getting her alone was a problem. He couldn't single her out for a private conversation. That would only arouse suspicion and get her back up more. And trying to catch her alone 'by chance' was proving impossible.

There was always someone else around, and he got the distinct impression she was working hard to make it so. Which only served to make him feel worse.

'It's not often that I admit to being wrong,' Connor said from his lounged back position on the aft deck sofa, making the most of the post-dinner entertainment in the form of Cherry and Dana dancing to some cringe-inducing tune across the way. 'But in this case, I think I might be.'

'Wrong?' Tim frowned. 'About what?'

'You. This trip.' Connor waved his whisky glass at their surroundings, gave Cherry a subtle wink as she caught his eye, and then his gaze landed on Tim, the sudden gravity in its depths piling extra weight on the guilt Tim was already carrying. 'It being good for you.'

'It *is* good for me.'

He raised one lazy brow. 'Yeah, it looks it too.'

'Just ignore me.'

'How can I? You spent the entire dinner acting like your cat just died.'

'I don't have a cat.'

'Maybe you should—it might encourage you to talk more.'

'A *cat*?' He gestured to his friend's drink. 'I think you've had a few too many of those.'

'Na-ah. There was a time we couldn't get you to shut up. Now it's like pulling teeth.'

'And you think a cat is the answer?'

'Desperate times call for desperate measures.'

Tim sipped his whisky, thinking how funny his closest friend should be saying all this when he'd been more than willing to talk a week ago. More than willing to a few hours ago too. Because when he was with Maria everything came alive, his body, his mind…his tongue.

'Glad you find it so amusing,' Connor said.

'I didn't say I found it amusing.'

'The look on your face says otherwise…'

That was what a certain moment with a certain brunette could do. But then he remembered all that came after. The way she'd run…what she'd said…the tears.

'So, you going to tell me what has you so distracted you didn't engage in any of the conversation over dinner?'

'The *conversation*?' Every time he'd risen above the mental replay of his chat with Maria to tune into the talk at the table it had been nothing but ego-stroking nonsense. 'Excuse me if I didn't feel the need to tell you that your efforts in the gym are paying off,' he murmured around his glass, taking a satisfying swig and sending Connor a smile laden with tease. 'Or that your shirt matches your eyes…which it does, by the way.'

Connor laughed and tossed a stray flower head from the table arrangement at his chest. 'All right, I guess I deserved that.' And then he leaned in, resting his elbow on the sofa between them. 'But I'm serious—you going to tell me what's going on in that head of yours?'

'You don't need to know.'

'I kind of feel like I do.'

Something about the way he said it had Tim's back stiffening. 'Why?'

'You're my brother in all the ways that matter for a start.' His friend threw back his drink and gestured to a hovering Trix on the other side of the saloon doors, but it was Maria who stepped out. And no matter that he'd seen her plenty this evening as she'd helped with the dinner service, she still had the power to make his skin fizz with awareness, his body tighten and pulse race.

She wore black tonight, a simple dress that skimmed her knees, but the way the fabric clung to her curves and set off the natural glow to her skin...it hadn't been Chef Rio's food that had had his mouth watering all evening.

'Another whisky for bed, please, Maria. And whatever the girls would like too, of course.'

'We're going to bed?' Cherry said.

'Already?' Dana blurted.

'I figured the three of us could continue this downstairs,' Connor said.

'In that case—' Cherry cracked a grin '—espresso martini, please, Maria.'

'Make that two,' Dana said. 'Gotta keep our energy up.'

Both women threw Connor a coy smile as Maria nodded and swept back inside. She didn't look at Tim. Not once. The story of the entire evening, and the reason for his mood too.

'I saw you two earlier,' Connor said and Tim's head shot around, his friend's grave tone setting off alarm bells.

'Who?'

'You and Maria.'

'When?'

'Cherry left her phone by the pool, and I was coming to

get it when I saw you. Figured it looked pretty intense, so I left you to it.'

Intense? Tim couldn't put it better himself. But how much had his friend witnessed? The kiss or purely the convo...?

'Didn't look like you were talking about the weather, if you get my drift...'

The kiss. *Definitely* the kiss. He cursed.

'Yeah, think I said that too. Is that what has you all...?'

'All what?'

Connor raised his brows. 'Moodier than usual?'

Tim pressed his lips together, his eyes finding Maria through the glass. She was busy making the cocktails in the saloon bar, Trix beside her, chatting away. There was no way they could overhear them. Not even Cherry and Dana could overhear them above the music, but he worried all the same.

'Don't make a thing of it, will you?'

'Why don't you tell me what I'm not making a thing of first and then I can tell you whether I agree. Because I know you, Tim, and you're the last person on earth I would expect to have to talk to about respect and boundaries and what's okay and what's not. She works on my boat and you—'

'It's not like that.'

'No?'

Tim raked a hand through his hair. 'She didn't want me to say anything.'

'This is getting worse by the second.'

'We've met before.'

'Huh? When?'

'She was working in the bar I ended up at after the party last week. Trix was working there too.'

Connor leaned forward, his eyes drifting to Trix and Maria still talking inside. 'Hang on, you mean the bar Trix's uncle owns?'

'Yeah, you know it?'

'I know about it, sure, but it's miles out of the city. Wow, you really did want to get away!'

'That's hardly news.'

'No, but—hang on, so you know *both* of them? And yet none of you said anything when you came on board.'

'I didn't know Trix by name, no. And Maria made it clear she didn't want me to let on.'

'Why?'

'For the same reason you're now getting all preachy with me.'

Connor's brows lifted into his hairline. 'I'm not getting preachy, but there is a line, bro... I take it you two weren't just talking about the weather the night you met either?'

'Connor...' It was a low warning.

'I'm just making sure I have all the facts.'

'The only fact that matters is that she isn't interested. Not any more.'

'Impressed her that much, hey?' he teased, but Tim didn't find anything about this situation funny. 'Quit looking so grouchy. I'm only kidding around, because I'm telling you now, what I saw looked mutual enough to me.'

He'd thought so too, but...

'The words coming out of her mouth suggest otherwise.'

'Did she say why?'

'She says it's the whole crew-guest dynamic, which of course I understand, but...'

'You don't believe her?'

No, he didn't. Worry over her position on the yacht didn't warrant tears. It had been deeper than that. So deep, it had caused her pain. And *that* he wanted to understand. Understand and take away. Because if she hurt, he hurt.

'I don't know. I just know I haven't felt this way since Ellie.'

'*Seriously?*' Connor choked on the dregs of his whisky.

'Don't look so surprised.'

'Seven years, man. Seven years and you meet a random woman in a bar and just like that…'

'I know how it sounds, but I'm telling you, it happened.'

'What happened?'

'That moment, you know, when you just *know*? The lightning bolt.'

'The what now?' He was looking at him like he'd sprouted three heads, every one of them spouting nonsense. Hell, maybe it *was* nonsense and somewhere along the way he'd lost his grip on reality.

He'd known nothing of her in that moment…nothing other than the fact that she triggered the same intense reaction Ellie once had.

But to feel it again…after all this time.

'Doesn't matter.' He downed the last of his drink with a hiss. 'Forget I said anything.'

'It matters plenty if it's got you thinking about enjoying life again.'

His gaze drifted back to Maria beyond the glass. She had all four drinks on the tray now and Trix was frowning at her, saying something. His neck prickled. Were they talking about him, *them*? Did Trix know? Was she offering her own counsel?

'If you want my advice, just apologise.'

He set his frown on Connor. 'For what, exactly?'

Because Tim knew well enough what he had to apologise for, Connor's take on it however…

'Buggered if I know.' His friend shrugged. 'But it always seems to work for me.'

Tim gave a tight laugh. 'Says the guy who's a self-professed womaniser.'

'Means I have plenty of experience in smoothing things over with the opposite sex, and I'm telling you, one should never underestimate the power of an apology, even when one has done nothing wrong.'

He'd done plenty wrong…pursuing her when she'd said no.

'Hell, maybe you just scared her off with your smile that's so out of practice.'

'Thanks.'

'You gotta admit, it is kinda rusty… But I'm serious, pull her aside and talk to her. Explain how you feel.'

Hadn't he already tried that and look where it had landed him, in even deeper bother with an even bigger reason to apologise. And for that, he did need to get her alone.

'A bit hard when we're always surrounded by people.'

'You want me to talk to her, tell her not to stress about the whole staff—'

'No! I don't want you to talk to her!'

'But it's my boat, I'm effectively her boss, maybe she'd feel more at ease hearing it from me.'

'I can't think of anything worse. And neither could she, I imagine.'

'So, you do it. Most of the crew are down for the night. Russell's up in the wheelhouse on anchor watch. Anya won't venture this way unless something crops up, and I'll distract Trix with some task downstairs.' He pushed up out of his seat. 'Consider the deck yours.'

Maria was on her way back and his racing heart knew it. 'Connor…'

'Come on, ladies,' his friend said, wrapping an arm around each of them. 'Let's take this party below deck… 'Night, Campbell.'

''Night Campbell,' they chorused, folding into Connor's side.

''Night,' he said through gritted teeth.

They passed by Maria, taking their drinks as they went, and leaving her standing there in the middle of the deck, a solitary glass of whisky left on her tray, its colour as rich as her eyes that flickered his way. He gave a small smile, she followed suit, though it stalled when the pumping tunes through the sound system cut to something softer, more sultry, more... *Connor!*

The man himself gave a thumbs-up through the glass, his smile as mischievous as his actions. The man was a goddamn menace.

But then he was gone, a menace no more as he took his women with him, and a dutiful Trix followed. God knew what task he'd assigned his chief stew or for how long she'd be gone, but right now, they were alone.

Just the glittering ocean and the moon and a thrumming beat for a backdrop...and he wasn't just talking about the music.

OhGodohGodohGod...

This was too much.

He was too much.

Too hot. Too broody. Too intense.

His dark shirt adding to the entire vibe as he lounged back on the cream leather sofa, legs spread, eyes watching, waiting...anticipating.

He wants his drink, doofus!

She hurried forward, keeping her gaze fixed on the table as she swapped his empty glass for the fresh one and prepared to leave. 'Can I get you anything else?' she asked, her voice too small, too distant over the pounding beat of her heart.

She needed to get a grip. Do her job and get to bed. And quick. Because hanging about after dark, with him, was a bad, *bad* idea.

'Maria?'

He was just another man, another rich man at that, and she really ought to know better. She wasn't a teenager daring to overreach. She was a grown-ass woman who knew her place in the world and knew well enough the trouble her feelings could get her into.

'Maria?'

'Yes!' She bit her lip on the outburst. Not cool. Not cool at all. 'Sorry, yes?'

'Will you look at me? Please.'

She released her lip and took a breath, exhaling as she lifted her lashes... Oh, God, those *eyes*. They unravelled her from within.

'What is it?'

It came out harsh, rude even, but man, she just wanted to get back inside and away from him and the danger.

'I owe you an apology. And I don't want to get it wrong this time.'

You what, now...? She was the one that had fled from him. She was the one snapping at him. She was the one who should be...

She frowned, her knees weakening. 'I don't understand.'

'Will you sit with me a second so I can explain?'

Her knees screamed, *Yes, sit!* But her head...

She glanced around at the deserted deck, the deserted saloon, the sea, the dark shadow of Refuge Cove in the distance...

'It's time you clocked off anyway, it's long past midnight.'

And didn't her dog-tired limbs know it, but so long as the guests were still up, she was still on...

'Surely you can quit treating me as a guest now everyone else has gone to bed,' he said, reading her thoughts so clearly.

'*You* haven't.'

'And I don't need you waiting on me, so please, take a seat. I'd make it an order if I thought you'd obey it quicker.'

Now that put a fire up her. 'Don't push it.'

He smiled. 'That's better.'

She gave a huff of a laugh, grateful that it had somehow broken the moment that had held her in its grasp. 'I'm glad you enjoy getting my back up.'

'I prefer it to you being meek, because the woman I met last week was anything but meek.'

Heat assaulted her cheeks. Why, oh, why did she have to be a blusher?

'That was different then,' she said, slipping the tray onto the table and perching herself on the sofa's edge. 'You were just a customer in a bar.'

'And now I'm a billionaire on a yacht you think I want you to behave any different?'

A billionaire?

Did he just say…? *Oh, sweet heavens*, what the hell was she doing?

And he wasn't bragging either, he was simply stating a fact…and she shouldn't be surprised, not when the yacht they were bobbing around on had to be worth hundreds of millions…but that was Montgomery's wealth.

'Maria?'

She wet her lips, forced her eyes back to his. 'You said you wanted to apologise?'

He gave a slow nod, the intensity of his gaze sending a flame through her veins, and she gripped her hands in her lap. Focused on steadying her breath rather than the way he was making her feel.

'Yes.'

'I can't even begin to imagine why. Unless…' Oh God, no! 'You haven't told Mr Montgomery about—about us?'

He shifted in his seat. 'That wasn't why I was apologising, no.'

'But you have, haven't you? Ohnonono, what were you *thinking*?' She launched to her feet, glaring down at him. 'I asked you not to.'

'I know and I'm sorry. It wasn't how you're thinking.'

He was lucky she didn't bite his flamin' hand off as he reached for her, trying to calm her but only infuriating her further. How Montgomery must see her now. How utterly humiliating. How easy. Because she *had* been easy. Giving herself to Tim on that very first night, agreeing to one night…

'And how exactly am I thinking?'

'I don't know, some boastful chat between guys...'

Exactly that!

'But it wasn't. He saw us together on deck earlier. Saw enough to know that something had happened.'

'And you just had to confirm it?'

'He wanted to know what was wrong with me.'

'Wrong with you?'

Another slow nod. She was beginning to find the gesture quite maddening.

'Why would he ask that?'

'He seems to think I'm more out of sorts than normal.'

'And you told him that was down to *me*?'

The guy was gonna get her kicked overboard!

And if they dropped her in Refuge Cove she'd be screwed. Hundreds of kilometres away from Melbourne. Would they expect her to find her own way back too? Money she could ill afford to spend. Could she even *get* a taxi from the cove? She had no clue.

'Don't worry, it's very much my problem, not yours.'

She sank back into the sofa. 'How? How can it be your problem when you've just labelled me the issue? Called me out to your closest friend. Do you think he's gonna keep me on board? *Upsetting* you?'

His mouth twitched, his eyes glinting in the low light. 'I didn't label you as any such thing. And he wouldn't dare fire you mid-charter because of how I feel about you.'

And there he went again, bringing up his feelings for her. Feelings she didn't want to listen to because they only triggered her own.

'We went through this today.'

'We did and that's why I want to apologise. Though I find myself having to apologise for a whole lot more now.'

'I suppose that's my fault too.'

He ran a hand over his stubble, the sudden laughter in his eyes surprising and dizzying.

'I don't think it's funny.'

'I'm not laughing.'

'Your eyes are.'

'Can I help it if I find your argumentative nature amusing?'

'*My* argumentative nature?'

His eyes still danced, a smile playing about his lips now as he reached for his whisky, but he didn't take it up. Instead, he turned the glass in his hand while he considered her and she wriggled in her seat, wishing he wasn't within arm's reach. That his hand wasn't distractingly close as he rolled the whisky around, his fingers calling to mind all the things he had skilfully done with them, all the things she wanted him to do still.

She cleared her throat, lifted her chin and her gaze with it. 'Some apology this is turning out to be.'

'You had me distracted. I'll try again, shall I?'

'Please, because then I might be able to say goodnight and get some sleep.'

'That keen to get away from me again?'

Her conscience squirmed while she kept her lips sealed. She knew how she sounded, but her walls were up and she needed them to stay that way.

'Not that I blame you.'

Huh?

'I'm sorry. Sorry for Connor discovering the truth. Sorry for making you uncomfortable. Sorry for the conversation he witnessed, because we never should have been locked in that discussion in the first place. I never should have pressed you for more when you've made your feelings clear, several times over. So, I'm sorry. But answer me one thing…'

'What's that?'

'Is this purely about the here and now, or is there something you're not telling me, because the way you ran from me today—'

'I told you, I'm part of the crew, there's a code of conduct to follow,' she rushed out. 'This job is important to me and I need the money. I get that you might not understand that with your wealth, but—'

'I'd never put your job at risk. Your position on this yacht is solid. I promise you that.'

Her stomach rolled. He was so sure. So blind to the impossible position she was in. Just like Fraser...

'How? How will you do that when the crew start gossiping about me?'

'Do you honestly think people here will judge you, judge us?'

'Of course they will.'

Though Trix had already made it clear she didn't care. And if she didn't, maybe the rest wouldn't. But none of that mattered because really, she was the one running scared. She was the one using the crew as an excuse, so she didn't have to admit the truth. That the only person who cared was her and she was the one losing all fight now as his sincere gaze burned into hers.

'Why do you care so much about what others think?'

'Spoken like a man who has never been the brunt of vicious gossip before.'

'Believe me, at my level, people have plenty of stuff to say, most of which is unfounded and derogatory.'

'Enough money not to care then.'

'If they mean nothing to me, their words mean nothing. It's as simple as that.'

She gave a muted huff. 'Oh, to not care, I'll envy you that.'

'Why? What happened to you, Maria?'

She swallowed, remembering the whispers, the judgemental stares...

'It doesn't matter.'

'It does to me.'

'The point is, it's different for you. No one will dare say anything to you.'

'And if anyone dared say anything to you, they'd have me to answer to.'

It was a growl, a loaded threat that stole her breath and warmed her through. She almost believed it too. Almost. But hadn't Fraser said the same? All those empty promises… He'd only intervened when the whispers had gotten loud enough to reach him, threatening to reach his family, his wife and his daughters, the community at large…

'And what would you do?' Her laugh rang with cynicism. 'Go to Connor and get him to silence them? Get him to give me a nice juicy bonus too? Or pay me yourself to make up for it?'

Because Fraser had. He'd thrown money at her repeatedly, instead of the love she'd craved.

'That's not what I'm saying.'

'No, are you sure about that?'

'I'd make sure you weren't financially impacted.'

'And my reputation?'

'Trix is your friend. She knows we met before we came aboard, that this isn't some…some weird financial arrange-ment.'

He looked confused and she couldn't blame him. She sounded irrational. She was being irrational, taking out her past on him, and that wasn't fair. He didn't deserve it.

No, what he deserved was the truth. He'd given her his. Opening up to her about his past, wearing his heart on his sleeve when he'd spoken of his wife, his daughter…and when he'd spoken of his desire for her…his want…

She could destroy that though. Obliterate his desire for her with her own truth.

So why wasn't she doing just that?

She'd like to think it was because she was used to keeping it a secret.

But she knew it had more to do with losing his respect than anything else. Which meant she cared what he thought. Cared too much.

'I'm sorry I made you feel that way, Maria.'

'You need to stop apologising.'

'I don't think I've—'

'I'm not the person you think I am.'

His head shot up. 'And what person is that?'

'I don't know, someone who deserves that look in your eye, the attention you're giving me...'

'I think I should be the judge of that, don't you?'

She stared at him, wishing she could just come clean. If ever there was a reason for him to keep his distance, her past was it. And then she wouldn't have to work so hard to avoid him and the danger he represented, because he'd be avoiding her enough for the two of them.

'And if this is where you say *you don't know me* again,' he said, 'I'll tell you the same thing I did earlier. I *want* to get to know you, if you'll let me.'

'No. You don't.'

'Why? What are you so afraid of?'

'Who says I'm afraid?'

'You did—when you ran from me today. People don't cry and run for no reason, they do it because they're scared...so tell me, what were you running from?'

And that was when she realised his hand now covered hers upon the sofa between them, his palm a soothing balm to her soul...a balm she couldn't accept, because she didn't deserve to heal.

'You wouldn't understand.'

'Try me.'

CHAPTER NINE

TIM HADN'T BEEN aware of taking her hand…

Until she pulled away.

Her warmth still clung to his palm, the echo of her touch tingling and taunting as the chill of her rejection washed over him. He curled his fingers into a fist and forced himself back in his seat.

He'd give her space, if that was what it took to get to the truth. What it took to get to know her.

She ran her teeth over her bottom lip, her lashes lifting as her eyes found his again. 'You'll judge me.'

'Do I strike you as a judgemental person?'

'No, you strike me as an honourable one, and any honourable person would judge me.' She took an uneasy breath. 'I've never talked to anybody about my life before I rocked up at Mickey's Bar. Not even Trix, and she's my best friend.'

Her obvious torment twisted through him. 'You can trust me, Maria.'

She wrung her hands in her lap and he ground his teeth, battling the desire to untangle her fingers and pull her close…

'I promise.'

She swallowed hard and turned away, pushing herself to her feet, but he sensed she wasn't running. Not this time.

She crossed the deck to the rail, and slowly he followed, not wanting to spook her but unable to keep his distance either.

He glanced down at her beside him, her hands gripping

the rail until her knuckles flashed white, eyes unseeing on the moonlit water. The breeze tore strands of hair from her bun, whipping them across her face. He could blame it for the sheen in her eyes, but he knew better—those were the same tears he'd witnessed earlier.

Damn it. He never should have pressed. He should've let it go, just as she'd wanted him to.

'It's okay, Maria. You don't need to tell me. You don't owe me. This was never meant to be anything more than one night. It doesn't warrant—'

'No.' She blinked back the tears, her eyes flitting to his. 'I do need to tell you, then you'll know the person I am and you'll know to let this go.'

He didn't believe it for a second, but if it made her feel better to think it then so be it...

'I'm listening.'

She licked her lips. 'You know enough to know that I wanted to escape my childhood... My parents—they didn't make me feel safe and secure like yours did you.' Her voice quivered with emotion. 'And I'm not using their treatment of me as an excuse either, I'm just trying to explain how I ended up choosing the path I did...'

'Okay.'

'They were angry people. All the time. Angry at their lot in life, angry at each other, angry at me. When words weren't enough, the fists joined in...'

Her eyes flicked to his again—had he cursed?

Probably.

But *hell*, the thought of it. The thought of her...

'Everyone knew it too,' she said softly, her gaze back on the horizon but lost in the past. 'Our neighbours all talked, and the more they talked, the worse it got. It wasn't like we could move away either, we never had any money and the police never got involved. It was just another domestic case to them, and I wasn't about to rock up at the station and get another kicking for my efforts.'

He clenched his jaw tight, his entire body vibrating with the desire to hunt these people down and hurt them like they had her. These people who should have been protecting her, nurturing her, *loving* her.

'When I was fourteen, Dad lost his job. That's when everything really turned to shit. I quit school and took all the work I could get. Cash-in-hand. For two years, I worked, giving them some but holding a little back, trying to save enough to get the hell out of there. Only...'

He saw the way her throat bobbed, her lashes flickering as fresh tears came.

'My father found the money and totally lost it. He accused me of doing all sorts to get it, accused me of being selfish too. Told me I was just like my mother, and I was no kid of his.'

'The heartless *prick*.' Acid laced his words, filled with vitriol for the man he'd never met but by God, he wanted to make suffer.

'Turns out, he meant it too. He never thought I was his daughter. All those years treating me like I meant nothing suddenly made so much sense.'

'Did your mum not do anything, did she not...?'

She was shaking her head. 'Mum was wasted most of the time and when she was sober she'd look at me like she didn't recognise me, like I'd somehow grown overnight and she had no idea how I'd got there. I used to fantasise about someone knocking on the door one day and telling them there'd been a mistake, that I'd been taken from my real family at birth and they were here to take me home. Now *that* was a story I would have got behind.'

She gave him a weak smile and he couldn't stop himself from reaching out now, easing away a stray strand that had caught on her lip and tucking it behind her ear.

'I'm so sorry you had to live through that.'

'Yeah, well, I didn't have to live through it any more. He threw me out that night, took the money he saw as his due, threw me some change and told me not to come back.'

He cursed again, his head shaking. It was like some god-awful movie playing out in his head, only it had been her life. 'Where did you go?'

'To the diner where I worked every Saturday. The lady who owned it, she was a sweetheart. Her sister worked in a big house out of town and they were looking for a live-in house-maid. The salary was a pittance, but it would put a roof over my head, food on the table... With her vouching for me, I got the job. I really thought I'd landed on my feet. The house was incredible, like nothing I'd ever seen before... And they were the golden couple, extremely good-looking and suc-cessful. He was a world-renowned cosmetic surgeon, often away. And she was a committed socialite with three daugh-ters all under ten. Two were often away at boarding school, the other had a nanny. They were always throwing parties at the weekend and having guests to stay, so we were forever busy. It was fun. For a time. And I was so relieved. Indepen-dent at sixteen. Living in a mansion. A solid income, and a life that was mine. No more beatings, no more screaming... I was finally happy.'

'What changed?'

She looked away completely, her neat bun a poor substitute for her eyes that she now hid from him.

'One day, my boss came home early from a business trip.'

Tim's heart sank to his feet, dread keeping it there.

'He wasn't in a good way. He'd lost a patient in the operat-ing theatre. An unexpected complication. I was cleaning his suite when he rolled in, whisky in hand, talking about how this wasn't supposed to happen, not in his line of work. That the patient had lied, but it was his reputation on the line.' She took a shuddery breath, her head dropping forward. 'He was so broken. I'd never seen him like that before.' She turned just enough for him to glimpse her profile, the sheen in her eyes, the tension around her mouth. 'And there I was, sixteen and young, but I'd seen enough in my years to know that whisky wasn't the answer. So I took the glass from him, telling him exactly that, and he thought—he assumed...'

She lifted a hand to her lips and a shiver ran down his spine. 'He didn't, please God tell me he didn't.'

'He did,' she whispered against her fingers. 'I was too stunned to respond at first, I just let him kiss me. I'd never been kissed before and I... I liked it. The idea that this man, this charismatic, successful, well respected, intelligent man could want me...want me when he could take his pick of all the girls. Everyone had a thing for him. And his wife, she was stunning. Stuck up and demanding at times, but stunning. It was her that made me stop. Remembering he was married and how wrong it was. Not to mention how flamin' stupid it would be...risking my job and my home. I pressed him away and he apologised, said he had no idea what had come over him. That he wasn't thinking straight.'

'And you believed him?'

'Yes. And I still believe it was true of that night.'

'But there were other nights?' he said quietly, wishing he could stop the whole sorry tale but knowing this was what he'd asked for all the same. Her truth. Because not hearing it didn't suddenly make it go away. Didn't make it untrue.

And if she'd lived it, he wanted to know it. No matter how much it hurt him too.

'It was another month before anything happened again, but by then we'd become friends, or so I thought. He would seek me out when he returned from work, and we'd talk. I told him about my parents. I told him how coming to work for him had saved me from that life, and he told me about all the fascinating people he would meet and the places he would travel to and how one day he'd like to take me too. He told me about his relationship with his wife, how it was all for show, that neither of them were happy but they stayed together for the girls. That as soon as the girls were old enough, they'd go their separate ways, and he'd be free to see whoever he wanted. He'd be free to see me.'

'So, you had an affair?'

'Yes,' she whispered. 'I'm not proud of it, but I believed him. I believed him when he said he loved me and that he wanted to marry me and that he would just as soon as the time was right. Until then we had to keep it a secret. No one could know.'

'I bet they couldn't.' He shook his head. 'How old was he?'

She swallowed. 'Late thirties.'

'And you were *sixteen*?'

'Seventeen when our relationship changed. And yes, I know how it sounds, like he groomed me or something, and it would be so easy for me to say that's what happened, but it wasn't. I knew what I was doing. I wanted him. For the first time in my life, I felt like someone truly saw me, truly wanted me. I fell hard and I fell fast and he was everything. Until I got pregnant. And then it all changed.'

'*Pregnant*? Oh God, he's Fae's father, isn't he?'

'Yes.'

'My God, *Maria*.'

'His reaction wasn't far off yours.' She gave a twisted smile. 'He wanted me to get an abortion. Said it was best for the baby and for me, but really he was just terrified of our affair getting out. It wasn't just his marriage on the line but the affection of his daughters and his standing in the community too.'

'Because he knew he was in the wrong.'

'We both were.'

'No, *he* was, Maria. You were only just of age, far too young…'

'Old enough to get pregnant and to know I wanted to keep it at all costs.'

'How did he react?'

She huffed. 'When he realised I wasn't going to change my mind he shipped me off to the city. Set me up in a flash apartment, got me the best doctors, paid me enough so I didn't want for anything. Told me everything would be okay so long as I kept quiet. He started to control where I went, who I saw, what I did… When Fae was born it was days before he came to us, and even then he barely looked at her. I realised then that he would never love her like he loved his other daughters. I also realised that he was never going to leave his wife. That it was all just empty promises, and we would forever be his dirty little secret.'

He winced as she used the same label he'd accused her of dismissing him as.

'Yeah…that's why I ran this afternoon.'

'I'm so sorry.'

'You weren't to know.'

He wished he had though. Wished to God he'd known the whole damn lot because it made so much sense now. Her fixation on her place amongst the crew, her protectiveness over Fae, her fear of messing up a life she'd worked so hard to secure for them both…

'If it had just been me back then I would have run then too, started over, but I had Fae to think about. And knowing that he was willing to pay to support us both…he could afford to give her the kind of life I couldn't, not in my wildest dreams. After the childhood I'd had, I was convinced this was what was best for Fae. She wanted for nothing. I showered her in love while he showered us in money. And for fourteen years, I let him keep a roof over our heads, pay for her schooling, even let him worm his way back in on occasion, but those visits became few and far between as Fae got older and started to ask questions of her own, wanting to know where he was, when he was coming back… He didn't like that.'

Tim cursed, the idea unimaginable to him as a father.

'Eventually, I realised he was doing more damage than good. Damaging us both. After Fae got caught up in a nasty encounter at school, I called him, told him what had happened, and instead of coming to her aid, offering his love, his concern, he offered up a relocation, a different school, and I was done. I told him if he didn't want to know his own daughter, we didn't want to know him in return. I told him I was selling up and taking the proceeds from the sale to start a new life, and I didn't want to hear from him again.'

'And he let you go?'

'When I told him I'd go to the press if he didn't, yeah. That was four years ago now.'

'And you haven't heard from him since?'

'No. And to think I once thought myself in love with him.'

'You didn't know any better.'

'I like to tell myself that but…'

'But nothing. That son of a bitch took advantage, and you know it. If Fae came to you now and told you she'd met a man your age, don't tell me you wouldn't be putting the blame firmly on his shoulders.'

Her eyes shimmered, but she didn't deny it.

He cursed. 'You must look at Connor with those girls and think…'

'Cherry and Dana are almost ten years older than I was, it's different.'

'You still thought it though?'

'For a moment, maybe.'

He inhaled softly. 'I'm sorry, Maria.'

'You need to stop apologising…'

'But I *am* sorry. I'm sorry your parents were horrible human beings that didn't deserve you. I'm sorry that your first love—'

'My only love, if you take Fae out of the equation.'

'I'm sorry it was so messed up. And I'm sorry Connor has brought it back, that I've brought it back by making you re-live it.'

'The past is the past, but I can't deny what I was. A mistress willing to be kept and controlled by a man.'

'What you did, you did because you thought it was right for Fae.'

'And what a mess I made of that too. Parents are supposed to protect their children from the bad stuff. She was in the centre of it. And she knew it. All her life she knew she was the forgotten child, the unwanted child...' Her voice cracked. 'And I tried to make him see sense. He didn't have to love me or be there for me, but he should have been there for her, he should have loved her like he loved them. Her pain was my doing.'

'No! Her pain was *his* doing. You're not the villain in this piece. He is. Surely you can see that. He was the married man. He was the one bound by vows. He was the one who betrayed his own family to be with you. And then to control you from afar...what man does that?'

'What mother lets him? For fourteen years I let him...'

'You did what you thought was right.'

'I sometimes wondered if he was right, it would have been better, kinder to have...' she swallowed, one solitary tear escaping as she shook her head. 'But then I wouldn't have Fae, and she is everything to me.'

'You can't think like that,' he said softly. 'And you need to stop hating yourself for it all.'

'I don't hate myself.'

'No?' He cupped her cheek, encouraging her to turn and meet his gaze. She blinked up at him, the vulnerability in her caramel eyes teasing at his heart. 'You were the one who told me I wouldn't want to know you when I knew the truth, but listen to me now when I tell you, you are worthy of knowing, Maria.' He stroked his thumb along her cheek. 'And I'm *glad* you told me, so that I can tell you, right here, right now, that I see you and I still like you…'

Her lashes flickered, the smallest smile quivering on her lips as a flush of colour reached into her cheeks. Her eyes warming too. 'You're just being nice.'

He gave a low chuckle. 'Like someone else once said, I don't do anything for nice's sake.' Then his eyes dipped to her lips… 'And I certainly don't do this.'

He bowed his head, slow enough for her to stop him if she wished, and brushed his mouth against hers, savouring her sweet inhalation and the soft parting of her lips.

'But I'll stop. If this isn't what you want, say so now. But don't tell me it's because I shouldn't want you, because I do.'

She'd never let anyone see the real her.

And yet she'd let him. And he was looking at her like…

Don't be fooled like you were with Fraser.

But he wasn't Fraser—a married man high on the thrill of the forbidden, of control and secrecy. He was a loving widower, a loving father, and now he was caring for her…in ways that she'd never dreamed of experiencing again. Not like this, with her heart laid bare, her past with it.

And the rush of feeling terrified her, but…

'No,' she whispered. 'I don't want you to stop.'

She buried her fingers in his hair, reaching up as he came down, their mouths melding together in scorching-hot harmony. A moan rose through her throat as she took all that he was gifting her. Acceptance. Heat. Passion as much as compassion.

And hadn't she suffered enough, denied herself enough?

Could she not enjoy a little slice of this, but on *her* terms this time?

Not for forever, but for now?

She leaned back, gazing up into his eyes that devoured her where she stood, and curled her toes into the deck. It would be so easy to forget the end and dream of the future when he looked at her like that. She sucked in a breath as unsteady as she felt. Boundaries. They needed boundaries.

'I want this. I do. But my life with Fae…'

'You don't want anything interfering with it.'

'Any*one*.'

He nodded. 'I get that.'

'Can you get on board with it though?'

His eyes danced, his mouth cocking to the side. 'We're very much *on* board, in every possible sense.'

'I'm serious.'

'So am I.'

And then he captured her lips in a kiss that stripped her of all thought and breath and left her in no doubt he wanted this. His hands roved over her body as she slipped her own beneath his shirt…

'We should take this inside,' he rasped, and she nodded, a pinch of reality breaking in. They still needed to be discreet and—

'Thank God!'

They leapt apart, spinning towards the voice as a chair clattered across the deck.

Maria's heart surged into her throat. *'Dana?'*

'Help!' The girl stumbled up to them, wild-eyed, breathless, a robe wrapped haphazardly around her body. 'Please! It's Cherry—she's not breathing right!'

Maria launched forward, Tim right beside her.

'Where is she?' he demanded.

'In our room.'

'Where's Connor?'

'He's there too.'

They shared a look as they raced inside, her heart beating ten to the dozen as they weaved through the saloon and down the stairs. All the way Dana sobbed, rambling that she didn't understand what had happened, what was wrong, why she'd collapsed…

Collapsed?

Oh, God!

The moment they stepped into the cabin, a chill washed over her. Montgomery stood with his back against the wall, half naked, deathly pale, his terrified gaze locked on the girl sprawled across the bed, limbs slack, skin ghostly pale.

Tim cursed. 'What the hell happened?'

Maria raced forward, dropping to her knees beside Cherry. The girl's lips were blue, her chest barely moving. She checked her pulse. Faint but there, far too slow.

'Did she take anything?' Maria glanced up at a frozen Montgomery, then Dana.

'I… I don't know!' Dana stammered out.

Maria eased Cherry's head back, checked her airway. Still clear, thank God.

'I don't think so. We were just drinking. Everything was fine and then—and then she zoned out.'

'Connor?' Tim gripped his friend by the shoulders, forcing his attention on him. 'Did she take anything?'

But Montgomery remained mute.

'I'm pretty sure she's overdosing,' Maria said, shifting Cherry's body into the recovery position. 'It could be alcohol, but her lips…'

Tim broke away from Montgomery, checking every surface; he pushed open the bathroom door—'Got it!'

He came out of the bathroom with a small compact, dusted

with the remnants of something, and a tiny packet of pills. Maria rushed up and took the packet. Blasted opioids!

Dana shook her head frantically. 'I didn't... I don't...'

'What's going on?' Trix came flying into the room, PJs on, toothbrush in hand. She spluttered out a curse full of toothpaste.

'Trix!' Maria blurted. 'Do you know if there's naloxone on board?'

Her friend shook her head, swallowed. 'I doubt it.'

'Connor?' Tim strode up to him, gave him a shake. 'Answer her. Naloxone?'

'I don't even know what that is.' Montgomery shook his head, swallowed. His bare chest heaving with the motion and exaggerating the scars he bore down one side. Scars she hadn't seen before today. 'There shouldn't be any drugs on board. You know I don't—'

'Trix, get Russell to issue a mayday,' Maria demanded, hurrying back to Cherry's side. 'She needs airlifting. Now!'

Trix nodded and ran.

Dana let out a choked sob. 'Is she going to die?'

'Not if I can help it,' Maria said, unwilling to give false promises.

Damn drugs and the fools who thought they would never fall foul of them.

'I should've noticed. I should've—' Dana's knees buckled, and Tim caught her before she hit the floor. Guiding her to a chair, he looked back at Maria. 'What can I do?'

'Just keep an eye on Dana,' she said, then she glanced at Connor, who was stumbling forward, his eyes fixed on Cherry.

'I don't allow drugs on board. If I'd known...' He dragged a hand down his harrowed face, looking every one of his forty plus years now.

'I've got her,' Maria said, trying to reassure him, but she

wasn't convinced he heard her. He was living in his own hell. She looked to Tim for help.

'Connor, it's not your fault,' he said. 'Go get some air, yeah?'

'I can't just leave her.'

'You'd be better getting dressed and greeting the rescue crew.'

With a last long look at Cherry, he staggered out.

'You knew exactly what to do,' Tim said into the sudden quiet.

'Mickey trains up all his staff…' And this wasn't Maria's first overdose encounter. Likely wouldn't be her last either. She blew out a breath. 'We're not out of the woods yet.'

'No.' He gave her a small, firm nod. 'But you just gave her a damn good chance.'

'Let's hope so.' Maria glanced down at the fragile blonde and prayed he was right.

Some evening. From dinner to impromptu therapy to a truly explosive kiss and now this… Her stomach was in knots, her hastily snatched dinner threatening to return.

She took the girl's hand and checked her pulse again.

'Come on, Cherry, you're a fighter. Fight this.'

CHAPTER TEN

As THE RESCUE helicopter lifted off, its blades slicing through the night air, Tim stood rooted to the foredeck. A tightness coiled in his chest—not just from the gravity of the moment, but from the woman beside him. The woman who had kept her head while everyone else was losing theirs. The woman who'd spent most of her life surrounded by people who should have loved her and cared for her and done nothing of the sort.

Aside from Fae, of course. The most important person in her world, who was lucky enough to be loved and protected by the best. Her mum.

But who was there to protect her…?

She had Trix, sure. And Bob across the hall. Mickey too. And he knew from his talks with the landlord that he was trying to do his best by his tenants. Even if that desire had led him down a path of poor decision-making. Something Tim could help with. Something he *was* helping with. But it wasn't enough.

Tim wanted to be there for her, and that driving need was as instinctive as all the other feelings she'd dusted off within him.

'You okay?' he asked as the flashing red lights of the helicopter disappeared over the headland.

'Yeah,' she said softly. 'I just hope Cherry will be.'

'She's stable,' he said, fighting the urge to take her hand in his. 'That's something.'

'And it's all thanks to you, Maria,' Connor said from the

other side of him—more composed now, but no less shaken. 'I mean it. You were incredible. If you hadn't taken charge like you did…'

'I did what anyone else would've done given the chance.'

Tim took in the set of her shoulders, the quiet strength in her stance despite the exhaustion lining her face, and admiration swelled within him. For *everything* she had done, not just tonight, but before then too. Breaking away and starting afresh. Twice over.

'I didn't do it,' Connor said.

'You were in shock,' she replied gently.

'Maria's right,' Tim said, placing a placating hand on his friend's shoulder. 'Don't be so hard on yourself.'

But Connor wouldn't be told. He radiated tension. Tension and guilt. And Maria could see it too, her concerned gaze flitting between them both.

'I'll just…' she gestured to where Trix had Dana wrapped in a blanket off to the side, the girl's hushed sobs only just audible now '…go and see if I'm needed.'

He nodded.

'Tell Dana our ride will be here in a few hours,' Connor said. 'If you and Trix can make sure all their things are packed up and good to come with us.'

'No problem.'

She looked back at Tim, some unspoken message in her gaze, and he gave her the smallest of smiles, his eyes following as she walked away.

'You're right about her,' Connor murmured. 'She is pretty special.'

The coil within his chest turned that bit further. 'She is.'

They watched in silence as Maria embraced Dana and Trix, the women all offering one another support.

'Did you manage to talk earlier?' Connor asked. 'Before everything…'

He gave a slow nod. 'Yeah, we talked.'

'And?'

And things had been better, but now...

'We cleared the air.'

'Good. That's good.'

Was it? She'd been happy to indulge in whatever this was so long as it didn't impact on her life with Fae—it was better than nothing, but was it enough?

Tim had never thought himself a greedy man, but when it came to Maria...

And now their trip had come to such a cataclysmic end, reality beckoned, her sacred life with Fae...

'Take *Celeste* on, won't you?'

'What?' Tim tugged his gaze from the women now heading inside to frown at Connor. 'How do you mean?'

'*I mean*, don't quit the trip because I'm leaving with Dana.'

'But Connor, it's your yacht...'

'So? The crew are all booked in, Rio flew in from the States to cater for this, and hell, Trix and Maria deserve some downtime after what I've put them through this evening.'

'You didn't put them through anything, you had no idea the drugs were on board.'

He gave a soft huff. 'I should have seen the signs.'

'We *all* should have seen the signs if that's how you're going to look at it.'

'But I froze down there. All I saw was...' he swallowed, his skin turning ashen as he pocketed his fists '...all I saw was them. Lifeless and...'

He gripped Connor's shoulder, felt the tremors rolling through his friend's body. 'Hey, it's okay.'

'It's not okay. I felt as helpless as I did then, only this time I should have been able to do something.'

'Rather than beat yourself up over something you could have no control over, why not see it as a sign?'

His brow creased up, his bloodshot eyes zoning in on Tim's. 'A sign?'

'Like maybe it's time to ease back on the partying, find some real meaning to life again?'

'Says the guy who's simply been existing for the last seven years.'

'Don't worry, I've had my wakeup call too.'

His brows lifted. 'You mean Maria?'

'Yeah, I mean Maria.'

Connor almost smiled, his shoulders relaxing as he eased round to face him fully. 'Which means you have to continue on without me, spend some time with her, see whether this could be something more…'

'And what about you?'

'I'll get Dana to the hospital, see Cherry back on her feet and then we'll see.'

'Mr Montgomery?' Captain Kali joined them. 'What would you like us to do, sir?'

Connor looked at Tim. 'What do you say?'

What could he say when he finally felt like he was living again?

'If you're sure.'

Now Connor smiled. 'Good man.' He turned to Kali. 'You're going to continue on to Gabo Island, Captain, just as soon as Dana and I leave.'

'Very well, sir.'

'I know I don't need to say it, but take good care of my friend here, see he gets everything he needs. But I also want you all to get some downtime in. Treat it as something of a pleasure cruise. You deserve it after tonight.'

'That's very kind of you, sir.'

Connor gave Kali a brusque nod, guilt still tugging at the edges of his smile. 'Assure everyone that their salary plus bonus will be paid in full for the charter.'

'Will do.'

Kali walked away and Connor raked an unsteady hand through his hair. 'If one good thing can come of tonight, it's seeing you make some changes for the better.'

'Right back at you.'

'If there's anything more I can do to thank you, to thank Maria too, you only have to say the word.'

'Actually...' Tim checked the master stateroom beyond the glass, the women were no longer in their eyeline, but Maria was still on his mind as ever. 'You don't happen to know a decent private investigator, do you?'

Connor cocked his head. 'Are we talking corporate or private?'

'Private. Very much private.'

'Can I ask why?'

'You can ask...'

His eyes probed, looking for the answer Tim wasn't prepared to give.

'Is everything okay? With you? Sasha?'

'Yeah, everything's fine, just asking for a friend.'

'Heard that one before.' He pulled out his phone and worked the screen. 'If it's personal, you'll want this one. She's good. Real good.'

Tim's phone buzzed in his pocket. 'Thanks.'

'No.' He pulled him into a hug. 'Thank you.'

Hours later, with the departure of Montgomery and Dana, and a skeleton crew manning the yacht, Maria and Trix had retired to their cabin to get some sleep before they set sail for Gabo Island.

But Maria couldn't sleep.

Her mind wouldn't stop taunting her with Cherry's lifeless body. How close she had come to losing her fight and the idea that somewhere in the world Cherry's mother would have been none the wiser. Helpless to save her.

Didn't matter that Maria knew Fae's stance on drugs mirrored her own, the fragility of life and that of your child's was a burden every good parent carried, and the night's events with Cherry had thrust that constant weight to the fore.

She wanted to call Fae just to hear her voice, but to call now would only give Fae cause to worry and that would entirely defeat the point of calling.

Trix gave a loud snore and turned over on the bunk beneath her. Her friend clearly wasn't struggling in the sleep department. But then she wasn't also battling the knowledge that not too far away Tim would be lying in his giant cloud of a bed alone…alone when she could be…no, don't go there.

Because heaven knew where they stood now. After all she had told him and the kiss they had shared…then the near tragedy…was it any wonder she was still abuzz with adrenaline and worry and going out of her mind?

Biting back a groan, she threw off her sheets. Maybe a dose of fresh air would cleanse her of the lot.

Unlikely, but it had to be better than this.

She slipped from the room and into the quiet hallway. After the chaos of the night, the deserted stairs and hallways were eerily silent, the low glow of the courtesy lights and the gentle creak and roll of the ship adding to the freakish vibe. That was until she broke out onto the swim deck and then the entire world opened up in breathtaking fashion.

With the moonlit ocean on her left, stretching for as far as the eye could see, and the dark shape of the headland with its secluded, crescent-shaped cove to her right, it was quite possibly the most beautiful sight she had ever seen. The mystical glow to the bright white sand against the granite rocks and the shadowy backdrop of eucalyptus trees that reached up into the star-studded sky above…it didn't look real.

She took a breath and another, the tension in her shoulders easing…

'Couldn't sleep?'

She gasped, her body jolting as she clutched a hand to her chest and spun to find Tim leaning against the wall of the yacht. His relaxed stance telling her he'd been there long before she had.

'Sorry, I didn't mean to startle you.'

She licked her lips. She'd been wrong before…*he* was the most beautiful thing she had ever seen. His hair in sexy disarray, his eyes so dark they were almost black, the moon highlighting every chiselled feature—his cheekbones, strong jaw, bare chest, each undulating ridge to his abs—before her gaze reached his black shorts and snapped back up again.

'I thought you were in bed.'

'I couldn't sleep either.'

He pushed out of the shadows and came towards her, his gaze raking over her. From her simple vest to her tiny shorts to her bare feet, she felt every exposed inch of skin as it tingled against the sea breeze. The tingles multiplying as his eyes swept back up, resting an extra beat on her breasts where she knew her body betrayed every salacious thought.

'Are you okay?' she whispered

'Yeah, you?'

'Yeah.'

His eyes narrowed on hers. 'Why don't I believe you?'

'Perhaps because you're lying as much as I am.'

'Do you want a hug?'

Her breath caught. Did she want a *hug*? She wanted so much more than a *hug*. But there was something about the question, the offer…

When had a man asked her that? Asked with such care and concern and…*oh, my God*… Wordlessly, she stepped forward and he opened up his arms, wrapping them around her as she leaned into him.

She breathed in his warmth, his scent, his solidity and

everything about her pulsed and settled. She listened to the waves rolling and his heart beating and took all the comfort he was offering.

'Are you cold?' he murmured, his breath disturbing the hair on her head.

'No.'

How could she possibly be cold with his welcome heat pressing into her?

'You're shivering.'

'I think it's just the adrenaline wearing off.'

And the shock of her reaction to him.

He gave a low hum, the vibration working its way through his body and into her own.

'Connor was right, you were incredible tonight. The way you held your cool and knew just what to do.'

'I told you, Mickey makes sure we're trained up. It doesn't matter how hard he works to keep the drugs out, they always find their way in. And it's better to be prepared than in denial about it.'

Another low hum.

'You weren't too bad yourself, you know.' She lifted her head to meet his gaze. 'You saved Dana from hitting the floor, gave her a shoulder to cry on. You were there for your friend, too.'

And he was here for her now…

His mouth tugged to one side, dark eyes burning into hers. 'Glad I'm good for something.'

'You're good for a whole lot more,' she said softly.

'Are you flirting with me?' It was a low growl, the sound teasing against her chest. 'Careful, Maria, because my restraint is hanging by a thread.'

She nipped her lip. Flirting? Not intentionally, no. She'd been serious. She'd never wanted to lean on a man, depend on a man, to the extent that she did him in this moment. And that was bad. Bad. Bad. Bad!

But the chemistry…

'You know what I want?' she breathed.

His hooded gaze fell to her lips.

'I have a fair idea, but why don't you tell me?'

'To take a stroll.'

'A *stroll?*' His eyes sparkled, his mouth twitching with laughter. He didn't believe her, not for a second. And she couldn't blame him. She didn't believe her either.

'I want to be on that beach, feeling the sand between my toes as I watch the sun rise.'

She turned in his hold, leaned back against him as she took in the moonlit cove and tried to press mute on the crazy flutterings inside. All the wants and the dreams that were trying to rise up under the power of his gaze.

It was just shock and the comedown from the night's events messing with her mind. Making her want for more. Dream for more. With a man so far out of her reach he might as well be on the moon up there…

'Then let's go.'

'What?' She turned her head to meet his eye.

'Let's go to the beach.'

'*Now?*'

'Sure, why not?'

'Because we're due to set sail soon.'

'Who says?'

'Captain Kali.'

'Only because she's following Connor's last instruction to continue the trip as planned.'

'Exactly.'

'But we're the masters of this voyage now—you, me, the entire crew—and if we want to set sail a little later, who's to say no?'

She chewed the corner of her mouth and he turned her back to face him.

'Do you honestly think...' he said, stroking the hair back from her face in that way she was coming to savour '...anyone would take issue with leaving a little later?'

She thought of Trix still sleeping and of the deckhands who'd been brought in to assist during the night when they should've been catching up on their Z's. They could all do with the lie-in.

'Will you clear it with Captain Kali first?'

'I'll go one better and get the RIB too.'

'We don't need the RIB, I can swim it.'

'Okay, Miss Olympic Swimmer Wannabe, I believe you, but we're taking the RIB.'

'Do you know how to handle a RIB?'

He stared back at her, unimpressed by the suggestion that he couldn't, and she smiled. 'Okay, let me just change.'

She started to move off and he tugged her back. Surprise had her rolling right into his chest as his mouth claimed hers. *Oh, my!* The flutters fused into a fire, spreading through her abdomen as her knees turned to jelly, and she clung to his shoulders for dear life.

'Now,' he murmured against her lips, 'you can go.'

She blinked up at him in wonder...wonder and fear. And not just of falling literally, falling metaphorically too. Because it wasn't just her knees that had gone all soft, her heart was racing that way too.

And that wasn't okay.

That wasn't okay at all...

CHAPTER ELEVEN

TIM WATCHED HER GO, his heart lighter for seeing her smile again.

Lighter still to see the playful spark in her gaze. He hadn't felt this attuned to another in so long, his mood so easily swayed by theirs. Somewhere his head was telling him to exercise caution, but his heart beat louder.

And that was what he was listening to twenty minutes later as he helped her onto the RIB. The first fingers of dawn reached into the bay, subtle hues of rose and amber stretching from the sky to the rugged green hills and glass-like sea. The air carried with it the scent of salt and eucalyptus and promised another beautiful day in paradise.

'Wow,' she exclaimed beside him, her face lit with it all as he sped towards the beach. Her hair and thin white shirt billowing back as her caramel eyes shone with the rising sun.

'Wow indeed.'

Her eyes flitted to him, her smile soft. She knew exactly to what—to whom—he was referring, and he didn't care. Not any more. He'd been so scared of sharing his heart with another for so long, that now he was open to the possibility he couldn't hold back if he tried.

'It's hard to believe that life can be so cruel when there is such beauty in the world.'

'I know what you mean,' he said, slowing the boat as they approached the shore and bringing it to a gentle stop in the sand.

'Okay, I eat my words,' she said as he hopped off to drag it further up the beach. 'You can definitely handle a RIB.'

'My parents were big on sailing. Most holidays as a kid were spent on the water.'

'That sounds amazing.'

'It was.'

He reached up to help her down and she came willingly, her hands soft on his shoulders, her eyes smiling into his... but there was a hesitation there. An uncertainty. Was she nervous to be alone with him here? Surely not—not after everything they'd shared, but then, maybe that *was* the problem... the weight of it. The intensity.

He slipped his hands around her waist, her warmth teasing at his palms as he swung her to the ground. He held her steady as she settled, her eyes still hooked in his, hands still soft on his shoulders. He caressed the exposed skin just above the waistband of her shorts, felt the tremor within her. Was that a trapped whimper too?

'So how does it feel?'

She released her lip, the flesh all plump and glossy and tugging at his gaze.

'Feel?' she whispered.

'To be on the sand.'

She looked down at her feet, wriggled her toes and gave a sweet little sigh. 'Like heaven.'

Her eyes returned to his, their golden depths more alluring than the sunrise.

God, he wanted to kiss her. Kiss her and not stop.

And she wanted a stroll, not to be ravished.

'We best move before I do the other thing on my mind.'

She gave a soft laugh as he pulled away, taking his offered hand and letting him lead her along the deserted shoreline. For a while, the only sounds were the morning chorus of the birds and the gentle lapping of the waves. Then she slowed and looked up at him.

'Thank you for this.'

'I didn't really do anything.'

'You made it happen.'

'I'm just glad you came.'

'Me too. It's been a long time since I've done something like this…'

'What? Watched the sunrise? Enjoyed a walk on the beach?'

'Both.'

'But you live so close to the sea…'

'Not close enough when you always have something more important to be doing. Working. Cleaning. Mum duties…'

'You and Fae don't go together?' he said, pausing to frown down at her.

'I think she's a little old for building sandcastles on the beach these days, don't you?' She was trying to brush it off, but he couldn't miss the underlying sadness in her voice. The way she released his hand and continued on without him…

'What do you do for fun together?'

'Watch movies, eat rubbish. I'll cook her favourite meals, and she'll eat enough for two.' She threw him a smile, but it didn't reach her eyes. 'We'll take a walk along Merri Creek when we get a decent bit of time off together.'

'And holidays?'

She looked away but he'd already seen the reply she wouldn't give—what holidays?

He swallowed his curse and focused on the moment they were in, taking her hand once more as they walked.

'Do you know why it's called Refuge Cove?' she asked.

Was she trying to change the topic? Probably. And he was willing to roll with it, but inside…inside, he was desperate to change her reality. And he knew he was interfering enough by addressing her living issues with Mickey. Something he couldn't bring himself to tell her because he knew her pride wouldn't stand for it.

But what about the rest? All those long hours working, the lack of time for her and Fae, none of that would change…

'I didn't think it warranted that level of thought,' she teased, and he forced a smile.

'You probably know how treacherous the Bass Strait can be…'

The look on her face suggested otherwise.

'It's considered one of the roughest seas in the world.'

'I'm regretting asking now…'

'Don't worry, the conditions are good, but if things change there are places like these along the way where we can seek shelter. Hence its name. Sailors have been using this cove to hide from the elements for years. And you can't deny, it looks appealing too.'

'Especially at this time of day…' she said, walking up the sandy bank at the edge of the cove and taking a seat so that she could look out over it all.

'Can we sit here a little?'

'Sure.'

He settled back against the boulder beside her and she surprised him by leaning into him, her blissful sigh music to his ears.

'It's so very beautiful.'

He kissed her hair on impulse. 'It is.'

'Too perfect to be true.'

'And yet, it is true.'

'Is it though?' she murmured, and he had to wonder, did she mean the view or *this,* the rising connection between them?

'I can pinch you, if you like…'

'I'm serious. Doing things like this, enjoying things like this…it might be normal for you, but for me it's the stuff of dreams.'

'I *used* to do stuff like this, but it's been a long time for me too.'

Her eyes were full of scepticism as they met his.

'I mean it, Maria. You've got me living my life again. Seeking out the joy in it. And for that, I'm grateful.'

But what about after? When—if—they parted ways, what would his life be then?

'If I had the money you did, I'd be making every holiday about seeing the world,' she said, folding back into his side. 'Taking time to properly see it and enjoy it.'

There came his wealth again…

'I wasn't always this wealthy, you know. My father was a builder and my mother an architect. My childhood was spent in your average street, at a mainstream school, no bells and whistles. Their hard work really paid off when I hit my teens, but that came with its own downside too.'

'Like?'

'Like being sent away to school. I wasn't lying when I told you I wanted to run back home. I missed them. But eventually I found my feet, my friends, Connor. And I knew my parents were only doing it because they wanted me to have the best education, and they knew they weren't around enough. But they always made up for it in the holidays. Taking extended leave from the business to travel and spend time with me.'

'You don't have any brothers or sisters?'

'No. I think they would have liked to, but it just never happened for them. It's probably another reason Connor and I are so close.'

'Where do they live now?'

'They have a small farm in the Blue Mountains. Mum loves her horses just as much as Dad loves his boats, and they split their time between there and their travels. Right now, they're cruising along the Danube River.'

'Still big sailors then…'

'Seeing the world one cruise at a time, though now they prefer someone else to be at the helm while they do it. More time for them to enjoy one another and see the sights.'

She smiled as she swept her windswept hair out of her face. 'Still very much in love too?'

'Oh, yes.'

Her smile turned wistful. 'Must be nice. To have that in your life all these years. No wonder you're so…'

His ears pricked, his heart too…

'So?'

She nipped her lip. 'Nothing.'

'You can't just say that and then…'

'You're not your typical billionaire.'

'Know a lot of billionaires, do you?'

She gave a husky laugh. 'Fair point. You just surprise me, that's all. You're…softer.'

'S-softer?' he choked out.

'Don't get me wrong, you're all chiselled too.' Her cheeks warmed. 'But the way you talk about your family, your daughter, your…' she swallowed, her voice hushed '…wife.'

'Billionaires are capable of loving just as much as the next man.'

'I know. I guess I just… I would expect you to mask it more.'

'I tried that once. Ellie would have none of it.'

She gave a tender chuckle. 'I think I would have liked her.'

'Everyone liked her. She had a heart big enough for the both of us and she insisted on showing it every day. After she died…' He watched the froth on the waves form and dissipate, felt his pain ebb and flow with it and realised Connor was right. Talking about Ellie made him feel better, not worse. Especially when Maria was so willing to listen. 'I guess I shut down again. People would ask how I was, probe and probe, and it would only make me clam up more. Then I met you and suddenly, it's all coming out again.'

'Why do you think that is?'

'I don't know.' He considered it. 'Maybe it's guilt.'

She stiffened. 'Guilt?'

'For meeting someone who made me feel like she once had.'

He sensed the way his words pulsed through her. But, good or bad, he couldn't take them back. And he didn't want to.

'Like it's some sort of betrayal. But by talking about her to you, it actually feels the opposite. Like I'm sharing the part of me that will always belong to her, with you.' He shook his head. 'Sorry, I'm making no sense.'

She pulled his arm around her front, cuddling in deeper. 'No, you're making perfect sense. I'm glad you told me about her.'

'I am too,' he whispered, realising just how true it was. 'Talking to you has made me realise I was doing her a disservice by not talking about her. Not letting people around me talk about her too. Not sharing those moments with Sasha. You've helped me realise that I can focus on the joy we shared for all the years we were together, rather than get caught up in the pain of the end.'

She looked up at him, her eyes glistening. 'I'm glad I've been able to give you that.'

'Me too.' He stroked her cheek, lost himself in her eyes that were so very different to Ellie's but no less evocative. 'You're special, Maria. And I wish someone had shown you the value of true love before now. Like Ellie showed me.'

She licked her lips. 'I think that might be one of the sweetest things anyone has ever said to me.'

And then she kissed him. Her hands lifting into his hair as she turned to him fully and he eased back into the sand, taking her with him. Glorifying in her kiss and the press of her body as she settled over him.

'Thank you,' she murmured, her palm resting against his cheek as she met his gaze.

'What for?'

'For making me *feel* special.'

His heart pulsed, his chest tightening around it. *God*, this woman. She owned him. His every thought, every feeling. And instead of running scared like his head told him to, he was surrendering to it. Because he knew the power of it, the rarity and its worth.

And yes, it had the potential to cripple him anew.

But he realised something else as he gazed into her eyes. He realised if he had his time over with Ellie, he wouldn't take a different path. He wouldn't choose not to know her, not to love her, because of the pain that came after.

And he wasn't willing to take a different path now. Though choosing the path for himself was one thing, encouraging Maria to join him on it...

'*This* is special, Maria. What we have. It doesn't come along often but when it does...'

'We need to make the most of it.'

'Yes. And I don't just mean now, I mean tomorrow and the day after and the day after that...'

She pressed a finger to his lips. 'Let's not talk about the future. If tonight has taught me anything, it's that life's too short to spend it dwelling on what might be. Can we just... live in the moment and enjoy it?'

He kissed her finger away. 'Sure.' Though he wanted to press for precisely that—a future. 'If enjoying it means more of that kiss right now.'

She swept her thumb over his bottom lip, her eyes tracing the move. 'Do you think we're alone enough?'

'There's no one around but the birds.'

'And the bees?' Her laughter caught in her throat as he slipped his hand beneath her shirt.

'Those too.'

He savoured her whimper as he caressed her skin, cupping

her breast in his palm and teasing its tautened peak over the top of her bikini.

'Tim…' she moaned, arching into his touch.

'Is that a request for more?' he murmured, rolling her under him and deepening their kiss. Desperate to drive her to the brink, right here, on the beach.

He eased back to gaze down at her, marvelling at her beauty as he slowly unbuttoned her shirt. 'Because I'm all for giving you more.'

Her eyes gleamed up at him, silently pleading—dark, hungry, full of need.

He swept the shirt away from her skin, his own need rising with the sight of her, all flushed and eager, her breasts shifting with every shortened breath she took.

'We don't have any protection,' she whispered, and he smiled.

'We don't need any protection for what I have in mind…'

Her mouth fell into a delectable but silent O.

'Do you want me to stop?'

She lifted her hands into his hair. 'Absolutely not.'

And so he didn't, not until she was crying out his name and he felt sure, so sure, she wanted it all too.

The now, the next, the future.

All with him.

'Well, hello there…' Trix gave her a flirty wave from her reclined position on a sunbed beside the upper deck pool, her bikini as bright and as yellow as the umbrella-adorned drink in her hand.

'Is that…'

'A piña colada done Trixy-stylee?' She eyed her over her sunglasses as she toyed with the straw. 'Why, yes, yes, it is. You want one?'

'Trix, it's not even noon!'

'Hey, don't you be judging me, rolling home after sun-up.'

She gave a giggle. 'Or should that be sailing home? Maybe a Sex on the Beach is more your style...'

'Trix!'

'Where's your Adonis anyhow?'

'He's not my Adonis, and *shh*,' she said, scanning the entire area for an unsuspecting eavesdropper. 'Someone will hear you.'

'You think everyone doesn't know? You'd have to be blind not to see the sparks coming off you both.'

'Oh, God!' Maria's cheeks burned as her stomach squirmed, not again.

'Hey, don't worry about it, no one here cares. We're all on holiday now remember, orders from the boss.'

'Still...' Maria dropped down onto the sunbed beside her, snatched Trix's drink from her hand and took a long drag on the straw.

'Hey, take it easy,' Trix said, shoving her glasses into her hair and sitting up to face her. 'It really is okay. Everyone's on cloud nine to be getting a hefty paycheck and a surprise break. It's fun all the way, darl, enjoy it.'

Fun. That was what it was. Fun.

A fling. Not a relationship that could end in disaster.

So why did it feel like her heart was hurtling headlong into precisely that?

She swallowed the nervous bubble, gave a smile. 'You're right.'

'That's my girl!' Trix tapped her knee and retrieved her drink, settling back into the sunbed as she took a sip. 'So where is he? Don't tell me you exhausted him and he's now taking a nap to recover?'

'I swear you have a one-track mind!'

'It's my mind, my problem.'

Maria shook her head with a laugh. 'He had a work call to make.'

'Working? On a day like this…sucks to be a badass billionaire, I guess.'

'Don't you think it's weird though?'

'What?'

'*Us not* working?'

'Weird, yeah, but in the best possible way. So I take it I've lost my roomie?'

'Your roomie?'

'You've seen the bathtub in that stateroom, right? With all those massage jets…' She wagged her eyebrows. 'You need to get yourself moved in.'

'We have two nights left, Trix.'

'All the more reason to get packing, don't you think?'

Maria didn't know what to think because her body was too busy overriding her head at every opportunity.

'Ohnononononono.' Trix shot back up. 'Honey, please tell me you're not getting in deep with this guy?'

'*W—what*?' she choked out. 'Why on earth would you say that?'

'Because you look like you're overthinking it, and if you're overthinking it, you're making it into more than it is.'

'Of course I'm not.'

'F is for fun, honey, it's also for fling, and a fling doesn't warrant all this thought and feeling…well, save for the orgasmic kind, of course.'

'I know what a fling is, Trix.'

'So why are you stressing?'

Why was she stressing?

Maybe because she'd got the distinct impression that Tim was starting to reach for more… That when he'd told her of his feelings, of how special their connection was, there was a part of her that had reached for it too.

And that was why she'd cut the conversation dead. Telling him not to talk of the future. Telling him to make it about the now. Because everything was safe in the now. Fae was at home, blissfully unaware of their fling, and their fling was as finite as the charter.

In a few days she would return home and life would go back to being as it had been. As it should be. In the meantime, she had a gorgeous man and a superyacht at her disposal...

'You know what, Trix?' She got to her feet and smacked her thighs. 'I've changed my mind, a Sex on the Beach it is.'

'Attagirl! And while you're at it, remind that badass billionaire of yours he's supposed to be on holiday too. Montgomery's orders.'

CHAPTER TWELVE

A SUDDEN RAP on his door had Tim's head snapping up. 'Yes?'

Maria burst in, a pineapple-topped cocktail in hand and the biggest smile on her face. 'Quick, quick! You have to come! There are whales!'

She grabbed his hand and tugged, her excitement making him laugh as he closed the lid on the surveyor's report and let her lead him out. He didn't want to tell her he'd seen whales before. Whales, dolphins, seals…the whole gamut. Swam with them, too. Her joy was too infectious.

As was the sight of her hurrying into his room like she belonged there. Whether it was the morning they'd shared, the cocktails or the downtime, he was just glad to see it.

'Look!' She pointed as they broke out onto the aft deck, her eyes sparkling and wholly captivating. 'Have you ever seen anything so amazing?'

Every moment with her, *yes*.

'Your first sighting?' he asked, dragging his gaze from her to watch as the knobbly head of a humpback broke through the deep blue surface several metres away, a small calf following a heartbeat later, its tail flipping up as it swam in perfect sync beside its mother.

She nodded, inhaling softly. 'It's so sweet how they stick so close together.'

'They'll stay like that for about a year,' he murmured.

'While she nurses it?'

'Nurses it, protects it, helps it to swim…she's effectively using her slipstream to tow them along—taking on more work so they don't have to.'

She gave a small laugh. 'A mother after my own heart.'

Another whale surfaced a little further out, sending a spray of mist into the air, and she gasped, her eyes widening. 'Do you think that's dad?'

'Unlikely, they're not known for sticking around. But I reckon he's their escort now.'

'*Escort?*'

'That's what they call the protector in the pod—the bull that keeps predators and other males at bay…'

'Wow, is it normal to be jealous of whales?'

His heart protested, beating against his ribcage. He knew she was teasing, but still…

'I wouldn't be too jealous. He's only hanging around to get one thing.'

Her eyes flicked to his. 'Oh!'

'Yes, oh.' He grinned. 'Sometimes another cow takes on the protective role but, judging by his slightly smaller size, I'd say he's a bull. They normally hang around in the background unless they see a reason to make themselves known.'

'You think they see the yacht as a threat?'

'Possibly.'

'You seem to know a lot about them—is this from your parents and all your holidays on the water?'

'Them. And Ellie.'

Her hand pulsed around his as she turned to look up at him, her smile as bittersweet as his own. 'Yeah?'

'She loved all marine life. We'd go diving several times a year. Different places, different things to see. She had her bucket list too.'

'Another mother after my own heart. I hope you managed

to tick off plenty...' she said, her voice thick with the unsaid—
in the short time you had.

'We did.'

And the desire to do the same for Maria—*with* Maria—
pulled at him. Incessant. Unrelenting. There was so much
she hadn't seen...

'If you love this,' he said, a plan forming, 'you're going to
love Gabo Island.'

'You've been before?'

'My parents used to take me as a kid and then I took Ellie—
it was one of her favourite places, Sasha's too...'

'Tell me about—'

She broke off, her eyes flicking to the right of him as Anya
appeared on the deck. She released his hand and backed up
a step, the move as telling as the sudden dip of her gaze and
the blush in her cheeks. So much for being at ease in front
of the crew...

'You know it doesn't matter how many times I see this
sight,' Anya said as she approached, the bosun far more interested in watching the whales than what they had or hadn't
been doing. 'I still struggle to tear my gaze away.'

'They're mesmerising,' Maria murmured, looking decid-
edly uncomfortable as she toyed with the straw in her drink.

'Any idea when we'll get to Gabo?' he asked, drawing
Anya's attention his way.

'Captain says we should arrive well before dusk.'

'Great. Can I steal the RIB again, take a trip out to the island?'

'If the weather permits, sure. Just gotta keep an eye on
the conditions, it can get pretty hairy around the island quite
quickly if the winds pick up.'

'Yeah, I remember, thanks.'

'No worries.' With a friendly smile and one last look at the
whales she moved on.

'Are you okay?' he said as soon as Anya was out of earshot.

Maria rubbed the back of her neck. 'Yeah. Sorry. I know we're all on holiday now and according to Trix no one gives a damn what we're doing, but I just…'

'It makes you uncomfortable.'

'Yeah.'

After everything she'd been through with her ex, the gossip she'd endured in his household, he could understand her not wanting to risk the same here. But the idea she would liken their relationship to that messed-up dynamic…he hated it.

'So how about another private boat trip?'

She blinked up at him in surprise.

'What? You didn't think I was planning a solo boat trip, did you?'

'I didn't know what to think.'

'How about thinking private island tour with a Chef Rio picnic?'

'I…' Her cheeks warmed as her mouth hung open, her eyes racing with so much.

'Unless you have something else you'd rather be doing?'

'No.' She licked her cocktail-laced lips. 'Of course not.'

'Then it's a date.'

And pressing a swift kiss to her brow, he left before she could think to back out…

Wild and remote, Gabo Island gave Maria the shivers.

This was the island Tim thought she'd *love*…?

Sure, the rugged coastline—with its pink granite cliffs and dense green scrub—had a certain raw appeal, but it wasn't for her. It was too isolated, too exposed—too lonely. The towering pink lighthouse on the headland was the only sign of man, and even then it served as a warning to passing ships to steer clear after so many had met their end there.

'You ready to go?'

She turned to find the man himself behind her, two large bags in hand. She hadn't seen him since her cocktail-infused PDA and her bonkers jealousy over whales of all things. She totally blamed the drink. Not the man standing before her in a fresh Henley shirt and cargos, looking fit to play model for some swanky fashion designer, not private tour guide to her.

'Y-yeah.'

'You don't sound so certain.'

'I'm just struggling to see the appeal...' She gestured to the island, making clear she meant *it*, not him. Like he could *ever* possibly think she meant *him*. Fool. 'Deadly island? Luxury yacht? You sure you don't want to stay on board and join the others in their impromptu karaoke night?'

'Do I look like the karaoke kind?'

'I don't know... I reckon you could bang out an awesome Tina Turner.'

'Now I definitely know you're joking.'

She laughed, already imagining it in her mind's eye. 'I'd pay to see it.'

'Never going to happen. Though if you'd rather spend the evening with the crew over me and the picnic Chef Rio has prepared...'

Well, when he put it like that...

'I'm good, let's go.'

He grinned his approval. 'Just tell me you've got something warmer to throw on later?'

He cast his gaze over her and her skin fizzed, her vest and jeans suddenly stifling.

'Anya told me to pack a bag—' she puffed out '—said we might get a little wet on the crossing.'

'It's possible, though I've seen the sea a lot worse.'

'Not what I want to hear,' she said, her body chilling just as quickly. 'Not when Russell's been filling me in on the numerous ships this island has claimed.'

'Cheers, Russell... But you trust me, right?'

She gave an affirming hum, realising just how much she meant it.

'Come on then.'

'You've got the radio just in case...?'

'Yes, I've got the radio.'

'And the weather is good?'

'The weather is good.'

'But it will be getting dark soon.'

'And that's when the real fun starts.'

'The fun?' She squinted at him. Was he joking, flirting, promising a repeat of that morning...? 'Does it beat seeing the whales this afternoon?'

His eyes twinkled like the ocean. 'I'll leave you to be the judge of that... Come on.'

He loaded up the RIB and helped her aboard the rocking vessel, keeping hold until she was safely seated at the rear, his care and attention as thrilling as his touch.

'Thanks.'

His smile was so tender, so... *Damn those cocktails!*

Though she wasn't drunk. Unless being drunk on a man was a thing?

'No problem.'

She pulled her bag onto her lap and watched as he set the boat in motion. His muscles flexing beneath his pale T, those capable hands knowing just what to do...whether they were working the boat or—

He caught her eye, his smirk sizzling. 'You shouldn't be watching me, you should be watching them.'

He motioned towards the island and she turned, her sheepish laugh fading as she took in the flurry of activity. Seals—so many seals! Some lounging lazily on the great pink boulders at the base of the lighthouse while others dived and frolicked in the surging waves...

'They look so happy!'

He grinned back at her. 'So do you.'

He was right. A ridiculous grin stretched across her face—one she hadn't worn in so long, but today it just kept on coming. Her shoulders didn't feel so bunched either. Nature's magic. Or Tim's.

Not something you wanna debate...

Though it was there, still pressing on her mind as he moored the RIB in the small jetty and they hauled their belongings ashore.

'Do you want to eat now, or fancy a tour first?'

'Tour,' she said without hesitation, eager to see what made this island so special—to him, his family. Ellie, too.

Eager to focus on something other than her racing thoughts too.

Don't you mean your feelings?

Over the next hour, he showed her everything there was to see, weaving in stories from his previous visits. How Sasha had picked wildflowers to make a posy for the small picket-fenced cemetery, its three weathered graves so old their inscriptions were illegible, but she'd wanted to give them something nice. How she'd grazed her knee at the stone monument honouring those lost in the 1853 wreck of the ship *Monumental City*, the very tragedy that had led to the lighthouse's construction—yet still insisted on climbing it to the very top.

Maria eyed the lighthouse in the distance. 'That's some climb.'

'One hundred and ninety-six steps. Believe me, I felt every one. But Sasha loved it—especially when she could tell her friends she'd climbed to the very top of the second tallest lighthouse in Australia.'

'What about the tallest?'

'That was the next year.'

She chuckled. 'Quite the little adventurer.'

'She was. Still is. I'll have to tell her that they've turned the Assistant Lightkeeper's Cottage into a holiday let now...'

'A holiday let?'

'You don't look convinced?'

'I guess if you like your solitude, it's perfect.'

Because they hadn't seen another soul. Though the light-house keeper had to be around somewhere. And Tim assured her that when the weather was good, the place would often have visitors passing through.

'I don't know,' he said. 'In a world that's forever changing, there's something quite reassuring about a place that stays the same. A place where you can step away from the noise, let go of the pressures in the real world, and just appreciate it for its natural beauty.'

'And enjoy the quiet that isn't quiet at all,' she murmured.

Because between them, the silence was alive with the crash of the waves, the call of the seabirds, the distant bark of the seals. And the grass...was that frogs? Whatever it was, the land hummed with it.

'Exactly. Ellie and I had busy lives, whether at work or out of it, there were always people around. Coming here was a total break from that.'

'What did she do for work?'

'She was a human rights lawyer.'

Wow, she almost blurted.

'When she wasn't fighting the good fight for the people, she was volunteering at homeless shelters and animal shelters. She had busy feet. Always had to be doing something.'

'She sounds—amazing.'

'Amazing, *and* exhausting.' Though his chuckle was full of fondness for the woman he had lost. 'Coming to places like this made her take a moment, you know.'

Maria nodded, because she could totally see it now. Through his eyes, through theirs—the island's magic unfurling with every memory he'd shared and every step they took. As for Ellie, *hell*, Maria was half in love with the woman herself.

He paused at the edge of a sandy cove and looked back at her, offering out his hand. She took it and together they looked out over the sea and the sun low on the horizon.

He inhaled softly. 'This is the first time I've been since I lost her...'

She looked up at him, all the emotion she'd been trying to suppress surging through her as she realised what this trip meant for him too. 'I'm glad you brought me.'

'So am I.' He gave her a smile, his eyes so full of something...something deep, something that had her throat closing over and her heart in a spin—was that Ellie in his gaze or...?

'We should eat.'

'Eat?' she blurted.

His smile lifted to one side. 'Yeah, you know that thing called food...'

'Sounds good.'

And if she was eating food, she couldn't be devouring him.

Heart, mind *and* soul.

'I think Rio thought the entire crew were coming with us,' Maria said, flopping back on the blanket and palming her stomach with a groan. 'I can't eat another thing.'

'It'll keep,' he said, reaching for the containers to pack away the leftovers and she made a move to help. 'Oh, no, you don't. It's my turn to look after you.'

Her eyes twinkled with the setting sun. 'If you think I'm going to lie here all idle...'

'Do you *ever* let anyone take care of you?'

'Nope.'

She wrapped the cheese and placed it in the cool box, the juice and leftover fruit too. All the while his eyes remained fixed on her, his body unmoving.

'I thought you were packing up,' she said.

'Right now, I'm trying to unpack you.'

She gave an abrupt laugh. 'You've unpacked me enough. No one knows me as well as you—' Her eyes jerked to his, then away just as swiftly as she dived for the bread.

'Is that true?' he said.

'Don't get a big head about it, I'm hardly worth getting all excited about.'

She reached across him to place the bread in the bag he held, and he took it from her, took her hand next. 'Don't say that.'

'I'm only teasing.'

She tried to pull away, but he wouldn't let her go, his hold gentle yet firm. His words too. 'Only you're not.'

Her eyes flickered under his gaze. 'Tim, seriously…'

'You are worth knowing, Maria. You are worth getting excited about. You're…' He ran his thumb along the back her hand and she licked her lips, her mouth parting and drawing his eye. Making him want, when what she needed was to hear— 'Damn, I want to kiss you. But I don't want you to think that's all this is…'

A crease formed between her brows as he reached into her hair.

'You fascinate me, Maria. And the more I get to know you, the more I like you, and the more I want—' Her eyes flared and he pulled back, scared he'd send her running with his need for a future as much as his need for her in the present. 'You should lie down and watch the cove. Your night's entertainment is about to begin.'

'My *what*?'

'You'll see.'

This was why he'd brought her so late in the day. To see the island at dusk. Not to seduce her and confess his feelings in the process.

But tonight, the appeal of the island had some serious competition in the woman now lying on her front beside him. The sunset in her hair, her eyes, her smile…

Stunning. That was what she was. So why couldn't she see it?

Her parents. Then Fraser. Her ex. The man who had chipped away at her for more than a decade, taking what he'd wanted. The man who now made his blood boil. Not since Ellie and her diagnosis had he felt such anger. And the more he thought of him and what he'd done, the more…

'You shouldn't be watching me—you should be watching them.'

His laugh fractured the sudden tension in his frame. 'Using my words against me.'

'There are whales…' She gestured towards the sea as a massive tail slipped beneath the surface. 'And oh, my God…' She pushed up off the ground. 'Are they—*dolphins*?'

It took him a delayed second to switch from the beauty in her face to the beauty in the ocean. And as much as the pod of dolphins made for a stunning sight, his eyes kept drifting to the one beside him.

He knew which one he'd choose, again and again and again.

CHAPTER THIRTEEN

WITH THE PICNIC packed away, the sun a teeny-tiny sliver on the horizon and the dolphins no longer around, Maria figured it had to be time to go. Especially with the sudden chill in the air and the breeze that had picked up since their arrival on the island.

But she had to admit, there was something special and intimate about being hunkered down on the grassy bank with Tim, a blanket drawn over them both, his body heat as warm as it was provocative.

'Do you—'

A sudden gust snatched at the blanket, cutting her off, and Tim swiftly clamped it back down.

'Okay, I think that's a sign for us to—'

'Shh,' he hushed against her ear. 'Look.'

She peered through the darkness at the waves rolling ashore. Nothing. 'I don't—' And then she saw it, a shifting shadow in the surface of the water. 'Is that…'

He nodded and with a break of foam, a sleek black-and-white body popped up.

'Oh!' she gasped, pressing a hand to her mouth as the little penguin found its feet on the sand, its waddle both cute and hilarious and tickling at her stomach. She scoured the shoreline looking for more, remembering how she'd once taken Fae as a kid to see the fairy penguins landing in St Kilda and how they'd come in droves.

A few minutes passed and nothing. He couldn't be on his own—surely. But then the entire surf came alive, a flurry of black-and-white bodies appearing as if on cue.

Wow! Out they popped, their flippers splayed, some landing gracefully and shaking off the spray, while others tumbled and skidded before they found their feet. The air was filled with chatter as they gathered on the shore before dashing to their burrows and their waiting young.

'Honey, I'm home!' she murmured, and Tim turned to smile at her.

'Can you imagine, all day swimming at sea to come home and have to sick up what you caught for your kids?'

'Way to spoil the moment.'

'Sorry,' he murmured, pressing a kiss to her hair. 'I'll be quiet now.'

She hummed her approval, her own words lost in the thrill of having his mouth so close. Torn between kissing him and the latest charge of penguins disappearing into the hummocky dunes, some coming quite close to where they lay.

'I thought sunrise at Refuge Cove was special, but this…' Then she saw a stray little fella left behind. 'Oh, no, why didn't he leave with the others?'

'He's probably waiting for his mate on the next raft.'

'You think?'

'Just wait…' He gestured as a new wave arrived and, sure enough, the little loner was no longer alone. With the rising cacophony of calls, he came together with another, their waddle as excited and as giddy as Maria now felt.

'Oh, my goodness, that is just….' *Sweet heavens*, she felt like crying. First whales, now penguins. What was wrong with her? 'I can't believe I'm getting all emotional over birds.'

'Or maybe it's the sentiment?' he said softly.

And of course, he'd think that after her foolish statement

with the whales and the jealousy… *He's not wrong though, is he?*

'If it makes you feel better, I'd wait for you too.'

Oh, my God.

He was teasing her, his eyes danced with it, but her head, her heart…

She forced a laugh. 'Who says I wouldn't beat you home?'

Home? She was supposed to be making light of his tease. Instead, her words hit hard. Because a home with this man in it…the idea of it…it was the stuff dreams were made of. And she'd quit dreaming years ago. Or so she'd thought.

He gave a low chuckle. 'Fair point.'

They cosied back down and watched more of the penguins come ashore, wave after wave arriving until the groups became smaller, the sounds on land growing with their homecoming…

'We should get back to the yacht,' Tim said, easing onto his side and stroking her hair over her shoulder. His touch the cure to every panicked thought.

'Or we could stay here?' she said, rolling onto her back to meet his eye. Her previous desire to return to the yacht taken out by the desire to live in this moment now—to dream a little longer.

'And have Trix think I've kidnapped you—you're okay, thanks.'

She gave a hushed laugh. 'I think she'd encourage you to do just that.'

'Really?'

'Oh, yeah, Trix is all for you having your wicked way with me.'

'She *is*?'

'She already has us moving in together—on board, I mean!'

She swallowed. *Watch what you're saying!*

'Sounds good to me…' and then he frowned. 'But you don't want to?'

Want? That room, that luxury, *him.* Always, *him.* 'It's your bed.'

'And?' His mouth twisted with amusement. 'You shared your bed with me, remember.'

'That wasn't premeditated.'

'And this is?'

She didn't get a chance to answer as his mouth closed over hers, soft and tantalising, the lightest sweep of his tongue, and everything about her cried out for more. 'That's a dirty trick.'

'Are you complaining?'

She forked her fingers through his hair and kissed him back. Wanting, needing, pleading...but fearing it too.

Because the more he gave, the more she wanted.

And the more she dared to dream it was possible.

Tim felt the entire world shift and settle around them as she curved her body into his, her kiss turning hungry, desperate, matching him breath for breath.

'Maria,' he groaned against her lips, his hands raking down her sides and slipping beneath her sweater. He palmed the curve of her spine, pressed her closer, wanting—*needing* to feel every inch of her. 'What are you doing to me?'

'The same as what you're doing to me.'

Damn, he hoped so.

Could he really be so lucky as to fall in love twice in one lifetime?

Love—was that what this was?

The world shifted again, only this time he felt the energy shift in the air itself. A chilling gust broke through their heated haven and she stiffened against him, her nails clawing into his shoulder as they looked up at the sky. Ominous clouds moved towards them, drowning out the stars in the distance— a *storm*?

Another sharp gust sent sand skittering across the ground

and he pulled her close again, shielding her from the swirl-ing onslaught. Amidst the sound of the island, the muffled crackle of the radio reached him from the bag. He cursed.

'Is that…' Maria started.

'The radio, yeah.'

He had no idea how long it had been going off, between the noise all around and the heat of their kiss…

He twisted to grab the bag, tugging it open.

'Mr Campbell, this is *Celeste*,' came Captain Kali's voice. 'We need you to respond asap. Mr Campbell, can you hear us?'

He snatched it up. 'Captain. It's Tim. We can hear you.'

'Mr Campbell, it's good to hear your voice! We have a cold weather front moving in fast. The crossing isn't safe in these conditions—you need to hold tight and find cover. Hope-fully, it'll sweep on through. We'll reassess in an hour. Keep the radio close.'

Captain Kali might as well have said, *Don't ignore me next time.*

'Copy that.' He kept his cool as Maria stared up at him, wide-eyed and pale. 'Come on.'

He stood, clipping the radio to the outside of the bag and hauling her to her feet.

'We need to get to the lighthouse,' he said, gathering up the rest of their things while she did the same. 'We can find cover there.'

Switching on the lantern he'd brought, he took her hand just as a fat raindrop hit the ground, followed by another…

'Best hurry.' He urged her into a run as another drop hit, then another. Before long, they were being attacked from all sides, wind, rain, sand, all of it obscuring the white trail to the lighthouse.

'It's not far!' he shouted, keeping a tight hold of her hand, the beam of the lighthouse as much an aid to them as the ships in the sea now.

It was less than a two-kilometre dash, they could do it in ten if they picked up the pace.

Finally, the dry-stone wall that marked the boundary to the light station finally came into view and he hurried through the gate, heading for the cottage straight ahead. There was no sign of life, just a solitary courtesy light switched on beside the door. He tucked her into the porch and knocked, knocked again.

'Hello!'

No answer.

He tried the door.

Locked.

He scanned the area, the property to his right looked just as shut down. 'Stay here, I'm going to find the keeper.'

'I'll come with you—'

'No, stay sheltered, look after our stuff.' He gave her his bags. 'I won't be long.'

Maria watched him go, her heart in her mouth as the weather closed in around her, relentless even beneath the porch. In no way did this feel like a passing threat.

She gathered the bags to her chest and pressed herself back against the door, squeezing her eyes shut. All the while praying it quit at wind and rain because if the heavens threw thunder and lightning into the mix she feared she might cry.

Captain Kali's voice crackled up to her and her eyes slammed open—the radio!

She dropped all but the bag with it attached and tugged it free, fumbling over the button to respond. 'H-hello? Captain Kali?'

'Maria, is that you?'

'Y-yes.'

'Have you found shelter?'

'We're at—at the lighthouse.'

'That's good. There's a storm rolling in and we can't hold position. We're moving the yacht to safer waters, we'll return just as soon as it is safe to do so.'

She knew it. *Freaking* knew it.

'Maria, do you copy? Maria?'

She licked her lips, took a shallow breath. 'Yes, we copy.'

'Stay safe, *Celeste* out.'

She gripped the radio to her chest, closed her eyes against the dark.

It's going to be okay, everything will be okay, it's just a bit of bad weather...just—

'I've got a key!'

Her eyes shot open—*Tim*.

He appeared by the light of his lantern, his drenched hair sticking to his face, his clothes like a second skin. He blinked away the droplets clinging to his lashes as he looked down at her, concern etched in every sweet line of his face. Never had she been happier to see someone. She wanted to leap into his arms but she couldn't even move.

'You okay?'

She clenched her jaw. Nodded. His eyes hesitated over her face, his concern still blazing as he unlocked the door and urged her in. He tossed their belongings inside and swept the lantern around. The room was basic but functional. A sofa, a fire, a wooden sideboard and a lamp. She slid off her shoes and moved to switch it on.

'There's no power to the cottage.'

'No p-p-power...' Her teeth chattered. 'How come?'

'They're in the middle of some critical infrastructure work, but the keeper says we're welcome to use the fire and anything else we need.'

'O-okay. Captain Kali radioed while you were gone.'

'What did she say?'

'She...she said a storm was coming and they needed to

move to safer water.' Maria tried to push out the fear as she forced herself to relay everything Kali had told her. 'She said they'd return when they could.'

'Okay. No worries.'

'No *worries*?'

'It'll be okay, Maria, honestly.'

She tried to nod but her head refused to move, everything about her was drawn tight. Her body chilled to the bone. A storm. A *freaking* storm on an island as exposed as this. Never mind dreams, this was the stuff of nightmares. For her at any rate.

'The keeper says there are candles and lanterns in the sideboard, wood for a fire and fresh linen that we can help ourselves to.'

He slipped into action while he spoke, finding the lanterns and the candles, lighting a couple before turning his attention to the fire in the grate. All the while she stood rooted, shivering in place. The wind was howling, the shuttered windows clattering, the rain beating wild against the walls…

'Do you want to take the lantern and see if you can find towels and some blankets?'

Did she want to…

'Maria?' He paused before the fire he was building to peer at her and cursed, shot to his feet. He was across the room in a heartbeat, his hands hot and sure on her arms. 'What is it?'

She shook her head.

'Tell me.' His thumbs stroked her through her clothing, the gentle pressure a reassuring hit of both heat and strength.

'I… I don't like thunderstorms,' she whispered. 'They terrify me.'

His frown deepened. 'You're serious?'

She nodded. 'D-don't look so sh-shocked.'

'I'm just surprised…'

'W-why?'

'Because last night with Cherry, you were fearless.'

'Last n-night, the heavens weren't cr-crashing down on us.'

'And they're not crashing down on us now… Oh, baby, come here…' He pulled her into his arms, kissed her hair, his 'baby' echoing through her, warm and as soothing as any lullaby. 'It's going to be fine. I promise. Keepers have survived here for well over a century, the building we're in has stood for all of that. You'll be fine, I promise.'

She nodded against his chest, feeling tiny and weak. And she hated being weak. Fraser had made her feel weak and she'd sworn she'd never feel like that again. Or let another see her like so. But with the rain hammering, the wind howling, the waves crashing against the rocks and the threat of an impending storm, she was crumbling, and she couldn't stop it.

'You're frozen. We need to get you out of these clothes.'

She nodded as he led her from the room with the lantern, pushing open doors and looking in cupboards, gathering up everything they could use—towels, pillows, blankets.

'I'll get the fire going while you get yourself dry, okay?'

Numb, she took the towel and blanket he offered her and watched while he built the fire. It flickered to life and he got to his feet, brushing off his hands and pulling off his T. He turned to find her in the same position. Still clothed. Still wet. Still stunned.

His eyes narrowed, his jaw pulsing as he let his T-shirt drop to the floor, then he closed the distance between them. Slow this time. Tentative. He raised his hands to her face, stroking away the wet strands from her eyes, her cheeks, her mouth…

'Do you want me to help you?'

She swallowed, her nod as juddery as her insides felt.

'Okay.'

He drew her to the space before the fire, the concern in his gaze burning with the flames that danced in his depths.

And she focused on those as he took the blanket and the towel from her trembling hands.

'Arms up, baby girl.'

She did as he bade, his eyes staying fixed on hers as he peeled her sweater over her head, her T-shirt too. Each item hitting the floor as his half-naked body came ever closer.

'It's going to be okay,' he murmured. 'I've got you.'

She nodded, her eyes drifting to his chest. The beauty before her soothing away the harsh reality beyond the walls, the noise drowned out by the thudding of her heart and the chill raced away by the fever in her blood.

His mouth twitched. 'What did you say?'

She hadn't said anything—had she?

'It sounded like "Refuge Cove".'

She nipped her lip as a tremor ran through her. Though this time she couldn't be sure it was fear or the desire to reach out and touch what was tantalisingly close.

'I was likening you to the cove…its beauty and its power to make you forget…'

'Forget?'

She looked up into his eyes, the smallest of nods. 'Forget how cruel life can be…'

And she wasn't just talking about the cruelty of the storm now, she was talking about him as a man with the power to make her feel again, the power to make her hurt again…

But in that moment, she didn't care. She lifted her palms to his chest, felt his body tighten and pulse beneath her touch.

'Make me forget.' Her voice was no more than a husky whisper. 'Please.'

His eyes dipped to her lips, a moment's hesitation and then his arms came around her, setting her skin alight as his mouth came down on hers. Hard and punishing, in all the best ways. More powerful than any storm could be—more powerful than any *man* had any right to be.

He unhooked her bra and swept it from her shoulders, popped the button on her jeans. And then he was on his knees, peeling the wet denim down her thighs. His hands hot, his kisses hotter.

She gripped his shoulders as he tugged each leg free. Stripped her socks too. He teased kisses over one thigh, then the other, smoothed his hands up the back of her legs, his fingers curling into the waistband of her knickers. He pressed a kiss to the lace and she gasped, her hands launching to his hair. He looked up, caught her eye, the fire in the grate nothing on the look in his eyes as he pressed another slow kiss to her sweet spot, teasing it through the lace with his tongue.

'Tim!' She rocked against the pressure, his eyes deliciously intense on hers and staying as he eased the lace down, letting it fall from her knees to the floor as he cupped her behind and brought her to his mouth. His tongue flicked across her throbbing clitoris, and her knees buckled, his hands taking her weight and holding her in place.

'You are beautiful,' he said against her skin. 'You are safe.' His tongue rolled over her. 'I've got you.'

He sucked back over the sensitised nub and she cried out, her fingers clawing, her stomach contracting.

'That's it, baby, let me catch you.' He slid his fingers between her folds, filling her as he teased her with his tongue, driving her to the brink so quickly she couldn't catch her breath. She couldn't—she couldn't...

Her orgasm hit with the first strike of lightning and she cried out his name as the stark white light slashed through the shutters.

'I've got you.' He held her steady against his mouth, took every wave her body offered up, stayed until her limbs had softened, and her breaths had slowed. He stood, holding her against him in one arm while he threw a blanket over the sofa, then he set her down upon it.

'I still need you,' she murmured as he straightened, uncaring of what she was saying, what she was admitting, 'Please.'

His throat bobbed, every exposed muscle in his body straining as he unbuttoned his jeans and slid them off with his underwear.

Naked and hers.

The thought pierced her brain, caught at her heart as he lowered himself over her. Desire blazing in his gaze as he stroked his hand down her side, cupping her knee to raise it to his lips. He kissed it softly, hooking it over his shoulder as his fingers dipped to caress her. Easing her back to the brink, until she was panting and desperate and couldn't take much more.

'Please, Tim.'

He was so close, he just needed to…

'Make love to me.'

And then he cursed, the tension in his face dialling up a gear as he froze and looked away.

'What's wrong?'

He dragged in a ragged breath. What had she done? What had she said? Oh, God, make *love*! She combed her fingers into his hair, rested her palms against his cheeks as she forced him back to face her. The tortured look in his eyes tearing her heart in two. Was it Ellie?

Her thighs slackened around him.

'I can't,' he said through his teeth. 'We don't have any protection.'

Never had she been more relieved. And with that came a spark of terror. She licked her lips. 'It's okay.'

His brows drew together. 'How?'

'I'm on the pill. I'm safe. I got tested after Fraser…'

There'd been no one else *since* Fraser—the meaning of that was enough to make the fresh wriggle in her gut worm its way deeper.

'I assume you're…'

He nodded. 'But are you sure?'

Sure? She kissed him until the wriggle quit. 'Yes.'

With a low groan, he rose up over her, his eyes piercing hers as she splayed her hands against his chest and lowered her gaze. She marvelled at every honed muscle accentuated by the light of the fire, all the way to where their bodies met, *almost* melded.

'Are you sure?' Another husky rasp, his body straining to take what it so evidently needed, but he was still Tim, determined to put her needs first.

Which was why she knew this was right. That this was what she wanted. That she, heaven forbid, would always want this.

She let her eyes drift back to his and she nodded, rolling her hips as he rocked his, each delicious inch claiming her heart as much as her body. There was no going back. She knew that now. And she surrendered to it. Moving with him as he filled her, their tempo building as fierce as the crashing weather outside.

They cried their release as the roll of thunder hit and she quivered in his hold.

'I've got you, baby girl.' He kissed her throat, her cheek, her lips. 'I've got you.'

'I know.'

Because she did know. He had her heart, soul and mind, and it made her quiver even more because there wasn't a damn thing she could do about it...

Not in the now, not until she could get away from him and then she'd run. As fast as her legs could take her. And keep on running until common sense prevailed and her life was safe and contained and all about her and Fae once more.

'I know,' she repeated quietly. 'I know.'

CHAPTER FOURTEEN

TIM HAD NO idea what time it was, or how long it had been since the thunderstorm had quit its rumble overhead. Their lovemaking had blended effortlessly into sleep into lovemaking into sleep again. Over and over like some fevered dream, only it was very much real, and reality would soon come calling. The light creeping through the slits in the shutters told him to get the radio back on. Though he had no desire to move. Not yet.

Not with her body entwined with his on the sofa, her fingers caressing his chest beneath the blanket he'd pulled up over them. She was sated, relaxed, no trace of the tension the storm had caused, but he couldn't forget it.

She'd been so pale, so lost in her fear...paralysed by it, too.

'Have you always been afraid of thunderstorms?' he asked, his eyes on the ceiling but his entire focus on her and the way her breath sighed through her.

'No.'

'Did something happen?'

'You don't want to hear about this.'

'I wouldn't ask if I didn't want to know.'

She looked up at him, wet her lips then tucked herself in deeper against his chest.

'When I was about seven, I ran away from home.' Her arm tightened around his waist...or was that him drawing her closer? 'I told you we never had any money, so things like uniform were always a trigger for a fight. I'd outgrown my school shoes but my parents refused to buy me new ones. Then one day the teacher called them up on it, she'd noticed they were hurting me… You can imagine how that went down. My father was humiliated, blamed me for telling tales.' She gave a bitter laugh. 'Like I'd want anyone to know that truth. Anyway, after he was done taking out his temper on me, they locked me in my room. I just figured, if I wasn't around any more, things would be so much better for everyone. I didn't get far. The weather turned nasty and I hid in the playground. They had this old helter-skelter and I hid in its base. I had no idea whether I was safe there, I was just petrified of the storm and didn't dare move. A mother with her kid found me there the next morning, they took me to the police.'

'And your parents?' he forced out, the words hard to form with the anger rolling through him.

'They were livid. Turned out running away only made it worse. I never tried it again.'

He cursed and hugged her tight. Kissed her hair, breathed in her scent, her warmth, her safe and reassuring presence in the now.

'The police *never* should have let you go back.'

'I didn't tell them what had happened. I didn't speak for days. Mum and Dad made up some excuse about how they'd thought I was with a friend. And who would have me anyway? There were no aunts or uncles or grandparents to take me away. The neighbours gave us a wide berth because of how they were, and their kids avoided me too.'

'No wonder you were so desperate to leave.'

Leave and land herself in bigger bother with just as big a piece of scum.

He wanted to rewrite her past, protect her from it all, no matter how impossible a wish it was.

'There was this one teacher though, Miss Smith, she was

real sweet. Used to bring me books and treats, tried to include me, but then her mother got sick and she had to leave. I learnt pretty quickly not to get attached again.'

'Until Fraser?' Just saying the name sent fire up his throat, a searing mix of anger and pain.

'And look how well that turned out…'

She pressed up off his chest. 'I'm going to try out the shower.'

Was that code for give me space? Literally pushing him away too.

She slipped out from under the blanket and stood. The cool slivers of dawn painted her naked body alabaster, her hair almost black as it tumbled down her back—wild from sleep, even wilder from his touch.

She turned to eye him over her shoulder.

'You wanna join me…it might be warmer with two.'

He cracked a grin—relief, desire, and something far deeper, far more instinctive surging through him.

He got to his feet and lifted her into his arms, treasuring her laugh. 'Best idea I've heard all day.'

It's a fling. Just a fling. A sizzling, mind-altering, fear-beating fling.

But even as she told herself the words she could feel herself wanting to deny it. Make it into more. The same old dream she'd had with Fraser, for a future and a happy ever after, trying to make its way back in. But she'd been young and naive enough to believe in it back then. She knew better now.

She knew to make the most of the fun and walk away when done.

And combing her hands through his hair as he travelled kisses down her body, the shower raining over them, she was certainly making the most of the fun…

'I can't get enough of you.'

His words, murmured against her navel, clutched at her heart, and she bit down on her lip—forcing them away, forcing his head down further too.

They mean nothing. They're just words. Empty promises gifted in the moment.

He chuckled, low and slow. 'Impatient, baby girl.'

Impatient to make him stop speaking—yes!

She couldn't listen to it. She couldn't believe it. But everything about Tim was trustworthy, and that made everything he said all the more dangerous. As for the endearment—baby girl—her entire body sighed.

'Yes! We have a radio to turn back on!'

'Ah, the radio...' he circled her clitoris with his thumb '... I think there's something more pressing to turn on this second.'

Her body trembled, his words and his skilled caress taking her to the precipice faster than she could think—

'Tim!' She flung her hands to his shoulders, her nails biting into his lats as her entire body rocked against his touch. 'Get up here.'

'Your wish is my command.' He was on his feet, turning her into the wall as he effortlessly claimed her, his growl as guttural as her cry. She palmed the cold tiles as he drove her to the edge with him. Never had she climaxed so easily or so frequently, not even with Fraser.

But then he wasn't Fraser, came the untimely reminder.

He was so much more.

And therein lay the bigger problem—Fraser hadn't been half the man Tim was proving to be, and Fraser had broken her. Dismantled her confidence, her autonomy, her independence and her worth. Until she'd become a mere shell of her former self.

It had taken four years to get to where she was now. Better. Stronger for what she'd been through. And Tim was all about lifting her up, making her into more, offering up his honesty and his care too. How could she possibly keep a lid on how he made her feel?

But if Fraser had broken her, heaven knew what Tim could do, given half a chance…

And it was that thought that pierced through her post-orgasm haze, sending goosebumps rife across her body.

'Do you hear that?' he murmured in her ear.

'Hear what?'

She twisted in his arms, her eyes shooting to the open door as above the noise of the shower, the continued rain and wind outside, there was an intermittent knocking…a rap of knuckles on wood.

'Hello!'

Her eyes widened at the stranger's voice. 'Is that—?'

'The keeper. Gotta be.' He scrambled out of the shower. 'I'll deal with him.'

He grabbed a towel and wrapped it around his waist, almost losing his footing on the wet wooden floor and a giggle burst through her. 'Easy, tiger.'

He smacked a kiss on her lips and legged it out. She laughed after him, the happy bubble swiftly bursting as she realised just how easily he made her forget where her head had been. Where it still should be. In the land of caution.

She took a deep breath, pushing out her thoughts and her feelings that all revolved around him, and stepped out of the shower. Through the closed door she could make out the rumble of voices, indistinct but ongoing.

Raking her fingers through her hair, she tried to tame every tangle, doing the same with her thoughts too, but it was no use, the end result was just as messy, just as confused, just as—stop!

She walked up to the mirror and gripped the sink. Lifted her gaze to her reflection and saw a woman she didn't recognise looking back at her.

So much colour in her cheeks, her eyes so bright and body flushed pink. The telltale trail of marks from their lovemaking—no, not lovemaking—sex.

That was what Trix would call it.

And so should she.

Sex. A fling. Finite!

'No one gets hurt,' she whispered, 'least of all you.'

'Maria!'

She looked to the door. 'Yes?'

'Breakfast is served.'

Breakfast?

She wrapped a towel around her body and padded out of the room. Coffee? She could smell *coffee!*

She followed the scent to the kitchen and found him sat at a feast-laden table, her eyes bugging out over the food as much as him dressed in fresh lounge pants and a T she didn't recognise.

'He brought you clothes, too,' Tim said, guessing at her thoughts.

'He did?'

'The T-shirt will likely drown you but the bottoms have a drawstring waist so you should be good.'

'That's very sweet of him, and this…' She took in the array of food—honey, jam, butter, fruit, a giant loaf, a carton of milk, a cafetière of coffee *and* a box of mainstream cereal. 'This is amazing.'

'The bread's freshly baked too, the keeper's own recipe. The rest are staples from his stores. He says to shout if we need any more.'

'Any more?' She slid onto a wooden chair and poured herself a coffee. 'There's enough to feed us twice over.'

'That's what I said. I think even Rio would be impressed.'

She popped a piece of bread in her mouth, having slathered it in honey, and moaned. 'Oh yes, Rio would wholeheart-edly approve.'

It was utterly delicious. And the coffee—heaven in a cup!

'Okay, so keep that sweet sensation in mind as I tell you the bad news.'

She swallowed. 'The *bad* news?'

'He heard from Captain Kali this morning, *Celeste* isn't coming back any time soon.'

'She *isn't*?'

The blood seeped from her face as the bread got stuck somewhere between her tonsils and her tensed-up stomach.

'The conditions are too choppy. The tender won't be leaving the jetty for another couple of days at least.'

'A couple of days...?' she repeated softly.

'Afraid so.'

She forced down the food with coffee. 'What are we going to do?'

'We could make the most of our extended stay...a change up to our vacation?' The spark in his eyes lit a fire in her stomach, and she pressed a hand to it. Now was not the time to be thrilled by him, now was the time to get the hell out, before...

'*Your* vacation—it was supposed to be a work trip for me, remember.'

'A trip you've already been paid for in full, so now you can afford the extended holiday. The keeper assured me we were welcome, said he'll even launder our clothes if need be.'

She licked her lips. 'I can't just stay here. I have a job to get back to. I have Fae...she's going to worry.'

'Trix will get a message to Fae. And surely Mickey can survive without you for a day or two.'

'Not without Trix as a backup he can't.'

'He must have other staff that can fill in. They're doing so now, aren't they?'

'They've already covered for me enough.'

Tim leaned back in his seat, his eyes narrowing. 'Okay.'

Okay. Nothing was okay. She was trapped here, on an island with a man she couldn't, wouldn't, *feared* she was already in love with.

'There's also the opportunity to get a flight off the island before then.'

'A flight?'

He nodded, his mouth forming a grim line. Had he guessed at her panic? Had he sussed it had nothing to do with Mickey and everything to do with him?

'The conditions should allow for an air transfer to Merimbula as soon as tomorrow morning.'

'Merimbula?'

'Yes. And from there we can fly to Melbourne.'

'And you—you can sort that?'

'The keeper can arrange the flight for us, and from Merimbula, my jet can get us back to Melbourne.'

'Your...' she swallowed '...*jet*?'

He nodded like it was an entirely normal thing to have on hand.

'When you say *your*, you don't mean your *your*, do you?'

'I don't fly it, if that's what you mean, my piloting skills are strictly limited to the water.'

'I meant the jet. Is it yours?'

'Yes. Why?'

Yes. Why, Maria? You already knew he was loaded, why be surprised at this tiny added detail?

But how easy it had been to forget how very different they were when they were stuck on a remote island, cut off from their realities. Realities she clung to now as she used them to bolster her defences.

'And you're happy to use it to fly me back to Melbourne?'

'In truth, I'd fly you anywhere you wanted to go.'

Her heart slammed against her ribs, her eyes flaring as she choked in protest.

'I mean it, Maria. Name a place and I'd take you tomorrow. Pick one of the places off that wall of yours and have at it.'

Her stomach fizzed over with her heart. 'You're crazy.'

'I'm not crazy.'

He reached for her hand across the table and she drew back, folding her arms as she stared at him. Shock and something else she didn't want to acknowledge stealing her voice and her appetite.

'I want to spend more time with you.' He frowned. 'I thought, after everything, you might want that too?'

Against all her better judgement, yes.

'I know you're worried about Fae, but don't you think what we have deserves a chance at something more? And you've always wanted to travel, I can give you that, I can give you *and* Fae that.'

'Not everyone can just up and leave when they feel like it, Tim.'

They had jobs, responsibilities…

She pushed away from the table, strode to the window. Her gaze on the rolling sea outside but her mind on the storm within.

'You're asking me to let you into our lives, to risk upending what we've built together, all for the sake of a fling?'

'Not for the sake of a fling, no. I'm asking you to take a chance on forever, Maria.'

His words were dancing all over her heart, firing up the flutters, no matter that she'd learned long ago to take such words with a pinch of salt. When would she learn?

'Forever?' she choked out. 'How can you have any faith in forever after Ellie? What you had together was beautiful and look what happened… Nothing good lasts forever.'

'And yet it's a risk I'm willing to take. Do you think know-ing what the future had in store would have stopped me from choosing a life with Ellie? No, it wouldn't. And I'm doing the same now. I'm choosing you, Maria.' He came up behind her, his hand soft on her shoulder as he turned her to face him. 'I've spent the last seven years with my life on hold, and I want to live it again. I want to live it again with you. Please don't give up on us without giving us a chance.'

'I…' She couldn't say it. Not when every fibre of her being wanted him, cared for him…*loved* him? 'I want to go home.' She beat back the rush of feeling as she lifted her eyes to his. 'Please, Tim. Take me home.'

His jaw twitched, his eyes burned, a second's silence, then, 'Okay. If that is what you want, that is what we'll do.'

Want? No, she didn't want it. She wanted him. She wanted this. She wanted it all for the rest of her life, but she'd been a fool to long for forever once, she wouldn't be that fool again.

'Thank you.'

They didn't speak of it again. Even when she'd slipped into his arms that night and their mouths had found each other. They'd made love but it was quiet. Dampened by the impend-ing end. Tim's head screamed at him to do something, to say something, to lay his heart bare, but he couldn't. He'd already said enough, and he didn't want to ruin what time they had left, hashing it out, only to get to the same depressing end.

Or worse, have her shut him out entirely.

At least this way, she'd spent the night in his arms.

But with every passing hour he'd felt her withdraw. In the morning, she barely ate, she barely spoke. Her smile reserved for the lighthouse keeper as she thanked him for all that he had done for them. On the transfer from the island, she only spoke when spoken to and with his jet she'd been full of polite praise. But there was no sparkle in her gaze, no playfulness in her wonder, no sign of the woman he had come to love so much in so short a spell.

Even when Connor called to tell them the news that Cherry was out of danger and doing well, she'd said how pleased she was to hear it, that it was a relief, but every word had been weighted with this. With them.

By the time his car pulled up outside Mickey's Bar, Muted Maria was driving him out of his mind.

He understood why she didn't want to rock the carefully curated life she had built with Fae. Why it was so sacred and man-free too. But he knew what they had, and he knew what it could be.

And as much as he didn't want to open himself up to potential heartache in the future, he realised he no longer had a choice. Whether she chose to end it now or he lost her further down the line, the pain would be no more real, no less visceral.

'This was supposed to be a fling,' she said as his driver cut the engine, her voice so quiet he had to strain to hear her. 'No one was supposed to get hurt.'

'I know that, Maria.'

'Then why did you do it?' Her eyes lifted to his, their pain crushing him. 'Asking me for more when you knew I couldn't give it.'

'I didn't ask you to make you feel guilty, I asked you because I hoped you felt the same.'

'It wasn't fair.'

'Life isn't fair. We've both learned that the hard way.' He took her hand in his, grateful when she let him. 'Please, Maria. Don't walk away from this, from me, not yet. Give me time to show you how good we could be together, how good life could be?'

'I *have* a good life. Here with Fae. It's safe and it's ours. Now, please, let me go.'

He stared into her eyes, his heart and soul screaming *No!*, but how could he refuse her?

His driver opened her door and she tugged her bag up off the floor.

'Goodbye Tim.'

And then she was walking away and there wasn't a damn thing he could do about it. Not if he wanted to respect her wishes.

But what about doing justice to your own?

With a raw curse he slid out after her. 'Maria!'

She paused on the footpath, her shoulders lifting with the smallest of breaths as he came up behind her.

'Maria?'

Slowly she turned, her eyes lifting to his. 'Yes?'

'I know you don't want to hear this, but I also know I'll regret it if I don't say it to you now.'

She swallowed. 'Don't do it, Tim, please d—'

'I *love* you.'

Her mouth fell open, her lashes quivered. 'No. You can't.'

'Why can't I?'

'Because you've known me all of five minutes,' she choked out.

'And? In all my years, I've only met two women who made me feel this way. My wife was one and I will always carry her with me. You're the other and the same will be true whether you walk away from me now or not. I will always carry you here.'

He covered his heart as she gripped her middle. 'You can't use me to replace her.'

He gave a sharp frown. 'That wasn't what—'

'No, because it sounds like it. And I won't be some substitute for your affections.' She threw the words at the ground. 'I won't.'

'How can you even suggest that?'

She was lashing out, he realised, trying to hurt him to get *him* to walk.

Which meant she had to be running scared. And that had to mean she cared.

'You know me, Maria, and in your heart of hearts you know that's not what this is.' Reaching out, he lifted her chin, forcing her to meet his gaze. 'What I feel for you is no less than what I felt for her. But make no mistake, it is different, because you are different. And I *do* love you.'

'Stop saying that. Please just stop!' Her eyes overflowed with her tears as she tugged his hand away. 'Fraser said it, too. *All* the time. How much he loved me. How much he wanted to be with me. And it was all lies. Just lies.'

'Maybe. Or maybe it was the truth and he did love you, but it sure as hell wasn't a healthy kind of love. It's not the kind of love I feel for you. Because nothing would stop me from choosing you. Nothing would stop me from protecting you.'

'I'm not *yours* to protect.'

'My heart disagrees.'

'Tim, please…'

'No, you need to hear this. I'm lucky to have been surrounded by love all of my life. By my family, by Ellie, by Sasha, even Connor, and I want to ensure you never go another day without feeling it too.'

'I do feel it. Fae is the most loving daughter one could ever hope to have.'

'And you can have me, too. I want to build my life around you, Maria. You, Sasha *and* Fae. I can't force you to see the truth in that, but I am asking you to give me the chance to prove it to you. To show you what we could make of life together.'

She shook her head, swiped at her damp cheeks. 'I can't.' She swallowed. 'I can't.'

And then she ran, pushing through the door to the bar and disappearing inside.

He moved to follow but someone stepped out of the shadows, drawing him up short. Fae!

She met his gaze, her eyes so like her mother's shimmering with something. Was that...*sympathy*?

'I'm sorry,' he said, because what else could he say. Fae had made her feelings clear that very first day they'd met, and now he'd brought her mother home in tears, confirming her worst suspicions.

'Me too.'

CHAPTER FIFTEEN

'MUM?'

Maria stiffened. She'd thought she was alone. The bar deserted. Else she'd never have dropped into a chair and sobbed into the table with her head in her arms. The last person she wanted to see her like this was Fae.

She hadn't gone upstairs because—Fae.

She hadn't risked her heart anew because—Fae.

No, that wasn't true. She hadn't risked her heart anew because—this! So, this!

The pain of loving someone, trusting someone, letting them in...

Not that she'd ever truly loved Fraser. She realised that now. Because this was so much more—*Tim* was so much more.

And she'd walked away because she was utterly terrified of being that broken woman again and look at her now. Broken anyway.

'Mum?'

This time Fae's footsteps accompanied her soft call and, peeling herself off the table, Maria swiped away her tears and turned.

'Darling, what are you doing here? I thought you'd be upstairs getting ready for your shift.'

'You're really asking me what I'm doing here when you're the one sat sobbing?'

She gave a weak smile. 'I'll be okay.'

'You don't look it, and you sure as hell don't sound it.'

'You're right,' she admitted weakly, getting to her feet. 'Can I have a hug?'

She opened her arms and Fae filled them, wrapping her own around her waist and resting her head against Maria's chest.

'I think you should go after him.'

She stiffened. 'Who?'

'You know who I'm talking about.' Fae leaned back to look up at her, her eyes awash with concern. 'I saw you outside together. I heard what he said.'

'You were eavesdropping?'

'Not on purpose. I was coming back from a walk, and I saw him run after you.'

She tucked Fae's head beneath her chin, unable to hold her daughter's gaze while inside her heart was shattering with his replayed words...

I want to build my life around you, Maria.

I love you, Maria.

I've got you, baby girl.

'I didn't want to get in the way,' Fae said quietly.

'You could never be in the way, not ever.'

'Are you in love with him?'

Maria choked on her tears. 'What—why would you say that?'

'Because look at you, Mum. I haven't seen you like this in forever, and even then, your pain was more about your frustrations for me, rather than yourself. This is all about you now.'

She gave a soft huff. 'When did you get so wise?'

'When you were so busy taking care of me you forgot to take care of yourself. But that has to stop, Mum. You need to start living your life for you again. I heard what he said to you. I saw how he looked when you walked away. I may not know much about relationships, and heaven knows, Dad did a total number on you, but I'm not sure walking away from him out there was the right thing to do.'

'You've changed your tune, not two weeks ago you couldn't wait for me to get shot of him.'

'That was before…'

'Before what?'

'Before he fell in love with you.'

Her heart gave a painful beat. 'You shouldn't believe everything you hear.'

'I don't, believe me, but he isn't Dad, Mum. He's nothing like him. Dad was all about himself. Taking what he wanted and dropping what he didn't. He was a liar and a user. Tim is none of those things.'

'You don't even know him, love, how can you possibly say what he is and isn't?'

'Take a look around, Mum. Do you really think Mickey suddenly came up with the money for all this work?'

'Huh?' She blinked, only now noticing the state of the bar. The dust sheets on the tables, the builders' tools stacked in one corner, a fresh 'Closed for Refurb' sign hanging on the door…

'The surveyor that came to the house that morning you left was just the beginning. Mickey's had people in and out for days. He's buzzing with ideas. I asked him what had gotten into him, and he said this guy just rocked up at his office. Asked him about the place, the history, what it meant to Mickey and his family, and then offered to invest. Offered him a deal he couldn't refuse. His time and his money.'

'I don't understand.'

'Tim didn't tell you, did he?'

'Are you saying it was *Tim*? That *he* gave Mickey the money?'

Fae nodded. 'At first, I was mad, I figured he was trying to buy your affections, just like Dad used to. I was going to ring you and warn you, but your phone was out of range. That's when Trix messaged to let us know about the storm. But having heard all that out there... I don't know, Mum. Those weren't the words of a selfish man, wanting to get what he could out of you.'

Maria cursed. 'I can't believe he'd do this. Of all the interfering, manipulative—'

'But that's just it, Mum. I don't think it was about that at all. If it was, he would have told you about his involvement in the bar, used it to convince you to stay instead of walk away.'

'Or did he walk knowing that he'd be back, for the bar, for Mickey, for me?' She cursed, ramming a hand through her hair as she eyed all the work in progress and seeing his mark in every one. Her home wasn't even *hers* any more. Just like her home with Fraser had been all his. *His* choice, *his* money, *his* suffocating presence. 'I can't believe this.'

'Where are you going?'

She hadn't realised she was running until Fae called out after her.

'To have it out with him.'

'He's *not* Dad, Mum!'

'He might as well be and I won't be put in that position. Not again.'

She pulled open the door just as his car started to pull away...

Tim's car came to a screeching halt, his driver's apology drowned out by the thundering beat of his heart. Because there was Maria. Standing in front of his car, her palms pressed to the bonnet, her eyes spearing his through the windscreen.

'What do you want me to do, sir?'

'Just hang back.' He unbuckled his seatbelt. 'I'll call when I'm ready for you.'

He pushed open his door.

'How could you?' she hissed.

Not a happy U-turn then…

'How could I what?' he said as he joined her on the pavement.

She gestured to the bar. '*You're* the investor behind Mickey's refurb.'

'The place was in need of a cash injection.'

'And you just took it upon yourself to offer it. Your involvement had nothing to do with *you* sleeping with *me*?'

He scanned the footpath as the odd passerby glanced their way and urged her into a side street, his voice low as he admitted, 'Of course it had something to do with you. Do you honestly think I could see the issues with the building and not do anything about it?'

'The issues with the—' she spluttered, her entire body trembling. 'Why? What the hell is it to you? Mickey's been good to us, the best landlord. He's looked out for us from the day we moved in and you dared to come along and pick at him! Not everyone has the kind of money you do to throw into non-essential maintenance!'

'Non-essential? That damp could make you ill. And it sure as hell isn't good for the building. Mickey *is* a good man, but a good landlord he is not. He's been charging too low a rent for years and the building has suffered because of it. In helping people, he's failed to help himself and safeguard the future of the place. I offered to help him, not just because you're his tenant but because this is his family's legacy, and the idea of him being forced out by some developer looking to make a quick buck further down the line didn't sit right with me. This way, he gets to give the place some TLC, bring it up-to-date, and *choose* when he sells. He gets to retire on his terms.'

'And then what, you take a huge chunk of the sale?'

'No, Maria. If I had my way, I'd walk away with nothing, knowing I've done some good here. But Mickey is a proud man; he doesn't want a handout, he wants a fair deal, and that's what he got. I wasn't about to injure his pride by pushing my own agenda. Now, if you're done taking down *my* pride, I'll be the one to say goodbye this time.'

'Wait!'

He paused.

'Why…why didn't you tell me what you'd done? All that time we spent together and you didn't mention it, not once.'

'You're asking me that after the way you're reacting now?'

'But if you'd told me…if you'd explained…'

'You'd still think the worst, because you can't look past Fraser to the man I am. And while you still see him, I can't—'

'I know you're not Fraser.'

It was a whisper, but it was enough to have him face her full-on. 'Say that again?'

'I know you're not Fraser.'

He pressed his lips together. Swallowed. 'And that terrifies you, doesn't it?'

'Yes.'

'Why, Maria? Tell me, why?'

He could see it in her eyes, but he needed to hear her say it. Yearned for it.

'He broke me. Ripped me apart, and it took me years to piece myself back together again. But you made me realise I never loved him at all. And if someone could hurt me that much without love, the idea of being hurt by someone I do love. The idea of being hurt by you…'

'Maria,' he whispered, his voice raw as he felt her pain, but also hope, hope for a future he'd all but given up on, 'I could never hurt you.'

'You can't know that.' She was trembling, the fear in her eyes unbearable. 'And to be that vulnerable again by choice…'

'It's okay to be vulnerable, Maria. We're all vulnerable in love. Don't you think I feel it too? That when you walked away from me just now my whole world didn't come crashing in…'

'I'm sorry.'

'I don't need you to be sorry, I just need you to see the truth.'

'And the truth is what terrifies me, because you are everything Fraser wasn't and you're everything I could ever want. Because I do love you Tim, and I know now that no amount of running away is going to change that.'

'Then how about running this way instead?'

He opened his arms to her and a slow smile spread across her face, a fresh well of tears coming too, and then she was in his arms. And as much as he wanted to lose himself in that moment, he knew he had to come totally clean first. 'There's something else you need to know…'

She stiffened in his hold. 'O-okay?'

'I employed a PI to look into Fraser.'

'*What*—why?'

'Why do you think?'

'But Tim, he's firmly in my past.'

'He's also clean as a whistle, but I'll get him Maria, I swear to God, I'll make him pay for—'

She pressed a finger to his lips. 'No. You won't. You taught me to let go of my past and my shame for being the other woman. You taught me to move forward. I've wasted enough of my life thinking of him, and I almost let my history with him ruin my future with you. He's done enough damage, and I don't want to think of him any more.'

'But Maria, what he did—'

'Was wrong. Yes. But karma will catch up with him eventually, and if it doesn't I don't care, because I'm happy. I'm happy because I have you. I know what true love is because of you. And I wouldn't change a thing in my life, because ultimately it gave me Fae and it gave me you. And I am the luckiest woman alive for it all.'

'How can I argue with any of that?'

'You can't.' She cocked one confident brow. 'You can kiss me though?'

'I thought you'd never ask…'

And then he swept her into his arms and kissed her until need threatened to push the boundaries of public decency. 'Now can we go inside so that I can show you just how much?'

'Fae's inside.'

'*Fae* is heading out.' Their heads shot around to find Fae sauntering past, one hand raised in a wave. 'Have fun, kids, don't do anything I wouldn't do.'

He chuckled. 'Does this mean she accepts me now?'

'I think it means she wants me to be happy and right now, she thinks you're the answer to that.'

'I'll always be the answer to that.'

'Cocky, much?'

'Just you wait until we get inside, baby girl. I'll prove it to you again and again if needs be.'

'Promises, promises.'

'And you can trust in every one.'

She searched his gaze as she cupped his cheek. 'I know. And I love you for it.'

'And I love you.'

EPILOGUE

One year later...
London, England.

MARIA HADN'T STOPPED SMILING. From the moment they'd touched down in Heathrow she'd been abuzz with nervous excitement. Today wasn't just about another new city on her bucket list. It was about Tim's daughter, Sasha, and her charity's annual gala.

She'd been primped and polished within an inch of her life. Hair, make-up, nails, dress—she'd barely recognised herself as she'd stepped up to the mirror, the bold red dress skimming over her figure in all the right ways. But she'd recognised herself in Tim's gaze. The familiar desire burning in his depths as he'd stood back and admired her. Just the memory of that look made her quiver now.

'Are you cold?'

His hand pulsed around hers on the back seat of their chauffeured car.

'No.' She met his gaze. 'Far from it.'

'Good, because we have a small detour to make.'

'A detour?' She glanced at her watch as the driver pulled over. 'Surely we don't have time...'

'We'll be perfectly on time, I promise.' He got out of the car, rounding it and pulling open her door. She frowned up at him. *What on earth?*

'Trust me.' He offered out his hand and she took it, letting him guide her out. The driver handed him a faux fur shawl which he draped around her shoulders, but she hadn't felt the chill of winter. She'd been too preoccupied by him. Her stunning man of mystery, suave and sophisticated in his black tie...much like the night they'd first met.

'It's our one-year anniversary,' he murmured as he led her to the river, where a string quartet were playing, the ground littered with rose petals, several flickering lanterns too. The buskers were way fancier in London!

But nothing could be fancier or more beautiful than the sight of Tower Bridge lit up across the Thames. It looked just like the photograph she had on her wall back home...which of course was why he was bringing her now. Always thinking of her. Always fulfilling her dreams.

'You mean since the day we met?' she replied, her eyes drinking in the view.

'Since the day we did a lot of things,' he said low and slow and snagging her attention. 'Which is why it feels right to do this now...'

'This?'

He stepped back and her stomach fluttered. 'Tim?'

He lowered himself to the ground, his eyes never once leaving hers.

'I would have asked you months ago, but I promised you time. So here I am, one year on, Maria, down on one knee, asking you, will you be mine?'

He raised his palm, an open box with a diamond twinkled at its heart, and she gasped. The sight becoming a blur as tears filled her vision and she struggled to find her voice.

'I have Fae's blessing.'

Her eyes shot to his. 'You do?'

'For as long as I make you smile, I do, yes.'

'Her words?'

'Yes.'

'And what about Sasha?'

He smiled. 'She helped me pick out the ring.'

'In that case…' She bowed down until they were eye to eye. 'Yes, Tim! A gazillion times, yes!'

She sealed her vow with a kiss and he rose up, drawing her tight against him.

'You best put the ring on,' he murmured against her lips. 'Sasha will be looking for it as soon as we arrive.'

She eased back enough to let him take it out and then he slid it on her finger, and she felt her heart soar and settle. She was his. And he was hers.

Of all the destinations on her bucket list, she knew their journey to Happy Ever After would forever eclipse them all.

* * * * *

If you missed the previous story in the
Sun, Sea and Swept Away miniseries,
then check out

What Happens at the Beach…

And if you enjoyed this story, check out these other great
reads from Rachael Stewart

Fake Fling with the Billionaire
Unexpected Family for the Rebel Tycoon
Reluctant Bride's Baby Bombshell

All available now!

ITALIAN TYCOON TO REMEMBER

JUSTINE LEWIS

MILLS & BOON

For Peter, who is unforgettable

CHAPTER ONE

THE REHABILITATION WARD was much quieter than the neu-
rology ward. There was no constant beeping, no clinking
trolleys, no one entering her room at all hours to take end-
less observations. Freya had finally been able to get a proper
night's sleep and she felt better than she had since the accident. Her physical injuries were superficial: a bruise on her
cheekbone that was fading, cuts on her right arm and hand
that were bandaged and stiff but not troubling her.

She almost felt normal.

Except she wasn't.

Not a bit.

There were many things bothering her, but they all came
back to one single problem.

The day's date.

Though the date only seemed to be a problem for her—
everyone else in the world was completely fine with it. But
then, they could remember the last five years of their lives.

'There's someone here to see you, Freya,' the nurse said,
knocking on the door frame.

Feeling well, simply confused, Freya was out of bed and
sitting in the armchair by the window of her single room
looking out at an unfamiliar London street.

A tall, broad-shouldered man walked in. He had hair as
brown as it could be without being black and a strong, de-
finitive jawline. She couldn't make out the colour of his eyes,

which wouldn't meet hers, but she remembered him from a few days ago. He'd been amongst the doctors and the nurses in her room when she'd first woken up. He had the kind of good looks that caught in your throat and upset your ability to breathe. He hadn't even spoken, but had still stood out from the rest of the medical professionals crowding into her room.

Her heart still fell when she recognised him. As gorgeous as he was, rather than recognising the face of a random doctor, she'd prefer to remember what she'd been doing for the last five years.

The man wore a blue business shirt, slim fitting but not tight. Just snug enough for her to be able to see he was in pretty good shape compared to the other doctors who'd been through her room over the past week.

'Hello,' she said.

'Hello,' he replied with a smile that she almost might've described as shy.

Neither of them said anything. He seemed to be waiting for her to speak first, but what was she supposed to say? He was the doctor. She was the amnesia patient. She didn't have any answers. Only a million questions.

'So what have you come to investigate?' she asked.

'What do you mean?'

'What's your specialty, Doctor?'

His brow furrowed and she was sorry. Nothing should ever crease a forehead as smooth as his. His face should be on a National Treasure register to keep it preserved for future generations to admire. Yet he frowned.

'I've seen the physician, the neurologist, the occupational therapist. Oh, goodness! You're the psychiatrist, aren't you? Or the psychologist?'

He winced.

'Oh, heck, I'm sorry. I know I should know the difference, and I do. Really. But I've just had a big bump on the head.' She smiled, so he'd know she was kidding. Amnesia humour. One good thing about having amnesia, and there weren't many, was that you could pretend to have forgotten things you'd never been sure about in the first place.

Still he didn't speak. He just looked at her with his big eyes. She now saw they were dark, a deep, delicious brown. She ran her tongue around her mouth, which was suddenly very dry.

'So?' she asked

'So?' he replied.

She had amnesia! Could he be a bit less judgemental?

'It's one of the two, isn't it? One of the head-shrinkers. Sorry, I'm probably not allowed to say that either. I don't know what words are acceptable five years in the future. But that's why you're making me do all the talking, isn't it? You want to analyse me.'

The man looked down and she took that as a yes. She really did want to talk to someone, try to make sense of what was happening to her.

'I guess I feel as happy as you can be when you've lost five years of memory. Five years of my life. I'm happy to be alive—don't get me wrong—but I'm also so frustrated and I think that's understandable. I'm allowed to be a bit upset, don't you think? How would you feel if you woke up five years in the future?'

'I'd be confused. Upset.'

'Yeah, and now imagine you live, not just in a different house, but in a different city. In a different country! And you're apparently a food stylist but you have absolutely no idea what a food stylist does. The last thing you remember is being sacked from your job as a photographer for a second-rate local newspaper in Pasadena, halfway around the world.'

The man looked around the room. After spying a plastic chair next to the bed, he sat. He crossed his legs and leaned forward, resting his chin in his hand. His large, smooth, tanned hand. Psychiatrists were the doctors, right? Psychologists were the counsellors. She'd seen a psychologist once, after her father had passed away. But he'd been nowhere near as gorgeous as this semisilent man sitting in front of her now.

Which type was he? She wasn't getting a strong vibe either way, but he was definitely one or the other judging by the way he just sat there, looking at her and waiting for her to fill the silence with her babble.

'And imagine you don't know any of your friends' names. Or your colleagues. Or your housemate, who apparently is also your boss.'

At this point, she would not even have bet money on the fact that her name was Freya McFadden. And that would have been sensible since her current financial position was also a complete unknown. In the States, she'd had few savings, probably enough for a plane ticket to the UK. She'd been working here in London, but who knew how much food stylists earned? Or how much her boss was charging her for rent. She didn't know a lot about London, but she did know it was hardly a budget-friendly city.

The hospital and rehabilitation ward were quite nice, which meant she wasn't destitute. But she had nothing to compare it with. She'd never been on a rehabilitation ward in any hospital before.

'So you probably want to know what I remember.' she said.

'It would help.' His voice was high, pained.

Her last memory had been of the night of her twenty-fifth birthday. She'd been out for drinks with her best friend, Jane, drowning her sorrows after being sacked that very day.

'Who sacks someone on their birthday?' she'd cried.

Her horrible boss had told her that her work lacked vibrancy. That it wasn't dynamic enough. That *she* wasn't dynamic enough. And then she'd remembered the words her recent ex, Lachlan, had said to her not two weeks earlier, that he needed to be with someone with more 'energy.'

'Energy?' she'd moaned to Jane. 'I don't lack energy. Or vibrancy. What is that code for? What are they trying to tell me? What's wrong with me?'

Jane had shaken her head, ordered them another round of cocktails and the next thing Freya knew she'd woken up in a hospital bed in London.

'As far as I remember, I live in a share flat in the sketchy part of Pasadena with my friend Jane. I work as a photographer at a small local newspaper. At least I did until I was sacked. I have a small group of friends who I've known more than half my life. I have lunch with my mother each Sunday.'

It was the same response she'd given for the past week and was still the wrong answer. Because she didn't live in Pasadena anymore; she lived in London. She hadn't worked at the paper for almost five years.

Her mother, Jillian, had flown straight to London after the accident and tried to fill in the gaps: the day after her twenty-fifth birthday Freya had bought a one-way ticket to London. It had been an impulsive decision, sparked by frustration and heartache, but her gamble had paid off. She'd found a job she loved and a nice group of friends. But for some reason, the knock she'd had on the head had made her forget everything that had happened after leaving Pasadena. What had happened to her in London? Why had her brain decided it was best left forgotten?

As best she could, Jillian had told Freya about her London life: Freya worked for Niccolò Rossetti, a celebrity chef Freya had never heard of, and she lived with him too. Jillian told Freya she had answered an ad for a food photographer and, amazingly, had got the job. She'd been working for Niccolò for almost five years and seen his career progress from strength to strength, prestigious award to prestigious award.

She had worked for him as he had gone from having one restaurant in Chelsea to three across London, alongside million-pound book deals and tours around Europe, the United States and Australia.

The sort of experiences it would have been nice to remember, Freya thought bitterly.

'Your memory will return,' Jillian said for the hundredth time as she squeezed Freya's hand.

But her mother had just been saying that to comfort them both. As the days passed, the looks on the faces of the doctors were becoming increasingly worried. The look of harrowing concern creasing the face of Dr Handsome sitting across from her now made her wrap her arms tightly around herself. What if she never got those memories back?

Freya looked down. She was wearing a pair of lovely brushed-cotton pyjamas, patterned with soft pink flowers. They were apparently hers, taken from the wardrobe in the bedroom she couldn't remember. They were gorgeous, but twenty-five-year-old Freya had never owned such things.

Dr Handsome was still watching her, still using some psychiatric trick of waiting for the patient to speak first. She obliged.

'The last thing I remember is drinking cocktails and crying because I'd been sacked. The next thing I know I'm here in the hospital and you and all the other doctors are studying me.'

And she had no idea what had become of her friend Jane after that night and her mother had told her they were no longer close. But her mother was talking about a different Freya, a Freya who had had five years to build and get used to this new life.

Dr Handsome put his ridiculously attractive face in his hands, rubbed it vigorously and let out a soft, pained moan. Somehow, she felt his pain in her own chest and tried harder, for his sake, to try to remember something. So much for putting your patient at ease.

'They say I work for this celebrity chef named Niccolò Rossetti. I haven't heard of him but he mustn't be too bad because apparently I live with him too.'

Her mother had told her that she lived in Rossetti's attic. But what did that mean? Were they friends? Did they hang out? Did she like him? Her mother told her they were good friends. But what *sort* of good friends? He hadn't been to visit her.

This doctor wasn't helping at all. Wasn't he supposed to know the right questions to ask her?

'I don't live with him, *with* him, but in his attic, which sounds a bit dark, don't you think? A little bit Jane Eyre?'

'I'm sure it's a very light, bright attic,' Dr Handsome said.

'Are you? Really? The only attics I've known have been for storage. They are for insulation and besides, it would be too hot.' She really was rambling now.

The doctor raised a perfect dark eyebrow and one corner of his mouth twitched. He actually had a lovely mouth. Pink and soft looking. Kissable.

Gah.

She was mixed up enough in the head without lusting after the gorgeous shrink. Wasn't there some name for the syndrome involving falling for your psychologist? Of course, if there was, she couldn't remember it. And she didn't need another diagnosis on top of everything else.

'Anyway, I think I'm glad I came here, I just wish I could remember it.'

The outline of the last five years was there, but it was far from coloured in. She knew facts, but not feelings. In particular, did she *like* her job? Did she *like* her boss? She supposed she must if they lived together. And besides, it didn't matter what people told her; it wasn't the same. It was like

hearing a story that had happened to someone else. Glamorous job, trips to New York and Paris. It sounded great, but
she was jealous of the woman it had all happened to because
it just wasn't her.

'Freya, there's something I should—'

'I'm trying, I am. Really. But it's hard, especially being
stuck here. I look out the window and it's so strange. I don't
know this city. It's like I've just stepped off the plane.'

'You want to leave the hospital?' he asked.

'Yes,' she quickly added. 'But also no.' Because the thought
of going out into London, into her other life, was terrifying.

His eyebrow did that sexy smirk-grin thing. Was he married?
He was bound to be. Was that something she could just ask?

'I want to leave, because it's stifling being here. But I'm
also afraid. I don't know London. I don't know my boss. I
don't even know how to do my job. I mean, what does a food
stylist even do? I don't have the first idea! And how preten-
tious do you think the average celebrity chef is? I don't know
what to say to him, how to act. Do you know any celebrity
chefs? Since when was that a job description? Do you think
that's what's written on his passport?'

The man tilted his head and regarded her. No doubt reaching some conclusion about how messed up she was. Strangely
with this doctor, she didn't feel worried; for the first time she
felt as though she could say all her fears aloud. There was
something about him that made her comfortable. But also,
truth be told, more than a little excited. Alive.

And being alive was good. Notwithstanding the black hole
that was her memory, she was immensely glad to be here,
living and breathing, and that she hadn't perished in the car
accident.

She leaned forward. 'Can I ask you something?'

He didn't respond. No words. And not the eyebrow thing
either. She took that as permission.

'Doctor, it's none of my business, but are you married?'

He coughed. The cough turned into a choke. She scrambled around for some water to offer him.

He waved her away and composed himself. 'I'm not a doctor.'

'Oh.' Then who the heck was he? 'What do you do?'

'My passport says chef.'

'Oh.'

'But I guess people do sometime add "celebrity" to the front.' He grinned, but the grin had a hint of a grimace.

Of course.

She remembered with blinding clarity how her mouth had never been too small for her foot to fit in. It was bad enough she felt terrified about meeting the Niccolò Rossetti; now she had to blurt all her fears out to him.

He knows you.

The voice in her head telling her that was fainter than a whisper.

He knows you can sometimes put your foot in your mouth. He also knows you can sometimes talk without thinking. But he must also know that you are kind and loyal and hard-working.

'Ah…'

'Freya.'

The way he said her name felt like chocolate melting in her mouth.

And if he didn't know her before, he surely did now after she'd blurted out all her thoughts and fears.

'I'm so sorry. Niccolò, isn't it?'

He nodded. She wasn't sure if she wanted him to speak or not; she longed to hear his voice and know what he was thinking but each time he spoke her insides quivered. And the way he looked at her wordlessly made her sad. Like he was confused. Angry. Disappointed.

'But you call me Nico.'

Nico. And there was that melty-heart feeling again. Nico sounded so familiar.

He doesn't mind—he knows you.

But she didn't know him.

'I really am sorry. I can't help it. It feels as though I've been dumped in someone else's life.'

'*You* don't have to be sorry.'

Why did he emphasise 'you'?

'No, I do and I am. You know me, but I don't remember you. And I wish I did. And you're my boss so I was just so rude. I'm sorry about the remarks before. I really am.'

She couldn't remember Niccolò, though the rude things she'd said to him not moments ago were seared on her brain.

She had so many questions about her life in London but she could hardly ask the man sitting before her with a slightly stern look in his eyes, even if they did know one another. There was still a wall between them. It was invisible, glass-like, but definitely there in the way he held himself aloof, the way he had hardly smiled. The way he pursed his beautiful lips together until they were white.

She was saved by a knock at the door.

An older man, wearing a bow tie and a tweed jacket, knocked at the door.

'Hello, Freya. I'm Dr Jamal.'

'Doctor?'

'Yes, I'm your neurologist.'

'Really?'

Dr Jamal looked familiar but she still glanced to Niccolò for confirmation, though she didn't know why.

'Yes, this is Dr Jamal.' Niccolò nodded.

'How are you doing today?'

Freya lifted her hands in a shrug.

'So nothing is clearer?'

She shook her head. 'My mother came this morning with her laptop and we flicked through photos. But almost all the photos Mum has are of my childhood, which I remember perfectly.' The taste of Nan's roast lamb, the bright purple of the hydrangeas in her garden. The smell of her father's aftershave. The sensation of their dog licking her toes. Those memories made water well in her eyes. She sniffed and swallowed them down.

She had yet to see any photos of her life in London. Her late twenties should be the most exciting time of her life and all she had were the recollections of others.

'I wish I could have forgotten the years from twelve to seventeen instead,' she grumbled. 'Puberty, acne and school. Why couldn't I forget *those* five years?'

The doctor laughed but Niccolò rubbed his forehead as though he was in pain.

'I think the best thing now is for you to go home. Ninety percent of traumatic amnesia patients will recover their memories within two weeks, and most will recover it within days of returning home.'

'Home? To California?'

'No. I mean Islington. But of course if you want to go back to the States we can get you in touch with the appropriate specialists. But…'

Dr Jamal looked to Niccolò and Niccolò shook his head. The doctor's forehead creased but he turned back to Freya.

'We find that most amnesia patients experience the return of their memory within days of going back to the place they are currently living. I worry that if you travel back to the United States before your memories of London have returned that the memories of your London life will remain forever blurred and confused. I would strongly advise you to return home with Mr Rossetti and check in with me in a few days' time.'

She had only met Dr Jamal a few times that she remembered, but she trusted him. Though she wasn't yet sure about Niccolò.

'Your paperwork is finalised and I believe Mr Rossetti is able to take you.'

She looked to Niccolò. Her boss. Her landlord. Stranger. She longed to go back to Pasadena. To everything and everyone she knew.

She was missing huge gaps of her memory here, but her life in Pasadena had not felt complete either.

Twenty-five-year-old Freya had climbed on a plane and travelled halfway around the world. She'd got a job with Niccolò and she'd stayed.

You have to trust that Freya. You have to trust yourself.

Besides, thirty-year-old Freya worked for a celebrity, lived in London and travelled the world. She was having the time of her life as a food stylist.

Whatever the heck that it was.

Jillian McFadden came back to the hospital shortly afterwards to help Freya pack up the few belongings she had with her. Jillian also brought a small bag with other clothes for Freya to change into. Clothes Freya didn't recognise. Not only were fashions slightly different five years in the future, but it seemed that her style had changed as well.

Back home, if she wasn't working, she'd wear jeans and T-shirts. Short skirts and tank tops. Her London wardrobe, or what she'd seen of it, was more sophisticated.

She put on a pair of soft but tailored navy pants and a bright pink sweater for the trip back to Niccolò's house. She couldn't quite bring herself to call it home.

When you get there, you're bound to start recognising things.

This also scared her. What if she didn't like the life she'd made her herself in London? What if she didn't like Niccolò? He wasn't giving off 'best-friend vibes' but rather 'aloof-boss energy.'

Freya followed her mother out of the hospital and onto a London street.

'Where are we?'

'University of London Hospital. Bloomsbury.'

The stone buildings around her were impressive, imposing. The roads were narrower than at home, frantic with cars and red buses that looked like they were out of a postcard. The street signs were different and so was the smell. It wasn't unpleasant, just different.

'And where…where do I live?'

Jillian took her hand. 'It's a beautiful house. In Islington.'

Islington. Was that in Monopoly?

'Have you been there?'

'I've been staying there.'

'You have?'

'Yes, and it's lovely.'

Her mother hailed a black cab as though she'd done it all her life and yet again Freya felt as though she was in a dream. She climbed in, expecting to be seated behind the driver, but of course she was not.

'They drive on the left here,' she muttered to herself.

Freya sat back and watched the unfamiliar streets zoom past. She'd hoped that as they got closer to the address her mother had given to the driver, she would remember, but nothing looked familiar. Surely she had driven along these roads many times, walked these sidewalks, but she remembered nothing. She felt like a tourist.

Not exactly like a tourist. Even a tourist who had mislaid their map was probably not feeling this confused.

Her stomach twisted tighter, anticipating arriving at her home. The one she shared with Niccolò. Nico. The hand-

some man who was not a doctor. Her cheeks burnt again, remembering anew her embarrassment at mistaking him for a
doctor and for mocking his profession. To be fair, she'd also
mocked her own, but that gave her little comfort.

She pressed her damp palms against her soft trousers. Navy
blue and well made. Better quality than anything she'd worn
at home in California. Was thirty-year-old Freya as attracted
to Nico as Amnesia Freya was? Surely not. Otherwise, she
would've been lusting after him for the past five years.

Or…

Could they…had they…? Was there something physical
between them?

She dismissed the thought as soon as it arose. Someone
would have told her if they had a relationship. Besides, she'd
have remembered something like that, wouldn't she?

Why, when you don't remember anything else?

The cab stopped outside a house on a quiet road, just a
street back from a canal. Jillian was right; Niccolò's house
was lovely.

With a white facade and two columns by the door, it looked
like a fancier version of many of the houses they had just
driven past. Something rose up inside her; not memory, but
expectation. This was her home!

They climbed out of the cab and Jillian took out some keys.

'Nico's at work but he said to say he'll be home later. He
wanted to give you some space,' her mother explained.

Freya nodded. She was grateful for that.

*You can move out, you know. Go back to Pasadena with
Mum.*

She could, but remembered the doctor's words: her memories of the past five years were more likely to come back if
she stayed in London, at least for the next while. However
the desire to avoid all of this strangeness was pulling her towards the airport.

'Do you really have to leave?' Freya asked as Jillian unlocked the front door.

Jillian frowned.

'I'm sorry, forget I asked.'

Jillian's trip to London at short notice after Freya's accident had already left a big gap back in Pasadena. Freya's ninety-five-year-old grandfather was ailing and her mother was his main carer.

'I'll stay if you need me,' Jillian said. 'But I think in the next day or so, things will start to become clearer.'

'How about I come back with you? I don't belong here.'

'You know what the doctor said. Coming home now, before your memory's returned, won't help your recovery. Besides, sweetheart, you're building a career here. You're happy, successful.'

'I could be those things back in the States.'

'Come on inside. I bet it'll all start to make sense.'

Freya took a deep breath and followed her mother through the heavy black door. She noticed the smell first. It was familiar, but then again this was her home and her mother was standing next to her. Yet it was more than that. Excitement sparked inside her. Her memories were coming back!

But when she stepped into the hallway, she got a jolt. Because nothing was familiar. It was beautiful, more beautiful than any place she ever imagined herself living, but it was not familiar.

To her left was a wide doorway, leading to a bright living room, furnished with soft fabrics and pastels. It looked comfy and inviting.

Freya, still clutching her bag, followed her mother down a wide hallway, lined on one side with floor-to-ceiling bookshelves, and into the kitchen and another living space.

Freya gasped. The room was gorgeous. It managed to be modern yet comfortable and traditional as well. Wooden benches, cupboards of pale blue, open spaces with bright prints covering the walls and the largest stovetop she'd ever seen. The room opened to a small garden, bursting with greenery.

'Wow!' she whispered.

'It's lovely, isn't it? You both renovated the place together when you moved in.'

'Together?'

'Well, yes, but I think he left many of the decisions to you.'

Weird. So weird. But it explained why she loved the house so much. Why it was to her taste.

'Come upstairs,' Jillian said, looking at the bag Freya was holding close to her body.

Her chest was tight as she climbed the stairs, that were covered in a thick, luxurious white carpet.

Expensive. This place is expensive.

She paused at the first-floor landing.

'Nico's room is that one and I'm in here.' Jillian pointed to a room to the left.

Freya glanced to the left, resisted the urge to look into Nico's room. 'I'm in the attic, aren't I?' She began to climb the stairs.

Her room was an attic in name only. It was hardly the dusty cramped space of fairytales, but was instead filled with light. Slanted windows that faced the sky were ajar to let the fresh spring air in. There was a spectacular view over nearby gardens and rooftops. If she'd had a pick of all the rooms in the house, she would have chosen this one. London looked magical from this angle. A door led to a bathroom, large enough for a claw-foot tub. Another door led to a small room or a large walk-in closet, depending on your perspective.

'The whole floor is yours.'

The bed was covered with a floral bedspread, but with a modern pattern. She loved it. It looked like something she might have chosen and yet...

Disappointment tasted bitter on her tongue and she held back some tears.

'Are you okay? Are you remembering something?' Jillian rubbed Freya's shoulder.

Freya shook her head.

Nothing.

She'd been hoping that this room, more than any other place, would trigger something. But nothing. It was like intruding into someone else's private space.

She had to start piecing together the last five years of her life. But where to start? Freya wasn't sure if she had a phone; she assumed she must, yet she hadn't been given it in the time she'd been in hospital.

'Mum, do you know where my phone is? Do I have one?'

Jillian grimaced. 'I believe it was crushed in the accident.'

Freya winced. She knew she was lucky to be alive but this detail about the accident made her shiver.

'Don't worry. Nico said he was going to get you a new one.'

That was kind of him. He must be a nice man; she had to trust that London Freya had had good taste.

'Cup of tea?'

The need for a hot drink was suddenly overwhelming. Freya followed her mother back down the stairs to the beautiful kitchen. It made sense the kitchen would be gorgeous; he was a chef after all.

Freya chose a chair at the table. Was this the chair she usually sat in? Or was it Niccolò's? Did they ever eat together? He was probably a good cook, but maybe he didn't like to cook at home. Did she cook? Had she finally learned to make more than cheese on toast?

Her eyes were drawn back to a green ceramic jug filled with large open blooms in pinks, yellow and reds. Gorgeous, but something she'd never had in her tiny apartment.

'Mum, what's Niccolò like?'

'What do you mean?'

'Exactly that. What's he like? You've met him. At this point you know him better than I do. I… I just don't remember him.'

Jillian reached for Freya's hand. 'He's lovely. He's been very good to you over the years. And he's very, very worried about you.'

That might explain the strained look permanently etched across his face.

'What did I tell you about him?'

Her mother laughed. 'All sorts of things. You've known him for years.'

Freya frowned.

'But we're close? I like him?'

'Yes, and yes. I can reassure you of that.'

Her mother couldn't answer all the questions she really wanted answers to: How were they when they were together? How did he feel about her? How did she feel about him?

Freya sighed. 'It's weird, suddenly living with a man I don't know.'

'But you *do* know him. You can trust yourself.'

Jillian placed a steaming mug in front of her. Earl Grey. Black. That hadn't changed. Freya clutched it like a lifeline.

'When did I move in with him?'

'Oh, a few years ago now. When he bought the place.'

They must have been good friends. More than just boss and employee.

Flatmates.

But was it anything else? Were they more than friends? No.

Freya dismissed the thought again with a chuckle. Niccolò was a gorgeous, glamorous celebrity. But most of all, if she and Niccolò *were* an item her mother would have told her. Niccolò would have told her.

She wouldn't live in the attic; they would share a room.

The list could go on. She nodded to herself, satisfied. They were friends, but not lovers.

Though how did London Freya manage to live and work so closely with a man like Niccolò and not be tempted...?

None of it made sense.

'How did I come to move in with him?'

'You were living in a dingy flat in South London and he suggested you move in with him to be closer to the restaurants. The office.'

It was his idea. Interesting.

'Can I please borrow your tablet?'

Her mother handed it over with a smile then moved about the kitchen, tidying up some things. Her mother looked more at home than Freya felt.

Google still existed, and still worked the same way. The homepage looked different, but that was hardly a surprise. She typed in his name, watching the predicted searches as she did.

Niccolò Rossetti.
Girlfriend.
Wife.
Shirtless.
Sexy.

The rest of the world was asking the same questions she was.

She'd move on to those searches once she'd figured out the basics. It wasn't dishonest, looking him up like this, was it? This was publicly available information, things that she should know if she was going to be living with the guy.

Stuff she had known. Once.

The basics were this: he was thirty-three years old, born in Puglia, Italy. That would explain his name and stunning

Mediterranean looks. He moved to London when he was ten years old to live with an aunt.

Her throat tightened. What had happened to make him leave his home to live with a relative? None of the reasons she could think of were happy ones and the website did not elaborate.

Niccolò started as an apprentice chef straight out of school and had worked his way around several restaurants in London and Paris. Some Freya had heard of but most she hadn't, though they sounded impressive.

The bio said he had opened his own restaurant about six years ago, in Islington. Freya didn't know a lot about the London restaurant scene but even she knew it was pretty impressive to open your own restaurant at twenty-seven. About four and half years ago he had landed a big book deal, and a television series followed. Since then, he'd written a book and produced a television series every year as well as opening two more restaurants. He was successful and getting more so. His style was everyday, practical food with an Italian bent. Fresh, healthy and easy.

His next anticipated project was a book and series titled *At My Mother's Table.* The mother he'd left behind in Italy.

She continued reading and watching videos as she drank her tea. Niccolò was seriously impressive. She'd been working closely with the sexiest celebrity chef in the world and didn't remember any of it. And Niccolò Rossetti did not have a face, or body, one forgot easily. A video of him kneading bread and smiling at the camera was still making her tingle fifteen minutes after watching it. It must have been some bump on the head to make her forget his brown eyes.

Freya glanced at her mother, who was cleaning up the kitchen with her back turned. She typed her own name into the search engine but then she gasped so hard her mother turned and exclaimed, 'What?'

Freya shook her head. She wasn't sure what she was expecting, but not this.

The search of her name brought up images of beautiful food, beautiful places. Some were instantly recognisable: a dining room with the Chrysler Building of New York in the background, another with the sparking lights of Paris. The photographs were bright, full of life and looked delicious. There were also links to interviews she'd given to all manner of people, including newspapers and magazines. The quotes attributed to her sounded like things out of another person's mouth, but most were about Niccolò: 'This is his best series yet... A fresh, modern take...'

As she scrolled down, the photos weren't just of the food, but of her. She was wearing clothes she didn't remember purchasing, standing in places she didn't remember visiting. Rome. Athens. Somewhere ice covered and Scandinavian looking. Her thoughts whirled. In some photos she was standing next to Niccolò. In others she stood next to strangers who looked glossy and fabulous.

It was a lot to get her head round.

In some photos she looked quite different. Her dark blonde hair, which was now straight and below her shoulders, was cut in a messy, textured, chin-length bob with highlights. A style she'd never been brave enough to try before. It suited her. She touched the screen with a single fingertip.

'Why didn't you tell me, Mum?'

'Tell you what?'

'That I'm famous.'

CHAPTER TWO

OKAY, SO SHE wasn't as famous as Niccolò Rossetti but she was quoted in goodness knows how many publications, and photographs she had taken were all over the web. As well as photographs of *her*.

Niccolò was really the famous one: as socially aware as he was talented, said one paper. Dark, sexy, looking as though he wanted to devour you through the camera, said another.

That he was called the sexiest celebrity chef in the world wasn't surprising, but that she worked for him was. Was she amnesic or simply hallucinating? If she did get her memory back, would she even believe it? What an amazing life she'd been living.

If I get back to work, back to my normal life, I might start to remember...

She sighed. Coming home to her house hadn't brought the memories flooding back; she was as confused as ever but now engulfed in disbelief.

'Are you sure this isn't a trick, Mum?'

Jillian laughed. 'Oh, love, no. Here—look.'

Her mother took out her own phone, scrolled through some photos and showed Freya a selfie she had taken right outside this very house. She was beaming.

'Now, go and lie down,' Jillian instructed. 'You've had a lot to take in and the doctor said to rest.'

Freya nodded. The morning had taken it out of her. She'd

go upstairs, get into bed and maybe when she woke up things would be clearer. It was a faint hope, but it was all she had.

She walked into the hallway just as the front door was opening to reveal Niccolò coming in. He was wearing well-fitted black pants and a black sweater and coat. Mouth-watering. That's what they said about his food but it also described him perfectly.

'Hi,' he said. His lips lifted into a hesitant smile.

What on earth did he have to be nervous about?

'Hi. I'm going to lie down. Is that okay?'

He stepped towards her and she leaned slightly back. His eyes opened wide then quickly returned to their normal gorgeous size. 'Freya, of course it's okay. This is your house.'

'I know. It just feels like a stranger's.'

'It's not, this is *your* house. How are you feeling?'

She shook her head. She didn't even know where to begin. 'Overwhelmed. Confused.' But also, if she was honest, a little excited that she may soon recover the memories of the wonderful life she seemed to have been leading. And a lot nervous.

'Oh, I almost forgot.' He passed her a white box. 'It's a new phone. It should be all set up for you.'

She took the box and their fingers brushed. An electric shock pulsed through her but she flexed her fingers to shake it away.

'Thank you for getting me a new one. What do I owe you?'

Niccolò looked hurt. 'Nothing.'

'I can't just let you get me a phone.'

'Insurance. Insurance will cover everything.'

'But…' She began one question, then thought of another.

Jillian had shaken her head anytime Freya had asked about the accident and clearly didn't want to think about it, much less talk. All Freya knew was that she had been a passenger in a car and a truck hadn't given way.

'Do you know how the accident happened?' she asked.

He looked around the hallway as though choosing an escape route.

'Where was I? Where was I going?' she continued.

'I think we should sit down.' He motioned in the direction of the living room; a room Freya hadn't yet been into.

She followed him in and sat on the sofa, hoping at least the cushion remembered her shape, even if she didn't remember it. The sofa was as comfortable as it looked. Niccolò chose the armchair across from her, even though the sofa would have fitted them both with room to spare. He sat straight backed and rubbed the five-o'clock shadow covering his chin.

'We were going to lunch. For your birthday.'

'We?'

He looked ashen.

'You were with me?'

'I was taking you to lunch for your thirtieth birthday.'

'Oh, Niccolò, you were in the car as well? Are you alright?'

He gestured to his intact and upright form. 'Not a scratch.'

'I'm so sorry.'

'Why are you sorry?'

'Because…' She wasn't sure what she was sorry about but he looked as though his best friend had just died. 'Who was driving?'

'Ah, I was wondering when you would ask that.' He grimaced again and her heart dropped. Her memory might be a mess but this much was clear.

'It was you. You were driving,' she said.

'I'm the one who's sorry, so, so very sorry.'

'But it wasn't your fault—the doctors said the truck didn't give way.'

Niccolò nodded but the look on his face broke her heart.

It was all his fault. She needed to know the truth at some point and he had to be the one to tell her.

Freya sat on the sofa, perching at the front of the seat, like she was a guest in her own home, and it nearly broke him. How many ways was it possible for a heart to break? The sight of her looking nervous and perplexed in hospital was one thing, but on this couch? In *this* room? Why had he suggested they come in here? Anywhere but here. This sofa.

He couldn't meet her eyes. It was too much. Her confusion, her uncertainty, but most of all the fact that she looked at him as though he were a stranger.

'I should have told you,' he began. 'I'm sorry I didn't. I'm sorry—'

'No. I know it was an accident. I know you didn't hurt me on purpose.' Her eyes were wide and worried.

For an instant something like hope swelled up in him. She must trust him if she could be so sure that he wouldn't hurt her intentionally.

'The doctors said a truck was at fault.' she said.

His heart fell again. Technically, yes, but he knew that if he'd been paying better attention, he would have been able to avoid the lorry. But he hadn't and he didn't.

'Are you sure you're okay?' she repeated.

Physically, he was fine. He wasn't sure he'd ever recover from the other scars. The last week had been like hell. Watching her being cut out of the car. Lifeless. Pale. Then watching her lie unconscious and unresponsive for days in the hospital.

Having to call her mother.

The joy at seeing her fluttering eyelids being shattered by the blank look in her eyes when she saw him.

'Freya,' he'd said, taking her hand. 'Thank goodness.'

'Who are you?' had been her groggy response as she'd snatched her hand away from him.

He'd had to leave the room to throw up. The guilt had been so paralysing he'd struggled for days to go into her room. Instead he'd hung around outside the room on the hard chairs, waiting for the doctors to give updates, for her mother to arrive.

Waiting.

Waiting.

But it was no more than he deserved.

She's home, sitting here, where she belongs. You should be grateful. It's all over.

Except it wasn't and never would be.

'Nico, darling, I thought I heard you come in.' Jillian appeared in the hallway. 'Can I get you something to drink? A cuppa? Something harder?'

'No thanks.' He moved to stand.

Jillian waved him down. 'You stay and talk. Tea?'

It had been both comforting and confusing to have Jillian here. Her presence reminded him of Freya, of before, but Jillian wasn't Freya. And being reminded that Freya wasn't his Freya hurt even more.

But he acquiesced and remained seated. Freya moved slightly but assuredly farther away from him and his heart broke a little again.

His chest did not seem to stop aching. How much could one heart withstand? It was a question he'd had cause to ponder often over the past week.

'I'm the one who's sorry,' she said.

'You have nothing to be sorry for.'

'My mother's been staying here. You're being so patient with me.'

'This is your home.' How many times did he have to say it? *Until she understands. Until she remembers.*

Freya looked slowly around the living room. After the kitchen, it was their favourite room in the house. It had a big, soft, comfy sofa and armchairs that were like sitting in a hug, a large television and an entire wall of books. She liked the view outside as well. The window was half a storey above street level, affording an easy view of the people walking past and the park across the road. Sometimes he'd catch her sitting where she was now, just watching the world go by.

Her eyes caught on one of the prints on the wall. It was a series of drawings of California. She'd chosen them. Would she remember those?

She's lost her memory. As far as she's concerned it's five years ago, she lives in Pasadena and has a dead-end job with a horrible boss and a best friend who is about to betray her.

You? She doesn't even know you.

'I know…but…' she protested.

'What can I do to make you feel more comfortable?'

A pained look crossed her face. 'You can put up with me. At least until my memory is back.'

'There's nothing to put up with.' He tried to smile but smiles these days were in short supply. The muscles in his face tightened each time he tried to smile reassuringly.

She grimaced even more. 'You know there is. I told you everything in the hospital. I don't remember anything about my job, what I'm supposed to do. I don't know how to be a food stylist.'

'Is that what you're worried about?' Of all the concerns, that was the last thing she needed to be worried about.

'Of course. You're my boss and I just told you I can't do my job.'

'Freya, you've had an accident—that was my fault, by the way—and you have amnesia. I understand you don't remember some things.'

'I've forgotten everything.' Her voice was soft and instinctively he reached for her with his hand.

She recoiled and he regretted not exercising more control. He stood, went to the window but couldn't help pacing.

'Yes, I'm your boss, but I'm your friend first of all. I'm going to look after you.'

She screwed up her nose as though she didn't believe him.

'But I don't… I'm sorry, it's just so strange. You're famous, I'm nobody.'

He barked out a laugh. 'You're not nobody—please don't say that. We're good friends. Best friends.' Though those terms didn't even quite cover what she was to him.

'Best friends? You and I?' She laughed.

'What's so funny?'

'Because how? What do we even have in common?'

So much. We laugh at the same things. We share the same jokes. We like the same things and we don't care when we don't. We tell each other everything.

Maybe not everything.

How could he tell her what had happened between them? She had no idea who he was. That was apparent from the hospital. She'd thought he was a doctor, for crying out loud.

She wouldn't believe him if he told her *everything*. Or worse, she'd be even more upset and confused than she already was.

He had to wait for her to remember, in her own time.

Though doing that worried him just as much. Was he lying to her by not telling her?

Even if he was, he couldn't tell her what had happened between them the night before the accident. It would be far too confronting, given that she didn't even remember him. Yet he also hated lying to her. Every decision he made felt like the wrong one.

Jillian returned and put two cups of hot tea in front of them. 'I'm just going to finish packing,' she said as she left the room.

Freya looked longingly after her.

'You wish she wasn't going?'

She nodded and he got the feeling she was holding back tears.

You and me both, baby.

Freya shook her head and refocused. 'What do I do?'

'What do you mean? Now?'

'What do I do in my job? For you?'

Everything, he wanted to say. Instead, he swallowed the lump in his throat and said, 'You really don't need to worry about that now.'

'Why not? Are you going to sack me?'

'What? No! Freya, your job is open for as long as you need. I just want you to know that you don't have to worry about your work. You should concentrate on getting well.'

He didn't want her to quit. He couldn't lose her. She wasn't just his right-hand man; she was the whole right side of his body. He owed so much of his success to her. Professionally, personally. He didn't know where he'd be without her.

Yet after what had happened the night before the accident, could she stay working for him? Living with him?

'No, I have to know. It'll help me understand.' She waved her hands around the room. 'This. All this. And why I live here with you.'

He drew a deep breath and tried to be as honest and direct as he could. 'You're a photographer, food stylist and social media manager.'

She laughed. 'Is that all?'

It took him a beat to realise she was being sarcastic. He cleared his throat. 'I hired you as a photographer and the rest went from there.'

'That makes sense—photography was my thing.'

'At *The Southside Chronicle*.'

'You know about that?'

He nodded. I know all about you. I know your favourite colour is the same blue as the colour of the walls in the kitchen. I know your favourite place in the world is the beach at Leo

Carrillo State Park and your favourite place in London is the rose garden in Regent's Park. Your favourite music is pop.

'You are going to be so excited to hear the new Taylor Swift albums,' he blurted without thinking.

'What?'

'Nothing, I'm sorry. You had—that is, you *have* a flair for designing food and know how to make it look amazing on film. You were a natural, and it went from there. I wasn't famous when I hired you. I was struggling with my first restaurant. You helped me become as successful as I am.'

She let out what sounded like a snort.

'You've been running my social media and publicity for years. We became successful together.'

'But I'm not—'

'Yes, you *are* successful. Look.' He took out his phone and pulled up a photo she'd seen earlier of her wearing an evening gown and holding a glass statue.

'That's you, getting a food photography award.'

She shook her head and buried her face in her hands.

'What else do you know about me?' she asked through her fingers.

'You love Taylor Swift.'

'Lots of people do.'

'She's released several albums in the past few years. We saw her at Wembley.'

'No way! That's awful!'

'No! You loved it. We had a great time.'

'It's awful because I don't remember. It may as well not have happened. No, in fact, it's worse than not happening because I'm jealous of myself.'

He stepped back towards her, wanted to hug her, and had to fight every instinct in his body not to.

'Your memory will return. The doctors are hopeful.'

You have to be strong for her. You know exactly what it

feels like, to wake up in a strange country and not know anyone around you.

It was terrifying when he'd first arrived in London. No English. His parents both dead.

'The doctors don't know. I think they expected it would've begun to return by now.'

His heart plummeted. He'd been hoping she wasn't worried yet. But clearly she was. The doctors began with plenty of optimism, but with every day that passed with no recollections, the less hopeful they became.

Freya had been diagnosed with traumatic retrograde amnesia. The physical brain injury she'd suffered in the accident had impaired her memory of events that had happened before the accident. However, the longer it went on, the more the doctors were worried she was suffering a type of dissociative amnesia, which may be due as much to psychological factors as to the physical injury. They were perplexed by the fact that it was specifically her memories from the past five years that were lost and not a random collection of events from her past.

This was Nico's greatest fear: that her condition had been triggered by what had happened in the days before the accident, rather than by the accident itself.

Freya did have memories. They had just stopped at a point that she had made a significant transition, when she'd been fired from her job at *The Southside Chronicle* and decided to move halfway around the world. And her memories recommenced when she'd woken up after the accident he'd caused. She had still been able to retain memories since regaining consciousness.

In other words, her brain had erased every memory of her life with him.

Which was fitting, since it had all been his fault. Nico had been subsisting on a couple of hours of sleep each night since the accident and was starting to get used to the sick feeling in his stomach. It was all he deserved.

Freya needed to rest, relax and not worry. And it was his job to see that she did.

'It's early days, and now you're home, things are bound to start coming back to you. I'm sure it won't be long.' He wished he believed what he was telling her.

She sipped her tea and pressed her lips together. Pink, full and soft as satin on his. He pushed the recollection deep down.

'What else do you know about me? What about us?'

He ignored the second question, the loaded, unanswerable one. 'I know that you're a ridiculously talented photographer, a lot of fun. Full of energy, ideas…' His tongue suddenly felt too big for his mouth and he paused.

She nodded. 'Then tell me about you.'

'Me?'

'I did look you up, but I want to know from you.'

'You looked me up?' *She's living with a stranger. Of course she looked you up.*

'Sorry, but I had to.'

'You don't need to be sorry. You should look up anything you want about me to make you feel more comfortable. But you can just ask me.' It was an invitation he wanted to withdraw as soon as he issued it. He could tell her many things, but not everything.

'Do you have a girlfriend?'

The tea churned in his stomach, empty apart from an apple he'd eaten six hours ago.

'No.' He said truthfully. *That* was what she most wanted to know? 'I don't. My last girlfriend was a few years ago and it wasn't particularly serious. I'm focused on my work and that doesn't leave much time for dating.'

She nodded, seemingly accepting his answer.

'Why did you move to Britain?' she asked.

'What did Professor Google tell you?'

'That you were born in Italy, but moved here when you were ten. But it didn't say why.'

He closed his eyes so he didn't have to look at her when he answered, 'I moved here to live with my aunt, my mother's sister. She brought me up after my parents died.'

'Of, Nico, I'm so sorry. I should've put two and two together.'

'No, it's alright.'

'They both died when you were ten?'

He opened his eyes but looked out the window instead of at her. It was easier that way. 'My father drowned in a boating accident when I was five. My mother passed away when I was ten.'

'Do you have any siblings?'

'No, but I'm close to my two cousins. I grew up with them. After.'

'That's lucky. I mean, none of it is lucky, but it's nice you're close to your cousins.'

He nodded and smiled. He knew what she meant. He'd always known what she meant.

'Was she good to you? Your aunt?'

'The best.'

His mouth tasted salty. His aunt, Cara, had arrived in Puglia shortly before his mother's passing and she and her husband had taken him in and raised him like one of their own children. However, there was no denying he was different. Dark hair, olive skin and a slight accent when he spoke English that he still hadn't quite shifted. Not that he wanted to. His Italian accent gave him an air of authenticity on British television that Freya called his Mediterranean edge.

Nico loved his adopted family fiercely, but that didn't mean he didn't miss his parents every day. He also wondered a lot about the place he'd left behind. While he'd returned to Italy for a few visits, he'd never made it back to Puglia and his home village.

'I'm sorry, I shouldn't pry.'

'No, please do. These are all things you know. You know me far better than Google.'

Freya frowned. 'I have so many questions.'

'And I want to answer them.' Just not *all* of them. 'I'm so glad you're home.'

His relief was physical. Yet as he saw her here, at this moment, sitting on the sofa, relief was tainted with guilt. He understood now why they called grief crushing; it weighed on him with each step and each movement, his body hurt, his limbs were heavy as concrete and his chest was tight. Sometimes it hurt even to breathe.

'Are you…? That is, has anything come back to you since you've been home?' he asked.

She yawned. 'No. Not yet.'

'Big day?'

'I was just on my way to have a lie-down.'

He jumped up. 'Go, don't let me stop you.'

She stood as well and lifted the hand that held the new phone. 'Thank you again.'

'Please, don't thank me.'

How could she be grateful when the fact that her old phone was pulverised was all his fault?

He shivered as she left the room.

They had been driving out to a new restaurant in Richmond for her birthday lunch when he'd failed to avoid the lorry coming onto the motorway. The police pressed charges against the truck driver but not against Nico. It might have been easier if they had.

There was nothing he could have done, the police had said.

Except they didn't know.

They didn't know that if he had been focusing properly, he probably could have avoided the lorry and the carnage afterwards. He should have avoided all of it. But he'd been weak. Done the very thing he'd vowed not to, and look where it had got him…

When Freya had finally woken up, three torturous days after the accident, he couldn't help thinking it was almost a blessing that she didn't remember anything.

He didn't want to stop her memory from returning—he wanted his best friend back more than anything—but he couldn't help thinking that it would be far easier on her if she didn't remember the day before the accident.

Because she would be far better off without him.

CHAPTER THREE

IT WAS DARK when Freya woke. A cup of tea was on her bedside table. She reached over and it was stone-cold. The clock at her bedside table flashed 10:00 p.m. The house was quiet.

She remembered the new phone Nico had gifted her and took it out of the box. Now if only she could remember her password… But the phone scanned her face and opened. She nearly dropped it. Heck, technology never stopped developing.

The good news was she recognised all the social media channels on her screen so started to look back over her posts. Much like the Google search, there were many photos of food and travel and people she didn't recognise but who she had tagged as friends. People who had tagged her.

She had friends. London friends. She scrolled through photos, partly curious, partly nervous. Nothing in her profile suggested she'd had any partners she didn't remember. And there were no photos of the same guy over and over. The creeping feeling came over her skin again. Something wasn't right. She hadn't had hundreds of boyfriends over the years, but had she really lived in London for five years and not found someone special? Even for a short while?

She wanted to remember things naturally, but on the other hand, not knowing how many other surprises awaited her was equally worrying.

She listened carefully for noise downstairs. Even though

she didn't think Niccolò would enter her room without knocking, she didn't want anyone knowing about the search she was about to do.

'Niccolò Rossetti girlfriend.'

Nothing.

Well, not nothing. There was plenty of speculation. Photos of him standing with women at events. He even had his arm around some of them, but he wasn't kissing any of them. There were no pap shots of him holding hands with anyone. Then another thought occurred to her and she slapped her forehead. Of course.

She typed in, 'Niccolò Rossetti boyfriend.'

Again, there were heaps of hits. She scanned the results but no, despite many men obviously wanting it to be true, interviews confirmed that Niccolò was in fact straight.

Freya fell back onto her bed. In moments, she was asleep again.

It was morning when she woke. Dr Jamal had told her that having amnesia was exhausting. He had also told her that as hard as it might be, she should try to carry on with her life as normal.

After showering in her beautiful bathroom, she went to her wardrobe. She didn't recognise most of the clothes, but found a T-shirt she had bought at Leo Carrillo State Park. This was hers. She remembered buying it from a little place up from the beach. She must have brought it with her from home. It was a little looser than she remembered, but she didn't know if the weight loss was from after the accident, or earlier. How had she lost weight living with a celebrity chef? This new life really was too good to be true.

Freya walked carefully and quietly down the stairs, not sure if Niccolò was home and if she would have to go through another awkward encounter.

It shouldn't have been awkward, but it was. He was a stranger. A beautiful, gorgeous, sexy stranger who was trying to tell her that they were friends. Best friends. He'd really said *best* friends.

Her best friend was Jane. Yet no one had mentioned Jane.

Freya stopped on the landing of the second floor. She looked through the doorway of the room she knew was Niccolò's. The door was open, though not wide enough for her to see in. Still, the fact that it was left open indicated a degree of openness and trust that confused her.

She wasn't sure which part of the scenario with Niccolò was weirder—that they were friends or that they were *only* friends. Hadn't London Freya wanted to sleep with him? How had she possibly managed not to?

Maybe he smelt bad?

No, she knew he smelt good. The whole house smelt good. Like clean carpet and expensive gift shops.

At that instant, Niccolò came through his bedroom door and she stepped back just in time to avoid a collision, but her face came within inches of bumping into him.

Caught!

The smell question was answered. He didn't smell bad; he smelt amazing, like clean and coffee and fresh croissants.

'Oh, sorry, I was just looking for Mum.'

'Please don't apologise. This is your house.'

Maybe it had been once, but didn't feel like it any longer.

'How are you feeling this morning?' He leaned forward, then leaned back just as quickly.

'I'm…' It was hard to explain, but was that because she couldn't remember the right words? 'Is there a word for "Okay, except that it feels like there is a big black hole in my head"? The Japanese probably have a word for it. Or the Germans.'

Niccolò grinned. He must think she was a fool.

'Physically fine. But tired,' she added.

He nodded. 'Jillian's in the kitchen.' He stepped back to indicate she should go first down the stairs.

Her mother was cutting up some fresh fruit and looked up happily when she entered, followed by Niccolò.

'Good morning! How are feeling?'

'Still no memory, if that's what you're asking.'

'Oh, sweetheart, it'll come.' She placed a bowl of freshly cut fruit on the table.

The three of them ate in silence. She looked from her mother to Niccolò and back again. This was ridiculous—these were the two people who allegedly knew her better than anyone in the world. She could ask them all the things she was worried about, couldn't she?

'Do I have a boyfriend?' she blurted.

'No,' Jillian said, shaking her head.

Relief flooded Freya's chest. She had deduced as much and it was good to have it confirmed.

'Have I had a boyfriend since Lachlan?'

Jillian and Niccolò exchanged a glance and panic rose again in her. She quickly waved her hands in the air as if that would erase the question.

'No, stop, no, don't tell me. I don't want to hear that I dated someone I don't know. I certainly don't want to hear that I've slept with someone I don't remember.'

She believed her memory would probably come back in time but if there were any really bad surprises, she wanted to know sooner rather than later.

'What I'm asking, is, is there anything, anyone I should…? Oh, I don't know how to put it.'

Niccolò set down his fork and looked at her. Brown eyes turned down. Worried.

'What's the matter?' he asked gently.

'I know I need to let the memories come back naturally. The doctors have said that they most likely will. But what I'm worried about is why my last memories are in California. Why not London? Why don't I remember London? Did something happen to me in London that I somehow want to forget?'

Niccolò drew a deep breath and she noticed his body stiffen.

'As far as I know, and I've known you pretty well, the most traumatic thing that has happened to you in the past five years was the car accident.'

Freya exhaled, but Niccolò didn't look at all relieved.

'Nothing awful or traumatic or heartbreaking has happened to you that I know of,' Jillian added.

It was a relief to hear and that was all she needed at the moment. But there were still some things she wanted to know.

'Am I still friends with Jane?'

This time Niccolò and Jillian didn't exchange glances but both looked at the ceiling.

'Oh, my.' Freya's heart fell to her stomach. 'Is she okay? What happened?'

Jillian reached across the table for her hands. 'She's fine, she's well. She's still in Pasadena. Married. They're about to have their second baby.'

'Oh, that's great. Who is he?'

It took Jillian slightly longer than a beat to say, 'Lachlan.'

'Lachlan. Not…' But she could tell by the looks of pity on Jillian's and Niccolò's faces that the answer was yes. Jane, her supposed best friend, was now married to Freya's ex.

Niccolò stood and went to the counter to get a box of tissues. Freya stared at them but didn't feel like she was about to cry. She felt numb. Lachlan had dumped her a few weeks before her twenty-fifth birthday, telling Freya that he thought he should be with someone more 'high energy.' Freya had

spent many waking moments since that point trying to figure out what he meant. She had plenty of energy.

Though her stupid boss at the stupid *Chronicle* had also
implied as much.

You're not dynamic enough. Your work lacks vibrancy.

But Jane? *Her* Jane?

'How long? How? What?'

Even though she couldn't articulate the questions, Niccolò
had the answers.

'It wasn't long after you got here. About the time we met,
actually. She was avoiding your calls and you thought it was
because she was annoyed with you for leaving. Which she
probably was. But then one of your other friends called you
up and told you.'

Jane and Lachlan. Dating. Married. And they had kids
together!

'You eventually managed to get her to answer your calls
and she said how sorry she was, that she hadn't meant to fall
for him, asked you to forgive her, blah, blah, blah.'

Freya might have giggled at his casual phrasing, if she
hadn't been so shocked by what he was telling her.

'Did I? Forgive her?'

'You decided not to go to their wedding. They invited you,
but you didn't go. We went to Paris for the weekend instead.'

We? She looked at him. Instead of going to her best friend's
wedding—admittedly to a man Freya had dated for a year—
she went with Niccolò to Paris.

Almost certainly a wise decision, but still a baffling one.
To Amnesia Freya.

'You haven't really spoken to her since. You occasionally
mention them but you're no longer hurting so much. You got
over them once. I know you will again.'

It was the past for everyone else, but for her it was still
the present. She expected to feel something physical, but she

didn't feel anything. Like her body was already accustomed to it. Even though her brain couldn't even process it.

Lachlan and Jane? Jane had hooked up with Lachlan?

'Are you okay?' Jillian asked.

'I'm sure I'll remember in time, but please, please don't tell me anything else. Not yet.' This was enough to deal with for the moment.

Freya tried to eat some more breakfast, and Jillian and Niccolò pottered around the kitchen like they were old friends.

'The car's coming to get me in a few hours,' Jillian announced.

'I've told your mother that she can come back anytime she wants.'

'Or maybe you can both visit me again?' Jillian said.

'Again? We visited before?'

Niccolò and Jillian shared another conspiratorial glance.

'A couple of times. We spent a few weeks in California last year, filming a show. We spent a fair bit of time in Pasadena.'

'Right.' Freya crossed her arms. This was getting stranger and stranger. She thought maybe it was just London she'd blocked out, but it really was *all* of the last five years.

Everything to do with Niccolò.

'I'll pay for your flights,' he said to Jillian.

'That's too generous,' Freya said and Niccolò frowned.

They both had to get better at this. She had to start believing that he was her friend and that she could trust him. But he needed to realise she wasn't the Freya he knew.

She couldn't trust anyone at the moment, not her old friends and not even her own memory. The only person she did trust was about to get on a plane.

Niccolò turned to her mother and held his arms out. 'I need to get to the restaurant. Jillian, safe travels. Come back as soon as you can.'

'Thank you for everything.' Jillian stepped into his arms and they hugged.

It was like watching a movie. Her mother and this stranger were hugging, quite affectionately. Jillian patted his arm several times.

She had to try to start believing that this really was her life. Then maybe her memories would begin to come back.

Once Niccolò had left for work, Freya sat on her mother's bed and watched her pack. One of the only things in this house she recognised was her mother's suitcase. In a few hours Jillian would be gone and Freya would be truly alone.

'I don't know what I'm going to do without you.'

'You're going to be fine. I honestly think it's for the best. You need to get back to your real life and having me here probably isn't helping you do that. I wouldn't be getting on that plane if I didn't truly believe that you'll be fine.'

Freya sighed. 'What do you know about Niccolò?'

Jillian smiled. 'For starters, you call him Nico.'

Nico. That sounded too familiar for someone she hardly knew.

'I know you care a lot about him. I also know, without a doubt, that he really cares for you. Couldn't live without you. He's been beside himself. He didn't leave the hospital for a week. Has hardly worked since the accident. That's why he has to go in today.'

'But why? Why does he care so much?'

'You tell me.'

'I wish I could. I don't have any recollection of him at all. He doesn't even feel familiar.'

Jillian frowned. 'He's always been great to you. I've always wondered…'

Yes. Freya had been wondering the same thing.

'Why we're not together?'

Jillian nodded.

You and me both.

She definitely found him attractive. She had a pulse. And good vision. *Even if you were blind, you'd still be mad about him. His voice feels like the sun's caress on your bare skin. Each time he stands close to you his scent makes your head spin.*

'I guess because we're friends, we work together... Those are reasons, right?'

'Absolutely. Very good reasons.'

And maybe since they were friends, she'd seen his less attractive side. And maybe that dampened any attraction she might have felt? Maybe she'd grown to think of him as a brother?

'Take me with you.'

'Sweetheart.' Jillian walked over to the bed and held Freya's chin.

'This place is too strange.' Freya's cheeks began to wobble.

'The best thing for you, and you know it, is for me to go home. You need to do this on your own.'

'But...'

'You're so brave. I'm so proud of how intrepid you were to pack up and come here with nothing and build this life.' Jillian gestured around the room. 'Your memories will come back.'

Freya hung her head, knowing her mother was right.

She had to stay. If she never got her London memories back, there would always be five years of her life that were lost.

She also knew that you didn't get so many years in your life that you could afford to give up five of them. She'd recently come close to losing the rest of her years altogether.

The doctors and her mother had been cagey about the finer details of the accident, but Freya knew it had been bad. The fact her mother had travelled all the way from the States, as well as the anxious look on the faces of everyone she met, hinted as much.

Besides, while she had family in Pasadena, she had no job and apparently no friends either. Each time she thought about Jane and Lachlan she became a little angrier. Then a little sadder. Had they been planning it all along? Had Jane liked him from the start? Had London Freya understood all of this?

A car came for Jillian in the early afternoon. Her departure left Freya alone in the house for the first time. She took out her phone, the magical box that held so many clues to the past five years but none of the actual memories.

On a whim, she typed 'Jane Caruso' into the browser and the first things that came up were wedding photos. Freya winced at the bright smiles across both their faces and put down the phone. How had it happened? Why had it happened?

You weren't at the wedding. You went to Paris with Nico instead. She felt her thoughts begin to spiral but caught them. Niccolò was right; London Freya had moved on from Lachlan and Jane once before and she would do so again. She shut down the browser and opened her emails.

She scrolled through weeks of advertising but an email caught her eye. A plane ticket. Heathrow to LAX. One-way. She double-checked the day's date and then the one on the ticket. The ticket was for three days earlier. She was meant to be going to LA three days ago. She'd clearly missed the flight. Why had no one told her? With everything going on, they clearly had other things to worry about, but still. No one had mentioned it. Was she going to visit her mother? Grandfather?

Maybe they didn't know?

Impossible.

They would have told her about it. Someone would have mentioned it.

Why was it one-way? There was no return date.

Her head ached. The paracetamol package next to her bed was empty.

Freya went down a flight of stairs, head aching. She opened the first door on her right at the bottom of the stairs. Nico's. She walked to the en suite bathroom and opened the first cabinet on the left and there was the paracetamol.

She didn't linger long in the bathroom but instead stood in the bedroom.

The walls were a cool grey, matching the thick, soft carpet. But the rest of the room was coloured with bright accents. A large fireplace sat on one wall, lined on both sides with white bookcases, which in turn were filled with brightly coloured books and other objects.

A bright red armchair looked strange, yet was a feature of the room. She had an urge to curl up and sit in it with one of the books from the shelves.

You shouldn't be in here.

Freya left the room quickly, leaving the door slightly ajar as she'd found it.

It was only once she was in the kitchen filling a glass with water that she realised she'd known exactly where to look for the paracetamol.

This house was her home. She'd lived here for over two years. So what if she knew where the painkillers were kept? Chances are she'd helped herself to some before. Or fetched them for Nico. It didn't mean anything.

Except it did mean that her memory might be returning.

You found painkillers in a bathroom cabinet? That doesn't mean anything, everyone does that.

Except that she'd always kept hers in her bedside table.

Freya groaned and rubbed her temples. So much for getting rid of her headache.

When she woke from yet another nap, the sun was low in the sky. She took an unfamiliar cardigan from her unfamiliar closest and wrapped it around herself. A delicious smell was coming from downstairs and she went to investigate.

Niccolò was sitting at the kitchen table with a laptop in front of him. He offered a broad welcoming smile when she walked in. Her stomach flipped. She smiled back.

'Hey, sleepyhead.'

'Hey yourself.'

His brown eyes sparkled. 'Hungry?'

'Starving.'

He served her a warm bowl full of an egg-and-tomato gratin, oozing with mozzarella cheese and with fresh bread on the side.

'This is amazing. Hands down the best thing that's happened to me all day,' she mumbled, mouth half full.

Colour rose in his cheeks. 'It's your favourite.'

'You made it?'

'Yes.'

'And I've eaten it a lot?'

He nodded very slowly.

He's afraid to tell me too much.

The realisation was sudden yet so obvious she wanted to slap her own forehead. He wasn't stand-offish. He was just afraid of saying something wrong. Was he hiding something or just trying to protect her?

You can trust him, a voice whispered to her. *London Freya trusts him—you should too.*

'I don't know how I lost weight, living with you.'

He laughed. 'I think you may have lost a little since the accident, but don't worry, I'll make sure you get it back.'

Their eyes met and her body warmed. He cared for her. Deeply.

A memory of Lachlan telling her she should think about losing a few kilos came back to her.

Traitorous Lachlan.

Stupid Jane.

Those were memories that she'd rather stayed forgotten. The thought of actually finding out what had happened between Lachlan and Jane and the extent of their betrayal terrified her.

Freya looked away and took another generous mouthful of the comforting food.

London Freya had had five years to get past Lachlan and Jane. London Freya probably didn't think them about them very often at all.

She wanted to be London Freya. She wanted to become that person. The person who was Niccolò Rossetti's best friend.

But how?

'I want to go back to work.'

'There's no rush.'

'No, there is.'

'Yesterday you told me you didn't remember anything.' His eyes sparkled and her stomach flipped.

'I remember how to take a photo.'

He pulled a face.

Her face reddened. He was right; what business did she have waltzing to his office or studio or whatever it was and taking photos? She didn't know what her job involved. This was the worst type of imposter syndrome—because it was real.

'As your boss, I can't let you return until a doctor says.'

'Are you my boss, or my best friend?'

'I'm both. How about this? You have an appointment with Dr Jamal the day after tomorrow. Let's see what he says then. In the meantime, rest. I have to go into the restaurant tomorrow morning but I hope to be back by mid-afternoon.'

'Thank you, Niccolò.'

'Nico.'

'What?'

'Nico. You don't call me Niccolò—you call me Nico and I'd like it if you did again.'

Freya opened her mouth as if to repeat it but seemed to have forgotten how to say his nickname too.

'I'll be home mid-afternoon. I'll take you for walk around, see if that triggers any memories.'

'You're a chef. You run a restaurant. People eat at night.'

The thought was so obvious she couldn't believe it hadn't occurred to her before this. He laughed.

'We run three restaurants, but we have managers and talented head chefs in both. I can't possibly cook in three places at once as well as everything else.'

'*We?*'

'What?'

'You said "we" run two restaurants. Who is "we"?'

'I meant "we", the team.'

'Right, of course.'

His face reddened. He stood and went to the sink.

Nico returned home, as promised, just before two the next afternoon. He'd stayed in the office just long enough to check in on everyone and make sure they were managing.

Which they were. His team was at pains to push him out the door and go home to where they all said he needed to be.

To *whom* he needed to be with.

Everyone who worked for him knew how important Freya was to his business. They also knew how important she was to him. He was sure they all wondered why, given the closeness he and Freya shared, why they were not more than colleagues and friends.

The answer he gave when anyone asked outright was that they *were* colleagues and friends. What he and Freya had was far too important to risk.

She was on the sofa when he walked in, curled over her

phone, looking confused. He noted the new crease that heart-breakingly hung between her eyebrows much of the time these days.

'Hey.' He stood in the doorway, waiting for her to invite him to sit beside her. He hated, hated in his bones the pain he felt when she leaned away from him as though she was afraid.

Afraid of him!

She'd never been afraid of him. Maybe polite and cautious during their first few meetings, but after she'd been working for him for a few days and realised, quite naturally, what was missing from his business and what she could do for him, he felt that they had been equals. Still boss and employee, but she'd had no difficulties telling him what she thought he should do, and he'd had no problem following because when Freya had an idea about promoting his restaurant she was almost always right.

'Oh, hi. How was your day?' She sat up and smiled when she heard him.

He allowed a little relief to creep in and sat on the other sofa. 'It was good. Everything's ticking along. Lacey and Raff are managing to get along with one another, thank goodness, and Simon, I think, is loving having a bit more control in Chelsea.'

He saw the moment he lost her—at the mention of people she didn't know and problems that two weeks ago she'd been fretting over but now didn't know existed.

'What I mean is, the team is managing.'

She nodded. 'Anyway, I'm dying to go out and explore.'

'Are you sure you're up to it?'

'More than up to it. I'm going stir-crazy in here. I slept half the morning. I feel more awake than I have in days. I do still like to walk, don't I?'

He nodded and allowed himself a smile. 'Yes, very much. But if you get tired, we come back.'

He both longed for and feared spending time with her. He missed her desperately, but every moment they spent together brought new, painful reminders that she didn't know who he was. Freya wasn't the Freya he knew. The Freya he knew couldn't stop talking and loved to share things with him.

This Freya was more like the one he'd first met, recently arrived in London, shell-shocked and still recoiling from the betrayal of her friends. Still raw after being dismissed from her previous job.

She's still the same person. You just have to be gentle with her. She hasn't had the five years of healing your Freya had.

She came downstairs five minutes later wearing no more than a cardigan over her outfit, jeans and a blue T-shirt.

Even her style had changed since the accident. They were still her clothes, but she matched them differently somehow. He opened the hall closet and took out her navy blue coat. She eyed him suspiciously.

'Trust me. This is the coat you wear when rain is predicted.'

She took it slowly and he was careful not to let their fingers brush. That was not a sensation he needed to remember.

Outside he turned left as always but she turned right. They stopped, looked at one another. Her brow furrowed again.

'I'm doing it wrong again.'

He sighed. 'Not wrong. You usually walk this way. That way doesn't go anywhere. This way goes along the canals.'

'You know which way I walk?' Her tone was cautious.

'We often do this walk together. We can go that way, but if we go this way you might remember something.'

She fell into step with him and they rounded the corner. The canal came into view.

'I walk this way often?' she asked.

'Yes, but more often in summer. You do a loop, along the canal, to the park and—'

He stopped himself. He felt every bit of the burden in telling someone about themselves. It felt so wrong. Such an intrusion.

'It's okay, you can tell me. I want to know.'

'I don't want to put memories in your head.'

She stopped and smiled at him. For a moment he saw the trust in her eyes that had been there once before.

'I want to know. I need to know. Tell me everything.'

'Everything?'

'Tell me about us.'

'Us?' he scoffed and hated the way he sounded so dismissive. But what was he meant to say? *We were friends for a long time, but one day that changed. And then I nearly killed you.*

He couldn't tell her.

Not yet.

Maybe not ever.

Don't tell me, I need to remember myself.

'Yes, *us*. We work together, we live together, everyone tells me we're friends.'

He nodded.

'Then tell me about *us*. For starters, how did I come to work for you?'

This he could answer. 'I advertised for a food photographer and social media expert.'

'And I answered?' Her expression was incredulous.

He laughed. 'You did.'

She pressed her left palm to the side of her face. It was a gesture he knew meant she was thinking hard about something.

'Why on earth did you hire me? Were there no other applicants?'

'You're a great photographer. And you had journalism experience. Of course I hired you.' And she'd been honest, brutally honest about her lack of experience. And that had been the clincher. It wasn't often he came across people who were up-front. Unafraid to tell the truth. Freya always had. And he'd come to value that honesty, to rely on it. No, to depend on it.

She was the person who kept him grounded.

'But plenty of people know more about blogging and social media than I do. And I know nothing about food.'

He smiled at the memory. 'I asked you about that. I asked what experience you had with food.'

'And?'

'And you told me you loved eating.'

She winced.

'But that's the best qualification. A passion for food. I liked that you were so honest with me. I was starting out myself. I didn't know what I was doing. I'd opened my first restaurant six months earlier and it wasn't thriving. I'd been calculating how many more days I could afford to stay in business. But after hiring you, I didn't have to. Freya, I wasn't famous when we first met. It might help you to remember that.'

Freya had known more about food than she realised. She had a sophisticated palate and a real eye for colour and smell, but her feel for what made a good dining experience was innate. Her instinct for what was good and what was great had set her apart and had helped him grow his business. That had made her an integral part of his success.

And her enjoyment of food was positively seductive. He remembered the first time he'd cooked her his mother's seafood stew and she'd closed her eyes and opened her mouth in an almost orgasmic expression. Much like the look she'd given him when he'd fed her last night.

'But how?' she whispered.

'You learned about food. You learned how to promote a

restaurant at the same time I did. We grew a successful business together.'

'Together?'

That was the wrong thing to say.

'We learned the business together. With your photos I landed a book deal. Then the television show.'

She scoffed. 'I'm sure it wasn't just my photos. I'm sure your innate sex appeal played a bit of a part.'

She gasped and her palm went firmly back to her mouth. Her cheeks turned the colour of tomatoes.

He laughed. Harder than he had in days. Harder than he had since before the accident.

'Sorry. I'm sorry. I know you're my boss, I just keep forgetting that. Along with everything else.'

Her boss. He was her boss. He sometimes had a certain amount of amnesia around that fact himself.

'They say I have a certain appeal.'

It was her turn to laugh. She mimicked him '"A certain appeal." I've read the reviews.'

'What else would you like to know?' he said but his tongue felt heavy. There were some things he wasn't ready to tell her.

We slept together and then I nearly killed you.

Some might say there was no cause and effect between the two things, but he knew the two things were connected. Because when he cared for someone, they died. It was what happened with his parents and it was what nearly happened with Freya.

'Why did I move in with you?'

'You were living down in Sutton.'

'Where even is that?'

'And you had weird flatmates who kept ferrets and stayed up partying all night. And it took you over an hour to commute. When I bought this place, I suggested you move in. It's closer. Much more convenient.'

He didn't add that she had helped him find this place when he'd got his second book advance and that he'd chosen it for the two of them to live in. Of course, they weren't together, just good friends. But he'd chosen the place because it was large enough for them to both share as friends, with each of them having their own floor.

'Can I ask you something else?'

'Of course.'

'It's a bit personal, but then I guess I live with you so I'd probably know. But it still feels strange to ask. Do you have a girlfriend?'

He smiled to himself. 'What did Google say?'

'Said no girlfriend. And no boyfriend.'

'Well, Google was right about that.'

'And when was…? Oh, don't worry.'

'Freya, you can ask me. You know me.'

'When was your last serious girlfriend?'

'Oh.'

He hadn't been expecting that question. Freya had known the answer to that and known that he'd been effectively single for the past five years. He'd had some casual flings, and had known she had too, but nothing serious.

'Um, four or five years ago.'

'Why?' she blurted.

It was a fair enough question.

'I've been busy. Running a multimillion-pound business isn't a piece of cake.'

She may not have intended to give so much away with her expression, but he knew it was her don't-mess-with-me-kiddo look.

'I've been busy. It's not easy to date when you're a chef—we work long hours.'

And some people just didn't want relationships. Some people just weren't made for them.

He was saved by the weather. The mist that had surrounded them developed into actual rain. He went to grab her hand, his instinct to pull her quickly in the right direction, but he remembered himself just in time.

'Come with me. I know somewhere warm.'

He led to her to the Red Crown, a pub where they had enjoyed countless casual evenings when he didn't want to cook and because she didn't.

They entered the warm room just as the rain was beginning to fall in earnest. Freya looked around and to his great relief headed in the direction of the table they preferred to sit at.

As though she remembered.

It's just a table. Anyone can see it's the best spot in the pub. It doesn't mean anything.

'Would you like a drink?'

'I think so. What's the worst thing that could happen—I might forget this evening?'

His heart fell.

'I was joking. Amnesia humour,' she said.

He should've been glad she found levity in the situation, but he wasn't.

Freya sat and he went to the bar and ordered red wines for both of them.

She looked appreciatively at the glass, picked it up and sniffed. 'Nice, thank you.'

He watched as she sipped slowly. Maybe the wine and being in a place she knew well would prompt a memory to surface.

'Can you please tell me about the accident?' she asked.

Nico pressed his lips together. 'You don't need to know about that.'

'I want to. I think I need to. But you and Mum have been so reluctant to tell me about it.'

There were good reasons for that. He could hardly bear to think about that day, let alone talk about it.

The car was on its roof. He couldn't remember it rolling, just like he couldn't remember climbing out of it, but he must have because he was standing on the road, barely a scratch on him, and she was still inside. He was frozen to a spot a few feet from the car. Too afraid to leave because she was in the car and he needed to be close to her, but even more afraid to step forward and see what was in the car. What was left.

Her hand hung, lifeless, from the smashed window, lying in the shattered glass.

He hardly registered the sirens above the noise of the traffic and the roaring in his ears but he saw the flashing lights, beating around him, making his eyes hurt.

'I was driving, I didn't see the lorry. I don't even remember the car rolling.'

'You have memory loss too?' Her eyes were wide.

I almost wish.

'There isn't much to say. The car was a wreck. It was a miracle I got out as I did.' That was all he could manage to say. He couldn't bring himself to think about that moment, let alone try to describe it. Why did she want to know about something that was so traumatic?

'It's not fair,' she sighed.

'I know. I'm so sorry.'

'I meant, it's not fair that you know more about me than I do.'

'You're right, that isn't fair.' A lock of wet hair had fallen across her face and without thinking he brushed it away.

Touching a hot stove would have been less painful.

She froze and he saw again the distance separating them. The way she looked at him like he was a puzzle. A stranger. Almost fearful. He was trying to make her comfortable, not to run.

'You'll have a break from me soon anyway. When I go to Italy.'

'Italy?'

He felt a stab in his chest. He hadn't told her.

Well, he had told her. They had planned the whole trip together. She'd spent the past year working on the plan with him, the places they would go, the dishes he might cook. She had even started writing the cookbook with him. This was the project they had collaborated most closely on, the one closest to his heart.

To both their hearts.

'I'm going to Puglia. Next week.'

'What for?'

'To research my next book and television series.'

'Why aren't I coming?'

'You were meant to, but I'm not sure you should be leaving London at the moment. I need to go soon or I'll get too behind.'

'But I'm fine!'

He bit back a response. Physically she may be well, but they both knew she was not fine.

She sipped her drink and played with the stem on the glass as she always did when she was thoughtful. 'Did I have any other trips planned? Anything else booked?'

'No. Just Puglia.'

'Are you sure?'

'Positive.'

The look on her face made him uneasy.

'Then when do we leave?' she asked. The expression on her face was expectant, full of excitement.

'You're not coming.'

'Why not?'

'Because you're not well enough.'

'I'm fine. I feel fine.'

'Dr Jamal says you should stay in London until your memory returns.'

'No, technically he meant I shouldn't go back to California.'

There was nothing wrong with her ability to argue. The thought should have comforted him, but instead it was simply frustrating.

'I don't want to rush you, overwhelm you.'

'But if Dr Jamal says it's okay, I can go?'

He ran his hand over his head. 'I think you should rest.'

'You don't want me to go with you?' Her shoulders dropped limply.

'Of course I do. We planned this trip together.'

But now everything has changed. Now I know that the more time we spend together, the harder it will be for both of us.

This would be the first time he'd returned to Puglia since he'd been hurriedly packed off to live in the UK with an aunt. It was a trip he'd only had the courage to make with Freya's encouragement.

To go there without her would be heartbreaking, but to take her with him would be problematic. She had the best chance of getting better here in London. Every moment he spent with her reminded him of what he was going to have to give up. Every moment he spent with her made it harder.

He had to let her go.

He had to learn to live without her.

The thought of letting her go was terrifying. But the thought of something else terrible happening to her was even worse.

The following morning, Nico was in the kitchen, hunched over his laptop, going over the travel plans when Freya came downstairs. He sat up straight when she walked in the door.

'Can I make you something?' he asked.

She shook her head. 'I need to do it. I need to relearn where everything's kept. I tried to make a cup of tea yesterday and I didn't know where anything was.'

'If it puts your mind at ease, you don't use this kitchen much.'

'I don't?'

'You eat at the office. Or out. Coffee?' he asked, standing.

'Yes, please.'

He went about making her a cup of coffee using the machine she'd bought as she watched on. Standing a little close for his comfort.

'I really feel fine about going to Puglia,' she said. 'I feel as though I'm getting somewhere.'

'You can remember things?'

'No, not exactly, but…'

'What?' His heart jumped but he wasn't sure if it was from excitement or dread.

She sat at the table. 'It's hard to explain without sounding silly.'

He shook his head. 'Nothing sounds silly.'

'It's like you sometimes feel after waking up from a dream. I can feel some things. I know a particular emotion has flowed through my veins, but I don't know why. I can feel that something has happened—the memory is so close, just on the other side of a door. But I can't open that door.'

He nodded. 'It sounds so frustrating.'

'You don't know the half of it. The other thing about amnesia is that you feel stupid. Most of the time. I know logically it isn't my fault. But I still feel silly. A lot of the time.'

'You don't have to come with me.' He put a macchiato down in front of her. Her favourite.

'I know. You've been so understanding, but I want to get back to work. And besides, I've never been to Italy. Oh, wait—have I?'

He laughed. 'No, you haven't. It was going to be your first trip.'

'Phew!'

'Why?'

'Because that's one less memory to have forgotten. Paris, New York, Amsterdam, Barcelona, all the places I've apparently visited in the past few years and I have no recollection of. So this will be great. I may not have all my memories but that doesn't mean I can't create new ones.'

It was difficult to argue with that logic. He longed to take her with him and yet what if she wasn't well enough? What if it disrupted her recovery?

'Please talk to Dr Jamal first.'

'Deal. But there's one more thing.'

'What?'

'Let me come with you to work today.'

Nico frowned. 'I'm not sure…'

'Just let me come with you. I'm going crazy just hanging around here. I just want to see where you work. Pretty please.' She made her fake pouty face and he was helpless to argue. He rubbed his temples instead.

'I won't do any work. I still don't understand what it is I do, but maybe coming in will help me remember.'

Again, it was difficult to argue. If coming home hadn't triggered any memories, maybe going to the restaurant would.

'Look at it this way—if you don't take me, I'll just try to find the place by myself. Are you really going to take the chance I'll get lost wandering around London alone?'

'No,' he sighed. He wasn't going to do that.

CHAPTER FOUR

FREYA WASN'T PREPARED for the number of faces that turned to look at her when she followed Nico into the restaurant. It was situated on a corner in what appeared to her to be a busy, slightly upmarket part of London. The front door opened into a large light-filled dining room with high ceilings, white walls and subtle bright touches. The restaurant was three-quarters full, even mid-morning. The bustling kitchen was half exposed to the dining room but the entire space fell silent when she walked in.

She didn't usually have this effect on people.

A woman wearing a white shirt and black apron rushed over to her, arms wide.

'Freya! It's so great to see you!'

She enveloped Freya in a hug and Freya stiffened. *This woman's a friendly colleague*, she told herself, but then a man lined up to greet her and Freya pulled back. The faces surrounding her were lined with confusion.

'How are you?' another woman asked.

'I'm...' She looked to Nico. *Please explain to them.*

'She's fine, tired, but is still having some memory problems. She's come here to see if it helps her recall things, but please, go gently. I know it's strange, since Freya's such an important part of the restaurant and because we all love her so much, but please give her space and time. She'll come to you when she's ready.'

There were murmurings of 'Sorry' and 'So good to see you' as the crowd dispersed.

At some point in his speech, Nico had placed a warm hand on her shoulder, protecting her, keeping her close. Freya had to resist the strong urge to turn her head and bury her face in his chest. Coming here was more overwhelming than she'd thought it would be.

Because we all love her so much.

A woman appeared next and wordlessly handed her a mug of coffee with only a dash of milk. She sipped it and it was exactly as she liked it. How did the woman know?

Because she knows you.

The feeling of being unnerved rose up again in her. She focused properly on her surroundings for the first time.

'Wow, this place is beautiful.'

He laughed.

'What's funny?'

'You had several arguments with the decorators and builders to get it just right.'

'I designed it?'

'You did indeed.'

'Who am I?' she whispered under her breath. She caught him hiding a brief smile.

'Our office is upstairs. NRHQ.'

'Eww, who named it that? Let me guess, me too.'

He laughed. She loved his laugh, the way his face brightened, making that dark and anxious face burst into a smile that made her feel like the cleverest and funniest person in the world.

She followed him up a narrow staircase, also painted white like the rest of the space.

Freya stood in the doorway and surveyed the office. One desk was neat and orderly. There was a computer and a stack of tidily piled notebooks. A clean coffee mug sat just so next to the computer mouse. The desk against the other wall also had a computer on it, but that was the only similarity. It was chaotic, with stacks of higgledy-piggledy cookbooks. And no less than three dirty mugs. She had a feeling which was hers, but was afraid to choose. How much had she changed in the last five years?

'Do you know which desk is yours?' he asked.

'I want to say the messy one, but… I'm afraid I don't know who I am anymore and I may have turned into a neat freak.'

'No fear, the filthy one is yours.'

'Hey! You might have cleaned it while I was in a coma. Washed my mugs?'

A cloud fell over his face.

'I'm just kidding.' She picked up one of the mugs and sure enough a layer of grime was nurturing a healthy bacterial colony. 'I take it back. I am a reformed woman. I'll wash my coffee mugs out from now on in case I'm caught in intensive care again.'

The colour drained from Nico's face. No mean feat since his smooth olive skin was far from pale.

'I'm joking. Again.'

'It's too soon,' he said sternly and turned to his desk, though Freya noticed his computer wasn't on.

He's been a mess.

Her mother had hinted at how upset Nico had been.

If your best friend was in a bad car accident, you'd be upset too.

Freya stepped towards him and before she could think better of it reached out and placed her hand on his shoulder.

'I'm sorry that my attempts at humour have been a little black. I'm struggling with my stuff and I'm sorry for not thinking more about how this is affecting you.'

He didn't respond and he didn't turn to face her. She squeezed his shoulder gently.

When Nico turned, his eyes were glassy. There weren't tears in his eyes but there was definitely fog. He smiled and replied, 'If you're going to clean your desk, that must've been some bump on the head. When are you seeing Dr Jamal again?'

'Ha ha.'

She still held his shoulder and now he was facing her she realised how close they were. She held his shoulder like they were in a chaste dance. With one step, their bodies would be flush. He was about a foot taller than her and had to look down to her. She noticed his Adam's apple bob in a deep swallow.

Did they touch often? Were they touchy-feely friends? It was hard to believe they could be and that she'd have kept her hands off his glorious body for so many years. Studying his face close up, she saw the smooth lines, sharp corners and soft skin. Eyes you could fall into and lose yourself in forever.

She searched those eyes for hints and clues about him. About *them*. But it was almost impossible through the wall he now had back up. He'd locked the door to his thoughts and he wasn't letting her in.

Nico looked away and the chance to discover more about him was gone.

'I have to get down there. Settle back in and hopefully...' He didn't need to finish that sentence. They both understood what he'd left unsaid.

The office was both bright and cosy. It looked out onto a small park and afforded a view of the sky. The walls were covered in maps and posters of food. They shared an office. And a house. Didn't they get sick of one another?

She picked up a cookbook that was sitting on her desk. She opened the hard, glossy cover.

Winter Warmth
By Niccolò Rossetti and Freya McFadden.
Photographs by Freya McFadden.

Wow.

She wasn't just a published photographer but an author too.

She flipped the pages. The book was full of beautiful photographs of food that were making her mouth water. Finished dishes of warm stews and curries, bright, healthy ingredients. Photographs of the cooking process. Tables laid out beautifully. She recognised some of the shots were taken in the restaurant downstairs.

You took these.

Freya sat at her desk for a while with her hand on the book, breathing deeply. She had done this. It was so far away from *The Southside Chronicle*, Jane and Lachlan and her life in Pasadena.

I need someone with more energy. You aren't dynamic enough.

What did they even mean by saying those things? Had Lachlan always preferred Jane? Had Jane always had a thing for Lachlan? Was it Jane who encouraged Freya to leave the country? Get her out of the way?

You sure did show them all.

She wondered if London Freya had posted a copy of this book to her old boss with a note inside saying, 'Vibrant enough for you?'

Probably not.

Had London Freya sent a copy to Lachlan and Jane with a note saying, 'I don't need either of you!'?

She doubted it.

London Freya probably didn't give Lachlan or Jane or anyone at *The Southside Chronicle* a second thought these days. Yet for Amnesia Freya the hurt was still fresh. The events still confusing. Jane? Her best friend, Jane? That betrayal was far worse than being sacked or Lachlan dumping her. This was Jane. Nico had been wrong; she *had* suffered a heartbreak since coming to London.

You could call her. Ask her why.

Freya stared at her phone. She hadn't spoken to Jane in years, apparently. They no longer had a relationship. And once Freya began to get her memories back, she'd also remember how she managed to put Jane and Lachlan out of her thoughts and move on.

She opened the heavy cookbook still on her lap. Niccolò's introduction spoke about the importance of food in the colder months for physical and mental health. He wrote about traditional winter feasts and celebrations. It was nice, inspiring stuff.

Then she read what she had written.

It's no secret that those of us from SoCal tend to struggle with London winters and I was no different.

These are the dishes that Nico cooked for me that first, cold, wet and lonely winter when I was struggling to make my way in my new home. These dishes will comfort you too. Some will give you strength, others solace. I hope they bring you the same joy they brought me.

How was she not *with* this man? The Freya who wrote that introduction sounded like she was utterly in love with him.

The computer on her desk was an unfamiliar model, but she found the on switch and managed to boot it up successfully. But what were the chances she'd use the same password?

Very high, as it turned out. It was still her old street name and the last digits of her mother's phone number.

Hundreds of emails popped up, from names she didn't recognise, with subject headings that made no sense. Proof. Drafts. Scripts. Finals. Italy. Puglia. Puglia. Puglia.

Her thoughts spun and it took a while to focus on one message at a time.

The emails were mostly business related, about the Italy trip, the cookbook and series they were working on. She would get to those when she had more of a handle on things. An email from Nico caught her eye and she opened it.

The itinerary looks fab, don't know what I'd do without you xx

Now, granted, the last boss she could remember had sacked her because her photographs were not eye-catching enough, but bosses didn't usually sign off emails with kisses, did they? Maybe this was another five-years-in-the-future thing?

She took out her phone. It was logged into her account. All her messages were still there.

She'd deliberately not looked at them before this, afraid of what she might see. Afraid of what she might assume or interpolate. Afraid they would just confuse her further.

Could she get more confused than she already was? No, she couldn't, she decided.

Nico Rossetti was at the top of her message list.

She closed her eyes, swallowed and clicked. There were hundreds. No, probably thousands of messages between them.

Some were administrative: Where are you? What time are we leaving? What's the address again?

And some nonsense messages that made no sense to her, but indicated a deep, close relationship between them.

Others were links to all sorts of things: newspaper articles, videos. There were memes, photographs.

Photos!

She opened that app.

There was a lot of food. But also places. It was like looking at the photos she'd seen online, only a million times more so. She didn't recognise any of the faces in the photos, except for Nico.

She scrolled and scrolled and lost track of time. So much for her vow to let her memories come back in their own time.

A photo of Nico appeared on the screen. He was standing in a kitchen, smiling at the photographer. Her. He'd been smiling at her. His entire face was lit up, his brown eyes focused entirely on her.

This photo.

She could fall asleep looking at that photo.

But had she?

He's always been great to you. I've always wondered why you two aren't together.

She'd been wondering the same thing. The more she got to know him the more she liked him. She was attracted to him, had been from the start. Surely London Freya must have been too. And if thirty-year-old Freya was falling for him as a stranger, wouldn't twenty-five-year-old Freya have as well?

We work together. We're friends. It seemed like a plausible explanation to Freya. It was what everyone else believed, but did she?

Her gaze fell back to the email with the airline ticket to LA. One-way. Nico didn't know about it; that was clear from their conversation last night. Was she leaving London without telling him? Why on earth would she do that? What was London Freya running from?

One week later, and after checking with Dr Jamal, Freya's carefully designed itinerary had landed them both in Bari, the largest city in Puglia, on the sparkling Adriatic coast. They'd picked their hire car up from the airport and driven into the city and to their hotel. He had asked her to drive, claiming that she was more accustomed to driving on the right than he was. That was true, but it wasn't the real reason. The real reason was that he wasn't about to get behind the wheel of a car with Freya sitting next to him ever again.

The plan was to spend a night in Bari before driving down the coast to Monopoli, the town they would base themselves in. From there it was a short drive to Tregua, the village where he'd lived the first ten years of his life.

Freya pulled up at the hotel and he looked over to her, blinking in the sunlight. She was looking a little washed-out after their trip but her eyes were wide with wonder, taking in the bustling street and the seafront across the road, filled with pedestrians enjoying an evening stroll.

The itinerary they had planned was mostly eating, drinking, visiting local markets. Talking to some chefs. It had been designed to be an amazing trip for both of them. Just the pair of them, drinking, eating, enjoying the sunshine.

Things they had done many times in the past. But that had been *before*.

Before the night they had shared.

Memories were a funny thing. Freya wanted hers back but he was being tortured by his own. By the thought of her lips, her hands on his face, the smell of her body, the way desire had rolled through his.

Every single one of his muscles tensed. He swallowed, regrouped and turned back to her.

'How about we freshen up before dinner?'

A cold shower and a change of clothes would fix everything and he'd be able to think straight again.

The effect of the cold shower and clean clothes lasted approximately five minutes, until Freya arrived in the hotel lobby wearing a green cotton dress with thin straps. The beautiful skin of her neck and shoulders was bare and luscious and he had to swallow hard and bite back the memories of the night before the accident.

He couldn't remember her wearing this dress before. He'd noticed that lately her style had changed. While she was still wearing items from her wardrobe, she wasn't wearing her favourites.

She must've caught him looking at her because she rubbed her arms and said, 'I know, I know. I'm so pale. Did I get any sun in London?'

'You stopped missing Californian winters eventually.'

'I did?'

He nodded. 'After three or four years.'

She winced.

'I'm sure you'll get your dose of vitamin D here over the next week.'

Nico led the way through the cobbled streets of the old town to the bar she'd chosen for them to try. Sounds of conversation and laughter floated out into the street as they passed open doorways. The bar was tucked away in a narrow alley and looked inauspicious until the aromas hit his nose. They ordered a selection of drinks and dishes, including curled octopus, calamari, king prawns. Bari was famous for its seafood.

'I thought this was just predinner drinks?'

He laughed. 'It is. We won't eat everything. We'll just try things. For research purposes.'

Her bright blue eyes were wide. 'How are we both in such good shape?'

He laughed again. 'We walk a lot.'

Conscious he was using the word *we* a lot, he pulled his notebook out and started taking some notes.

'Research?'

'Always.'

'What are you writing down?'

'Everything. The setting, the set-up, the menu.'

A selection of shareable dishes arrived and he couldn't help but salivate. Though at least it was a change from salivating over the gorgeous woman across the table from him.

She drank her ruby spritzer slowly and swirled it contemplatively.

'I imagine you already told me all about it, but could you humour a poor gal with amnesia and tell me again? What happened to your parents?'

He nodded, buying time while he decided if he would tell her the long version or the short version.

This is Freya. She knows the long version, so you may as well tell her.

It wasn't a story he brought to the surface of his consciousness often. Hardly ever.

'I was five when my father died, ten when my mother passed.'

'What happened?'

He took a deep breath. 'My father drowned. He was fishing and the boat capsized. I saw it from the dock. I screamed for help but they couldn't make it in time.'

'You saw it?'

He nodded.

'And you were five?'

He nodded again and she exhaled a profanity.

The look on Freya's face was almost identical to the one she'd given him nearly five years ago when he'd first told her the story. As though she could physically feel his pain.

'Oh, Nico, I'm so sorry.'

'There was unexpected wind and the boat capsized. I called for help, but not fast enough. I remember just standing there, watching, being unable to move and...' It didn't do to dwell on that feeling, panicked, unable to run or scream. Feeling like his feet were stuck in concrete. 'It was a bit like a nightmare.'

'Only real.'

He nodded. 'Mama was devastated. They loved one another so much. She left her life in England to live with him here. Her family wasn't overjoyed by the idea of her giving up everything for a poor Puglian fisherman. But they ran a restaurant together, they had me and...'

'And they were happy.' It wasn't a question. She knew.

'So happy. And when he was gone, she died of a broken heart almost five years later.'

'Not really?'

'Yes. That's what they said.'

'Is it really a thing?'

'Yes, it is.'

'I believe you.'

She reached over and took his hand. A gesture his Freya had done many times before, but it was the first time for *this* Freya.

What he didn't say, what his Freya had known, but what this one did not, was how it was all his fault. He wasn't foolish enough to think that he'd caused the boat to sink, but he hadn't been able to get help fast enough. He had just watched it happen.

And she also knew that after his father had died, Nico's own love hadn't been enough to keep his mother alive. She had died of sadness. Her grief had killed her.

He could not protect the people he loved. The day after he'd let his guard down with Freya was the day before he'd almost killed her. This was why he didn't let anyone too close to him. His work and ambition were a convenient and believable excuse, but the real reason was far more important: how could he let anyone love him when he knew he couldn't keep them safe?

After sampling the dishes at the bar, they walked to their next destination, a restaurant overlooking the port.

They were taken over to the best table in the place, with a view of the water and the boats bobbing up and down. They were treated to a spread of various dishes, orecchiette with broccoli, tuna tartare, smoked burrata and a Puglian speciality, *spaghetti all'assassina*. Or burnt spaghetti.

'Not actually burnt?' Freya asked.

'The fresh pasta isn't boiled, but cooked directly in the pan, in a sauce and then a broth.'

Freya knew this. He'd cooked the dish for her several times and she'd loved it. She couldn't wait to sample it on this trip.

But that was before the accident.

'Do I like it?'

He swallowed, though it wasn't the wine moving down his throat but fear. It scratched and burned all the way to his gut.

It was her memory. She'd forgotten what it was like to be herself and he mourned for her and himself all over again.

Such a stupid little thing, the dress she was wearing, her favourite drink, her favourite food. It shouldn't mean anything but it did. Because it shocked him again just how much was missing, how much might be lost forever.

Suddenly the weight of what was ahead for both of them in the coming weeks or months was too terrifying to contemplate. Fortunately, Freya was oblivious to the fear washing through him. She looked around the restaurant and sighed.

'Is this what it's usually like?'

'What? We've never been here.'

'No, I mean, travel, food. Us.'

Us.

His thoughts snagged on that word.

Was there even still an *us*? Would there ever be again? If she regained her memory, she'd want to leave anyway. Just as she had before. Leave London. Leave him. And this time he wouldn't be able to stop her.

'Pretty much.'

'We're so lucky. Is it possible to be jealous of yourself?'

'Your memories will come back.' He was reassuring her as much as himself.

He wanted her back—his Freya—yet at the same time was terrified about what that would mean when it did happen. Would she remember everything? Even the day before the accident?

Was it horrible for him to want her *not* to remember that?

Yes. He was horrible. It was all his fault.

Everything that happened was his fault and one way or another he'd have to live with it.

'Was I happy?' she asked, looking into her dish.

'I think so.'

Except at the end. At the end he wasn't making her happy. He was unsure how long she'd felt that way, but it had been long enough.

'You think so?'

'I mean, yes, you were. For most of the time at least.'

Her brow creased. 'Did it take me a long time to get over Lachlan and Jane being together?'

'Oh. I see. You were a little angry at first, but no. I don't think it took you all that long.'

She pulled a face. She'd been outraged when she'd first found out about Jane and Lachlan. If she could forget both of them and their betrayal for good, that wouldn't be a bad thing.

'Then what did you mean when you said, "For most of the time at least"? Was there something else that went wrong?'

'No, nothing like that. Your mother and I told you.'

'Then what?'

'I think…' He made a show of twirling his pasta but he was really choosing his words very carefully. 'I think as your thirtieth birthday approached you were thinking a bit about the future. About your next steps.'

'I was? Wasn't I happy working for you?'

'Freya, it's been a long time since I said you worked for me. I always say you work with me.'

She let out an incredulous laugh.

'It's true. You have to believe it. So much happened over the past five years, to you. To both of us.'

She sat with this thought for a while and looked out over the water. The sparkling Adriatic had darkened as they'd been eating.

'What on earth could I possibly want to do apart from this?' She waved her arms around the beautiful setting they found themselves in.

He shook his head. 'I honestly don't know. I didn't want you to leave.'

Oh. He'd said too much. But he didn't want to lie. It was impossible.

She put down her fork. 'I was going to leave?'

This conversation was tying his gut in as many knots as the spaghetti on his plate.

'I don't know. I hoped not. It was just something you mentioned the night before the accident. What your thirties might bring.'

'Oh.'

She nodded as though she understood. He hadn't lied. Not exactly. There was a fine line between answering her questions honestly and replacing her memories.

He watched her eat and think. She twirled her shoulder-length blonde hair absent-mindedly around her index finger, creating tiny curls. He rubbed his own fingertips together, remembering the silky sensation of her soft hair in his hands. Her blue eyes wandered over the bustling restaurant and then to the relative calm of the sea. Her eyes were still beautiful, still thoughtful and intelligent, but now were missing some of their familiar spark.

She's a lot like the Freya you first met. Young, uncertain. Hurting.

Yet she'd always been more than that. Also full of fire and passion, energy and enthusiasm.

She's still your Freya.

His heart sank.

She'd never be *his* Freya. And he had to stop letting himself think otherwise.

'The memories will come back. Probably when I least expect it,' she said.

And that was one thing he was afraid of.

CHAPTER FIVE

FREYA OPENED THE shutters of her hotel room wide and had to shield her eyes from the bright morning sun. The heat and sun reminded her more of California than London. The change of scenery was good for her, no matter what Nico might think.

She felt better in the Mediterranean sun. Her memory might not have returned but the air and the light here were invigorating. And that had to be a good thing.

Dr Jamal had assured them both that a trip away should be fine and not disrupt her recovery too much. He'd also assured her that if she felt well enough to drive then she could. Nico had been reluctant for her to come, but he couldn't argue with the doctor, who was adamant that if Freya felt well enough to go, then she should. Getting back to work, getting back to normal, was the best thing she could do now.

The doctor's unspoken words were, *I expected your memory would have returned before this. You'd better just accept the situation and start adjusting.*

So adjust she would.

And if her memories never came back, well then, she'd just have to make new ones.

As apprehensive as she was to recover her memories, the thought of never getting her memories back at all was more worrying. But only just. Why had her brain only blocked out the years she had been in London? The years she had known Nico. Dr Jamal had again brought up the possibility that she was suffering from dissociative traumatic amnesia due to a psychological event, rather than the physical one, so the fear that something awful had happened to her while in London lingered at the back of her mind. Nico was the last person she could tell about those fears, especially since she had insisted so vehemently that she was fine to come with him to Italy. She had bluffed her way onto this trip, but she had no idea what her role actually was. What was she meant to be doing? Nico was taking notes. She was just eating and drinking, which was fine as far as it went, but it didn't seem like work.

You should be taking photographs.

She'd packed her camera, her London camera, but hadn't actually taken it out of its case since she'd returned from the hospital. She hadn't even taken any photographs with her phone.

Your work lacks vibrancy.

You aren't dynamic enough.

I need someone with more energy.

London Freya must have pushed those voices aside and got on with her life.

Why couldn't she have forgotten her stupid old boss and her awful ex and their cryptic insults and remembered all the adventures she'd had with Nico? Stupid memory. Stupid amnesia.

She showered and went about the task of choosing an outfit. It was lovely having London Freya's wardrobe to choose from, though it felt a little as though she was playing dress-up. She chose a calf-length navy blue linen dress that California Freya would never have picked for herself, but which she had to admit looked very sophisticated on her. She paired it with some white sandals and hoped it would be suitable for whatever the day held.

Nico was already waiting in the lobby when she came down. She caught a smile quickly pass over his lips before he suppressed it by pressing his gorgeous lips tight together. As if to suffocate the smile.

Instead of pondering the significance or otherwise of his expression, she pressed on.

'Where are we going for breakfast?'

'A place just down the street,' he answered.

'Is it good?'

'You've always wanted to go there. You struck up an on-line friendship with the chef.'

'Oh.'

She had had just as much of a hand in organising this trip as he had. And going to this restaurant was probably something that two best friends would have enjoyed doing, less so something Nico felt like doing with Amnesia Freya.

'I'm sorry,' she said.

'What for?'

'You and Freya planned this trip together and you get stuck going on it with me.'

'Newsflash, you are Freya.'

She sighed, 'But I'm not your Freya.' She stepped out onto the busy morning street.

Nico grabbed her hand and pulled her back. 'You will always be my Freya, no matter what.'

She managed a weak smile.

He held onto her hand as though he was used to holding it. As though it was something they did.

She wanted to lean into him. Smell him, taste him.

His scent was familiar somehow. Was she remembering it from before, or just from the last week? He smelt of laughter, lightness and…longing.

How had London Freya withstood it? Being next to this gorgeous man day after day? Or had she felt nothing for him? The more time they spent together, the closer she felt to him.

The more she was drawn to him and the harder it was for her to step back and away. He drew her to him like a sun.

What had London Freya thought of him? What had she felt for him? How could she have been immune to his olive skin and kind eyes? Or those full lips that quirked ever so slightly in one corner when he looked at her? How had she possibly kept her lips away from his?

Nico led the way through a bustling market, filled with colourful fresh produce and the smell of freshly baked bread and down a lane lined with overflowing shops. The city was beautiful, full of so much colour and life, but it was hardly registering when all she could think about was what on earth had been going on between her and Nico.

He stopped outside an unassuming cafe. Before either of them said anything a man emerged from behind the counter.

'*Ciao*, Niccolò!'

The men shook hands and then he turned to Freya.

'*Bella* Freya!'

She smiled, nodded and wasn't prepared for the hug he pulled her into.

'How are you feeling?'

She shrugged. 'Okay.' It was the only possible response.

'Freya, this is Gino. The owner of the cafe,' Nico said, before speaking in Italian to the man. Freya assumed he was letting Gino know that she hadn't regained her memory because Gino then tilted his head in the universal sign for sympathy.

'Never mind, you will still enjoy your meal!' Gino said happily in English.

Gino brought them coffees and a selection of pastries with every conceivable filling.

She eyed the spread in front of them. 'Is this our only breakfast or should I leave room for a second breakfast?'

'We're going to have a walk around one of the markets, but eating is optional. And then we're driving down the coast.'

'To your village.' She remembered this from the itinerary he'd shown her. Tregua was the village he'd grown up in, to which he hadn't returned since he was ten. After his parents had died. She didn't know why he hadn't visited since his father's family still lived there and he had travelled to Italy. She wondered if it was because of the way his father had died. Freya shivered at the thought of how powerless he must have felt watching his father drown.

Freya had been there when her father had passed away, but he had gone slowly, of cancer. They all got to say their good-byes and there was nothing left undone or unsaid. And that was still awful. But to be five years old and to blame yourself? She wanted to reach for Nico, pull him to her.

Though that was an equally confusing thought.

'Yes, and then Monopoli.'

'Why aren't we staying in the village?'

'It's very small, there isn't a hotel or anything and I don't want to intrude on my aunt. She's nearly eighty. She's my father's aunt, so my great-aunt. Anna.'

Freya nodded.

'How do you feel about going back? Excited? Or nervous?'

He smiled. 'Honestly? I'm not sure. I am excited but I've been thinking a lot about the past lately. And that isn't all pleasant. Sorry, I shouldn't be telling you all this.'

'Why on earth not? You told London Freya.'

'London Freya?'

'That's what I've been calling my other self.'

He screwed up his face as though he didn't like what she was saying.

'You can tell me what you're thinking and feeling. I know the past few weeks have been all about me and my health, but you're allowed to have feelings too. You can talk to me. I don't need my memories back to understand that this will be a difficult time for you. I think I would feel excited and curious but also apprehensive and sad.'

Nico stared at her, his brown eyes wide and his jaw slack. She slipped her hand into his and squeezed. It was warm and strong and she wanted to keep her hand in his forever. She felt his hand tighten around hers for the briefest of glorious moments then he let go, closed his eyes and drew a deep breath.

'Yes, I feel all those things. I've been thinking about my parents a lot since we've been here.

'That's understandable.'

'And missing them more than I have in ages.'

'That's also understandable. They'd be so proud of you.'

Nico looked down and she heard him sniff back emotion. Then he shook his head. 'You don't know that.'

His sadness hit her in the chest. 'I do. I may not remember you, I may not know you like London Freya does, but I still know that you're a wonderful person, that you have done some amazing things. Including how you've been looking after me.'

Her mouth went dry when she said those last words. She was parched and she looked around for some water. There was none on the table so she turned to catch Gino's eye.

She didn't spot Gino, but she did spot her own reflection in the mirror behind the counter. She caught Nico's reflection too. He was looking up again, leaning forward.

Looking at her.

His mouth hung open slightly, his head tilted just a little, and the look in his eyes was unguarded. Dreamy.

He's looking at you.

Her stomach flipped and she had to look away, feeling like she'd seen too much. Intruded on something that wasn't for her. She blinked and Gino appeared next to her, bringing a bottle of water as though he'd read her mind.

When she turned back to Nico, he was studying his coffee and his face was once again blank.

They left the cafe and strolled along the cobbled street to the busy market, fully in the swing of the mid-morning bustle. People of all ages were buying their fresh bread, meat and vegetables. The sounds and the smells were something to behold.

But the colours!

Without thinking twice, she took out her phone and took some snaps of the fresh fruit, lined up in neat boxes of colour. The flowers of every hue, the breads and the vast array of seafood.

She noticed Nico, watching her, rubbing the day-old growth on his chin.

Oh, to do the same. To run her fingertips across that gorgeous stubble. To press her lips to it. Rub them along it.

She bit back a huff of frustration.

It didn't make any sense: she was attracted to Nico. Pure and simple. There were so many things she didn't know at the moment, but that was one fact that she knew without a doubt.

So wouldn't London Freya also have been attracted to him? Unless the bump on her head had triggered new feelings in her. Could amnesia do that?

She wanted to call Dr Jamal but how could she ask such a thing? Could amnesia make you lust after your best friend who you've had a completely platonic relationship with for nearly five years? Could a bump to your head change someone's desires so completely? Maybe a head injury could make you see the world in a different light. Maybe trauma could also make you realise how short and fragile life was and compel you to make the most of it.

She took some more photos of the market and looked on while Nico chatted to the stall owners in Italian.

Maybe London Freya was attracted to Nico but knew he wasn't attracted to her. Even as she asked herself the question, answers started popping into her mind. The look he'd given her when she'd walked into the hotel lobby last night in the green dress. The way he'd reached for her hand when she'd stepped onto the busy road.

The way his eyes widened when their faces were close.

The way he was looking at her in the cafe when he thought she couldn't see. Were they the actions of a worried, caring friend or something else? Something more intimate?

But maybe she was going about this all wrong. Maybe it simply didn't matter how London Freya felt about Niccolò. What mattered was how this Freya now, Amnesia Freya, felt about him.

She was hopelessly, crazily attracted to him. She had to make a conscious effort not to touch him when he was near. Not to lay a palm on his strong bare forearm. Not to touch his shoulder to make a point. She couldn't take her eyes off him, even in their picturesque surroundings.

Her memories may never return. It had been nearly four weeks since the accident. Over three since she'd regained consciousness. She knew that the more days that passed, the less likely it was her memories would return. She had to get on with this new life.

So instead of trying to remember what their relationship had been like, she had to forge a new one. She wasn't sure exactly what that relationship looked like, but she was hoping it involved them being more than just friends.

Nico looked around the village of Tregua, hoping to see something familiar. But it was all different. Some things were bigger, some smaller. And the most important things were not there at all.

It shouldn't have surprised him; it had been over twenty years since he was last here and even though so much about this place had not changed in millennia, everything felt different. Only one thing was the same. The smell. Every place in the world had its unique scent, and Tregua was no different.

Lemon. Dust. Salty air. Frying fish.

The house Anna still lived in was a short walk away. Or so he thought. The village was set around a small circular harbour. The fishing boats were tied up as they always were in the late morning, back from the dawn trip. The ancient houses were painted white so the whole place sparkled in the sun. The part of the town where they had lived was close to the water and the fishing docks.

'Oh, Nico, it's gorgeous.'

You're gorgeous, he wanted to say, but instead went with the far more sensible 'Anna's house is a street back from the sea.'

'Yes, just round the corner from the main square with the church,' she said and they both stopped walking.

She was right.

'How did you know that?'

'I don't know. Didn't you say?'

He had indeed told her; he had described the village to her several times when they were planning the book and the trip. But that had all been before the accident.

'We talked about it, but that was a while ago.'

Even he was struggling to reconcile his childhood memories with this place, she remembered.

Her face became brighter than he'd seen it in weeks. Her beautiful eyes were wide and excited. Pink colour bloomed high on her cheeks. His heart rate hitched.

'Do you remember anything else?'

She looked around frantically, as though searching for a lost item so she could leave the house. Kids ran around with a shiny brown labrador, and several elderly men sat on wooden chairs in the shade. Her face closed over and she shook her head.

'Sometimes I don't know what is real and what isn't,' she said and he understood so completely he couldn't help but pick up her hand.

It was what he'd wanted to do, what he'd longed to do for years: walk through this village holding her hand, knowing she was with him and that the past didn't matter.

For a brief moment he gave in to the longing and let himself believe that dream was still possible. Hand in hand with Freya, back here, and everyone was alright. His father, his mother. And Freya. He indulged that fantasy for few minutes only, then pulled his thoughts back to reality.

'Forget me and my faulty memory for a moment. You spent the first ten years of your life here. What do *you* remember?'

'Feelings, mostly. Smells. Tastes.'

That was why the cookbook was so important. It would be a way of bringing back his parents in some little way. A tribute to them. And it was also why it had taken him so long to come back here and do this. It was only with Freya's gentle encouragement that he'd felt brave enough.

And now? Even though she was here, holding his hand, it was far from what he'd imagined.

'I remember certain things, but I don't know how they fit together. A kitchen. A bedroom. A garden. But I don't know if they belonged to the same house.'

She grinned. 'I sometimes feel like that too. I recall disjointed images, but I don't know if they go together or the order they came in. Or even if they're real.'

'Exactly.' He couldn't have put it better himself. He squeezed her hand.

When they reached the point where the entire bay came into view, he stopped.

'This is it,' he whispered.

The bay glistened blue and turquoise, belying the tragedy that had happened here.

'It's beautiful,' she said.

'This is the bay where my father died,' he said before he could stop himself.

'Oh, Nico. Here? I'm so sorry.'

It had been a bright day, just like now. Clear and calm. It had been a freak accident.

'I should have been able to do something.'

'Nico, what? No! You were five. It can't have been your fault.'

He shook his head. 'I could've done more.'

'I'm sure no one could have prevented it. There would've been other people around. Adults. Everyone would have done everything they could.'

She could try to comfort him as much as she wanted, but he knew. He'd been there. He'd seen it.

He turned from the water, still holding her hand, like the life raft that should have come for his father.

Tourism had become one of the biggest industries in Puglia in recent years, but it was barely encroaching on Tregua, which remained primarily a fishing village.

He glanced around, from the street that led to the square, down to the docks.

'The restaurant is down that way.' He pointed down to the boat sheds. The restaurant, which had been in a converted shed, was directly on the water. 'The only place you can get fresher seafood is on the boat itself.'

Freya tugged on his hand. 'Your father used to say that.'

Nico stopped and closed his eyes as a rush of emotion surged through him. Even though it was a statement, not a question, he still said, 'Yes.'

He'd told her that many times. In fact, he recalled his father's words anytime he was lucky enough to eat seafood by the water.

'Did I remember that as well?'

He nodded.

It turned out today was a big one for both their memories.

'Our house was just this way.' He turned down a lane.

'Is it still there?' she asked.

'I honestly don't know. But most of these buildings are at least a hundred years old so we'll see.'

'Are you okay to go to your house?' she asked.

'Yes, it's why I came, after all.'

'But it's still hard.' She squeezed his hand and he longed to twirl her entire body to his.

They walked slowly down the laneway, taking in everything. The kids running past them, the occasional Vespa speeding by. People going about their days.

And there it was.

He stopped and she did too, studying it as he did. A single-storey cottage, so much smaller than in his memories. A blue door, a single window at the front and whitewashed like most of the other cottages.

'Do you want to knock?' she asked. 'Say hello? Tell them who you are?'

What would be the point? It would be different and muddle his memories. Or it would be the same and that would somehow be even worse.

'Not just yet.' He'd wait until the lump in his chest was not as large, not as unpredictable. 'It's still standing' he said, stating the obvious.

'Is that good or bad?'

'Good, I think. I'd have been devastated to find my childhood home knocked down. But it's still strange.'

This village might have been his home. If his parents had lived, he had little doubt he would have followed them into the business, stayed in this village his entire life.

And you'd have never met Freya.

But he also wouldn't have nearly killed her.

CHAPTER SIX

WHAT A DAY they were having and it wasn't even lunchtime.

Nico was overwhelmed with childhood memories and emotions and she was ill equipped to help him, with her own memories fighting their way to the surface in odd and unexpected ways.

They must have spoken so much about this place; why else would she have remembered something as random as the directions to Nico's childhood home? Just her luck to remember Nico's past when she couldn't even remember what she'd been doing two months ago.

No. It was more than that. She was remembering things that Nico had told her. She was remembering a story she had been told. A story that was close to her heart. It was important.

Tregua was Nico's hometown and it had somehow formed part of her memories, yet she'd never been here. How was that possible?

They went to find Anna's house next.

'You've kept in touch with her?'

He pulled a face. 'I tried to. We wrote occasionally but I was a pretty typical teenage boy and not a great pen pal. And it was hard, being in London. Each time I'd try to write I'd have to think about this place and…it wasn't always easy. But she still lives in the same house she always did.'

'And even though you kept up your spoken Italian you lost the confidence to write.'

They both stopped walking and her throat felt as though it was closing over. She shouldn't know that. She looked to Nico for confirmation.

He squeezed her hand. 'Yes, exactly.'

She was suddenly conscious that his hand was still wrapped around hers. Warm, reassuring. The really strange thing was that it didn't feel unusual. Did they usually hold hands? She understood they were close friends, but what sort of friendship involved walking around holding hands and nothing more? Not a purely platonic one.

They walked past a small market in the square, a fraction of the size of the one they had visited in Bari, with one butcher, two fishmongers and three vegetable stalls.

'The church looks different because it was built by the Byzantines,' he said.

'Yes, but the rest was built by the Venetians. The whole region is very rich in history. The Greeks, Romans, even the Normans. So many civilisations have stamped their mark on this place.' She stopped, heart in her throat. She'd done it again. California Freya couldn't have pointed to Puglia on a map, but London Freya knew its history.

More information had popped into her head from nowhere. *No, it came from somewhere. It came from you. You knew all of this stuff.*

Nico no longer seemed to notice; his eyes were drawn to one of the small streets leading away from the square.

Anna was sitting outside waiting for them. The woman squinted when she saw Nico, needing to reconcile the ten-year-old she'd known with the gorgeous grown man walking towards her, but Nico knew immediately.

'Anna!'

They hugged and she held his cheeks to examine him, then hugged him again.

Freya stood back and watched but was soon drawn into an embrace as well.

'*Bella* Freya! Welcome!'

They were ushered into the house, through to the kitchen. Delicious smells emanated from a steaming pot on the stove.

Colourful cast iron pots—a food stylist's dream—hung from the walls. It was a casual, relaxed kitchen that looked lived-in and loved. For generations.

Freya didn't know much Italian but could pick up a few words. Nico translated now and then, but she didn't need to know every word to understand what the conversation was about. They talked about his life in London, his restaurants. Once they'd finished eating and were mopping their bowls with the fresh bread, the conversation changed to his parents. Nico brushed away some tears but Anna let hers flow freely.

'She's telling me how much she loved them both, how she still misses them. What a tragedy it was.'

Freya didn't need a translation; everything was clear from Anna's tears.

Anna then picked up some framed photographs and showed them both. Nico explained that they were of her children and grandchildren.

After a while the topic of conversation changed again, but this time Nico made no effort to translate and he looked uneasy.

Freya could tell by the way Anna kept looking from her to Nico and back again that they were talking about her. Nico said something and Anna let out a sharp laugh and shook her head vigorously.

'What's going on?' Freya muttered to Nico.

'It doesn't matter.' He shook his head and Anna laughed again.

It clearly did matter. Nico's face was burning.

Anna grabbed Freya's hand and said, '*Bella, Bella.*' Followed by some more Italian that was far beyond Freya's progress on her language app.

She's asked him about our relationship.

With much of her memory missing, Freya was getting very proficient at piecing things together with context clues alone. By the way Nico's face was now the colour of one of the jars of homemade tomato sauce on Anna's shelf, Freya knew Anna had asked something personal.

She's asking about our relationship and he's blushing.

But what did it mean? She wanted to yell. What was he saying and what was the truth?

What are we to one another?

Freya had chosen a beautiful hotel for them in Monopoli. It was perched on one of the limestone cliffs and their adjoining rooms overlooked the turquoise waters. She knocked on the door between their rooms and opened it slowly.

'Have you seen this view?' She opened her arms. 'We can actually smell the ocean.'

He could feel her excitement in his chest. 'You chose this place.'

'I have good taste.' She grinned.

'You do,' he said but with a serious tone. It was wonderful to see her confidence returning. She might be remembering the past in strange and random glimpses, but the main thing that had changed about her since arriving in Italy was that she was less timid, less hesitant.

Less worried. Much of her anxiety and fear seemed to have been left behind in London. Her true personality was beginning to shine and that was better than any memories returning.

'Anyway,' she said, ignoring his compliment. 'Do I have time for a swim before dinner? The hotel has a pool.'

'Sure, this is Italy, remember—everyone eats late.'

Freya shot him a wide smile and disappeared back into her room, closing the door behind her.

He wasn't just warm. He was hot. And felt itchy under his skin. A swim seemed like the best idea he'd heard all day.

Except when he arrived at the pool deck fifteen minutes later it was to find Freya lifting a loose dress over her head to reveal a red bikini. The fabric stretched over her body like it had been woven around her curves. The swimsuit wasn't immodest, but certainly not substantial enough to be providing much support. Not that she needed that. Freya's body was perfectly stunning. In or out of clothes.

Or red string bikinis.

As soon as her face appeared out of the dress, she caught him looking at her.

Like a thief.

'Hey,' he said quickly. 'A swim sounded like a good idea. I hope you don't mind me joining you?'

'I, um, no. Of course not.'

He dropped his towel on the lounger next to hers and took his T-shirt off as fast as he could. Then as quickly as he decently could he jumped into the pool before she could see exactly how much he liked the red bikini. The water was refreshing after the long day and the drive, but was not quite cold enough to dull the throbbing in his veins he had each time he looked at Freya.

An ice bath wouldn't have been enough.

She swam some lazy laps, not making eye contact with him, and left the water first. The water dripping from her bikini-clad body reminded him of the morning after *that* night. He had to remain in the pool a while longer, thinking about the least sexy things he could imagine before he could safely climb out. He was conscious his wet shorts would cling to his body and hide very little.

He dipped his head below the surface, and when he emerged, he faced away from her. He gave her a few minutes to dry off and when he looked in her direction again, she was wearing the white cotton dress and was stretched out on the lounger.

He sighed with relief and pulled himself out of the pool, not exactly cooled off but certainly cooler than he'd been thirty minutes ago.

You've had an emotional day, that's all.

He'd visited Tregua and Anna and talked about his parents with someone who had known and loved them both. No wonder he wasn't able to control himself; he'd had a very stressful day.

He wrapped a towel around his waist and perched on the lounger next to Freya's.

'What were you and Anna talking about?' she asked.

'I'm sorry I couldn't translate everything.'

'There's no need to apologise—it was *your* visit. I'm honoured you took me with you.'

She sounded so honest and earnest and of course he'd taken her with him. There was no one else in the world he'd wanted to take with him on this trip, and particularly on that visit.

He was so churned up inside. So many memories were rising back into his conscious thoughts. Some things he'd purposely tried to forget because it was so much easier to look forward and not back. Many other memories had been unintended casualties of suppressing the bad memories. And so many things he'd simply forgotten. Today they'd all come up to hit him in the face.

'We talked about her family. She has four kids, and they have kids of their own. Most still live in Tregua or here in Monopoli.'

'Wonderful.'

It was. It made him wonder, not for the first time that day, what his life would have been like if his father hadn't died, if the three of them had stayed in Puglia. What would he have become? Would he have joined his father on the fishing boats or his mother in the kitchen? Or done something else entirely?

One thing was certain: he never would have met Freya. Either way, a whole lot of hurt would have been avoided if he'd been able to act faster on the day his father died.

Everyone's lives would've been different.

'She suggested I go down to see the restaurant.'

'Will you?'

'I know I should but…'

'It would be hard.'

For an instant he saw her again, the woman who understood him without him having to explain himself. His Freya.

She's not yours.

He had to keep reminding himself. They were not together and never could be. Even if he could see the outline of the red bikini through the white dress, now transparent from the water. Even then.

Freya looked at him with a wry smile. 'She asked you if we are together, didn't she?'

Caught again.

'Not exactly.'

'Then what exactly?'

'She asked us *why* we're not together. Totally different thing.'

Freya raised a single, perfect eyebrow.

'Why *did* we never get together?'

His rib cage tightened around his heart and lungs. Sitting next to her now, with her outrageously sexy bikini clearly visible through her wet white dress, he honestly had no idea.

They should be up in his room, lying together on his bed, with him peeling her bikini off with his teeth, her long fingers edging down his shorts…

Because you messed it all up. That's why you're not together and never will be.

'We're friends, colleagues.'

She nodded as if she also knew that was the official reason. But not the real reason.

'Are you in love with someone else?' she asked.

Her question nearly made his heart stop beating.

'Someone else?' he choked.

She crinkled up her face. 'Yes.'

Was he in love with someone else?

How could he have been when for as long as he could remember it had only been her? Stolen glances, guilty longings. Repressed desires. He knew they could never be together. There was too much between them and too much at stake, but that didn't mean that he didn't wonder.

'No. Freya, it's like I said. We're good friends and colleagues. We had—have—something really good. We never wanted to mess up the good thing we had going, I guess.'

She nodded again, but it wasn't the nod of someone who agreed but of someone who knew they weren't being told everything.

'I'd better get ready for dinner,' he said and stood. 'See you around seven?'

'Yes.' She smiled up at him and his stupid heart broke all over again.

He walked away but as he got to the corner he glanced back. She was still sitting on the lounger, her knees tucked up and her arms hugging her legs. Her face was resting on her knees.

He couldn't tell her what had happened, but he couldn't keep not telling her.

We never wanted to mess up the good thing we had going.

Until the night before the accident, when they had.

The night before her thirtieth birthday. It was only a few weeks ago but he'd lived a lifetime since then.

Nico had planned a surprise party for Freya at the restaurant for the following night, the night of her birthday. They were closing the place for the evening. He and the rest of the team wanted to show her how much she meant to them. Lately she'd seemed restless and he'd wanted to lift her spirits. He was excited, but anxious that she'd find out about the party and it wouldn't be a surprise. He'd been excited about Italy, about the coming weeks and months, but also sensed somehow that Freya was worried about something. He couldn't put his finger on why she was unsettled and she wouldn't say. He put it down to the fact that significant birthdays often stir up thoughts of change within people.

That night he'd arrived home around nine, after he'd assured himself the dinner service was going smoothly. Freya was home before him and waiting for him in the living room. She was wearing her favourite boots, but with a gorgeous pink silky dress he hadn't seen before. The neckline dipped lower than she usually wore it, and he averted his eyes to the spread on the coffee table next to the sofa. There were wineglasses and a plate of cheeses and crackers, though he didn't want to eat anything after she told him her news.

She was leaving.

'Back to California?'

'I just need a change.'

'From what?

She told him she'd been thinking about her future as a major birthday approached, just as he'd thought.

'I want more.'

'What could be more than this? The life we have here, the business we've been building?'

'I love my job. I love my life here, but I need more.'

More. That word again.

'A pay rise? Name your price.'

She smiled and shook her head. 'It's not about that.'

She clenched and unclenched her hands and then said softly, 'I need to know what I will mean to you in the future.'

It felt as though something had reached up from inside him and squeezed his gut. Nervous, sickening.

The question he had always been most afraid she'd ask.

She wasn't talking about another trip or writing another book. She wasn't even talking about opening another restaurant.

She was talking about something far, far bigger. It was a conversation he'd occasionally think about, and then shut down that thought. Because the idea of what she was talking about was scary enough but the reality? He'd be risking everything.

'I'm about to be thirty, and one day—I'm not saying it has to be tomorrow—but one day I'd like to get married and have a family.'

He adored Freya. She was the most fun, happiest, most integral part of his life. And if things had been different, if *he* had been different, then he may have already told her all this and they would already be embarking on the journey she was talking about: love, romance, a family.

Some days it took every ounce of his self-control not to reach out to her.

Not to tell her how much he wanted her.

He'd made it through the past few years with much selective blindness…and many, many cold showers and long runs.

He loved Freya, but it was precisely because he thought so much of her that they couldn't be together. Not romantically. She was his best friend.

'Do you ever think about us?' she whispered.

Constantly, consistently and mostly chastely. Because when I think of more it all becomes too confusing.

'Of course I do.'

Her eyes opened wide. 'And?'

'And we work together. And live together. And you're my best friend.'

'I know, and it's wonderful and I'm probably crazy to put it all on the line, but I want more, Nico. With you. And I want to know if you think there's even a chance that you might too.'

'Of course I do.' Despite trying otherwise, his words were full of pain. He wanted her, but he couldn't have her. What if he lost her? What if something happened to her? What if he hurt her too?

'You do?' Her beautiful forehead creased. 'You don't sound particularly happy about it.'

'Freya, you're my person. I adore you. Of course I think about you. About us.'

'But?'

'I'm your boss.' That was the truth, but just the start of what lay between them.

'I'll quit.'

He laughed. 'Freya, I'm not going to let you give up your career for me.'

Even if she didn't work for him, there were still so many reasons why changing the nature of their relationship was a bad idea.

He drew a deep breath and turned to face her properly and explain that a romantic relationship would only lead to heartache. Or worse.

But somehow when he turned, the cushion next to him sunk and his hand brushed against hers in the dip between them. They'd touched before. They'd hugged many times. And each time he'd been prepared. Or they hadn't been in the middle of a conversation like this and he'd been able to quell the sparks and bury the desire back away where it belonged.

But this time he simply hadn't been able to.

He dragged his fingertips across her knuckles. The most sensitive part of his hand brushed against the least sensitive of hers. A wave of heat whispered through him, but her eyes widened, irises open. Alert.

Seeing her reaction, his eyes widened as well. Thoughts opened, clicked into place, like a row of doors all unlocking at once.

He couldn't lose her! He couldn't let her go. He couldn't live without her. And not because she was his friend, not because she was his most trusted colleague, but because he didn't want to go a day without seeing her first thing in the morning.

And his entire body began to shake at the thought of going to bed each night for the rest of his life without the comfort of knowing she was asleep under the same roof as him.

He closed his eyes and leaned towards her. Their noses brushed, their breath mingled but still he held back from the line he was moving towards. The line he knew he shouldn't cross.

Freya's breathing quickened and his heart beat in his throat. He didn't want her to go but couldn't give her what she was asking.

Yet how could he pull himself away?

He rested his unopened mouth against hers, breathed in the same air, pausing on the edge. Even when he ran a hand up her smooth arm, he didn't open his mouth and neither did she.

He felt her sigh, heard her whimper. Only then did he finally open his mouth, causing her to open hers, sliding into one another, coming together.

And then she kissed him and he was lost.

And then everything went wrong.

Their evening in Monopoli followed the same pattern as the night before: drinks and nibbles at a bar, followed by dinner at a nearby restaurant where Nico ordered a variety of dishes and they both tried all of them. It was decadent and delicious and once again she was jealous of herself and the life she'd been living for the past few years. It seemed so wonderful that sometimes she almost wanted to laugh out loud.

But it wasn't all perfect. Right now, they were in a picture-perfect restaurant, enjoying a spread of mouth-watering food, attention from the staff. They could talk about the food and the view but not about what was really worrying her.

Nico could give her all the excuses he wanted to—*We're good friends, We don't want to ruin a good thing*—but she'd seen the way he looked at her. She'd seen his reaction to her bikini earlier, she'd noticed the look on his face when he thought she wasn't looking and she knew there was something he wasn't telling her.

She wanted to scream at him to tell her, but then she remembered the promise she'd asked him and her mother to make: don't tell me about past lovers, I don't want to know.

But she hadn't meant *him*.

Or had she?

What if he did tell her yes, they'd been lovers? Yes, they had slept together. How would she process that? Particularly when every time she saw him, she wanted to touch him, reach for him, taste him.

This afternoon, by the pool, she'd almost had to look away as he climbed out of the pool. His chest was broad, flat and bronzed. Slick with the water from the pool, glistening in the setting sun. As chiselled as his jaw, as well defined as his cheekbones. The man was all smooth surfaces, sharp lines and soft shadows. She salivated, and not because of the magnificent desserts laid out on the table before them, but because of the man across from her, licking his lips and half closing his eyes as he tasted them.

Besides, did it matter if they had been lovers if she couldn't remember? Wouldn't it be better to create some new memories, ones that were not lost?

Freya decided to try a little experiment with the *limoncello* semifreddo. She heaped her fork inelegantly with a too-big serving and made sure it missed her mouth. She licked most of it away but was confident she'd left a smudge just next to her lips.

She continued the conversation without missing a beat, but Nico's attention began to drift and he was staring at the food she'd left on her face.

'You, um, you've got some cream on your face.'

'Oh, embarrassing,' she said and used her napkin to wipe the right side of her lips. 'Better?'

'No, it's on the left.'

She wiped the left-hand side of her face but deliberately missed the food.

'Now?' she asked, feigning confusion.

'No, it's...' He waved to her face and again she attempted to wipe it away, deliberately missing again.

Nico leaned forward. She closed her eyes and moved in. She inhaled as deeply as she could and as she felt his thumb brush against the delicate skin next to her lips she opened her eyes, meeting his gaze in a flash. His pupils widened and he inhaled sharply. His brown versus her blue, locked for a moment in a deep, entangled gaze. With a quick movement he wiped her mouth clean and sat back, as though he'd been scalded.

'Thanks,' he murmured.

Her heart was racing.

He looked at his plate and pushed his food around for a few minutes.

What was wrong with this man?

This wasn't how platonic friends behaved, was it? Accelerating heart rates, shortness of breath, dilating pupils?

No. It wasn't.

Their friendship might be platonic on his side, but it wasn't on hers. If there were reasons they weren't together, she didn't remember them. And what if her memory never came back?

She couldn't wait around to find out. So what if London Freya was too scared to take their relationship to the next level? This Freya, Italy Freya, had only just survived a life-threatening accident.

Italy Freya knew how precious life was, how precious memories were. Italy Freya wasn't worried about preserving a friendship she couldn't remember, or a job she didn't even know how to do. Italy Freya only knew one thing for sure: that when she looked into the chocolate brown eyes of the beautiful man across the table from her, her insides turned molten, just like her heart.

Their hotel was a short walk along the wall of the old fort, by the sea. On their walk back, she stopped and pointed across the bay to the twinkling lights beyond.

'It's gorgeous. Thank you for letting me come here with you.'

Nico stopped walking too. Freya took a deep breath, turned and stepped up to him, holding his gaze in hers. He looked down at her, eyes full of confusion, but the unmistakable heaviness of longing.

'What? What is it?' he asked.

At this moment, overlooking the Adriatic, there was only him. There was no friendship that she remembered, no career she felt she needed to protect. Only Nico. The only memory that mattered was of him sitting by the pool, his bare chest glistening with drops of water in the sunlight. Of him looking at her longingly when he thought she wasn't noticing. Of him brushing her lips when she had cream on them.

She took his hand in hers. He looked down but didn't snatch his away. That was a good sign. She squeezed. He squeezed back and an ache of longing spread through her body.

She mustered every seduction tool she had and stepped closer. Only a breath separated their bodies, so close she could feel the heat emanating from him. Freya slipped her tongue oh so briefly over her bottom lip and was rewarded by his pupils expanding to the edges of his irises.

Why was he fighting this? It was clear to everyone in a ten-mile radius that they were attracted to one another. The magnetism was probably throwing out all the nearby compasses.

Usually by this point the guy had taken all the hints she'd laid down, but Nico was unbreakable. Stoic even. The muscles in his jaw tightened and he pursed his lips together.

'Look, we're friends, right?' she said.

'The best.'

'Then please tell me something honestly.'

He nodded slightly, as though in agreement, though hardly happy at the prospect.

'Are you attracted to me?'

He coughed. 'What kind of question is that?'

'A real one. An honest one. Because I'm attracted to you. I have been since the first time I laid eyes on you and I just don't understand.'

He cleared his throat again. 'What don't you understand?'

'I don't understand how I did this for five years! How we were next to one another every day and we never kissed.' *Because kissing you is all I can think about.*

Nico closed his eyes tight, as though blocking something out. As though he was in pain.

'We never came close? Never touched one another?'

'Freya, please.'

She felt his frustration in her gut but it only propelled her forward. She slid her palm up his forearm, pushing the hair against its natural direction. She cupped his elbow in her hand.

'We never did this?'

He winced but she was no longer expecting an answer. At least not a truthful one.

'What about this?'

Her hand continued its journey up his hard, muscular arm and her fingers slipped under the hem of his shirt sleeve, to the soft skin beneath it. It was like the finest velvet beneath her fingertips and she stroked her fingertips in small circles, loving the sensation on her skin, as well as the clear frustration creasing his brow.

'Because it seems like such a shame. Such a waste,' she whispered.

He tensed further beneath her touch, but didn't step back or even pull away. His breathing was as ragged as hers.

Freya slid her hand across his arm and to his chest, where it came to rest at the neckline of his shirt. Her fingers were safely resting on the linen fabric, but her thumb brushed ever so lightly against the sensitive skin just below his throat.

Nico let out one last grunt of frustration and the next thing she knew he'd pressed his lips to hers. No ceremony, no hesitation—his mouth was open and his tongue was seeking out hers. She opened her mouth and her arms and met him with the same fervour. Rushed, hot, insatiable. Desperate. Like he needed her to breathe.

He held her in his arms, pulled her to him, slid one hand expertly up her neck, into her hair and tilted her head just perfectly so as to give his lips maximum coverage of hers.

Everything started to fall around her—her knees, her inhibitions, the world—but he held her close and tight, even as she felt his body shake against hers.

His kisses became shorter, his breath rough.

She pulled back, panting, head spinning. 'I guess that's my answer.'

Nico stepped back, the realisation of what he'd just done hitting him again and again. She could see from the look on his face he'd done the very thing he'd been fighting against. The very thing he'd clearly vowed not to do.

'I'm sorry.'

She held up her hand. 'Uh, you have nothing to be sorry about. I'm the one who unleashed that.'

That.

Uncontrolled, runaway passion.

It was no wonder he'd tried to keep that in its box. Desire like that had a power all its own.

And then she knew.

She may not have remembered, but she *knew*.

He had kissed her before.

Those were not the actions of a couple doing it for the first time. They were the movements of a couple who had been trying not to do that for an even longer time. He was not kissing like a man who had never once thought about kissing her.

She took his hand and silently started to walk the short distance to the hotel, body still vibrating, blood thumping, thoughts swimming in one, single direction. Directly towards Nico's bed.

His hand was loose in hers; she was conscious she was practically dragging him along with her. But she didn't care. There was a doorway up ahead and she was going to pull them through it before it closed.

The street outside the hotel was deserted. She paused at the entrance.

'Come to my room.'

'Freya, I can't.'

'Why not?'

'Because it's too complicated.' He screwed up his eyes, closing them to her and all the possibilities that were so clear to her.

'Maybe it was once, but I'm not that Freya anymore. I know that life can change in an instant. I know how precious it is and how you have to live every moment.'

'And that's exactly why. Because life is precious and I don't want to ruin it.'

'I'm not scared of ruining a friendship I can't remember.'

He groaned. 'It's more than that.'

'Why? What is it? I know there's something you're not telling me.'

He took both her hands in his and drew a deep breath. Her heart swelled at his earnestness, at the way his eyes softened at the edges. 'I don't want to hurt you,' he said.

That was not what she was expecting him to say. 'I don't want to hurt you either. But I don't see how sleeping with me will hurt either of us.'

'Because it *will*.'

Not the way I do it, she almost said, but didn't think this brand of humour would be welcome when Nico was clearly struggling with something.

'But why?'

'Because it already has. I can't do relationships.'

She wanted to laugh, but the look in his eyes stopped her. He didn't 'do' relationships? What did that mean? What kind of clichéd line was that from a man who was anything but? His glare warned her otherwise. Whatever his reasons were, London Freya, as his best friend, clearly understood them. This Freya was suddenly on uncertain, even dangerous ground.

If he didn't do relationships, then why had he kissed her before? Not just now, but the other time, that time her body remembered but her brain steadfastly refused to acknowledge.

She opened her mouth to confront him with her suspicions but stopped mid-breath. She had asked him not to tell her about past boyfriends. They'd sat with her mother at their kitchen table and she had made him promise not to tell her about her past lovers.

I need to remember that sort of thing myself.

Besides, they were not a couple. Everyone had been clear on that topic and she didn't get the feeling that Nico would lie about something like that. Or that everyone else would too.

If they had kissed before, if they had slept together, then they had also broken up.

And she wasn't sure she wanted to hear about *that*. It was enough to still be getting her head around Jane and Lachlan; she didn't want to know that Nico had also dumped her. She wanted to take him to her room and forget that London Freya had ever existed. Now it was just them. The two of them, this night.

But she didn't make a move.

She could barely make sense of her thoughts when Nico said, 'Good night.'

'Yes, good night.'

He stepped towards the doors. When she didn't follow, he turned.

'You go ahead. I just need a moment.'

He looked up and down the street, as if assessing whether it was wise.

'I'll be fine. Go!'

He lingered for a moment, clearly unhappy about it, but the street was quiet, the town more so. She needed air. The thought of going up to her room, with Nico's room right next door, was a little too stifling.

Freya walked down to the corner and the wall overlooking the water. She breathed in the smell of the sea, the salt and the night air.

There was something familiar about the smell that she couldn't quite place. Smell and taste were often so evocative. Jane's perfume, her mother's fabric conditioner, her grandmother's house. All familiar smells guaranteed to bring memories to the surface.

And this smell.

She sniffed her jacket.

No. Not the sea, but Nico. The smell was Nico on her. His lips, his skin, just the merest of scents left behind on her.

She breathed in it again, hoping for all the answers to come, but they didn't.

Stupid, stupid brain. Stupid accident.

What on earth did 'I can't do relationships' mean?

Because it already has.

Something hit her—not a memory, but a realisation.

Because it already has.

He'd been talking about them. He meant that he'd hurt her in the past and he didn't want to do so again. He had broken up with her. No wonder he didn't want to tell her everything. Suddenly everything was so much more complicated than it had been ten minutes ago.

Hours later, asleep in bed, a sound woke Freya. Deep, pained, primal.

Was it inside? Outside? An animal. What animals were there in Puglia that made such a sound?

Freya sat up and looked around the room, her eyes adjusting to the light. She heard it again. A low moan. Someone in pain. And it wasn't coming from outside, but from next door. Nico's room. She swung her legs off the side of the bed and stepped onto the cool marble floor. Could she just barge in?

She turned on her bedside light and waited. Then she heard it again.

'Mama. Mama.'

Deciding there was something very wrong, she pushed open the door to his adjoining room, grateful he hadn't been so angry with her about the kiss as to lock it.

'Nico, Nico. Are you okay?'

Just enough light was creeping into his room from hers to allow her to make out him in his bed, tossing from one side to the other.

'Mama?' This time it was a question and it broke her heart into pieces.

'Nico, sweetheart, you need to wake up.' She had no idea where the 'sweetheart' part had come from but it seemed to do the trick. He woke with a gasp and a grunt.

'Nico, it's just me. Freya. Are you okay?'

He sat up abruptly, grabbed at his bed for something that wasn't there, then finally focused on her.

'I'm sorry, I didn't mean to wake you. Except yes, I guess I did. You sounded so distressed,' she said.

Recognition, realisation crept over his face and he fell back onto his pillows and groaned again. This was a different groan, though, laced with embarrassment and frustration.

Freya looked around the room, picked up an empty water glass and filled it in the bathroom sink. She handed it to Nico, who eyed her and the glass sceptically before sitting up again and accepting it.

He was shirtless and wearing goodness knows what under the sheet. She was suddenly conscious of the thin, strappy singlet and shorts she had on.

'I'm sorry I woke you,' he said.

'I'm sorry about whatever was happening to you in that dream.'

'No, I'm sorry.'

'Don't be silly. I was looking for an excuse to get into your room. You know that.' She smiled, hoping he appreciated the joke.

He smiled and she relaxed a little. They would be okay.

'The joke's on me, I guess.'

He patted the edge of his bed and she sat at the foot. She resisted the desire to sit at waist level and slide her arms around him. Climb on top of him.

'What was your dream about?'

'The same as usual.'

'Which is?'

'My mother…my father.'

'Oh.'

'It's strange being here in ways I hadn't anticipated. I've dreamed about them every night. Sometimes they're happy dreams—we're sitting at our kitchen table or playing with our dog or at the beach.'

'I'm guessing this one wasn't one of those.'

'No. It was my mother. It was the day she died.'

'Oh, Nico.' Freya wanted to hug him but settled for reaching out to the closest body part, his lower leg, and rested her hand on it.

'I don't know what's wrong with me.'

'Nothing's wrong with you! It's completely normal to be feeling like this being back here. I've been doing lots of reading about memory, funnily enough. Everything I've read suggests going back to places that were meaningful is likely to bring things to the surface. Places, smells, people all act as triggers. Coming here may not have been doing much for my memory loss, but it's stirring up all sorts of things in you. It's understandable.'

He shook his head. 'I knew bringing you here was a bad idea.'

'Nonsense. I *have* been remembering things, here and there. You know that.'

And everything I've remembered relates to you.

'My memory will come in time.' And because it was dark and because he'd already shared things with her she said, 'To be honest, I'm starting wonder if I want my memories back.'

'Why?' Nico sat straighter, pulled his legs and the sheets around him, but at the same time leaned forward.

I'm scared to know what happened between us.

'I'm scared about what I've forgotten. I'm worried that I must have blocked them for some reason.' *I'm worried you broke my heart and that's the thing my brain doesn't want to remember.*

He dropped his head. 'No, I've told you. You were happy. You were well. You were not distressed.'

And yet he'd hurt her. And something *had* happened between them. Her brain might not have remembered but her body did.

'You said I was thinking of my next steps on my birthday. What did you mean?'

'Ah. You weren't unhappy. I promise. You were thinking about moving back to California.'

'I was?'

'I didn't want you to. I *don't* want you to.'

And yet?

'You said it was because you were turning thirty. Thinking about your next steps, whether they would be in London. Or the States. Or somewhere else.'

'Did I have something lined up?'

'I don't think so, no, but Freya, you were never short of offers. You'd get one or two a week from people trying to poach you.'

'I did?'

He laughed. 'You did. More than anything, I truly hope you remember how great you are at your job.'

Nico leaned forward further and Freya realised she had as well. His knees and a white sheet were all that separated them. His gaze dropped and she saw it land on her pyjama singlet, which left very little to the imagination. She held her breath.

A second later, Nico realised where he was and what he was looking at and shuffled back on the bed. 'I'm sorry again for waking you.'

She shook her head. 'Don't mention it. Are you alright now?'

'I'm fine,' he said, though she wasn't sure she believed him.

CHAPTER SEVEN

NICO STRUGGLED TO get back to sleep after his midnight talk with Freya.

He lay awake, staring at the ceiling. The slowly turning fan was not enough to hypnotise him back to sleep. When the sunlight began to creep in around the shutters he gave up, got up and showered. His mind was a tangle of the dream that had woken him and Freya, barely clothed, sitting at the end of his bed, resting her hand gently on his leg but sending sparks all through his body.

And of course, the kiss. The kiss he'd been helpless to avoid and unable to stop. The kiss that had excited him and terrified him in equal measure.

She would remember eventually. Snippets of her memories had been returning to her all day. About Tregua. About his home.

Most worrying of all, even if she'd forgotten the details of their relationship, she hadn't forgotten the one thing he really needed her to: her attraction to him.

He had to tell her.

Tell her what? You made love and then you crashed the car?

The voice in his head scolding him he should have told her already was getting louder and louder. It was only just overruled by the fact she had told him she didn't want to hear about her ex-lovers, that she needed to remember things like that on her own.

But when did protecting her become lying?

Freya's room was still quiet by the time he'd dressed. The only firm plans for the day were for later in the morning. He slipped a note under her door and then set off alone.

The early-morning streets were already bustling with locals going about their day and the market was already in full swing, but he set off in the other direction, away from the sea, away from the centre of the old town. Searching for something though he wasn't sure what.

Freya was exactly right about his dream. It was understandable he'd been flooded with memories of his parents since he'd arrived back in Puglia. It had literally been one of the aims of the trip: to remember the food from his childhood. He'd anticipated the seafood, the orecchiette and the *panzerotto*, but he hadn't anticipated dreaming about being in his mother's hospital room as she passed away. Or what returning to the place where he'd watched his father drown would do to his already shaky equilibrium.

This was the reason he'd avoided returning here for so long. While he'd been to other parts of Italy, he seemed to know on some level that coming back to Puglia, and Tregua in particular, would be difficult.

It was Freya who had gently encouraged the trip, suggesting every now and then that it would be good for him. He'd thought she meant that it would be a good business opportunity, a good series and book to write, but he now wondered if she'd had something deeper in mind.

It was only with her support and the knowledge that she'd be with him every step of the way that he'd agreed to the trip. But, of course, since then everything had changed. He was now looking after Freya and dealing with the guilt of that accident.

No wonder he was also being tortured with nightmares from his past. Being in his mother's hospital room as she struggled for breath, standing alone by the harbour, frozen to the spot as the boat sunk. Unable to yell.

He shook himself back to the present. He had to focus on why he was here in the first place. It wasn't to worry incessantly about Freya, and it certainly wasn't to kiss her. It also wasn't to be sad about his parents; he had come here to *work*. To research his next book. His next series. To decide what he was going to write about and what recipes of Puglia he would showcase.

At the thought of food, even despite the churning in his gut, his stomach predictably rumbled. Freya had researched a range of places she wanted them to try, but he wasn't with Freya. He was alone.

Nico looked through the window of a nearby cafe. It looked established, not glitzy or polished, but importantly it smelt fantastic. And he needed coffee. He wandered in and caught the eye of the elderly man behind the counter. Nico lifted his chin and the man nodded his own head towards a nearby table.

'*Caffè?*' he asked.

'*Si. Espresso. Per favore.*'

The man approached him with a perfectly made espresso with a thick crema on the surface.

'Your espresso,' the man said. 'Would you like something to eat?'

Nico did and asked to try a *pasticciotto*, a pastry filled with ricotta and custard.

When the man returned with the pastry he said, 'You're Niccolò Rossetti, aren't you?'

Nico was accustomed to being recognised in London, but hadn't expected to be recognised here.

'Do I know you?' Nico asked.

The man laughed. 'No, I know your show and your books. You're famous.'

'But not here, surely?'

'Why not? You are from Puglia.'

It took Nico a moment to let that sink in.

'There are not many famous chefs from Puglia. And even fewer from Tregua.'

Nico nodded. Emotions were swelling up inside him. It was strange to think of himself as well-known in the part of the world he had left as a ten-year-old.

'Are you here for a holiday?' the man asked.

'A research trip. My next book is going to be about Puglia. And my family,' he added.

The man nodded. 'That's wonderful. I'm sure your parents would be proud.'

Nico starred at the man, still searching for recognition. 'Did you know them?'

'Oh, no, but I do know why you left. And I remember the accident in which your father perished.'

Nico closed his eyes. He needed to get used to being reminded. He needed to not shut down each time it was mentioned. He felt the man's thick hand on his shoulder.

'I know that they would be proud. We are all proud.'

Nico opened his eyes and smiled at the man, then gestured for him to sit at the table. 'If you have a moment, I'd love to hear about this place.'

The man's face lit up. He introduced himself as Constanzo and he pulled out the nearest chair.

The two men spoke for ages about the business, how long he'd run it, where he got his produce. Nico learned that Constanzo's cousin owned the bakery that made the pastries, that business was slower in the down season but that they got a decent tourist trade in high season.

The whole encounter was so unexpected and pleasant and distracted Nico from his other concerns momentarily, until he realised he needed to leave.

'Do you mind if we stay in touch? We will be coming back in a few months to film and it would be great to see you again.'

'Of course! And next time bring *Bella* Freya.'

Nico froze.

The man knew Freya. Of course people knew her. She was nearly as famous as him. He told his audience about the dishes she loved the most, talked about her incessantly. She was the person behind his photos and behind the camera.

The person behind his success.

But if Freya returned to the States, the next time he travelled to Puglia he would be alone. Suddenly the delicious coffee and pastries were like lead in his stomach.

Nico said goodbye to Constanzo and strolled back through the streets. The sun was getting higher in the sky and he knew that he should get back to the hotel, but his feet dragged. His head ached and his limbs were like stone. Between the nightmare and everything else he hadn't managed to sleep much the night before. Every time he would come close to sleep his mind and body would turn back to Freya and the kiss.

Even when he managed to turn his brain to other things his body would have other ideas, and tingling excitement would rush through him. His limbs would ache with longing to hold her in them.

The last time they'd slept together the fallout had been catastrophic. Very nearly tragic. He couldn't let it happen again.

A buzzing sound distracted Freya from kissing Nico. Hooking her legs around his.

The buzzing was persistent. She tried to ignore it, as it felt so good rubbing her body against his. But the buzzing wouldn't stop.

She rolled over and suddenly Nico was gone and all that was left was her alarm. She fumbled around and pressed

Snooze but lay there for a moment, trying to piece together the dream while she could still remember it. The feelings of fear, longing, excitement swirled together, unattached to actual events, but then the events began to come into focus, to slide into order.

She had been talking to Nico, in their living room at home. She told him she was thinking of moving back to California. She'd worn a new pink dress; one she'd purchased for that very conversation. Casual yet seductive. It had had the desired effect because when she'd asked him what she meant to him, he'd kissed her. Again and again. And they had made love. Right there, on the sofa. And then in his room.

Except it wasn't a dream; this had happened. Suddenly it was all there. Her memories. Her past. Maybe not everything but most things. The important things. The most recent things.

The night before her birthday. The night before her accident. Her and Nico. Together.

Freya lay on her back, staring at the fan slowly spinning on the ceiling and doing nothing to cool her down. A thin sweat covered her skin and her heart raced.

She struggled to catch her breath.

Over an orgasm that had happened weeks ago. She shook and panted, even though she was only remembering it.

They had slept together. She'd known from the beginning that there was something between her and Nico and it hadn't all been in her imagination.

Why hadn't he told her? Was he trying to trick her?

No, that didn't fit.

He was so protective, so cautious. Even though he'd been the one to initiate the kiss last night, she hadn't just led him on; she'd practically dragged him into it.

He'd been the one to pull away. He'd been the one to refuse

the invitation to her room. If he wanted to take advantage of her, he could have done so many times over.

Apart from the sex, there was something else he wasn't telling her, something that was buried in her lost memories or maybe something she'd never understood at all.

Her alarm buzzed again and she groaned. They were meant to be visiting an olive oil farm and factory. She needed to get up and dressed but was still out of breath. Her head was still whirling. She tried a few more memories, but only had glimpses of working in the restaurant. Of some of her colleagues. Of some faces and some names. Not everything, but so much more than she'd remembered yesterday. She got out of bed and went to the bathroom. She showered and under the hot steamy stimulation of the water more memories crept back, but still in disjointed fragments. Mostly of Nico.

Wrapped in a towel, she shuffled over to her suitcase and smiled at the clothes she'd packed, recognising them for the first time. These were not the clothes she'd planned on bringing, the ones she'd purchased for the trip, but old ones that had belonged to California Freya. Short denim skirts, tight T-shirts. Clothes she'd worn in Pasadena, but ones that she didn't wear in London.

Freya sat back onto the bed, suddenly more exhausted than ever.

The doctors were right; her memories hadn't all come back at once. She tried to remember helping him write the cookbook or taking the photos, but could only remember Nico. Him sitting next to her in their office, him asking her to taste a soup he'd made or some fresh focaccia. She couldn't remember designing the restaurant or their house, but somehow her memories of Nico and their relationship were coming into focus. How she'd loved him for so long. How she'd been so scared of losing his friendship if she told him how she felt.

How she'd vowed to herself that more than anything it was important that they stay friends.

How he never seemed to catch on to her too-subtle hints. How he'd looked the night he'd opened his third restaurant, more delectable than any dish he'd served, dressed as he was in a crisp new suit. The sound of his laughter one time they'd sat in the Red Crown one night. She stared absent-mindedly out the window as these old memories played across her mind. One leading to another and then another. But like a film she hadn't finished watching, she didn't know the ending.

The memories were all somehow connected to Nico. He was the centre of her world and had been for so long, so it was only natural that now the essential memory of the night they had spent together had come back to her, others did too. She marvelled again at the strangeness and fickleness of the human brain.

Some memories were happy, some sad, but the thing she was most grateful to have slowly returning was the sense of confidence, certainty and grounding that had been missing for the past few weeks. She was good at her job; she was a great photographer. And a vibrant and energetic person. Jane and Lachlan? Those memories were still vague, yet she didn't want to dwell too long on retrieving them. Some things were best left forgotten.

The sound of a text message from Nico asking where she was alerted her to the time. Let him wait, she thought, but at the same time, she needed to see him, to see if he looked different to her than he had last night.

She dried herself off slowly, studied her face in the mirror and marvelled at the sense of familiarity. It wasn't a stranger looking back at her anymore. She knew this person. She knew who she was.

She was Freya McFadden. Photographer. Food stylist and publicist to Niccolò Rossetti.

Most importantly, she finally remembered her plan: if Nico wasn't prepared to give her what she wanted, she would leave London to find a man who was. A man who didn't have the same hang-ups as Nico, someone prepared to give her all the love she deserved.

It was with this newly remembered sense of certainty that she returned to the suitcase to decide what to wear. She moved items around, trying to find just the perfect outfit. Something that showed Nico exactly what he was missing out on. Her fingers brushed over the pink dress.

The dress she'd worn that night. She laughed. Freya of a week ago had known this dress was special, even if she hadn't realised why.

She'd wear it. She had to. If only to see the look on his face.

She slipped it over her head, smoothed it down and looked at herself in the mirror. Freya of a month ago had paired it with stockings, boots and a jacket. But spring in Italy was perfect for wearing it on its own, with its cap sleeves, flattering bias cut and a neckline that was almost indecent. Because she was no longer going to play fair.

Freya drew in a deep breath, closed her eyes and let her new ability to access her memories revisit that night.

The night before her thirtieth birthday.

On her twenty-fifth birthday she'd been living in Pasadena, sacked from a job she hated, feeling as though the world was passing her by. On the eve of her thirtieth, her life was radically different; she had taken herself across the globe, forged a new life for herself, but a similar sense of stasis hung over her.

Her life was great, she loved working with Nico but something had changed in the past few months.

She'd realised she was in love with him.

Of course, any fool probably could have seen that long ago, but she hadn't. She had been so impressed and in awe of him when they'd first met and never imagined having a relationship with him. But as they'd gotten to know one another, become friends, things had changed. Freya had dated in London. She'd had a lot of first dates but never wanted to take things further. No one she'd met had ever quite matched up to Nico.

She had become very good at pushing aside the realisation that she loved Nico. It was too awkward. They were colleagues, flatmates and friends. And it was probably just a silly crush. And her life was great—she had a great job; she travelled the world. Her life was wonderful. Was she really going to give up all that by confessing that she loved him?

Maybe, she thought, as her birthday got closer, maybe she was. It was the eve of her next decade. And she had to do something.

So she'd bought the dress, set the scene, poured the wine and waited for him to arrive home.

She knew he was throwing a surprise party for her the next night. She hadn't let on that she knew but there wasn't much that happened in the restaurant she didn't know about. It was a lovely, thoughtful gesture and she suspected all her London friends would be there.

It would be the perfect time to say goodbye if everything went wrong with Nico. The perfect way to end her time in London.

Not that she wanted to leave, heavens no—she was hopeful that her declaration would have the opposite effect, but she had a plan B lined up just in case. A plane ticket to LAX.

Nico was cautious about relationships. He blamed himself for his parents' deaths but surely they could move past that together. There was so much they had done together in the past few years: opened two restaurants, launched his television career and written several books.

They'd overcome all sorts of obstacles with hard work, tenacity and sheer talent. They could build a romantic relationship too, as long as he felt the same way about her.

Freya had also bought a one-way plane ticket home. It was the superstitious part of her. So she couldn't chicken out at the last minute. She was going to tell him she loved him. Everything.

How she felt. What she wanted. What she needed.

And she was going to tell him that if he didn't feel the same, she had decided to go home to California.

She'd set the scene in their living room as best she could. Some white wine, and a big deep breath. He was sitting next to her, looking at his phone and choosing some music.

Before she could talk herself out of it or think twice, she said, 'Nico, I have to tell you something.'

He was singing away, putting on new music, and didn't turn. 'I know, Adele.'

'No, that's not it.'

'Not Ed Sheeran again? Okay, it is your birthday.'

'No, Nico, we need to talk.'

'Okay, Adele it is.'

He wasn't seeing her; he wasn't listening to her, even now. He never would. He'd never see her that way. He wasn't even listening to her properly now.

She took his phone from him and turned off the music.

'I need a change.'

He narrowed his yes, finally realising she wasn't talking about the music. 'What sort of change?'

'Maybe a change of job. A change of city.'

He tilted his head to one side, as though he didn't believe her. 'Two weeks ago, you told me you had the best job in the world.'

That had been true. They'd been in Cape Cod eating lobster next to the ocean. She had a job she loved and he was her best friend. Was she crazy to throw it all away?

No.

'It is, and I love it here, but I need more.'

'Puglia is coming up.'

'That's not what I mean.'

'Then what are you talking about?'

If she didn't tell him now, then she may never get this close again. She had to tell him how she felt or give up waiting for him.

'I can't keep going on like this.'

'Do you *have* another job?' He leaned forward and she smelt the last breath of his aftershave and the smell of the kitchen at the restaurant. Her body reeled with longing.

She shook her head.

'Then what?'

'I'm about to turn thirty.'

He grinned. 'I know that but…why does that mean you want to quit your job?'

Ordinarily it wouldn't. But when you were hopelessly in love with your boss it made it difficult to get on with your life.

'Because I need to make some decisions about my future.'

'And?'

'And…' Freya inched closer to him on the sofa. 'I need to know what I'm going to be to you in the future.'

Oh, dear. It was out there. There was no going back now. This wasn't quite how she'd imagined saying it; it wasn't poetic or persuasive, but the words rushed out of her in a large breath. She felt a moment of relief before a surge of panic while he processed her words.

'Do you ever think about us?' she whispered.

'Of course I do.'

'And?'

'And we work together. And live together. And you're my best friend.'

'I know, and it's wonderful and I'm probably crazy to put it all on the line, but I want more, Nico. And I want to know if you do too.'

'Of course I do.'

'You do?'

She couldn't breathe. It was so strange. It was probably like being told you'd won the lottery. Disbelief.

'Freya, you are my person. I adore you. Of course I think about you. About us.'

Then he stopped talking.

'But?'

'I'm your boss.'

'I'll quit.'

He laughed. 'Freya, I'm not going to let you give up your career for me.'

I'd give up everything for you, she thought, but didn't say it.

Instead, she leaned towards him. Her hand was next to his and then his fingers brushed against hers. His face close, his eyes staring deep into hers, searching.

'I'm crazy about you,' she said.

They held each other's eyes, started falling into one another's gazes. She looked at his lips, subconsciously ran her tongue over her own. She'd waited so long for this moment and couldn't quite believe it might be about to happen.

Their faces were closer than ever and then his lips touched hers gently. Yet he didn't open his mouth and nor did she, waiting, longing, hardly able to breathe.

They held the moment, poised on the precipice. She let her declaration sink in a little further, waited as he steadied his breath, but it didn't steady. Instead it became as ragged as her heartbeat. Freya was light-headed by the time Nico finally began dragging his lips slowly across hers, the friction sending a wave of tiny sparks through her limbs. His lips explored hers as he ran his hand up her arm. Slowly but not hesitantly. They took the time to become accustomed to one another's taste and then without knowing how, her mouth was open and so was his and as the room began to swirl around her she fell back onto the sofa. Nico didn't take his mouth from hers, not for a moment. She ran her tongue slowly over his, exploring but most of all tasting the most sensuous dish they had ever shared.

'You are so beautiful,' he gasped through kisses, and her heart soared.

It was happening! If all your dreams came true, would you actually burst? It felt as though she might; desire and need were gathering and colliding in her in a mix that would have to find release or she would explode.

'You smell so good.' It was all she could manage to say, and a total understatement. He felt good. He felt amazing. His body on top of hers was the most wonderful thing she'd felt in her life and she would die happy, right here.

'You have no idea how many times I've thought about doing this,' he muttered into her neck.

'I think I have a pretty good idea.'

His hands slid under the hem of her dress, over her stockings, higher, and she moaned. She ran her hands over his back and lower, lower to his trousers and onto his bottom. He stilled at that point.

My hand is on my best friend's butt. And it feels as magnificent as it looks.

There was a moment when she feared they had reached the end of the line. The point where he would get off her and tell her it was all a mistake, but then she felt his moan in her neck and his lips on the swell of her breast and she was no longer afraid.

'I have a good idea,' she said.

'You have lots of them.'

'Yeah, but this is one of my best.'

'Does it have anything to do with us getting out of these clothes?'

'Great minds,' she said.

He unzipped her boots and dropped them onto the floor. She lifted his sweater over his head, and the shirt under quickly followed. He worked her stocking down with care and kisses and she did the same with his pants.

'Protection?' she asked.

'Upstairs.'

She groaned. She didn't think she could wait that long. It had been years.

'Later,' he said. 'Let's do this first.'

His fingers and lips explored her folds and knew exactly where to rub and the perfect pressure. The want inside her grew until it was almost overwhelming. She could hardly breathe as he kissed and stroked and caressed and licked and reached into places she hardly knew she had. Her heart pounded in her ears, a roar travelled through her body, his fingers and his mouth flew her into the air then placed her carefully back down to earth again.

'Wow,' she gushed.

'Wow is right.'

'We are such idiots.'

He laughed.

'We could have been doing this for years. Think of all the practice we could have had.'

'Practice? I think we're pretty good at it already.' His kisses trailed across her cheek and to the soft spot below her ear. She leaned her head back and released a moan. His laugh was hot against her neck.

'I don't want to lose you,' she said.

'You won't,' he replied.

Freya was sitting in the hotel lobby when Nico finally returned from his walk. She stood when he walked in and he stopped mid-stride. She was wearing the pink dress. That dress. The one that clung to her hips then swirled around her knees. The one with the neckline that he was helpless to drag his eyes up from. Though he tried his hardest as he walked towards her.

'Good morning, I hope you got back to sleep.'

A sly smile crept over her lips and dread gathered in his stomach again. 'I did. As it happens, I had a good sleep. With some interesting dreams.'

'Good, I'm sorry again that I woke you.'

'How many times have we slept together?' she replied.

Nico looked around. The clerk at the desk lifted his head but looked away when Nico caught his eye.

You knew this moment was coming.

'Can we go somewhere more private?' Nico asked.

'Tell me honestly. And don't even think about lying.'

'I'm not going to lie—I've tried not to lie.'

She let out a snort. 'Just tell me.' She stood with her feet apart and rooted herself to the spot.

Nico leaned in to whisper but in doing he became dangerously close to her. She smelt of roses and a warm shower, and worst of all, he could see straight down her dress to the lacy bra underneath. His traitorous body began to harden.

'It was just the one time.' And it was amazing. *The time that I will remember above all others, until the day I die. If I forgot every other time in my life, it would be alright as long as I remembered that night.* He hoped he could tell her all of that with just the expression in his eyes.

But her hands remained on her hips and she looked at him with one eyebrow raised.

'Okay, more than once, but just that one night.'

She nodded, as if in agreement. She'd remembered and guilt gripped at his stomach, almost making him double over. Her memories were returning. He should have been overjoyed and yet...

'Can we please go somewhere more private and talk?'

She nodded. 'Your room.'

He'd have preferred somewhere less intimate but was not about to argue. Once she'd heard what he was about to tell her she'd never want to be in his room again. Or in his life.

He followed her into the elevator and back to their rooms, trying not to notice the way her bottom looked under the fabric of the dress. Once in his room, he opened the door to the balcony off his room. It was fitting that the Adriatic Sea, the backdrop to all his failures, would bear witness to this conversation.

He didn't deserve her and he couldn't keep her safe.

'Why didn't you tell me or anyone that we were together?'

'Because...'

'*Were* we together?'

'It was new and we hadn't really talked about anything. And that's the truth.'

'But why didn't you tell me?'

'I wanted to, but you said you didn't want to know.' Even as he said it, he wanted to wince.

'I did say that, but I didn't mean *you*.'

'I couldn't tell you—you didn't *know* me. You had no memory of me at all. It would have been too confronting. You needed to remember for yourself.'

Freya stepped back and hugged herself, despite the warmth of the day.

'Later. You could have told me later. You could have told me when I asked about what kind of relationship we had.'

'I've thought about telling you every day, but it was just that one time.'

She rolled her eyes, as well she might. The fact that it was one night didn't make what he had done forgivable.

'The night before my birthday. The night before the accident.'

'Yes.'

'But you *didn't* tell me.'

'I didn't want to hurt you or confuse you. I didn't know what to do. I struggled with this decision every day.' He rubbed his face with his hands. 'I tried to convince you that we were friends, you didn't even believe that. Besides, I didn't see what the point of telling you would be.'

She threw her head back and groaned. 'Because I'd know. I'd understand.'

He shook his head.

She turned from him and looked around the room. 'I'm not saying it was the right thing. Just the least-worst thing,' he said. There were so many things he should have done differently.

'It might have been confronting but it would've been the truth.'

'I'm sorry. Truly. I… I didn't know what to do. Above all else, I was trying to protect you.'

'Protect me from what?'

Now she knew about their night together, he had to tell her everything. Then maybe she'd understand why he'd struggled so much with this secret. That all he'd ever wanted to do was to protect her.

'How much do you remember?' he asked.

'Not everything. But I remember a lot more than I did yesterday, and more every minute. I remember I told you I was thinking of leaving London and I asked you how you felt about me. And we kissed. In our living room.'

'And do you remember what happened after that?' he asked.

He remembered. He thought about it every hour of his life. The sofa, their limbs, knowing there were more comfortable places to be doing it, but also knowing that they had already wasted so much time. Knowing that neither of them wanted to wait a moment longer.

'Do you remember the day of the accident?'

She shook her head. 'Nothing. But Dr Jamal said that memory may never come back.'

Nico dragged his hand over his face again. Her remembering the night they had spent together was not the worst thing. That was not the thing he dreaded telling her.

'Tell me about the accident,' she began. 'I know it wasn't your fault. The police told me that. And the doctors.'

This was where he was meant to fill in the blanks for her. Tell her what had been happening when the lorry had failed to give way and smashed into them. When he had failed to notice and swerve.

'Are you going to tell me or are there more secrets?' she said.

He hated to tell another lie but what choice did he have? 'We were just talking.'

She cocked her head to one side. 'What were we talking about?'

He could lie. Or tell her he didn't remember either. He had been knocked around in the accident too. Nothing like Freya but the shock and grief he'd felt after the accident had been all too real. The sleepless nights he'd been experiencing since. The nightmares. He drew a deep breath. He simply had to do the least-worst thing.

'Your hand was on my knee.'

All the colour left her face. 'Are you saying it was my fault?'

'No! Not at all. I turned to look at you.' *And my heart swelled and I wanted to reach for you. I couldn't take my eyes off you, couldn't believe how lucky I was. And I spoke to you and then the truck hit.*

'I was looking at you and I wasn't paying attention to the

road and I didn't see the truck.' That was the truth. At least most of it.

'But you had right of way.'

'I should've been able to avoid the accident. I should've been able to see it coming.'

Freya looked into the distance.

He wasn't prepared for what she said next.

'So, we were together.'

'Yes, we were in the car.'

'No, I mean we had sex, and then we were together in the car.'

'Yes.'

'So, were we in a relationship? *Are* we in a relationship?'

'No.'

'Did we break up?'

'No, but—'

'It was a one-night stand?'

'No, but Freya—'

'You regret sleeping with me.'

'I wouldn't say it like that.'

'Then how would you say it?'

Her words cut him more perfectly than the finest sous chef could manage. She was so angry. And understandably so.

'We made love, and it was wonderful, but I don't think it should happen again. I don't think we should have a relationship.'

'Why?' Her tone was laced with anger and hurt, but most of all bafflement. 'I was there that night. Parts of my memory might still be returning but that night I remember with perfect clarity. In a million megapixels. The memory of it woke me up this morning.'

Nico grasped the rail on the balcony. He couldn't look at her. He couldn't face himself.

'Because I hurt you. I never wanted to hurt you.'

'Then you shouldn't have slept with me.'

'No, I meant the accident.'

'It wasn't your fault.'

'But it was. I was driving and I couldn't keep you safe. Don't you see?'

'All I see is that you thought you had gotten away with sleeping with me. Amnesia, how convenient.'

'No, Freya, please. I couldn't save my father. I couldn't save my mother. And the moment our relationship changed I almost lost you too.'

'I don't get it. Is it the amnesia, or is this just not right? Help me.'

'You're my best friend and I care for you and I don't want to lose you.'

'But you just don't want the commitment or the responsibility of a full, loving, committed relationship.'

He closed his eyes tight with frustration. That wasn't it at all.

Except…

'I don't know how much you remember about everything, about me, about before.'

She shrugged. The doctors had told them both that her memories would come back in pieces, that even when she thought she remembered her past that there still might be gaps.

'When I was five, I stood on a dock, just down the coast from here, and watched as my father's fishing boat capsized and sank. I watched as he waved for help and I couldn't do anything. By the time help arrived, it was too late. That was my fault.'

'Nico, no.'

'No. Please listen. When he died, they told me I had to look after my mother. I tried and tried and I did my best, but when I was ten, she died of a broken heart. I couldn't stop that either.'

Freya bit her bottom lip and was looking like she was going to argue but mercifully let him say the next thing.

'And a few weeks ago, I slept with my best friend. And it was so wonderful and so distracting, I forgot for a moment that I can't look after people. But I was driving her to her birthday lunch and I was too busy looking at her and marvelling at how beautiful she is that I wasn't paying attention and the next thing I knew we were cleaned up by a lorry and I was standing there watching her being cut lifeless from the car.'

'Nico—'

'And I thought you were dead. I thought I'd killed you. And we didn't know for days if you would ever wake up, and then we waited some more to see if you would. And then when you did you didn't remember me at all and as much as that hurt, it was also a blessing because if you didn't remember me then I couldn't hurt you anymore.'

His mind seemed to leave his body as he said the next words. It was the only way to get them out. It was the next-to-last thing in the world he wanted, yet the last thing was still so much worse. 'You were right all along—it would be best if you went home to California. Trust me, you'll be better off that way.'

CHAPTER EIGHT

FREYA NODDED, STOOD AND smoothed down her dress.

'I assume you still want to go out today?'

'You don't have to come,' he said.

'Of course I will. It's my job. It's why I came here in the first place.'

'Freya, really.'

'No, I came to work and I'll work,' she said calmly, and was shocked to realise it wasn't an act. She was calm.

Or numb with shock.

There was a fine line between the two.

He cared for her, but felt too guilty about his parents' deaths to have a relationship with her. From anyone else that would sound like a bad excuse, but Nico was her friend and she wanted to give him the benefit of the doubt and believe it was more complicated than that. Even though he hadn't told her everything about their relationship, she didn't believe he'd done it maliciously or to manipulate her. She could see the conflict behind his eyes.

She hadn't fully processed what Nico had just told her and wasn't sure if she ever would but an instinct kicked in. Self-preservation. What he'd just told her had been too momentous to process, let alone overcome. Together with all the revelations of the past few hours she needed time, space and energy. She couldn't deal with it all now and she was damned if she was going to fall apart. At least not yet.

They had things to do.

'I'll meet you downstairs in fifteen minutes.'

Nico's jaw dropped and she smiled to herself. He didn't expect she would be up for the trip, but the fact that she was meant he had to be as well.

You can suffer through this with me.

She'd come here for work and they were going to work and she wasn't going to let this or anything stop her from doing so. Whether she was just repressing everything that had happened this morning or in the past few weeks she neither knew nor cared. She was going to do her job.

Freya gathered her things, brushed her hair and prepared to face the day. She picked up the keys for their rental car and considered them. Now it made sense that he wanted her to drive. She was accustomed to driving on the right side of the road, but Nico was a good driver. She remembered that much. And she doubted Dr Jamal would have recommended a recovering amnesiac be in charge of a car. And yet, here she was. She tossed the keys into the air and caught them with a sigh.

Out of Monopoli they drove over rolling green hills, along narrow roads lined with dry stone walls. Freya opened all the windows to the car and let the sweet spring breeze blow over them. Their first spot was an ancient olive grove and the adjacent factory, where they met the proprietors of the boutique specialty olive oil. The olive mush was dried out and then used as a dry fuel and organic fertiliser.

'I always wondered what they did with the rest of the olive bits once they squeeze out the oil and now I know!' she said to Nico, glimpsing a small smile cross his face.

The next stop was at a fortress garden, a medieval garden that had been fortified to protect it from the waves of invading forces that had occupied Puglia over the centuries. Much of the castle was in ruins but the garden was still flourishing and produced all manner of vegetables, flowers and herbs, including very old varietals.

All day she remembered how much she loved her job, how wonderful it was that she got to sightsee and eat for a living.

No other job will be as good as this one.

Maybe not, but she wanted more in her life. She wanted love. Not simply friendship, but passion. And if Nico wasn't the person to give it to her, she needed to move on. It was hard—it would be hard—but it would be more difficult in the long run to stay.

'Are you sure you don't want to drive?' she asked when they returned to the car.

'Are you not feeling well?'

She thought about lying, of forcing him to get into the driver's seat, but realised that wouldn't solve anything.

'I'm fine.'

'You're more comfortable driving on the right than I am.'

She stifled a snort.

Nico didn't want to deal with his guilt. It was so overpowering, so ingrained, and he maybe didn't have the capacity to. For the first time she not only remembered Nico's unwillingness to begin a relationship but understood it. His claim that he couldn't be in a relationship wasn't simply an excuse; it was a deep-seated fear, one that she hadn't been able to shift, not after five years of closeness. And after everything that had happened in the past few weeks, she now understood she had no chance. Nico would only ever be her friend. If she wanted marriage and a family, if she wanted that sort of life, she had to untangle herself from him—both her life and her emotions. Because she couldn't love anyone else while she lived and worked for him.

Somewhere on the road back to Monopoli, with a lump deep in her chest, it was settled.

Freya would return to the States. Maybe she'd try New

York. San Francisco. Chicago. Going back to greater LA seemed like a backward step after the past five years. A new city would be full of new challenges and best of all, no memories.

That's what she needed, a clean slate.

New place, new people.

She wished she could share this thought with Nico but it was far better not to. He was focusing on the map and giving her directions.

She didn't hate him. For the first time all day she understood him. Understood why he hadn't told her everything that had happened between them. He couldn't change who he was and nor could she. It was sad, but acceptance settled down on her.

She would have to leave London.

They had a booking at a nearby trattoria for dinner. Just the one meal as they'd been grazing on food all afternoon. He ordered a glass of local wine and she ordered a cocktail.

They tried each other's drinks and meals as a matter of course, and the friendliness of the gesture hit her for the first time.

We've been sharing drinks and meals for years. It was the best way to try as many dishes as possible. And a surefire way to increase intimacy.

And they did it again now.

Her brain may have accepted that she would be leaving him, but her body had other ideas. Each time their hands brushed, her heart raced and her skin buzzed.

She had to leave London. And Nico.

But not just yet. They still had a few more days.

Across the table from her, Nico ate his meal, his lids low over his dark eyes he was so consumed by enjoyment of the taste. She shivered. What was it like to make love with him?

Her memory of that night was patchy, incomplete. She remembered feeling nervous, exhilarated, but not the look on
his face or the sounds he made. Could she? Could they? Just
one more time? Could they make love one more time when
her memories would not be clouded by amnesia? One more
time to remember him by?

Freya was only half paying attention as Nico discussed
the notes he had taken from the day, the recipes he'd like to
cook, places to return to.

'We should go back the olive oil farm when we come to
shoot,' he said.

'You should,' she corrected. She saw the confusion cross
his face and the moment of realisation.

Life was about remembering the bad things, over and over,
she thought.

'Yes,' he said and coughed.

I don't have to go! she wanted to scream. *You're the one
sending me away!* She rubbed her temple; her head was sore
from stress and tiredness.

If they could make love just one more time, so they both
remembered, she could have an intact memory to take with
her into the future. Being with her one more time might make
him remember all the reasons why he didn't want her to leave.

She lowered her head. No. That was a fantasy. Unhelpful
thinking. Nico had made his mind up. It was a mutual decision; he couldn't give her the type of relationship she wanted,
and she'd decided she needed to leave.

'New York it is,' she muttered.

'New York?'

'Sorry, yes, I was thinking aloud.'

'You're going to New York?'

'It's just an idea. I don't know about LA. It seems like a
backward step. New York would be a bigger adventure.'

He nodded but looked away.

'I had an offer from a place there last year, didn't I?'

Nico's eyes darkened.

'Do you not want me to talk about it? I'll stop, but I'd appreciate your advice.'

'It's fine,' he grunted, though he was clearly anything but.

Pain gripped her temples like a vice. She took a sip of water but it was no match for the agony that was closing in on her. She closed her eyes and put her head in her hands but the pain began to spread. She hadn't had a migraine like this since she'd been in the hospital.

'Are you okay?' She sensed, rather than saw, Nico lean across the table.

'I'm tired. I need to rest.'

'We'll go. Wait here while I pay.'

His voice was rough, quick, but the command was unnecessary. Her vision was blurred by the pain spreading under her skull. She took deep breaths and drank some water but the pain didn't subside. So much for managing to cope with all the stress she'd been under in the past day.

Nico returned to the table, took her by the elbow and led her out of the restaurant. He hailed a cab and helped her into it. 'I could have walked,' she said.

'No way, Freya. You're unwell. I've pushed you too hard.'

She hated being coddled, particularly as she'd made more progress today than in the past three weeks combined, but with the vice tightening around her skull she lacked the capacity to argue. Back at the hotel he guided her into the lobby and up to their rooms. He swiped into his room and led her through the adjoining door to hers. She kicked off her shoes and fell on her bed. She sensed the room getting quiet and darker; Nico must have closed all the blinds and curtains.

The next thing she was aware of was Nico sitting gently down on the side of her bed. 'I've got you some pain medication. Do you think you can sit up to take it?'

She rolled herself over and pushed herself up. The disorientation wasn't as bad if she kept her eyes closed. She took the tablets he offered her.

'I don't want to leave you alone.'

'It's just a migraine. I've had them before.'

'Yes, but not three weeks after a coma. Not the day you get a whole lot of memories back. I knew it was a mistake to bring you here.'

She wanted to tell him there was no way he was going to stop her, that coming here, however unsettling, had still helped her. But all she could do was groan and lie back down.

'Need to sleep.'

She felt him get off the bed and step away.

He was gone. It was painful, yet also a relief. When he was around her, she couldn't think straight. She had wild ideas of trying to seduce him. Of ignoring the inevitable. As much as she wanted him to lie down next to her and pull her to him, she still knew how risky it would be.

She pulled the spare pillow close to her chest instead, took some deep breaths and in moments she was asleep.

The sound of a someone clearing their throat awakened him. Nico straightened up in the chair and as he did, he felt a strain in his neck and winced.

Freya was sitting up in her bed. The curtains were still drawn but the brightness of the sunlight creeping around their edges let him know the morning was well underway.

'Please tell me you didn't sleep there?' she said.

He grunted. 'I wouldn't call it sleep, exactly.' He'd sat in the armchair googling 'coma,' 'amnesia' and 'migraine'. Some sites had been reassuring. Others had told him to take her to hospital immediately. Eventually he'd messaged Dr Jamal, who had thankfully called him right back and reassured him that as long as she was comfortable and coherent that she would be fine but as soon as she had difficulty walking or speaking, he was to take her hospital right away. Nico's body flowed with relief to see her sitting up, looking bright and speaking normally.

'You were there all night?'

'Of course.'

'Of course nothing. I told you I was okay.'

'You weren't. I was worried about you.'

'I'm fine.' She spun her legs over the side of the bed, still wearing the pink dress. He watched her stand and his mouth went dry.

'Will you be alright if I go and have a shower?' he asked.

She laughed. 'I'm fine. I'm going to have a shower too. By myself.'

They looked at one another. He was about to tell her to be careful again but the glare she gave him warned him not to.

She didn't want his concern, and maybe that was what he deserved. He'd been the one to get her into this mess.

'I'm still allowed to worry about you,' he mumbled to himself.

'Pardon?'

He shook his head. He didn't want to argue, but he knew he had little right to play the concerned-lover card. At best he was her friend, at worst, her boss. He'd slept with her, nearly killed her and yesterday had told her that it had all been a mistake, that they did not have a future together. It was un-derstandable she didn't want him looking after her.

Yet, he couldn't help saying, 'I think you should take it easy today.'

'I'm great, really. The migraine is gone, my head feels much clearer. I just need some coffee. Something small to eat.'

They both showered and when he knocked again on her door, she called him to come in. She'd ordered breakfast to be delivered to her room and was sitting on the balcony with a mug of coffee in her hands.

Without meaning to, he let out a sigh, a deep half groan from the centre of his very being.

'What?' Freya looked startled.

'Sorry. I'm just tired.'

It wasn't a lie. He hadn't got much sleep last night. But he wasn't sighing about that.

He was sighing because Freya was wearing a skimpy halter top and short denim shorts. Her long legs were stretched out onto the chair next to hers. Her dark blonde hair was tidied up loosely on the top of her head and he could see every inch of her gorgeous smooth skin soaking in the morning sun.

She was beautiful.

She always looked beautiful, but seeing her sitting like this now was like a punch in his gut.

'Do you want some coffee?'

An intravenous drip of the stuff, he thought, but said, 'Thanks,' and pulled up the spare chair.

'So, I guess I should help you find my replacement.'

It felt as though someone had poured concrete down his throat.

'I can do that,' he mumbled.

'I can help, is what I'm trying to say.'

'There's no need.'

He was blunt, but he had to be. How else could he be? His best friend was leaving. Forever. He didn't want to think about it. He couldn't think about it. He might move on from the denial stage at some point but not yet.

She turned to him and put her hands on her hips. 'What's up?'

'Do you really have to ask?'

'You want me to leave. You told me to.'

'I know, but I'm not overjoyed by the idea.'

'Then?'

'We both know it's for the best. It's what you wanted, re-member?'

She flinched. *Remember* was a word he should strike from his vocabulary.

'We talked about it. Before and yesterday. You'll be happier back in the States. I support your decision.'

'Except for the groaning.'

'I wasn't…'

Freya raised her eyebrow.

'Look, we just have a few more days left here. Can we think about the future when we get back?' he asked.

Freya twisted her mouth. He knew the expression. It meant, *Okay, I'll humour you for now but this isn't over.*

He didn't need her to say it aloud. He knew this was all far from over.

CHAPTER NINE

THEIR ITINERARY HAD them spending the day in Monopoli, which was just as well. He didn't want Freya to drive after her migraine and he certainly didn't want to drive her anywhere. They wandered around the narrow streets of Monopoli's old quarter and explored shops, markets and cafes. They visited the picturesque harbour, surrounded on three sides by ancient stone walls and embankments. Freya chatted happily as they went, pointing to things she saw but also remarking on random things she'd done in the past as her memories gradually came back to her. His heart swelled at the sight of her face, delighting in the memories of the past few years. Memories of their time together. He didn't think it was possible feel such relief; Freya was back.

She was also recovered from her migraine. Happy. Laughing. And surely the flirtatious looks she was giving him were all in his mind. *What about the wink she gave you when you were looking at the vegetable market?* An involuntary twitch? Almost definitely.

The idea of making this next television series without her was incomprehensible.

So he wasn't going to think about it.

Not yet.

Maybe he could convince her to stay. Help her get a place of her own in London, put a little distance between them, but at least not lose her across an ocean. But even the thought of

Freya living somewhere that wasn't their house also twisted his stomach into all sorts of uncomfortable knots. The thought of her living with someone else... Being with someone else...

So he wouldn't think about that either.

But while he was doing his best to convince his brain not to think about her, his body had other ideas. His heart beat rapidly anytime they came within inches of one another, anytime he breathed in her scent. His limbs tingled and his stupid muscles tensed and jerked in all kinds of unfortunate ways.

They returned to their hotel after lunch for a rest to avoid the afternoon heat. He was looking forward to putting a small amount of space between them and having a break from the way his pulse quickened each time he accidentally brushed his arm against Freya's or when she smiled at him knowingly. Suggestively.

'See you in a bit,' he said at the door to his room. If he could only have an hour or two alone, but somewhere where he knew she was safe, then he'd be able to sort out his head and think sensibly again.

'Yes.' Freya turned to her door but then spun back around. 'You don't want a relationship. For reasons I don't fully agree with but that's beside the point—they're your reasons. And I'm going back to the States, so I don't think starting a relationship is a good idea either.'

'What are you saying?' *Please don't be going where I think you're going. Not now. I don't think I have the energy to resist you.*

'I'm saying we like having sex. We're clearly good at it. We may as well give it another go.'

He laughed, but it was driven by nerves, not amusement. 'You say it like it's easy.'

'Isn't it? I don't recall you having any difficulties in the past.'

That did it. The heat in his chest went from slow flame to forest fire in an instant.

She stepped towards him and he filled his lungs with her, loving the way the breath carrying her scent filled up his body. Ordinary air was nothing after breathing in the air she inhabited.

Freya moved closer, brushing her body against his. Her halter neck showed the smooth skin of her shoulders and chest. Delicious, lickable skin.

'Freya, you're not making this easy.'

'It's not meant to be easy.' She slipped her soft hand into his and drew her fingers in and out of his. The friction between their fingers shouldn't have felt as indecent as his body thought it did.

'But should it be this hard?' The air dragged painfully over his throat.

'Probably. Because we care for each other. No matter what else is going on, we still like one another.'

Against all reason, Nico closed his eyes and dipped his face closer to her neck. He felt her breathe in as well, felt her hand tighten around his. With her free hand she grasped his waist and pressed herself against him. She shivered and he realised his lips were tracing their way lazily from her throat up her neck and to her face.

Her hips were pliant and strong against his and he shifted back and forth to enjoy the full effect. He groaned.

'Are you sure?' he whispered, unable to make more of a sound.

'I wouldn't want us to miss this last chance.'

'Freya…' He couldn't. Not again. Because if they did this again, he didn't trust himself to be able to say goodbye.

'For old times.'

'It was one night.'

'And three times.'

She remembered. She remembered it all. There was no point hiding anything from her, or from himself. They had made love. Glorious, amazing, powerful love.

'Freya, you know as well as I do that this isn't a good idea.'

She raised one perfect eyebrow. 'I didn't realise how much you like to play hard to get.'

He grunted. 'I don't like it one little bit. I hate that I can't resist you.'

'*Hate*'s a strong word.'

But what he felt for her was just as strong.

'You're very persuasive,' he said.

'You don't have to resist.'

'You know I do.'

He had to protect her. This was risky, outright dangerous. She'd realise that one day. But right now, it was too late. The train had left the station. It had nearly left the tracks entirely. He moaned. Every last scrap of his inhibitions was destroyed by the tidal wave of desire that was surging through him. Her breath on his skin, her hot lips on his, her own moans reverberating through him.

She tugged his hand towards her room and he was powerless to pull away. She opened the door to her room and it closed behind them with a click.

'If not for old times, then for goodbye?' he said. For the last time.

'Just one more time for the sake of my memories,' she pleaded.

He couldn't argue with that, but he couldn't argue at all. He couldn't speak. It was all he could do to breathe. He longed for his mind to take a picture-perfect memory of this moment. Of the sensation of her fingers sliding under his waistband. Of her lips on his hipbone as she eased his pants off him. Of the taste of her breasts as he kissed her until she cried out. Of all of it. Of each sound, each smell, each caress, hard, sweet, soft and even the bitter pain. All of it. To preserve all of it in his memories and mind forever. And ever.

His head spun, his body pounded, and they moved until they were both lost.

I want to do this for the rest of my life.

It was amazing. More amazing than he'd ever allowed himself to remember. He was flying, dancing, everything... Swirling and falling with her. His best friend. His Freya.

They landed, body and soul, and as his breath returned so did his senses.

What had he done? He looked down at her; her eyes were closed but the look of bliss on her face was unmistakable.

And terrifying.

This was most definitely not the plan.

He'd promised himself he wouldn't do this. Not again.

He was a cad to the hundredth degree.

Freya lay facedown on her bed, panting, body spent, head whirling. Nico lay sprawled next to her, also panting, his arm resting unconsciously across her back.

'That was even better than I remember,' she muttered into the pillow.

If that was their one last time then it was worth it.

And yet it wasn't.

What a stupid idea to think that one last time would be a harmless way of saying goodbye.

How could she *ever* have forgotten how it was to be with him?

'What was that?' he murmured. His voice deep and rough and never sexier.

'Mmm,' she replied. Hardly her most articulate answer but all she wanted to say to him at that point. She was even dreading sitting up and looking him in the face, afraid her eyes, her entire expression would expose her true feelings.

That was amazing. Let's do it again. Immediately.

But they couldn't. That wasn't the deal. One time was meant to be enough. One time was meant to be the end.

Except now they had done it, the memory may as well have been tattooed across her brain. Making love to Niccolò Rossetti was the best thing she had ever done in her life.

And it was over.

Maybe some things were better left forgotten.

'Are you okay?' he asked, rolling over.

'Never better.' It was both the truth and an outright lie. 'You?'

'Oh, Freya,' he sighed and she knew that was as much of an answer he was going to give her.

He may have enjoyed it as much as she had but it was different for him. He wasn't even contemplating taking their relationship to a different level. He never had been. For him it wasn't about saying goodbye, but about satisfying her. Almost like a favour.

You practically begged him.

The bubbles of bliss floating through her were washed away by a wave of shame.

You feel far more for him than he does for you. That's never going to change.

You won't be the one to change him. You're just Freya McFadden, who lacks the right energy. Who isn't vibrant enough.

She felt pressure building behind her nose and eyes and jumped out of bed.

'I'm just going to have a quick shower before dinner,' she said and rushed to her bathroom before the tears had a chance to flow.

She pulled herself together in the shower.

Work. Concentrate on the work.

It was what she'd always done. Five years of sexual tension had been tempered by good ol'-fashioned honest hard work.

So that was what they would do now. Go out, drink, eat and pretend that it was hard work and that sharing wine and gourmet food on the Adriatic coast didn't resemble a very romantic evening.

There would be no time to think about the afternoon, about damp sheets, the cool sea breeze brushing over their naked skin. No time to remember how it felt to move on top of him or the way his face melted with desire.

No time at all.

Except for when they were walking down one of Monopoli's narrow cobblestone lanes. Or waiting for their food to arrive. Or taking a sip of her spritz.

Or pretty much every moment of the evening.

Their conversation was stilted, which didn't help to keep her mind off what they had spent the afternoon doing. They had made love. It had been wonderful—she'd never felt closer to him—so why were they both struggling so much now? To carry on even a basic conversation? Why was he not even meeting her eyes?

The food was wonderful, everything she had imagined it would be. Worse yet, her work brain was beginning to engage and before she'd even realised what she was doing she was thinking of ways to display the food, how to photograph it, the background colours, the themes she would use to show it all off to its best advantage.

You won't photograph this food or this city. Or this place.

Her chest clenched and she pushed all her feelings down. Despite wanting to sleep with Nico more than anything else in her life, she was now beginning to wonder whether her mind had erased the memory of the night before her birthday for a good reason. It was possible to want to remember something so much and also need to forget about it completely at the same time.

Their conversation over dinner was awkward even though they had the meal to provide some topics of discussion, but it was practically nonexistent on the walk back to the hotel. When they reached their room doors and Nico said, 'Do you want to come into my room?' Freya was momentarily lost for words.

Her stomach was full, her limbs loose from the wine. Her body wanted to reach for him, pull him to her. To lose herself in him again. And again.

But it wouldn't be again and again. It would just be one more time. Or maybe two. And that wasn't enough.

You're not enough. That's what it comes down to. Not vibrant enough. Not the right energy.

'Nico, it was one last time. I promised.'

'I promised too,' he said and a shy smile crept over his lips.

She stood on her toes and pressed a quick kiss to his rough cheek.

'Good night. See you in the morning.'

She locked the door to her room before she could change her mind.

If closing the door on her hotel room was that hard, how could she possibly manage to close the door on their entire life together?

CHAPTER TEN

SHE SLEPT POORLY, but she still slept. This was their last day in Monopoli and Tregua. Tomorrow they would drive across Italy's ankle to Taranto and the parts of Puglia neither of them had been before.

New places. No memories. A clean slate. They couldn't get there fast enough as far as Freya was concerned, but first Nico had to make one last visit to Tregua and Anna.

Until he returned in a few months' time.

But today would be Freya's last trip. She would have to take many notes and photographs to hand over to Nico and whoever it was who replaced her.

Work. Concentrate on the work.

'Do you want to drive?' she asked, not to goad him but in the genuine hope that after last night something might have shifted inside him. That he might be less afraid. That he might be brave enough to get behind the wheel with her sitting next to him.

But he shook his head. 'I'm better at navigating.'

'You're not, you know,' she muttered quietly enough that he only gave her a puzzled look.

Like last time, she drove until the lanes became too narrow for her to drive comfortably down and parked the car. They didn't have far to walk; Tregua was small. Small and unspoilt. It didn't have the tourist numbers that Bari or Monopoli had, though the village was no less beautiful. Perhaps more so because of its authentic, unspoilt nature. She drank it all in, tried to commit it as best she could to her faulty memory. This would be the last time she came here. Because in a few days she'd say goodbye to Nico forever.

Nothing had really changed in the last month. She'd known deep down all along that she wasn't enough for Nico, that she would never be enough to shift whatever it was inside him that was holding him back. Nico was never going to love her as she loved him. The feeling twisted inside her, threatened to overwhelm her but she talked it back down. *You will be okay; you will move on. You will find someone who sees how special you are.*

But when they arrived at Anna's and she welcomed Freya in, Freya found she couldn't step over the threshold. She no longer belonged to this part of Nico's life.

'Why don't I give you both a moment?' Freya said.

Nico and Anna protested that it wasn't necessary.

'I know, but I'd like to take some photographs, for the person who takes over from me.' She noticed Anna give Nico a puzzled look but she didn't care.

Let him tell her I'm leaving, she thought. *I don't think I can.*

As soon as Freya left, Anna rounded on him.

'What did she mean?'

'Freya's moving back to the States.'

Anna shook her head. 'Why on earth would she do that?'

'She wants to start the next stage of her life.' *And I can't be the man she wants. She deserves more than I can give her.*

Anna frowned. 'But her life is in London. With you.'

'I can't give her the life she wants.'

Anna laughed. 'The pair of you! You have a beautiful life. Sure, you live in rainy London, not beautiful Puglia, but I see the pair of you. You have a wonderful business, a great friendship.'

'It's complicated.'

'What's complicated? You just tell her. Even I can say "I love you" in English.'

I love you. Was it that obvious?

'I have told her,' he said.

Anna's face brightened with delight but then her shoulders fell.

'And she didn't say it back?'

'No, she did.' *And moments later the lorry hit us and the next thing I knew they were cutting her from the car.*

'And she doesn't remember?' Anna guessed.

'No, she doesn't. She remembers most other things, but not that.'

Dr Jamal had always told them both that patients such as Freya often didn't regain memory of the accident or the time immediately before it. And he couldn't tell her this. Not now. Not when saying it in the first place had nearly killed her.

'So you just tell her again! Simple.'

'No, I can't.'

'You said it once. You just say it again. So she remembers, so she knows. Niccolò, it's deceitful not to tell her.'

'I'm not lying. I'm protecting her.'

'Protecting her from what?'

From me. 'Telling her won't do any good.'

'Phfft,' Anna said. Disagreement sounded the same in every language. 'She deserves your honesty.'

'She also deserves to have a long and happy life and I can't give her that.'

Anna screwed up her face.

'It's for the best,' he pleaded.

'The best for who?'

'For her.'

'Rubbish, she loves you.'

'As a friend.'

Anna laughed. 'Is that what you think? I thought you were smarter than that.'

Nico shook his head. Freya loved him as a friend. Even as a lover. And maybe she even thought they could be something more but that would pass. It was natural she saw him as a life partner, a husband, the father of her children, because they were so close. But she was worried about turning thirty. Assessing her life. Thinking of the future. So it was natural her gaze fell to him, given that they were so close. But when she moved away, she'd realise that he couldn't give her everything she needed. That he couldn't keep her safe.

So he had to let her go, to find someone who would love her completely, unconditionally, forever. Someone who could protect her.

'I can't hurt her.'

'But if you let her go, aren't you doing just that?'

No. He'd be saving her. 'I need to protect her.'

'Oh, you silly macho man. Where did that idea come from? You must protect each other and the best way to do that is living on the same continent to begin with.'

'I couldn't look after my mother,' he said. Anna knew the truth; she'd understand *this*.

'What do you mean?'

'After my father, she died. I wasn't enough for her.'

'I don't understand what you're saying.' She took his hand in hers but didn't laugh.

'It isn't just that, though. I couldn't look after Mama.'

'You did look after her.'

'Then why wasn't she happy? Why did she die?'

'Her heart gave out.'

'Exactly. She died of a broken heart.'

'Well, that's just a saying. She had several heart attacks.'

'At forty-eight?'

'Yes.'

'That's too young.'

'It happens. Especially with diabetes.'

'What?'

'Diabetes. *Diabete*,' Anna said it in English and then Italian.

Nico leaned forward. It sounded the same in Italian as it did in English.

'Your aunt never told you?' Anna asked.

He shook his head. 'No.'

'Maybe she assumed you knew. Your mother had many underlying issues, which I suppose she kept from you. You were so very young.'

'I was ten.' He remembered everything!

'Yes, which is young to understand that your mother has debilitating health concerns. We always thought she had more time.'

He remembered his mother wasn't always well, was often tired, but he never connected that to her heart failure.

'None of it was your fault. But if you take anything away from this, get yourself a good cardiologist now and watch your cholesterol. You have those genes too.'

'They told me she died of a broken heart.'

'That's just a saying,' Anna repeated and held up her hands. 'It's what people say to show that she loved your father very much. But losing him didn't kill her. Losing him made her cling even more strongly to life because she had to look after you. She never wanted to die. She never wanted to leave you. She loved you so much.'

Anna got up to make them both a coffee. Nico insisted he do it, but he didn't feel the joy he thought he would pottering around this kitchen from his childhood.

A medical explanation was all well and good, but he knew the truth; losing his father had destroyed his mother. There was more than one way to die of grief. If his father had lived, his mother would have as well. Nico was certain of it.

Freya arrived back at Anna's, her face bright and clearly invigorated by what she had seen.

Maybe she'll decide to stay after all?

It was a vain hope. He didn't want her to leave, but he knew she wanted more from her life than he could give her. Marriage. Children. Things she would be amazing at. The life she should have.

But not with you.

'Are you heading straight back to Monopoli?' Anna asked.

'Yes, but I thought we'd go lay some flowers for Papa at the harbour first.'

'Why there?' Anna asked.

'Because that's where the accident was. Where the boat sank.'

Anna shook her head vigorously. 'No, it's not. The accident was off the point. Way off.'

'No, it was at the harbour. I saw it.'

Anna laughed. 'You didn't see it. You couldn't have. No one did. He was too far away from the shore. And it was too early in the morning, it was still dark.'

'But I…' No. He'd *seen* it. It was bright daylight. He'd been standing at the harbour's edge, a block from here, in Tregua. He remembered his father crying out.

He was aware that Freya had taken his hand in hers, but everything else around him was strange. Why would Anna lie to him?

'You think you saw it?' she asked.

Nico nodded.

'You were how old?'

'Five.'

'Five. You were home in bed. It was early morning, their regular fishing trip.'

'I saw it. From the harbour.'

Anna shook her head again. 'Your mother never would

have let you out of bed, let alone out of the house. You must have dreamed it. Wait.'

Anna left the room. They heard puffing and banging and she came back five minutes later with a dusty scrapbook.

'What's this?'

'In my day we kept newspaper clippings.' She flipped through the book; found the page she was looking for and opened it for him to see.

The newspaper had yellowed. It was almost thirty years old, but it was still entirely clear. Even Nico's Italian was good enough to understand the headline.

Three missing presumed drowned off Tregua Point.

It was there, if not in black and white, at least in brown and yellow.

Anna read it aloud in Italian and he translated as she went in English, for Freya.

'The fishing boat is believed to have capsized off the point and all three men are presumed to have drowned in what was the biggest storm to hit Tregua in a generation.'

There'd been a storm. Not a bright, cloudless day as he'd always remembered.

'Three men? He wasn't alone?'

'No. Did you think he was?'

In Nico's memory his father had been alone. The sky had been blue.

But that memory wasn't real, he realised with a creeping disbelief that he'd ever thought it was. It was a childhood confection, a misunderstanding. Or even, as Anna had just suggested, a dream.

A dream that had become a memory.

Anna kept reading but he'd heard enough. He couldn't reconcile what he'd just learned with his own recollections; it was too confusing.

Freya took over the conversation from that point on and told Anna they needed to get going. He didn't want to argue but couldn't have even if he did. He needed to go down to the harbour. He needed to see it again.

'Come and visit me when you come back. Both of you,' Anna said.

They left Anna's cottage and he turned towards the harbour. Freya followed, understanding exactly what he was doing without the need to speak. The harbour was small, narrow, neat. An adult who was a half-competent swimmer would be able to swim from one side to the other, especially on a bright day. Now he really allowed himself to think about it, actually analyse his memory, he realised boats didn't just sink on bright days, and not in harbours as busy as Tregua's, where dozens of boats would have been at the ready to help someone in distress. Being so young he'd never questioned how it really happened.

'Do you mind if I go up to the point?' he asked.

'Of course not, but you're not going alone.'

She didn't ask if he wanted to drive and he didn't even consider asking her to stay behind.

If a part of Nico had hoped that things would become clear when they reached Tregua Point, that somehow the place would resemble that in his memory, he was disappointed. He had no recollection of ever visiting the place, a cliff that was several kilometres outside the village and only accessible by a long walking track when the road ran out. Tregua lay well in the distance, partially obscured by another headland.

'This can't have been the place,' he muttered but trusting his memory less and less.

Freya kept at a short distance, close enough if he needed

her but far enough away to leave him with his thoughts. Off in the distance white tips capped the waves of the sea. Below them he could hear the roar of water crashing into the cliff.

Freya sucked in a sharp breath. He went over to her but when he saw what she was looking at he dropped to his knees.

On the ground was a small granite marker. Inscribed on it, in Italian, he could make out the date of his father's death.

The names of three men.

The worst storm in a generation.

He hadn't seen the boat sink after all.

He'd been home in bed.

Freya crouched next to him.

'I don't understand. I saw it,' he said.

He expected her to say the obvious, that he couldn't have seen it, that he was wrong, Anna was right.

'What do you think happened?' Freya asked.

'I think logically Anna and the newspaper and this plaque are right. But why is it so different in my memory?'

'I don't know. But I know that our memories are not always as reliable as we want them to be.' She smiled sadly at him.

'We can't trust any of them?' he asked.

'I'm not saying that at all. We do have to trust it, but at the same time know that sometimes our brains make us remember things that didn't happen. And sometimes it lets us forget things that did. Sometimes it does this to protect us, or to make sense of things. I don't think our memories are malicious, but as I've learned in the past few weeks, they can be affected by trauma. Your father's death was traumatic. And you were so young.'

'But why did I think I saw it?'

'Maybe you imagined it to try and make sense of it. Your imagination became your memory. Or you dreamed it and have been remembering the nightmare. I still remember some nightmares I had as a child, better than real memories. I don't know why that is.'

His memory was so strong, so vivid. Not being able to move his legs, screaming but no help coming. His father waving. It couldn't have been just a dream.

Freya touched his hand and it was so comforting he had to resist the urge to rest his head on her shoulder.

'You were five. Many people don't remember anything from when they were five at all.'

'I think I'd remember seeing my father's death.'

'Yes, but that's just it. You do remember it, so clearly. The only thing is you weren't there.'

His temples throbbed.

'I have another theory—do you want to hear it?' she asked.

He didn't want to; he sensed by her soft tone that he wasn't going to like it, but he had to hear it. He nodded.

'I think you blame yourself, not just for your father's death, but your mother's too. And of course, our accident. You're carrying a lot of guilt. So much guilt. And I don't know why, but I do know it's not good for you. And I know it isn't warranted.'

He shook his head. It didn't matter what Anna and Freya told him; he'd still played a role in all of this. It was impossible to deny it, his memories and feelings were so strong.

'Nico, you were five. How could you possibly have saved your father, even if you had been there?'

'I cry for help,' he answered, his voice cracking. He could hardly get a sound out, his throat was so closed over.

'What?'

'In my memory, I am crying for help, but no one comes. I can't yell loud enough. I can't run fast enough. My feet are stuck to the ground.'

'Like in a dream?' she asked softly.

No.

He couldn't reconcile all of this.

They were trying to tell him he hadn't watched his father die after all. That was just his own memory playing tricks

on him. It was hard to erase the images in his mind of the
boat sinking in the harbour with what must be the truth. Even
though it never happened like that, it still felt real to him. It
had been the product of his five-year-old imagination. Or
maybe even a nightmare. But it hadn't happened.

'My mother had diabetes.'

'Oh, Nico.'

'Anna told me. She had several health problems apparently.
That is why Anna thinks her heart gave out.'

'I'm sorry.'

'Anna says I didn't cause her death.'

Freya grabbed his hand. 'Nico, of course you didn't cause
her death. You can't have caused her illness.'

'She died of a broken heart. That's what they said.'

'Who?'

'Adults. People around us.' He didn't even know anymore
who they were, only that they were older than him and knew
more about the world and its strange ways.

'Nico, I don't think people do die of a broken heart, at least
not years after a traumatic event. Your mother had underlying problems. It wasn't your fault.'

'But I couldn't make her better. I wasn't enough.'

He looked at her, searching for understanding in her beautiful blue eyes, hoping for her agreement. Needing her to tell
him he didn't have everything wrong.

But Freya shook her head. 'I'm not a mother, but I know
that if I were I would do everything in my power to stay
alive for my child. Especially if he'd lost his father as well.
I wouldn't give up.'

'That's what Anna said.'

'There you go.' Freya stood and brushed herself off as
though it was all over, as though everything made sense.

But nothing made sense at all.

CHAPTER ELEVEN

FREYA DIDN'T SPEAK on the drive back to Monopoli and their hotel, leaving Nico alone with his thoughts. The news that he hadn't been responsible for the loss of either of his parents should have been a weight lifted from him, but instead his mood was dark.

Give him time to process it all. It's a lot to take in.

'I need a shower and a rest,' he told her at the door.

Alone.

It was implied, if not spoken, because yesterday afternoon had been a one-off. A last hurrah. They were not in a relationship and never would be. She'd practically promised him that last night.

For goodbye.

So I remember what it was like.

He didn't feel the same way about her. He cared for her as a friend, but she would never be enough to change his mind about everything else.

Freya showered as well, contemplated putting the pink dress on again, but shoved it to the bottom of her suitcase. There was no point. Besides, now that she knew she wore it the night they'd slept together, she couldn't wear it again without obviously signalling to him how she felt about him and what she wanted.

He knows what you want, he knows how you feel and yet you're not enough.

She sat on the shared balcony and loaded the photos she'd taken that morning into her laptop. She flicked absent-mindedly through the photos of Tregua. She would have to collate them and possibly edit some before handing them over to her replacement.

They were good. Some of them were *really* good. Just looking at some of them brought all the sensations of the day back to her, the smells, the sensation of the sea air on her skin.

She was a good photographer.

A *really* good photographer.

Freya clicked on some of the other files. Unlike a few weeks ago, she now actually remembered taking these photographs, compiling the cookbooks, choosing which ones to include, everything. Unlike that time in the office when she'd picked up the cookbook and felt as though it had been written by someone else, now she *knew* she was the author and photographer. She knew she had taken these photos.

And they were good.

She was good.

Vibrant. Original. Everything that stupid editor at *The Southside Chronicle* had told her she wasn't.

Full of life. Energy. Value.

Why had she let silly words spoken by other people invade her thoughts for so long? She was a talented photographer and a brilliant food photographer. She was really good at this job she had carved out for herself with Nico.

She would find amazing work wherever she went.

But she didn't want to go anywhere else.

I want to be with Nico.

She was so lost in her thoughts she didn't realise he had joined her on the balcony until he cleared his throat. Freya jumped.

'Are you okay?' he asked.

'Fine, yes. How are you feeling?'

'Okay. Tired, I guess.' He rubbed the back of his head. He still looked thoughtful though maybe slightly less tormented.

'Nico, it's a good thing what you've found out today.'

'Is it?'

'Of course it is. Now you know that none if it was your fault.'

'Knowing is different to feeling.'

He wasn't wrong. Like the photographs in the cookbooks, she knew she had taken them, yet she didn't *feel* that she had. Nico felt guilty about his parents' deaths and it may take him some time to be able to put that to one side.

And she didn't have time.

She'd waited five years for him to want her. She couldn't wait another five. Or ten. She loved him, but she couldn't wait forever.

You're worth more than that. You deserve it all.

'It wasn't your fault.' She spoke softly even though she wanted to scream it over the balcony and the sea beyond them: *None of it was your fault and now you can love me!*

He shook his head.

'You heard what Anna said about your mother. You saw the plaque on the point. You didn't see your father's boat sink.'

He looked down.

'You don't believe any of it?'

'No, I do, but…'

'What?

'I couldn't protect *you*.'

His words silenced her words and stopped her heart.

'I can't hurt you again. I can't go through that again.' Nico looked up and straight at her. His brown eyes were wide; she'd never seen him like this. Never. He dragged his hands through his hair with such force she was almost surprised he wasn't left with fistfuls of hair in his hands.

'I watched them cut the car from around you and pull you out. You were unconscious. I thought you were dead. And then you were asleep for so long and when you opened your eyes you had no idea who I was. None at all. You didn't even know you were in London. You'd forgotten it. Every amazing thing you'd done. You didn't know who I was. You thought I was a psychiatrist! And worst of all, you'd forgotten who you were. You were so scared, so frightened. And I couldn't help you. When I spoke to you it made things worse. I made things worse—you were terrified of me. I'll never forget that look in your eyes, Freya. I have to let you go, as much as I hate the idea. I can't stand the thought that I will hurt you again.'

Shame flushed her cheeks. She'd been thinking of herself so much these past weeks that thoughts about Nico and what he'd been going through had been cursory. She knew he was upset and worried, but this? The force of his emotions sent her reeling. Poor Nico, poor wonderful Nico. She stood on shaky knees.

'But don't you see, if you let me go, you will hurt me. Even more than the accident.' *You will devastate me. Ruin me.*

'No, you'll be fine, because you'll be safe. I can't keep you safe. I can't keep anyone safe.'

'None of it is your fault! Nico, why can't you see that?'

'I'm just trying to protect you.'

'I'm a grown woman! I can decide for myself. Let me make my own mind up about whether I want to be hurt.'

He scoffed. 'I'm not going to hurt you. I'm not going to watch you nearly die again. I can't do it, Freya. You're better off without me.'

She closed her eyes to gather her thoughts but as she did felt pressure build behind them. No. No tears. She had to stay calm. She had to convince him.

'Nico, I'm not. And I never will be better off without you. Because I love you.'

Her throat closed over then, because she also remembered and knew in her heart that this wasn't the first time she had uttered those words to him. And if that didn't convince him, then what could?

'I love you, Nico.' Her words were rough, barely intelligible, but she could tell by the way his mouth was hanging that he had understood.

Tell me that you love me too. Tell me!

He shook his head, only slightly and only once, but it told her everything she needed to know. The bottom dropped out of her world. The Adriatic may as well have risen up to wash her away.

'I can't. I'm sorry.'

Can't? Sorry? She wanted to yell, but the tears were streaming in earnest now and all she could do was sniffle.

'Freya, my wonderful Freya, you will thank me one day for letting you go.'

She scoffed but that only propelled more tears down her face.

He's not going to change his mind. Freya recalled the rolling feeling in her stomach she'd had the night before her birthday when she told him she was considering leaving London. This was the outcome she'd always expected. She'd hoped for the other, but she'd prepared herself for this. Nico had had five years to realise how he felt about her and he hadn't decided he loved her. If the events of the last few weeks hadn't changed his mind, her standing here crying wasn't going to either.

It really was over.

What else was there to say?

She grabbed her sleeve and wiped her face.

'I'll get going then. I can move my things out of the house while you're still here. I can be gone by the time you're back in London.'

'Freya, stop. Stay. There's no rush.'

'There is. I need to move on. We both do.' And staying a moment longer would just drag things out for both of them.

She wasn't going to hang around waiting for the outcome to change when she could see now that nothing would ever change it. He was never going to change his mind.

She wasn't enough.

'Goodbye, Nico.'

She stepped up to him, lifted herself onto her tiptoes and remembered not to inhale as she touched her lips briefly against his cheek. 'Goodbye.'

She went into her room and closed the balcony door behind her.

Freya started with logistics. Changing her flight back to London. Booking a removalist. She would leave most of the furniture behind but there were some things she wanted to take with her. Some prints. And a stack of books. She would store it all in Pasadena while she figured out her next steps.

Pasadena. The thought of moving back there was not overly appealing, but it would be a soft landing before she decided where to go next.

Or would it be, as she'd always thought, a backwards step?

Go forwards, not backwards.

But right now, she was exhausted, dehydrated from all the crying and lying facedown on the bed was all she was capable of.

How had things got so messed up?

The accident, for starters.

If they hadn't crashed and her brain short-circuited at that precise moment what would have happened?

No wonder she'd gone back to the night before her twenty-fifth birthday. She'd thought of it as her brain's way of protecting her by blocking out the memory of Jane and Lachlan. Getting sacked from the job she hated. But it wasn't just that.

Her brain was also protecting her from a pain even worse than those things. It was protecting her from the reality that even though she and Nico had slept together, he never intended them to be together. That he didn't love her back. That it had all been a mistake.

No wonder she was physically fine. No wonder Nico was physically and mentally fine. No wonder the doctors were so baffled. The knock on her head hadn't been much but the news that Nico would never love her had been the real trauma.

Nico's childhood was far more complicated than she had realised even after five years of knowing him. He blamed himself for his father's death. He'd spent his life believing he'd witnessed the boat accident that killed his father, even though it was absurd to believe that a five-year-old could have saved a sinking boat.

It wasn't logical, but if he'd spent his entire life believing he had witnessed his father's death, was it really any different from *actually* seeing it?

No wonder he was so terrified about hurting her. But even now he knew that the events in his childhood were not as he'd believed, he still felt guilty about her accident.

He was never going to move past it.

And she had to accept that.

All of it.

She was leaving.

She was going to go home. It had been her plan all along, hadn't it? That was why she'd booked the plane ticket. The accident, the amnesia, had just muddled it all up for a while but now everything was sorted.

She would leave. Build a new life without him. Make room in her heart for someone else.

She and Nico would always be friends, but with the distance between them that she needed. And so what if all she'd learned was that they were great together? That he desired her as much as she did him? So what if their bodies practically ignited when they were together?

There was so much more to relationships than great sex, deep friendship. Deep understanding, trust and connection. So much more.

There had to be.

And she was determined to find it.

Nico picked up the car keys from where Freya had left them on the balcony table. He wasn't sure if she'd left them deliberately or not and now wasn't the time to ask. She didn't want to speak to him and it might be a while before she did again.

She'll realise it's for the best. Just give her time.

Regardless of what he'd just learned about how his parents had died, the car accident *had* been his fault. He'd been driving and too distracted by Freya to pay proper attention to what had been happening around them. And if he continued his relationship with Freya he'd continue to be distracted. And dangerous.

And if they had the family she wanted... Even in the warm afternoon sun he shivered at the thought that anything could happen to Freya's hypothetical children.

He couldn't do that. Any of it.

She needed to be with someone who could keep her safe. He wasn't that man and one day she would realise it. Maybe not immediately, but when she lived to be ninety, surrounded by a gaggle of grandkids she would thank him. The man who saved her life by letting her go.

With Freya safe in the hotel room, he decided to take a drive by himself. He drove down the coast but after a few wrong turns found himself pointed back in the direction of Tregua. The universe was telling him something. He was going back to London in a few days and he still hadn't done the one thing he really needed to do: visit his mother's old restaurant.

He had more memories of that place than any other in

Tregua. It was where he had grown up, spent so many of his waking hours as a child. It was where he'd learned to run a restaurant. It was where he'd decided he wanted to be a chef.

He parked the car close to where Freya had stopped that morning, close to the waterfront but before the streets became too narrow. He preferred to travel on foot anyway; it was easier to see things and besides, he'd always walked these streets as a child. It was now late afternoon and people were emerging from their houses again after the heat of the afternoon.

He would be too early for the evening meal, but maybe they served drinks. Would he dare go in? It wouldn't be the same and he wasn't sure how he felt about that. Some things were best left as memories, but then as he'd learned today, some memories weren't real at all.

Walking along the waterfront was different now with the knowledge that this wasn't where his father's boat had sunk. He walked past bustling cafes, a few shops and then somehow reached the end of the strip without having seen his mother's restaurant.

Something wasn't right. He turned and walked back to where Via San Sebastino met the harbour and then along another three houses. The restaurant was there, except it also was not.

It was entirely different. And it wasn't just his memory. It was closed, utterly neglected. And the entire place smelt wrong. Like rotten fish.

It hadn't been cleaned in years, let alone painted. He looked in one of the windows, the glass almost too dirty with salt scum to see inside. Nico went around to the side door, where deliveries were sent. It was the door they would enter and leave from each day. He pulled and pushed on the door. It was locked, though it wouldn't have taken much to break the lock or shatter the decayed wood the lock clung to. He couldn't break and enter. He rested his forehead against the door.

As his head touched the peeling wood he remembered standing here, like this, once before. There was once a spare key. In fact, not even a spare key, but the *actual* key. Kept in the mailbox, which was also never locked. He looked to the left; it was still there. Rusted but intact. He lifted the lid and reached gingerly inside and his fingers found a single key.

No one would care if he entered. No one had cared for this building in years. The lock was a little stiff, but the door opened easily. He stepped slowly inside, inhaling the strange smells and adjusting his eyes to the dimly lit room.

The place had been sold when his mother died and he'd understood it had continued to operate as a seafood restaurant. At some point in the past twenty years, it had been abandoned. The dust was several years thick on all surfaces. The stoves remained and chairs and tables, but the pantry and shelves had been emptied. The restaurant shouldn't look like this. All his mother's work, for what? To be run into the ground? Abandoned. Unrecognisable.

It's all your fault.

A stack of menus sat on the counter. Unfamiliar. He picked one up.

Isabella's. The new owners had kept the same name, his mother's, though the menu was not as he remembered.

How is this your fault?

Because if his father hadn't died, his mother wouldn't have died and she would have continued to run the restaurant and…

His parents' deaths were not his fault. Knowing that was one thing, but shaking the feeling of it was another. Twenty years of crushing guilt was a heavy burden to simply shrug off in a single afternoon.

Besides, the car accident was his fault. His alone. He'd nearly killed Freya; he could have killed someone else.

You could fix it.

He could. He could buy it, restore it. Put in a manager. He'd have to spend a lot more time here in Puglia. He could do that; he could afford to.

He turned around to speak to Freya, to ask her opinion, but she wasn't there.

She was gone. Forever.

He buried his face in his hands.

It wasn't just this place. It was the restaurants in London. She was a part of almost everything he'd done in the past five years. He loved Freya.

He didn't want to do it without her—and not because things were better and smoother when she was around—but because he did it all for her.

He loved her.

And not just as his friend. He loved her. Body and soul. She was his person, his first thought of the morning and his last at night. He didn't want to do anything without her.

Except what if he hurt her? What if he hurt her again and this time it was worse? She was safer back in the States. Safer away from him.

Nico sank into one of the rickety chairs. Even covered in dust and grime he recognised it from over two decades ago. How could it be that his mother was long gone but the chair remained? Life's absurdities, vagaries and randomness hit him again.

Why would Freya be safer away from him, the person who cared about her more than anything in the world? She wouldn't. He may not be able to keep his loved ones safe all the time, but it was far better that they were with him, close to him, rather than on the other side of the world. Wasn't it?

Freya zipped up her suitcase and dragged it off the bed onto the floor. A car would be here shortly to take her to Bari and her flight home.

No. Not home. To London. London would only be her home for as long as it took her to pack up her things and book her next flight.

As she wheeled the suitcase out and the door to her room clicked closed behind her, she supposed she should let Nico know that she was leaving. She'd said everything she needed to say and was sure he had as well, but five years of friendship made her pause.

She wanted things he couldn't—or wouldn't—give her. She was worth all that. She was worth everything. She was worthy of the life she wanted. Friendship, passion, success. Love.

She was worthy of it. All.

She had made this decision once; she was strong enough to walk away once and she was again now. Especially now. Nico had seen with his own eyes proof of why he wasn't responsible for his parents' deaths and yet still wasn't able to love her.

He still felt guilt over the car accident, which also wasn't right. The lorry hadn't given way. It wasn't his responsibility to take care of every other person in the world.

It was this thought that made her decide to say a final goodbye.

She knocked on the door and waited.

No answer.

She knocked again and held her ear closer to the door, listening for noise inside. There was none. She didn't have time to wait and there was, after all, nothing more to say.

She picked up the handle of her suitcase and wheeled it out.

She handed her keycard in at reception and went out to the street, now hot in the afternoon sun. The streets were quiet and her car arrived on time.

This was it.

It's time for your next adventure, she told herself as the driver lifted her suitcase into the boot and she climbed into the back seat.

The cab pulled away and she looked into the distance. *Don't think about him. Think about the future. Where will it be? New York? San Francisco?* She heard what she thought was a bang but the driver carried on, unconcerned. Then there was another.

This time it was definitely at the back of the car. She turned her head but then jerked forward as the driver braked. The driver yelled something in Italian and even though Freya's Italian was pretty much limited to food she knew it was a curse.

A bang at her window made her scream.

Then she finally saw who it was.

He was panting, sweaty.

'Stop, please,' she told the driver but there was no need. He'd pulled over and was yelling at Nico.

She rolled down her window. 'I came to say goodbye, but you weren't there,' she said.

'I want to open a restaurant. Here,' he gasped.

'What?'

'I want to reopen my mother's restaurant.'

She closed her eyes and sighed. 'That's great, Nico, but I'm on my way to the airport. I'll miss my flight.'

'But I had to tell you.'

Her heart leapt and then crashed. Opening a restaurant in Puglia was a wonderful idea. Ambitious and it would be so much work. But what a wonderful thing to do to honour his mother and his heritage.

But it wasn't their project. It was his alone.

'Nico, I'm happy for you but I don't work for you anymore.'

'But...'

'No buts. We've been over this. I'm leaving.'

The driver held up his hands and said something else she didn't understand.

'Please leave,' she said to the driver, who then said something else and Nico spoke to him in Italian. They started to argue. The driver shook his head and began to accelerate.

As he drove away, she heard them.

The three words.

'I love you.'

She tapped the driver's shoulder. *'Arette*. Stop. Please. *Per favore.'*

Nico was at her open window again.

'What?'

'Freya, I love you.'

The driver swore again. She felt the same way. She needed to keep going or she'd miss her plane. This was the second plane ticket she'd booked to build her new life and he was getting in the way of this trip as well.

I love you.

He'd said it before. She wasn't sure when or how she knew, but she'd heard him say it before.

Maybe in a dream.

Maybe in a coma...

'I thought you were scared,' she said.

'I was wrong.'

'Let me out,' she said to the driver.

Nico took her suitcase from the boot of the car and a handful of notes from his wallet that he handed to the driver, whose face went from annoyed to delighted.

'If this is just a ploy to get me to stay... Nico, I swear...'

'It isn't.'

'You can't just say things like that.'

'Why not? It's true.'

True...

'Is it?' She loved him as well, in all sorts of ways. As a friend. A lover. A soul mate, but that didn't mean enough.

'I've never doubted that you care about me. But you know I want something more.'

'I want to give you more. I want to give you it all.'

On a warm street outside a hotel in Monopoli under the afternoon sun, Freya's heart stopped.

'You just told me you couldn't. That I wasn't enough.'

'Freya, no. You were always enough. It was me who doubted.'

'And what? You're not scared anymore?'

'No, I'm terrified. I'm terrified I'm going to fail you. But I'm more scared of not being with you. I'm more scared of letting you go.'

Her heart, her poor, broken heart began to beat again slowly. It was more optimistic than her brain, which still didn't let itself believe.

'How can you suddenly be so sure?'

'I went back to Tregua. I went to my mother's restaurant. It's been neglected.'

'And?'

'It was such a waste. I'm not sure why it is like that or what happened, but I want to rebuild it. The thought of doing it without you was overwhelming and not because of all the ways in which you help and support me but because I do everything I do because of you. If there's no one to share it with it doesn't seem worth it.'

'But you think you're going to hurt me—how will you deal with that?'

'If I let you go, I've already lost. It was something Anna said to me—I've given up before I've begun because I'm scared.'

This was a lovely speech but was he just reacting to the fact that she was about to leave?

'Nico, I want everything. A life, a marriage. A family. And if you aren't going to be able to manage…'

'I want those things too. With you. And only with you. For the rest of our lives.' Nico picked up her hand, ran his large thumb over the sensitive skin at the base of hers. 'I love you, Freya. So much it sometimes hurts.'

And she knew. She met his eyes with disbelief but also with questions. 'The accident.'

He cast his gaze down but the pain written across his face was apparent and made her stomach drop. He nodded.

She remembered it all, the drive, him holding her hand, the feeling of pure joy that enveloped them in that car. And him saying the words *I love you, Freya. So much it sometimes hurts.* She remembered the exquisite feeling in her chest and then darkness.

'I never got to tell you that I loved you too. But I do. I love you so much. And for so long. And I realise now I'll love you forever.'

'Oh, Freya, I'm so sorry.'

'No, you've nothing to apologise for. Losing my memory made me forget all the reasons we couldn't be together and I only saw the reasons that we should.' She lifted her ankles, pushed herself up onto her toes and he ducked his head to meet her halfway. Lips met lips, souls met souls.

'You fell in love with me twice.'

She laughed. 'It's true, I did.'

'I can keep being brave and keep stepping up. Day after day, I will do my best.'

'I know you will—that's never been in doubt. You are the best man I know.'

'And Freya,' he said as he took her face in his beautiful hands. 'I will fall in love with you over and over again until the end of time.'

EPILOGUE

PEOPLE WERE RUNNING everywhere: a camera crew, the people laying out the tables and chairs, children making mischief in the chaos. He realised it had been a while since he'd seen Freya and his heart hitched but a moment later, she emerged from the restaurant, his mother's restaurant, newly painted and restored, carrying a platter to lay on one of the trestle tables.

Whose idea had it been to throw a first-birthday party so big that the entire village was invited? Oh, yeah, that's right. It had been his.

The reopening of the new restaurant had been a while coming; purchasing the site, getting the necessary approvals and then opening it had taken time. And they had both been pretty preoccupied in the meantime, first with making a television series and writing a cookbook at the same time as planning a wedding. And then busier than ever with the arrival of their first child, a daughter named Isabella.

She sat with her grandmother, and watched the preparations. Izzy was convinced the restaurant was named after her and they had done nothing to persuade her otherwise. When she was older, she would understand the significance of her name and this restaurant.

The people of Tregua had been so welcoming and positive when he'd first tentatively discussed plans to reopen the restaurant, conscious that any project with his name attached to it would bring more people and attention to their unspoilt village. But his hometown had first welcomed the film crew when he made the television series and then loved the special focus that Nico had brought to the village. Other restaurants and hotels in the area had also benefited from the increase in visitors from around the world and they proudly showed off their village.

But today, the first anniversary of the opening of the restaurant, he was open to locals only. To say thank you. And for one day, not to be Niccolò Rossetti, celebrity chef, but just Nico, local boy. Son, husband and father.

Loving Freya had been easier than he'd ever thought, and loving Izzy had at times been stressful and worrying, but overwhelmingly the most amazing part of his life. And now with a second child on the way, his heart was full.

He caught Freya's eye and she weaved her way through the crowd over to him. He held out his arm and she stepped into it.

'Are you okay?' she asked.

'I was about to ask you the same thing.'

'I'm great. And everything seems under control. I meant, how are you feeling?' She patted his chest gently. 'I meant, how are you in here?'

'Full, even though I haven't eaten.'

Her smile was radiant.

'Me too. What next?' she asked.

'Next? Next is our very special project.' He put both arms around her and rubbed her growing belly. 'And that, I think, is quite enough to be going on with.'

They had purchased a house in Tregua and planned to spend a few months a year there, at least until the children started school, to let the kids know their Italian heritage.

Freya took out her camera.

'You don't have to work today. It's a holiday.'

'I'm not working. I'm capturing memories. For you, me and Izzy. And for everyone else here today. And for this bump.'

He watched Freya, his darling, precious and amazing Freya, walk through the happy crowd, taking photos of the restaurant, the staff, the guests and most of all her mother and daughter. She circled her way back to him.

'Say "pecorino",' she said.

He laughed and the camera clicked, saving the moment forever.

* * * * *

If you enjoyed this story,
check out these other great reads
from Justine Lewis

Dating Game with Her Enemy
How to Win Back a Royal
Swipe Right for Mr. Perfect
The Billionaire's Plus-One Deal

All available now!

MILLS & BOON®

Coming next month

SECOND CHANCE UNDER THE MISTLETOE
Kandy Shepherd

'It's less than two weeks until Christmas. Can we make the effort to get to know each other in that time? Even acknowledge that we could become friends of a sort? You know, bond over our shared care of Clem and her baby?'

'Friends? Do you think so?'

Jon paused. 'Perhaps not quite friends, although we were friends long ago.'

'We were never just friends,' Natalie said slowly.

An awkward silence fell between them. Was she remembering the fierce passion that had immediately flared between them, the overwhelming obsession they'd had for each other? First-time love. He had never forgotten it. Although he'd had serious relationships since, even been married, nothing had ever come anywhere near the intensity of those youthful feelings. No one else had engaged his emotions so deeply. 'You don't know how to love,' his second ex-wife had accused. But he had loved Natalie, deeply and completely. Perhaps there hadn't been any love left in him for anyone else.

Continue reading

SECOND CHANCE UNDER THE MISTLETOE
Kandy Shepherd

Available next month
millsandboon.co.uk

COMING SOON!

We really hope you enjoyed reading this book.
If you're looking for more romance
be sure to head to the shops when
new books are available on

Thursday 23rd October

To see which titles are coming soon, please visit

millsandboon.co.uk/nextmonth

MILLS & BOON

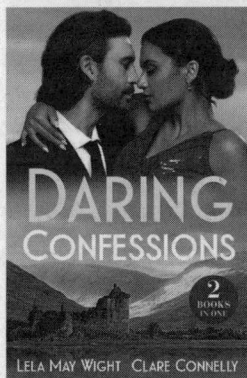

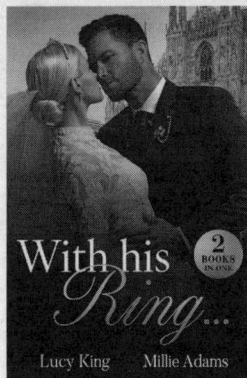

afterglow BOOKS

Afterglow Books is a trend-led, trope-filled list of books with diverse, authentic and relatable characters, a wide array of voices and representations, plus real world trials and tribulations. Featuring all the tropes you could possibly want (think small-town settings, fake relationships, grumpy vs sunshine, enemies to lovers) and all with a generous dose of spice in every story.

♪ @millsandboonuk

⊙ @millsandboonuk

afterglowbooks.co.uk

#AfterglowBooks

For all the latest book news, exclusive content and giveaways scan the QR code below to sign up to the Afterglow newsletter:

SCAN ME

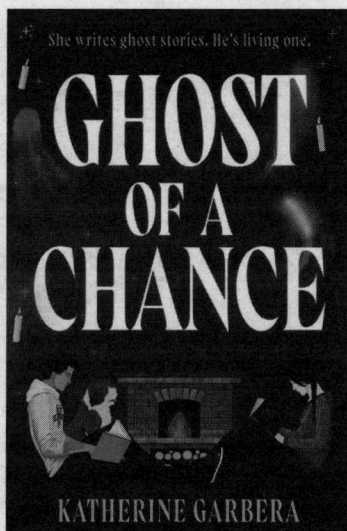

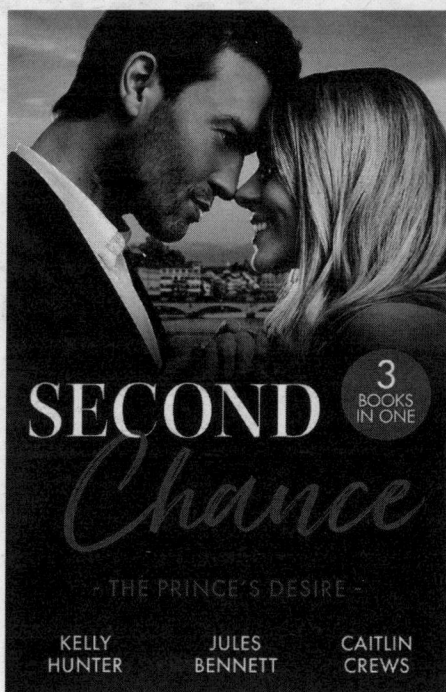

LET'S TALK
Romance

For exclusive extracts, competitions and special offers, find us online:

- **f** MillsandBoon
- **X** @MillsandBoon
- **◉** @MillsandBoonUK
- **♪** @MillsandBoonUK

Get in touch on 01413 063 232